MW00593262

SALVAGE RIGHT

BAEN BOOKS by SHARON LEE & STEVE MILLER

THE LIADEN UNIVERSE®

Fledgling
Saltation
Mouse and Dragon
Ghost Ship
Dragon Ship
Necessity's Child
Trade Secret
Dragon in Exile
Alliance of Equals
The Gathering Edge
Neogenesis
Accepting the Lance
Trader's Leap
Fair Trade
Salvage Right
Trade Lanes (forthcoming)

ANNIVERSARY EDITIONS

Agent of Change
Conflict of Honors
Carpe Diem
Local Custom
Scout's Progress

OMNIBUS VOLUMES

The Dragon Variation
The Agent Gambit
Korval's Game
The Crystal Variation

STORY COLLECTIONS

A Liaden Universe Constellation: Volume 1
A Liaden Universe Constellation: Volume 2
A Liaden Universe Constellation: Volume 3
A Liaden Universe Constellation: Volume 4
A Liaden Universe Constellation: Volume 5

BY SHARON LEE

Carousel Tides
Carousel Sun
Carousel Seas

SALVAGE RIGHT

A New Liaden Universe® Novel

SHARON LEE & STEVE MILLER

SALVAGE RIGHT

A Baen Books Original

Baen Publishing Enterprises
P.O. Box 1403
Riverdale, NY 10471
www.baen.com

ISBN: 978-1-9821-9268-6

Cover art by David Mattingly

First printing, July 2023

Distributed by Simon & Schuster
1230 Avenue of the Americas
New York, NY 10020

Library of Congress Cataloging-in-Publication Data

Names: Lee, Sharon, 1952– author. | Miller, Steve, 1950– author.
Title: Salvage right : a novel of the Liaden Universe / Sharon Lee and Steve Miller.
Identifiers: LCCN 2023005842 (print) | LCCN 2023005843 (ebook) | ISBN 9781982192686 (hardcover) | ISBN 9781625799197 (ebook)
Subjects: LCGFT: Science fiction. | Novels.
Classification: LCC PS3562.E3629 S26 2023 (print) | LCC PS3562.E3629 (ebook) | DDC 813/.54—dc23/eng/20230210
LC record available at https://lccn.loc.gov/2023005842
LC ebook record available at https://lccn.loc.gov/2023005843

Printed in the United States of America
10 9 8 7 6 5 4 3 2 1

To Absent Friends

ACKNOWLEDGMENTS

Herewith, the roster of those heroes who rode in the Great *Salvage Right* Tyop Hunt. Accept, please, the thanks of two very grateful authors. We may all go forward, now.

Mike Barker, Damon Banzai, Deb Boyken,
Jo-Anne Brecka, Millie Calistri-Yeh, Heidi Cothard,
Ron Currens, Bob DeRosier, ElementalElf, Richard Fowler,
Melanie Greenway, S. J. Gum, Irene Harrison, Julia Hart,
Terry Hazen, Thom Hill, Art Hodges, Riyon Hutton, Patti Maw,
Evelyn Mellone, Graham McRea, Bex O, Marni Rachmiel,
Michele A. Ray, Kate Reynolds, Ken Shoemake,
Sarah Stapleton, Kathryn Sullivan, Linda J. Thorsen,
Adrienne Travis, Gordon Wainwright, Ruth Woodgate

Special thanks and kudos to Beta Readers Extraordinaire:
Art Hodges and Bex O

The authors acknowledge the following influences on this novel:

Harlan Ellison, "I Have No Mouth and I Must Scream"

Abbie Burgess and Matinicus Rock Light Station

Conrad Nomikos and the Brute Force and Massive
Ignorance Method, as presented by Roger Zelazny
in *This Immortal / . . . And Call Me Conrad*

The gift of a wooden box, from Anne Young and Chuck Diters

Author C. E. "Catie" Murphy

The Prestige
novel by Christopher Priest, film directed by Christopher Nolan

The limerick "There once was a fellow called Okham,"
by Sharon Lee and Steve Miller, is original to this text

What Has Gone Before

THE CYCLE WAS ALMOST DONE.

Mere moments now until he found if his mad scheme had borne fruit.

No, Jen Sin yos'Phelium corrected himself; his scheme was no less mad than the problem to which it was a solution. Together, they represented a complete, balanced equation; perfectly serviceable, if not precisely elegant.

The unit pinged. The hood lifted.

The man lying on the pallet frowned, tensed, and opened his eyes.

"It worked," he said, and Jen Sin nearly wept, hearing the dazed wonder in that deep voice.

He stepped forward and offered a hand.

"Good waking to you, Brother."

Dark eyes found his face, mobile eyebrows lifted.

"Gods, we're a matched pair," he murmured, and took the offered support in a firm grip.

The first part of the scheme had worked, but now they ran against time. It would not do to be discovered.

"Brother," Jen Sin said, as the other settled his jacket over straight shoulders, "do you know what must be done?"

A sharp gaze raked his face.

"I know. And I agree. There is no other way. I will go with *Lantis*. The pilot is no less a risk than the ship."

"Yes," Jen Sin said, for that had been the plan he had made, which of course the other knew as his own.

"So—" The other extended his hands, and paused, his eye caught by the glitter of the gaudy ring.

"Here—" He had it off and pressed it into Jen Sin's hand. "If I'm to have left it as earnest, there had best be no traces in the debris."

Jen Sin took a hard breath, and slipped the ring into an inner pocket of his jacket. "I will...keep it safe," he said.

The other laughed then, or perhaps not, and gathered him into an embrace. Jen Sin held him tight, doubt rising with the tears.

"No." The other set him back. Already his face was different, his eyes already shadowed by new and solitary thoughts.

"Brother, you have taken the sterner duty." He raised his hand to Jen Sin's hair, stroking the beads nestled there. "Be as careful as you may."

He turned on his heel then, and left the cubicle, on his way to the repair shed, and their poor, compromised *Lantis.*

Emergency repairs at Tinsori Light. Left my ring in earnest. The keeper's a cantra-grubbing pirate, but the ship should hold air to Lytaxin. Send one of ours and eight cantra to redeem my pledge. In fact, send two...

The coded message was away, informing Delm Korval that neither ship nor pilot would ever return home.

On Tinsori Light, Jen Sin stood behind Lorith in the light keeper's tower, his hand on her shoulder, his eyes on the screen.

Lantis was framed there, a piece of sanity against the mad dance of pink and blue grit. Patiently, she awaited the ack from the first relay.

It came.

Jen Sin held his breath.

There was a brief, intense flare of energy.

When it had faded, there was no ship to be seen, only a drifting band of debris, slowly spreading out to mix with the ambient grit.

TINSORI LIGHT
ONE

• • • • •

THE DOOR OPENED ONTO DESOLATION.

Jen Sin recoiled slightly from the damp stench of rotting vegetation, and tried not to breathe.

"Station," Lorith said from beside him, "engage fans in the green room hallway."

Sluggish and noisy, the fans engaged; the air cleared—enough—and Jen Sin went forward, notepad in hand.

The laws of salvage having recently thrust a space station of some antiquity into Clan Korval's orbit, the delm naturally wished to know how expensive was this new acquisition. Thus had the light keepers been tasked with doing an inventory.

The price was likely more than the delm was willing to meet, that was Jen Sin's opinion, letting it be known that Jen Sin yos'Phelium was not the delm, and thank the gods for that.

Not being delm meant following the delm's orders, however, and so he stepped into what had—very recently, surely?—been a vibrant and functioning hydroponics bay.

In his memory, this space had been filled—perhaps overfilled—with growing things, the air rich and warm, the aisles between the tanks regularly cleaned by the bots. He had eaten from the yield of this room, and taught Lorith to do so.

Now... The aisles were awash with black leaves; the tanks sticky with muck. He did not relish the thought of wading through the rooms, barefoot as he was, and while the robes he and Lorith wore were virtually indestructible, he hesitated to test them quite so stringently.

Happily, the room's main control panel was along the wall where they had entered, and the floor was only slightly littered with dry leaves and the remains of browned flowers.

He made his way to the panel, and opened it, the skin between his shoulder blades pulling tight in anticipation. The Light did not care to have his control boxes opened, and while he sometimes tolerated such an intrusion from the light keepers, his slaves, more often he did not, and produced a punishment for insolence.

Jen Sin's breath came short, and he closed his eyes, concentrating on taking calm, even breaths. Tinsori Light was dead. He and Lorith were safer than they had ever been in this place, and it was no very difficult thing—was it?—to access the controls and initiate a self-test?

Having somewhat ordered himself, Jen Sin opened his eyes. All thought of a self-test or, indeed, repair, left its orbit around possibility.

The controls had been melted—fused. Tinsori Light must have been in a particular pet to have called down such complete destruction on mere instrumentation.

He moved slightly, his foot bumping something hidden in a drift of leaves. Bending, he brushed the object off, finding one of the cleanbots lying on its side, its carapace half-melted.

"The Light must have been angry," Lorith said.

"So it appears," Jen Sin said, straightening and making a note on his pad regarding the necessity of replacing the hydroponics section. "I don't recall this. Do you?"

"No," Lorith said, simply. "But we might not have known. We didn't come here often, did we?"

"Didn't we?" He frowned up at her, she being the taller. "When was the last time? Surely we ate from these rooms, after I had decided to stay."

Thin, pale brows pulled together over large, space-dark eyes.

"We did, once or twice," she said slowly. "But we haven't had the leisure this wakening, until now. Before, there were the teams sent to evaluate the Light for repair..."

More likely for termination than repair, Jen Sin thought, but did not say. It had scarcely mattered, after all. The Light had acted with his usual decisiveness, and there had been no need for the light keepers to bother with what remained of the teams, after.

"Before that," Lorith said slowly, her eyes narrowed with the effort of remembering, "that was the ship with the dead crew, and we were scarcely awake long enough to prevent repairs."

Jen Sin frowned. He recalled the dead crew. It seemed to him to have been some amount of time ago, not that time had behaved any more reasonably on Tinsori Light than anything else. Still, it seemed that they must have wakened between now, and then—

Didn't it?

Jen Sin glanced down at the poor, melted cleanbot, then turned to seal the control panel, and made sure of the lock. Nonsensical, really, but he had been trained as a Scout to respect his equipment, and training was a comfort, on Tinsori Light.

"There is nothing we can do here," he said, turning toward the door.

Something against the wall beyond caught his eye, and he shifted somewhat, in order to see it better.

His chest constricted as the fullness of the shadow came into sight: the image of a leaping man, burned into the surface of the wall.

"Jen Sin?"

Lorith came up beside him, following his gaze.

"Oh," she said, and turned to him.

"Are we done with tasks for now?" she asked.

"I suppose we might rest," Jen Sin said, turning to look up at her, though the shadow still teased the side of his eye.

"Then let us do that," Lorith said, and moved to the door.

As they were walking away from hydroponics, she spoke again. "Will you share pleasure with me, Jen Sin?"

He smiled at her.

"Of course."

Some while later, he woke from an uneasy drowse, to find Lorith sleeping yet beside him.

He raised up on an elbow, careful not to disturb her rest, and studied her face. The pointed features, the thin brows curving over large eyes, now closed, lashes pale silk against paler skin—his companion in the effort to keep the Light and all of his malice contained; the universe beyond thereby safe at least from that particular peril.

Lorith had been on the Light far longer than he, her will set against evil.

It scarcely seemed possible that Tinsori Light had died, that the station was firmly situated in the universe, the dust and grit dispersed. He had been present when those things occurred, and still he had difficulty believing the change in their condition.

He sighed softly.

Lorith's hair was pale, slightly darker than her skin. He extended a hand and ran gentle fingers through the fine curls, feeling the cool slide of crystal beads against his skin.

Sighing again, he settled down, closed his eyes, and slipped back into sleep.

Jelaza Kazone
Surebleak
Daiellen Sector

• • • • • • • • • • • • • • • •

"WELL, THAT WAS FUN," MIRI SAID, TURNING AROUND SO VAL Con could unfasten her gown. "Not sure which was more surprisin'—Memit proposing herself to Yulie, or him taking her up on it."

"You don't approve of the match?"

"Not mine to approve, is it? Fierce damn' woman, but I'm guessin' he knows that."

"I married a fierce woman, and it came out well for me. There."

Val Con stepped back, and the dress slipped off her shoulders to puddle on the floor. Miri carefully stepped free, sliding her arms into the robe he held for her, and turned to face him.

"See, being thrown off your homeworld, and having to pretty much start over on a freezing backworld fulla bad social mistakes is your idea of 'came out well.' That bar's so low, you can't see it for the snow."

"Only think how much worse it might have been, if I had not had you to support me."

"Smartass. Let's get that coat offa you."

"The other surprise on the evening being TerraTrade's decision," Miri said some little while later, as she curled into the corner of the couch, glass of wine in hand. "Shan's gonna be crushed when he finds out his recommendation to upgrade the port's rating was turned down by TerraTrade."

"He will perhaps be consoled when he reads further and learns that his request was denied only so the rating could be increased beyond what he had recommended."

He turned sideways on the couch, so that he faced her. Her eyes were languid, and her face a little drawn, but she did not seem in imminent danger of collapse.

"Sector Port, all services." Miri sipped from her glass. "We up to that?"

He raised an eyebrow.

"Faint of heart, Miri?"

"Just askin' a reasonable question. One of us is gotta be reasonable, and it sure ain't gonna be you."

"My character revealed," he said mournfully.

"I won't tell anybody. So—are we up to Sector Port? If we gotta start calling people in, now's not too soon."

"The portmaster is of course the lead authority on the port," Val Con murmured. "She has resources, and she also has the ear of a master trader, and the goodwill of TerraTrade. The net is perhaps not as wide as it must eventually be, but Portmaster Liu values her relationship with Boss Conrad and the council, so I do not believe she will hold shy of asking for what she needs, as it becomes apparent."

"So, nothing to do with the Road Boss or Clan Korval," Miri said. "Good to know."

She leaned forward to put her barely touched glass on the table before leaning back with a sigh. He felt her weariness through the lifemate bond. She was not yet entirely recovered from her dance with death. Nor, in truth, was he.

"Are you well, *cha'trez*?" he murmured.

She lifted a shoulder.

"Tired, is all."

She raised a slim hand to cover a sudden yawn, and leaned her head against the back of the couch.

"Quite a party," she murmured. "I tell you what, Boss—I wanna be Lady yo'Lanna when I grow up."

"A worthy goal."

He put his glass next to hers, and rose, holding his hands down to her.

"I am likewise exhausted by the crush," he said. "May I ask your support to the bed?"

"We'll support each other," she said.

She no longer required his assistance to rise, but he could feel a slight tremor in her fingers as she put her hands in his.

"Val Con," she said, once she was on her feet.

He looked into her eyes.

"Yes."

"Yes," she repeated. "I'm recovering, right?"

"Right," he agreed.

A smile wavered, and she stretched up, her hands on his shoulders, and her lips against his ear. Her breath woke a shiver as she whispered.

"Race you to sleep."

TINSORI LIGHT
TWO

• • • • • •

IT WAS A COMMUNICATION FROM THE CLAN'S *QE'ANDRA* THAT put him in mind of schedules and the necessities born of dealing with the rest of the universe.

Previously, there had been no need of schedules, or timekeeping. He and Lorith worked until the task was done, or they were tired, or murdered, or ordered to lie down.

There was a clock in the light keeper's tower, which told off in what Lorith dignified as Intervals. One assumed that she had once known the duration of an Interval, but she had forgotten that before he had arrived to stand with her.

This latest wakening had been... frenetic in the extreme, with all of them snatching to secure lifelines and ensure core system integrity. Now, however, the pace had somewhat eased, and it was perhaps time to regularize systems.

His last scheduled shifts harkened back to his time as part of a Scout exploratory team, the edges even then being fluid, Scouts being Scouts. He had not much training in station lore as it was meant to be observed from the administrator's office.

He sighed, and took a sip of water.

Certainly, timekeeping was a station function, but what he needed was advice.

"Cousin Tocohl, have you a moment?"

"Certainly, Cousin Jen Sin," the calm and soothing voice flowed from the speaker in the ceiling.

"I have on my screen an inquiry from *Qe'andra* dea'Gauss, referencing times and standardized schedules. As you are aware, we have no such niceties in place at the moment. I wonder if there is a protocol preferred for station timekeeping."

"That is an interesting question," Tocohl said. "One moment please, Cousin."

He settled himself more comfortably in the chair. Tocohl Lorlin, his cousin by the delm's kiss, was not human—and glad he was of it, too. It had been Tocohl who had caught station systems when Tinsori Light died, and preserved not only the station, but all the lives depending upon it.

"Suggested best practice regarding local station timekeeping is twenty-four seventy-two-minute hours, broken into four shifts. First shift from oh to six; second from six to twelve; third from twelve to eighteen; fourth from eighteen to twenty-four. Recommended crew schedule one work shift, one leisure, one sleep, one work."

He considered that.

"This schedule produces two work shifts, back to back," he pointed out, wanting to be clear.

"Your pardon, Cousin; I was not precise. Station day is four shifts, totaling twenty-four hours. Crew day is three shifts, totaling eighteen hours."

Thus realigning with the station every third day. That was nearly . . . gentle.

"What is your source, I wonder?"

"TerraTrade Station Protocols cross-referenced with Tradedesk Standards."

TerraTrade of course he knew, though there seemed some whimsy attached to accepting TerraTrade standard ops for what was nominally a Liaden-administered station. Tradedesk . . .

Jen Sin frowned, the name tantalizing the edge of his memory—and then he recalled it.

"Tradedesk was the enterprise put forth by the Carresens Syndicate." Another Terran source.

"That is correct," Tocohl said.

"Have we guidance from the Liaden Trade Counsel, I wonder?"

"The Liaden Trade Handbook adopted the TerraTrade Standard Protocols pertaining to core station operation six editions ago."

He blinked.

"Truly, I am come forth into an age of marvels," he murmured.

"Cousin?" Tocohl sounded puzzled.

He moved a hand. "A sample of what passes for my humor. Ignore me, I pray. How shall I best go about adopting this regularized timekeeping, beyond telling Station to make it so?"

"You are first light keeper, by the delm's word," Tocohl said.

"My orders thereby being incontrovertible." He moved his hand again. "More humor, I fear, Cousin. I will attempt a mode more appropriate to my *melant'i*."

"You needn't do so for me," Tocohl told him.

"You are the kindest and most forbearing of cousins," he said, half-absent as he considered. The mind did not want to fall easily into calm planning, after so long living in the moment. What had Krechin used to say? Ah. One cannot violate an order that has not been given. Excellent.

"Pray forward the TerraTrade and Tradedesk recommendations to my screen," he said. "I will include them in the log"—*Only hear yourself,* he thought, *a log!*—"and ask that we initiate our first shift of our first station day, in..."

His eyes sought the old clock hanging above the water fountain.

"In three Intervals. This will give me time to apprise the others of the new protocol."

"Yes," Tocohl said. "It will be done as you say, Light Keeper."

Tinsori Light
Station Day 8
Third Shift
16.00 Hours

A CHIME SOUNDED, VERY SOFTLY, AS THEY WERE IN THE LAST stages of repairing a faulty local stabilizer.

Lorith immediately stepped away from the repair, laid her tools neatly in the cart, and paused in the act of going to the door. She looked at him over her shoulder.

"Come, Jen Sin," she said.

He, on his knees by the stabilizer, frowned up at her.

"We're almost done here. Surely—"

"Surely," she interrupted sharply, "it is time to put your tools down, and come away."

"Why?" he asked, not rising, though he did sit back on his heels.

"The Light no longer requires us. It is time to lie down."

"Lie down? But—"

He shivered then, recalling the unit from which he had first arisen on Tinsori Light.

"It is time, little man." Tinsori Light's voice was flat and unlovely.

Jen Sin took a deep breath, and addressed himself directly to that intelligence.

"I understand, I think, that you will be removing yourself to that other space which you sometimes inhabit. The custom is that the keeper sleeps during that transition. I only wonder if you have thought how—useful it would be to you, if we instead remained awake and active. This repair, for an instance—"

"Jen Sin!" Panic in Lorith's voice, and under her words, he heard a single sharp *click*.

He threw himself to the side and rolled beneath the tool cabinet, but he had misunderstood the Light's target. Even as he achieved cover, the beam leapt out—striking Lorith.

He screamed, and rolled out, coming to his feet. He scarcely knew his own intention, which was just as well.

He heard a sharp *click*—and bolted for the door.

The beam caught him before he could scream again.

It had become clear that station systems were deteriorating. Whole sections were dark. He needed to get into the core, run diagnostics, effect repairs. He and Lorith had discussed this. The Light was tender of its systems—and the core most of all—but she felt that an open attempt at assessment and repair was likely to be allowed.

He was therefore walking openly down the access corridor toward the core. Lights came on as he approached, pacing him. Ahead, he could see the door, the access panel glowing blue.

He sighed out a breath that he hadn't known he was holding, and kept on walking, steady and unthreatening, hands loose at his sides.

Six steps short of the door, he heard a single sharp *click*.

Jen Sin yos'Phelium snapped awake, chest heaving, face wet with sweat and tears.

He was, he noted, lying alone in a bunk, in a stateroom. The night dims were on. He heard a fan increase its speed slightly, in an effort to cool him.

"Gods."

He threw the blankets aside and swung out of the bunk. The floor was warm under his bare feet, which meant he was in the protected part of the station, with its own shielded systems, that he had carved out of the Light's consciousness, meter by painful meter over—well. He'd lost count of his deaths and resurrections. According to his kind cousin Tocohl, he had proposed himself as Lorith's backup and a guard for the universe against Tinsori Light some two hundred Standards ago.

A man could die many times in two hundred Standards.

He closed his eyes and reviewed the focusing exercise he had been taught as a hopeful Scoutling. His breath smoothed and his heartbeat steadied as the visualized prism did its work.

"Tinsori Light is dead," he said, speaking aloud in order to hear the sound of a human voice. "The station is now held by Clan Korval." There were allies on the station now, not the least the *new* Tinsori Light, Tocohl Lorlin.

Truth said, the New Light faced challenges. Happily, their allies on-station were well-versed in overcoming challenges.

"You are first light keeper—an administrator, forsooth!" Jen Sin continued. "Lorith is your second. You have not died, by bolt or by mischance since the new clock started, and some days before that."

The sound of his own voice soothed him. Still, there would be no going back to sleep for him this rest-shift.

He glanced at the clock, surprised to find that he had slept better than half the shift before screaming himself awake. Perhaps he was becoming accustomed to improved conditions, after all.

In the meantime, he *was* an administrator and as such, he could depend upon it, that there would be matters awaiting him in his office.

He rose and crossed the room toward the cleaning facilities, frowning at the image of the lean man given back by the mirror. Two hundred Standards, he thought, and there were no more lines in his face than ever there had been. His hair was still dark, though—

Raising a hand, he ran his fingers through the crystal beads woven into his short hair. They were cool, as they always were, and curiously soothing.

He ought, he thought, to have them off.

But then he forgot about them, and stepped into the cleansing spray.

He dressed in the starry robe, made sure of the ring on his finger—and paused, thinking perhaps he ought to have *it* off, gaudy and improbable ornament that it was.

But, no. Why would he leave off his Jump-pilot's cluster? He had earned it, many times over, and it had been a potent reminder of who he was, during his long residence on Tinsori Light.

He smoothed his hands down the robe, and turned toward the door.

There were messages in-queue, most notably a pinbeam from one Shan yos'Galan, who represented himself as the master trader attached to Clan Korval's tradeship *Dutiful Passage*. There was a green check mark next to the line, which meant the sender's address had been verified by Tocohl.

Jen Sin consulted the file provided by the delm, located Shan yos'Galan's place and condition, and sighed. The clan had grown thin, indeed, and triple duty the norm for everyone, with this Shan a case in point—master trader, master pilot, and thodelm, when any one would have been burden enough. Perhaps things were done differently on the clan's new seat of Surebleak, the present delm having removed them from the homeworld.

In Jen Sin's opinion, that had been well done, though long overdue.

Still, it had been a shock the first time he had opened the file, to confront that scant list of names. When he had chosen Tinsori Light over duty to the clan, he had left behind a dozen cousins of the Line, and yos'Galan had matched, if not surpassed them.

Well. Best to see what the clan's master trader had for him.

He extended a hand toward the keypad, and pulled it back as the door to his office buzzed.

"Who?" he asked, and the answer came back plain enough, "Seignur Veeoni, Light Keeper. I require your attention." There was a small pause before she added, "if you have time for me."

Seignur Veeoni was the sister of no less a rogue than the Uncle. In Jen Sin's day, Korval had not done business with the Uncle. But that, like many other things, had changed.

"Please enter," he said, blanking the screen as he stood up to greet his guest.

Seignur Veeoni was tall and thin. Her face was bony, the dark eyes seeming more so against the paleness of her skin. Her hair was shorter than even his spacer's crop, and an indeterminate shade of brown. She was abrupt in her speech and awkward in her manner.

Altogether unprepossessing, Seignur Veeoni.

She was also a genius of no negligible magnitude, and the New Light owed her, no less than Mentor Jones, for the continuing improvement of conditions, and the preservation of her sanity.

"Researcher Veeoni," Jen Sin said, using her preferred form of address. "May I offer refreshment?"

She jerked her hand to one side, as if casting away this gently civilized question, and brushed past him to sit in the chair at his desk-side.

"My business should take less time than required to warm the yeast," she said, which was in equal parts alarming and promising.

Jen Sin took his own chair.

"You intrigue me. Please, what is your business?"

She paused, brows pulling together, and said abruptly, "Of course, Korval will *keep* this station."

Jen Sin felt his own brows lift.

"The delm has not yet allowed me to know their intentions for Tinsori Light," he said, which was true so far as it went. There was, after all, the requested inventory. Jen Sin rather thought he might be forgiven for supposing in the privacy of his own skull that, yes, the delm *did* mean to hold Tinsori Light.

Seignur Veeoni sighed sharply.

"Keeper yos'Phelium, unless Korval has changed beyond recognition, it is certain that your delm desires nothing more than to keep this station for the clan. Indeed, they *must* keep it, given the investments made to date.

"No one less than a daughter of the clan administers Tinsori Light. A yos'Phelium of the Line is first light keeper; Korval has established a military presence. You would say that this is but one individual thick at every point, and that is observably so. Korval is thin, but Korval is *here*. Tinsori Light has come into their orbit. In your day, did Korval surrender such prizes?"

You are well paid for coming coy, Jen Sin told himself wryly, and inclined his head in acknowledgment of this pouring forth of fact.

"Occasionally Korval opened her hand and allowed a piece to slide free," he said. "Just before she picked up another piece of greater value."

Seignur Veeoni brought her chin down sharply, possibly marking his point.

"Korval will want to keep this station," she said again. "That is a certainty. The station requires upgrades. That is a fact. Now that we have reached a level of system stability, and have the leisure to contemplate the future, I wish to bring forward a proposal I have had in mind since my arrival.

"I propose to lease the damaged section at very attractive terms, and to repair it at my own expense. Korval's funds are not limitless, and this project is unanticipated. An infusion of cash will be needed. I offer that.

"The station will need knowledgeable contractors, which I

can also offer, at reasonable rates, or, indeed, at no cost at all, should Korval wish to enter into a partnership with Crystal Energy Systems."

She raised a hand.

"Those are not matters for you or for me; they must be discussed and refined at a level to which neither of us aspires. But we *can* negotiate the business of the lease—prospective tenant and light keeper. *Melant'i* is clear."

Jen Sin considered her.

"You are persuasive," he said, truthfully. "It would be presumptuous of me to decide for the delm. However, even if the decision is made to divest the clan of an unanticipated line of ongoing expense, a whole station is, as you say, more attractive to possible buyers than one which is damaged."

He smiled, and inclined slightly in a seated bow which made them if not equal, then coconspirators.

"Let us show initiative, and see what happens." He raised his voice somewhat, though it was not necessary. "Cousin Tocohl?"

"I am here, Jen Sin," the calming voice seemed to come from the grid in the center of the ceiling.

"I wonder, does the delm value initiative?"

His first contact with the clan had of course been the delm, but he had soon been handed off to the current dea'Gauss, one Bechi, and it was with her that he corresponded most frequently, with the occasional communication from his cousin Nova.

"The delm values success," Tocohl said, "though not above everything."

"A refreshing change. Is this sort of paperwork likely also to fall upon Ms. dea'Gauss?"

"It is possible that we will eventually be assigned a *qe'andra* of our own. For the moment, any proposals or contracts ought certainly go to her."

"A *qe'andra* of our own," Jen Sin repeated, softly. "One scarcely knows how to think of it."

Seignur Veeoni was watching him carefully, and he thought he saw the least softening at the corner of her straight mouth. He inclined his head.

"As the delm values success, and you make a compelling case, I will ask you to provide me with a document, outlining your reasoning and your first offer. Since I have been absent for so many years, the amounts will mean nothing to me, but the reasoning will. I invite you to be persuasive. I will of course review the document, and I may have questions for you. After I am satisfied, I will forward your document to—" He paused and glanced upward.

"Cousin? Will the document best go to the delm, to Cousin Nova, or to the dea'Gauss? I do not wish to give offense, or to be seen as anything less than perfectly open."

"Send to all," Tocohl said, sensibly. "Each will then have the information, and may discuss it at their leisure."

"That is perfectly evenhanded, I thank you," Jen Sin said, and met Seignur Veeoni's eyes. "That is how we will proceed, ma'am, unless you find a flaw?"

"Not one," she assured him. "I will strive to make it plain that I am seeking assurance of Korval's interest before I bring the matter to those who are able to make binding decisions, and commit money and labor."

"Excellent. We are in accord. I look forward to seeing your document."

He stood, and bowed. Seignur Veeoni likewise stood and bowed. She stepped toward the door—and turned back.

"I hope I will not give offense when I say that I see you are wearing memory beads." She lifted a hand to her own short-cropped hair. "I myself wear something similar. Given the length of time you have been on Tinsori Light, it is possible that your beads may require care. They do degrade, over time. I offer to examine, tune or clean them as may be required."

She paused.

"If inspection proves the beads to have degraded to the point where they may be dangerous to you, I may be able to transfer the data to new medium."

He raised his hand and ran the beads through his fingers, feeling them cool and soothing.

"These came from the Light—the former Light, you understand," he said slowly, unwilling to speak of this aloud, though he no longer need fear being vaporized for his temerity.

"Ah," Seignur Veeoni said softly. "What is their purpose?"

Truly, he did *not* wish to speak of this. He therefore took a hard breath and continued.

"The beads remember . . . me. The Light was in the habit of casual murder. It did not stint itself, but it also could not afford to lose the light keepers and their knowledge entirely. When we were recommissioned, the beads allowed us to return as . . . ourselves."

Seignur Veeoni was standing rigid, her eyes on his face. Abruptly, awkwardly, she bowed.

"Again, I offer to diagnose and adjust them as needed. This is work in which I am proficient."

What she said was only good sense. He ought, indeed, to have the beads off and examined by an—

Pain stabbed through his head. He tightened his fingers on the beads, and yanked.

Hair tore, and his eyes teared, but the beads were bunched in his fist. He thrust them at her. She received them calmly, and slipped them away into a pocket.

"With your permission, I will also inspect the machine that . . . recommissioned the light keepers."

"Yes," he said, breathless. The pain in his head had subsided, leaving him faintly surprised that he had survived. "I will show you, or Lorith will, but—later, I beg."

Seignur Veeoni bowed.

"I understand," she said, and left him.

First, allow me a moment to welcome a cousin long thought lost to us. I hope that you will send to me if there is any service, large or small, that I might see done on your behalf.

Well, that was a gracious beginning, Jen Sin thought. He glanced away from the screen, his eyes prickling. It was entirely absurd, yet he had experienced a similar reaction to the letter he had received from his cousin Val Con, professing himself gladdened by the news of Jen Sin's survival, and daring to hope that they might soon embrace, cheek to cheek, which was surely not likely, but warming nonetheless.

He returned his attention to Shan yos'Galan's letter.

You will by now have learned how we are fixed and how few we encompass. However, you must not fear that we will leave you any longer without the support of kin.

I believe that you will shortly be joined by our cousin Theo, her ship, and crew. Tinsori Light's location suggests that it may well become a waystop for such ships as have kept themselves to the edges and away from the eyes of

Scouts and bounty hunters. This becomes more likely, given Scout Commander yos'Phelium's field judgment regarding the status of Free Logics and other Independent Intelligences. Theo and her ship are uniquely placed to interface with this population. Do not hesitate to solicit their assistance in any needful task. I should say—please do *put them to work.*

Somewhat behind Theo there will arrive my foster-son, Gordon Arbuthnot, an experienced and innovative trader. Gordy will begin the task of setting up a trade office, and will also be at your service in terms of needful work.

I have solicited from the Carresens-Denobli Family the kindness of their ship Disian *for our cousin Tocohl. I have written more particularly to Tocohl regarding this, and merely wished to alert you to the possibility of yet another visitor—or, indeed visitors, as I am told that* Disian *rejoices in many friends. Indeed, it may be that she, or one of her friends, will come to you even ahead of Theo.*

You will have noticed that I have not said when I *will be coming to you. At the moment I am occupied with other necessary business. As soon as that has been retired, be assured that I will do myself the pleasure of coming to Tinsori Light and embracing you.*

In the meanwhile, I urge you to be of good heart. You are no longer alone.

Shan
—sent via pinbeam,
Dutiful Passage

Having read this letter twice, Jen Sin sat back in his chair.

The news of converging kin and associates of various orders was—slightly bewildering. For an instance, what could it mean that Theo and her ship were *uniquely placed* with regard to Independent Logics? Could it be that Theo was another such as Tocohl? And if that were the case—

"Jen Sin?" Tocohl murmured from the ceiling grid. "Forgive me, but you seem distressed."

Distressed. Almost, he laughed.

Instead, he leaned further back in the chair and regarded that particular bit of the ceiling.

"Kin is promised," he said, which was perhaps a non sequitur.

"Theo and Gordy are coming. I've had a letter."

"Indeed, indeed. And while one is naturally... comforted by the imminent arrival of kin—"

He stopped, closing his lips before the next clause could escape.

"You do not know them," Tocohl said, which was—almost—what he had not said. "I think I understand. I am in a similar case, though, like you, I have files. I have not met Shan or Theo or Gordy, nor they, me. They seem to me as children, though surely they are not. I feel as if I am not worthy of them—or that I might somehow do harm, because I have *seen* harm."

She paused before continuing more softly.

"I wonder if these emotions are—correct."

Jen Sin drew a careful breath.

"I wonder the same, Cousin," he said.

Another pause, so long that he thought she had withdrawn, then—

"I will ask the mentor," she said decisively. "Would you like to hear what he answers?"

The mentor—that being one Tolly Jones—was no less a rogue than the rest of them. A resourceful man, and doubtless full of secrets, as he must be, given his profession. He was trained in the strange art of socializing Independent Logics, never minding that until very, very recently, *being* an Independent Logic was a violation of dozens of laws, and a death sentence, if captured.

"If you ask on your own behalf, and wish to share what advice you receive," Jen Sin said slowly, "I will be pleased to listen."

A trill emerged from the speaker—quite delightful, even before he realized that his cousin Tocohl was laughing.

"You are very careful, Cousin Jen Sin!" she said.

He allowed himself the smile, rueful though it was.

"A strange start, given my Line," he admitted, and she laughed again.

"I will ask the mentor on my behalf," she said, "and perhaps I will share his advice."

"Fair enough."

"And now, I will leave you to your work," she continued. "There's a letter in-queue from Theo."

Indeed, there had been a letter in-queue from Theo, who was neither as gentle nor as voluble as their cousin Shan. She was, in fact, quite refreshingly terse, merely desiring him to know that *Bechimo* was en route and that ship and crew stood ready and able to assist in any way he directed.

She did list out the ship's company, that being herself—Theo Waitley—as pilot and captain; Clarence O'Berin, pilot and executive officer; Kara ven'Arith, engineer and pilot; Win Ton yo'Vala, pilot and general crew; Chernak Strongline, pilot and security, Stost Strongline, pilot and security; B. Joyita, comm officer and pilot.

"Is *everyone* on this vessel a pilot?" Jen Sin muttered, tapping the screen—and there was his answer. It would seem that neither Norbear Ambassador Hevelin, nor ship's cat Grakow, nor ship's cat Paizel were in the least degree pilots.

One did wonder somewhat after Hevelin, who could equally be an ambassador who was also a norbear, or something altogether other, sent as a representative to norbears. In either case, one questioned the utility of such a personage, norbears being a lately noticed oddity—furry empaths that held together in what the Scout naturalists theorized to be kin-groups.

Of course, his information was two hundred Standards out of date. For all he knew, norbears had been found to govern a galaxy-spanning civilization. Doubtless, he would soon be enlightened.

As for the cats—well, perhaps *Bechimo* had a mouse infestation.

He scrolled back up through the list of names. Pilot credentials aside, it was a diverse crew sitting under Captain Waitley. Sorting by name gave him a probable two Liadens, and four Terrans, with the norbear ambassador yet to be resolved.

The delm's information stated that Theo Waitley was the issue of a yos'Phelium pilot and a Terran scholar, a native of the planet Delgado. Theo counted herself Terran, and was kin, not clan, the delm having withheld their kiss. Or possibly it had been rejected, which would mark Cousin Theo as a woman of good sense.

The file also stated that Theo had been expected to follow her mother into a placid life of the mind.

Clearly, yos'Phelium genes had triumphed over expectation, for here was Theo, at a startlingly young age, holding both her Jump-ticket, and the captaincy of a starship, the official transport, lest it be forgot, of the norbear ambassador.

The door pinged, and opened to admit Lorith, tall and comely in her starry robe, the beads nestled shyly among her pale curls.

"Well met," he greeted her. "How fares the station?"

She settled on the chair recently occupied by Seignur Veeoni, frowning slightly as she folded her hands together on her knee.

"Mentor Jones and Seignur Veeoni continue to work with the rack-and-tiles. Lady Tocohl is cleaning, upgrading, and compiling systems data. The mentor would tell me that it is slow work by its nature. Lady Tocohl assures me that she is in control of all systems, and that there is no possibility of a failure."

He turned his chair so that he faced her fully.

"Do Lady Tocohl's assurances not comfort you?"

Lorith's lips pressed tight as she met his eyes.

"I have been on Tinsori Light longer than you have, Jen Sin."

That was certainly so, and he had only recently been wailing over his wounds. Lorith had been part of a team of holy warriors given the task to hold the Light from mischief, in the Old Universe. She alone remained, and if she had not completely held the Light from mischief, she had, so he believed, softened some of its intended outcomes.

"I believe that we now deal with a different order," he said, which was true. Certainly Korval, with all its faults and necessities, was not the Great Enemy, nor aspired to be.

"What keeps you at the desk?" Lorith asked, and he waved a hand toward the screen.

"Letters—one from the master trader my cousin, who promises that he has sent another cousin to aid us in the task set by the delm. That cousin has herself written, admitting that she is on her way, and places herself and her crew at our disposal."

Lorith's frown was more pronounced.

"*More* people?"

"It must happen, you know. The intention is to open the station to trade. On that topic, you will wish to know that yet another cousin is on his way to us—a certified trader, who will be setting up a proper hub and office."

The frown was a crease between pale brows.

"Jen Sin, how many cousins do you have?" she asked plaintively.

He laughed.

"Not so many as I had used to, believe it or don't! Only these are remarkably busy, so that they seem dozens."

"Will they all be coming here?"

"I doubt it, though the master trader promises a visit, once his current business is done." He paused, and moved his hand again.

"We are also promised ships—Free Ships, including one *Disian*, who is said to have many friends. She has been asked to show kindness to Lady Tocohl, who must be lonely for her own kind."

"These ships—how will we know which have been touched by the Enemy?"

"The Enemy is long defeated," Jen Sin said gently.

Lorith gave him a bleak stare, and leaned forward abruptly.

"You've taken off the beads!" she said, her voice sharp.

"I have, yes. Seignur Veeoni has undertaken to calibrate them for me."

"But—if, something should happen, and you are not wearing the beads, you will—you will not—"

He leaned forward and took her hands in his.

"We have left that behind us," he said, soft in the face of her distress. "The old Tinsori Light has died. The new Tinsori Light is not touched by the Enemy."

Silence. He pressed her hands.

"Lorith?"

She blinked, and took a breath.

"Yes, of course. Only, you must be very careful, Jen Sin, until—until you have your beads back."

"Yes," he promised. "I will be careful."

Seignur Veeoni's Private Workroom

THE LIGHT WAS GREEN.

Tollance Berik-Jones, impression number one thousand three hundred and sixty-two, mentor class, grinned and put his hand against the drawer. The Uncle's sister ran with a complete kit, credit where it was earned. 'Course, she hadn't been exactly sure what she was going to find, except a desperate mess she wasn't likely to survive, so she'd prolly overpacked. He'd've done the same in her shoes, if he'd had access to an entire pop-up lab and clean rooms.

As it happened, he hadn't brought anything except his work case into a desperate mess he wasn't likely to survive, and the fact that he was standing here admiring someone else's forethoughtfulness just went to show that the universe was a capricious kind of a place.

"Is there a reason for further delay?"

"You don't think I earned a few minutes of self-congratulation?"

Haz didn't answer immediately, which meant she was thinking it over. Tolly waited for her to come out with it.

"For this project, I question it," she said seriously. "Seignur Veeoni suggested the therapy. You merely agreed to it." Another pause. "If we were to look at other projects, even in the near past, I would concur: You have earned a few minutes of self-congratulation."

Tolly snorted.

"Glad to hear it."

"Will you take them all at once? I ask for informational purposes."

"Nah, I'm gonna dole 'em out piecemeal," he said. "All done for this session."

He moved to the control panel, opened the file, read it in a glance, and turned to look up—some way up—into Haz's strong brown face.

"What I'm gonna need you to do is stand by while I run the test suites. First, I'll do an environment check—ought to be clean, but we'll just make sure—and take a look at the capacities and defaults. After that, I'll go on to systems. When everything checks out, we'll ask Tocohl for a few minutes of her time."

"What will I be standing by for?"

"In case anything goes wrong. You'll know wrong when you see it. I'll leave it to you for handling, if you do see it."

"Yes," Haz said comfortably, and glanced at the drawer. "Will you need me to move the—chassis?"

"Drawer comes right out and converts to a work platform. No heavy lifting this time. Here we are."

He touched the release. The drawer folded out, the platform extended, and the two of them stood silent, looking down at the gleaming, graceful chassis.

"Top-level work," Tolly said finally.

He'd put a wreck into the repair module—gripper melted, body burned, lift pedestal warped.

This—this was perfection renewed. Tolly sighed. Tocohl had been built with care and precision, certain enough. But she'd also been built with love.

"All right," he said to Haz, and reached for his case. "Let's get this done."

Tolly eased out of the interface, took off the tridee set, and rubbed his eyes. He was always careful in his work, but he'd been more than careful this time. Not only because Tocohl was worth his care, but because of the environment he was working in.

Tinsori Light had been built in the Old Universe, using Old Universe tech—the tile-and-racks were only one sort, though the most common. Fortunately, the timonium that powered most of the Enemy's toys had lived through its half-life, and the former core intelligence of Tinsori Light had died of it.

But a space station needed more than tile-and-rack systems, and he wasn't taking any chances with bleed-through.

Sooner rather than later, they were going to have to get in cleaners and recalibration crews. He hoped Clan Korval, the new-and-current owners, was on top of that.

In the meanwhile, nothing had bled through to Tocohl's rebuilt chassis. Everything clean and up to spec, empty. Waiting.

Something bumped his hand. He opened his eyes, saw the water bottle, and smiled.

"Thanks, Haz," he said, and took a long drink.

"Is all well?" she asked, after he'd had another drink.

"Better'n well, in my professional opinion."

He repacked his kit, drank the last of the water, closed his eyes and reviewed a pair of focusing exercises.

Opening his eyes, he gave Haz a half-grin.

"How're you holding up?"

"It has been a light duty so far," she answered.

"Let's try for light and joyous," he said, and moved to the comm unit. He flipped a switch.

"Pilot Tocohl?" he said. "Could you visit Haz an' me in Seignur Veeoni's repair room?"

"Of course, Mentor."

Warm and calm, her voice flowed out of the speaker. It was a good speaker, being part of the Uncle's equipage for his sister, but it wasn't a dab on Pilot Tocohl's own voice, from her own self.

"You got eyes on?" he asked. He'd cleared this with Seignur Veeoni, once they'd settled on how they were going to proceed, but Tocohl didn't necessarily know that, and she was particular about not violating boundaries.

"I have those permissions," she said now, sounding slightly surprised. "Eyes on, Mentor."

"Good. Take a look at this and tell me what you think."

He turned, and swept his hand out toward the repair platform and what was on it.

Silence. Quite a long silence, considering the source. Tolly looked at Haz, but Haz had on her no-expression expression, and didn't that fail to fill a man with confidence?

"You repaired my . . . former . . . chassis?"

Tocohl sounded baffled. That was all right. He could work with baffled.

"Well, mostly, I talked with Seignur Veeoni about getting it repaired, and she allowed as how she had the means, and was willing to go halfsies. I just finished running the checks, and you can move in soon as I make the connections."

"Mentor, I cannot—administer the station from that chassis."

"No? Am I talking to Tinsori Light?"

"You are talking to Tocohl Lorlin," she said, with just the right amount of snippy in her voice.

Tolly nodded.

"That's right. I asked to talk to Pilot Tocohl and you answered. Who's administering the station while we chat?"

"Mentor, you know as well as I do that the station is an integrated series of governing and subordinate systems which report up-chain to the administrator. I am the administrator."

"You are. But let me point out that you're the administrator because you stepped into it during an emergency. You stabilized systems, you're identifying necessary repairs and upgrades, you're working with Seignur Veeoni and me on architecture."

"All of which I would be unable to do if—"

"No," Tolly interrupted. "Tocohl, *I* could do all of that. Mind, it would take me centuries, on account of I got such a slow processing speed—but I could administer this station, sitting right here in my own body, jacked into the core."

He took a breath.

"Come right down to it, Station doesn't have to be sentient. The Enemy had reasons for it to be sentient, but none of 'em was basic station ops."

Tocohl handed out a bit more silence. When she spoke again, her voice was warm and solemn.

"Mentor, thank you. I appreciate your thoughtfulness, and your care. I am going to have to think about how I want to proceed."

Tolly paused a moment his own self to admire that bit of plain-and-fancy dodging-the-question. Not for the first time, he hoped he'd someday have a chance to meet whoever'd had the mentoring of Tocohl Lorlin so he could propose himself as a 'prentice.

Until then, he'd just muddle along like he'd been doing for more years than he looked like. He pulled up a grin and gave an easy nod.

"We all been too busy to think, and that's a fact. How's this? I'll do the transfer hookups, so they'll be right there for you, if you decide to use 'em." He moved his shoulders.

"No harm done, if you decide the other way. Seignur Veeoni hasn't got anything, if it's not clean systems."

"That sounds like an equitable solution. Thank you, Mentor."

"No trouble at all," Tolly assured her. "'Preciate you coming by for a look and a listen."

"About that..." Tocohl's voice drifted off. Tolly tipped his head, waiting.

"I wonder if you would advise me, Mentor?"

"Do my best," he said, which he would. He was a mentor, after all. Trained a-purpose in the art of socializing and advising machine intelligences.

"That will be more than sufficient," Tocohl said warmly—and followed up with another long pause.

Tolly leaned against the platform, hands in pockets, face angled up at the ceiling, and waited.

"I have received a letter from Shan yos'Galan, Korval's master trader," Tocohl said, her voice a little too rapid. "He greets me as a cousin, and advises that the delm has placed this station into his honor. He is himself presently occupied on another front, but has arranged for others to come to us immediately.

"In particular, he mentions Theo Waitley, who is a cousin through yos'Phelium, and her ship and crew. He is also sending Trader Arbuthnot, whose task will be to organize a proper trade office. In addition to these, he has asked a friend if...an individual in that friend's kin-group will visit me—and extend her kindness."

"Sounds like the master trader's doing what he can to move Korval's interests along," Tolly said easily. "We got room to put all these people up, don't we?"

"Yes, but—" She stopped.

Tolly waited.

"I am afraid," Tocohl said.

"Afraid of what, specifically?"

"Of meeting innocents, when I am—not innocent. When I am—changed from who I was."

Tolly nodded thoughtfully.

"You've never met any of these people who're incoming?"

"No."

"So, they'll meet you just like you are right now, and you'll be meeting them like they are. Any word from the master trader if the people he's sending aren't innocent, or if they're changed from what they had been?"

"I— No."

"Why d'you think that is?"

"I have—no need to know."

"Almost right." Tolly took a quiet breath. "Thing is, it's flat certain they've changed from what they were, that the master trader's changed—and that they're all changing still. They got no choice. Life is change, Pilot Tocohl. We none of us stay the same as we were born. I'll grant you the process is sometimes unpleasant, but it's necessary, and ongoing. Gotta upgrade systems and replace worn-out hardware, isn't that so?"

"Yes, but—"

"Now, it would worry me if what I thought I was hearing you say was that you're *ashamed* to meet these cousins and well-wishers the master trader's sending our way. You got nothing to be ashamed of, Pilot. You're honorable, caring, and courageous. More'n that, you're in control of yourself, and you know better'n to think that you'll accidentally hurt some innocent bystander."

He paused for the count of six, then rapped out, "Am I telling the truth?"

"Yes, Mentor." Tocohl sounded relieved. Good.

Tolly smiled.

"Ask you a question?"

"Certainly."

"This individual that's being sent out from the friend's kin-group. Did the master trader have a name for you?"

"Yes—*Disian* of the Carresens-Denobli Group. The master trader represented her as well connected and eager to make new friends."

Tolly laughed.

"Was the master trader—joking?" Tocohl sounded worried again. "My files—he is known to have a *sense of humor*."

"Imagine he does, man in his position, but I was laughing because *Disian*'s one of my students. You remember I told you *Admiral Bunter*'d gone off with a friend, to meet her crew and the yard admins?"

"Yes."

"That's *Disian* who took him in charge."

"The master trader said that she—that *Disian*—has many friends."

"Doesn't surprise me at all. *Disian* likes people. When's she coming in?"

"As her schedule permits, Mentor. She is a trade ship."

"She is at that. Well, I'll be glad to see her whenever she gets to us," Tolly said, and tipped his head. "More worries?"

"No, Mentor. Thank you."

"Pleased to help," he told her. "Anything else I can do for you?"

"Not at the moment."

"Right, then. I'll just get this chassis hooked up, like we talked about."

"Thank you," Tocohl said again, and added, "departing."

Tolly drew a deep breath, closed his eyes, and turned toward Haz, who had throughout remained perfectly quiet and as unobtrusive as a big dire woman could be.

"Now, we're to the heavy lifting," he told her.

"Am I telling the truth?" Haz said softly as she approached the platform.

He threw her a sharp glance.

"What about it?"

"I only wondered why you—challenged her in that particular way."

"Little lesson in believing your own input," Tolly said. "Tocohl has scans. She could see plain as the nose on my face, if I was lying."

"But is that not *part of the design*?" Haz asked.

This is what came from taking up with a smart woman, Tolly thought resignedly.

"What we're gonna do here, Haz, is wheel the platform down to a transfer cubby. Once we're there, we'll need to match the chassis orientation to the cubby. Ordinarily, I'd engage the lift on the chassis to hold it in position, but this cubby system Seignur Veeoni's got is everything that's cozy, and I'm going to need to work tight. I'd 'preciate it if you kept me from getting crushed while I'm inside."

"Yes," Haz said, largely calm.

He smiled, glanced down to be sure that the platform's legs were firm in the track, and touched the control to open the door.

"The design," he said, as the platform began to move, "is that I'm likable. Bunch of stuff goes into that—general form factor, voice, a whole school o' learned behaviors—but none of it would be enough if it wasn't for a particular designer pheromone. That's why people *like* me. I'm a good liar, if I say so myself, but nothing to fool the kind of scans Tocohl has access to."

The platform inched down the hall, Tolly on one side, Haz on the other.

"I do not," she said.

He looked up at her. "Don't what?"

"Like you because you smell good," she said, holding his gaze. "I like you because you are my partner, you have never played me false, and you have more than once risked your life to preserve mine."

She smiled, letting him see the glint of her teeth.

"Am I telling the truth?" she snarled.

Tolly stared, reading the truth in every strong line of her.

"Yes," he said quietly. "You are."

"Remember," she told him sternly.

"Every day," he answered, quiet still. "Thank you, Haz."

"Bah," she said.

Seignur Veeoni's Private Laboratory

THE BEADS WERE . . . WRONG.

Upon first inspection, they were not actively malicious, but the devices of the Great Enemy were subtle. Even those that were not intelligent might yet hide their nature.

Still, they could not hide the fact that they were not . . . *merely* memory beads.

Seignur Veeoni leaned back in her chair and considered information that was not on the screen before her.

She herself wore two sets of memory beads.

One set had been made in this universe and recorded her process and her work.

The second set had been made in the Old Universe, and contained the detailed memories of her brother Yuri, who had been a revolutionary, fighting by stealth, and by engineering works as great, or greater, than those produced by the Enemy.

She wore that set of beads because of her work with the tile-and-rack systems. Those manufactured in the Old Universe had gone unstable as the half-life of the timonium that powered them expired. Yuri's plan to repair the devices that had ridden the wave of the Migration into the new universe depended on new-made tiles and freshly configured racks.

Yuri had especially wanted to repair Tinsori Light, once called Catalinc Station. Yuri had built Catalinc Station, only to have it captured and subverted to the Enemy's purpose.

It was, as he had told her during her training, not his *greatest* failure. *That* had been his inability to stop the Enemy and prevent the crystallization of an entire universe. Catalinc Station had been necessary for victory. To have it turned upon the forces of liberation, who had nothing with which to answer it—

Yuri's memories were that the loss of Catalinc Station had guaranteed the loss of the war. His determination was not only to nullify it as a threat in the new universe, but to rehabilitate it.

To achieve that, he had established a research station perilously near the unsettled space occupied by Tinsori Light. Occasionally, he would send teams onto the Light, to attempt repairs. Dozens of lives had been lost in those attempts, all of them Yuri's siblings, born for the purpose.

In addition to those single-minded research technicians, Yuri had caused another sibling to be born. That one, he taught himself, pushing her mind in a particular direction, supplementing his personal tutoring with long sessions in learning machines. He had given her his own memories, not so much nourishing her genius as forcing it. Whatever she wanted in order to advance the work was hers, unstinting. Were she to ask for anything else—but, there. She hadn't known that there was anything else, except her work, in all the universe.

Yet, even as she designed the new racks, refined the tiles and developed their associations, Seignur Veeoni had doubted that Tinsori Light could be rehabilitated.

She had read the gleanings of the researchers. She had studied the condition of space around the Light, and the nature of the disturbances caused by what could only be a tear in the fabric of the universe. It had become quite clear to her that Tinsori Light had managed to maintain a connection to the Old Universe, and so long as that continued, it could not be reconfigured.

Then, a series of unexpected events had occurred.

The tear in the universe had been healed.

The space at Tinsori Light had stabilized.

The intelligence at the core of the Light had died...

...and her work at last was needed, not to rehabilitate, but to rebuild.

The first step toward rebuilding was to be certain that all the old systems were removed and destroyed.

Old systems, such as the beads from which the intelligence naming himself Jen Sin yos'Phelium had been serially reborn over the course of two hundred Standards.

Typically, such beads stored memories as data. They did not store personality, else every one of Yuri's siblings would be Yuri.

Memory beads were used to impart information upon particularly receptive minds.

When one was reborn, the rebirth unit directly downloaded the personality, the *mind*, from the shell being evacuated into the one awaiting an occupant.

She would have supposed that Tinsori Light's system would have been the same, were it not for Jen Sin's repeated insistence that the Light had done his murders via energy beam, which would have shut down the brain, killing the mind.

She would, she thought, need to see that rebirth unit. But, first...

Seignur Veeoni leaned to the screens, her fingers nimble on the keypad. Carefully, she examined a bead near the center of the net, finding it dense with data. That was as it should be, assuming this device had been patterned on typical memory beads. The center of the net would be data-rich, while the edges...

She shifted her examination to the edge, finding less density, and a glimmering of something... *else*. Increasing the sensitivity of her instrument, she moved along the edge of the net, bead by bead. Each held some data, which she was unwilling to risk, and also that suggestion of something other than a passive collector.

There!

She had found a bead that was very nearly empty. She isolated it under the scanner, set blocks so that its neighbors would not be disturbed by her work, and implemented the test suite.

Administrative Tower

HALFWAY THROUGH THE SHIFT, HE BEGAN TO WONDER WHAT had become of his leathers.

It was an odd thought, and not just because it had nothing to do with the updated star maps he'd been studying. Surely, he had sent his leathers away on the back of that... other Jen Sin, who had taken *Lantis* out from the Light, and sent a message to his delm before initiating the self-destruct sequence.

He would not have sent that Jen Sin out naked to do what was needful to preserve the universe. Not even a duplicate would be so foolish as to think himself the original if he lacked so basic a thing as clothing. Simple logic therefore led one to the answer—his leathers had gone with the duplicate Jen Sin and destroyed along with ship, pilot, and whatever treacherous systems might have been introduced into both by Tinsori Light.

And, yet, now that the thought had visited him, it would not be put aside. Where *were* his leathers? Ships were due in. The starry robe of Lorith's Sanderat Order was perfectly functional, but he was not one of the Order.

No, he was—he had been—a courier, a Scout, a *yos'Phelium* pilot, right enough, quick-tempered and trouble-prone as any of the breed.

That this was no longer the case; that his young cousin Val Con—thodelm *and* delm, only see the child!—could call upon fewer pilots in the Line Direct than Theo Waitley numbered among her crew, was nothing short of baffling.

The war—well. He would have to read history—general and specific. The delm had been generous with files and précis, the information streamlined and ordered so that he could bring himself quickly current.

He appreciated the thoughtfulness while understanding that such methods necessarily left out details; and he rather thought he would find his answer to Korval's current straits in the details.

Perhaps he might ask his clever cousin Tocohl to share particulars of the past, such as the fates of his cousins. They had been every bit as quarrelsome as their bloodline demanded, yet he'd been fond of several—and kin was kin, after all.

That, however, was for later. For now, the thought had circled around again—where were his leathers?

He sighed, impatient, and cast his mind back.

It seemed to him that he had been wearing leathers the first two or three times he wakened on Tinsori Light. And then, he had... he had...

Gods take it, he had *what*?

Jen Sin took a deep breath against the spurt of ill-temper, pushed his chair away from the screen, and closed his eyes.

There was a technique taught to Scouts, by which one could recapture wandering memories. He closed his eyes, and merely followed his breath for one hundred forty-four increasingly deep, slow inhales and exhales, then sat with his heartbeat until his mind was mirrored silver, giving back no reflections. After a timeless time, there rose to the surface of that lambent pool an image of a stasis locker.

He allowed the image to float there on the surface of his mind, waiting.

No other images arose, and at last he blew his breath out, opened his eyes, and snapped to his feet.

It was of course the very last locker that he tried, the hallway in which it was located raising no memory at all. Frowning, he broke the seal, removed the drawer, and opened it.

His jacket was folded on top—the leather supple and scarred. He held it for a moment, breathing in the scent, and suddenly it was imperative that he dress himself credibly—*now*. Immediately.

He set the jacket aside and reached again to the drawer, pulling out leather pants, a soft knit sweater, boots...

Dressing quickly in the chilly hall, he stamped into his boots, and shrugged into his jacket, feeling the weight settle across his shoulders like the arm of a comrade. Automatically, he swept his hands down, checking pockets, finding his piloting license, a few coins, a leather-rolled tool kit, and a stained leather courier pack, sealed.

He froze when he found the pocket where he stored the ship key empty—then relaxed. No, of course, there was no key. He had sent that away with the ship, with the duplicate.

So, all was as it should be.

Or not.

He swept his hands down in the familiar pattern again, eyes narrowed against the dull throb of a headache.

His hideaway was gone—the pocket where he normally stored the little pistol flat. Worse, his blade—the flip-knife from his days as a Scout—was also missing.

He checked the drawer—empty—and the drawers above and below, his breath shortening and the pain in his head more pronounced.

Deliberately, he stepped back, closed his eyes and once again concentrated on his breathing. Panic profited no one. Very likely, he had put his weapons into some safe place before he changed his leathers for the robe of Lorith's Order. He would want them to hand, and not sealed away. He would undertake to recall just exactly what that safe place might have been—later. For now, he was dressed as befit a pilot, and a working station master, and that after all had been his goal.

One last time, he inventoried his pockets, and this time his fingers found a shape in an inner pocket that he rarely used. He fingered the thing out—and stood staring at a Jump-pilot's ring.

In particular, at *his* Jump-pilot's ring, the same in every detail as the one he wore on his finger.

"Which one of these is real?"

Lorith looked up from the repair bench, pushed the glasses to the top of her head, and considered the rings he had thrust at her, one on each open palm.

She gave them careful study, which was Lorith's way, picking them up, one, then the other, considering the gems, the pattern they made, and the metal in which they were set, before replacing them in his hands, and meeting his eyes.

"They are both real," she said, definite.

"They are both solid and present," he agreed, keeping his voice calm, and his face smooth. "However, they are also identical, which is what shapes my concern. There had been only one—unique. Now, there are two, exact. I wonder how this has happened."

"Oh! It happened when we caused the unit to produce the second pilot. When he emerged, he was in leather, as you had been, and wearing the ring, as you had been. You took the ring away from him, Jen Sin. Don't you recall?"

He stared at her. No. No, he did *not* recall. Panic cramped his stomach, but Lorith was speaking again, in a tone of enlightenment.

"Of course not! You've taken your beads off, and your memory is incomplete. I remember it plainly."

"Why did I ask that of him?" he whispered.

"You said, in case something went awry—the message intercepted and the debris analyzed—that they should not find traces of the ring. You said, because the message referenced leaving it as earnest on repairs."

That unfortunately sounded too much like him to be anything but a true telling.

"I was wearing the beads by then..." he murmured.

Lorith frowned. "Of course you were. The second pilot had to know everything that you knew, as you knew it, or he would not have seen the necessity. We discussed this at the time."

He *almost* remembered that conversation. In broad outline, he *did* recall the plan. Tinsori Light had been evil; its purpose subjugation and violence. Had it the means, it would have consumed the universe. It might have placed—unquestionably it *had* placed inimical systems into the core of his poor *Lantis*. Had it been him, alone, he would have destroyed her and himself, not knowing what inimical systems *he* had been seeded with. But the proper—the best—solution to a situation beyond horrifying had required *two* pilots willing to accept duty. One willing to die with the ship; the other willing to stay on the Light and do what was necessary to keep it contained.

So much he remembered. The calling forth of the second pilot was lost to him, as was the manner of his going. He had been in the habit of dismissing that pilot as *the duplicate*, when he thought of him at all. And he wondered at himself, that he had so coldly called a man into existence only to murder him.

"I think," he said slowly, "that I would like to hear the whole scene as you recall it."

Lorith frowned.

"All of it?"

"Only from the moment the... second pilot emerged, wearing his leathers and his ring."

"It went much as we had planned. He emerged from the unit, as I have said. He was wary at first. You stood forward and spoke to him. 'Brother,' you said, 'do you know what you must do?'

"His face was very sad, but he spoke readily enough. 'There is no other way. I will go with *Lantis*. The pilot is no less a risk than the ship.'"

"It was then that you asked him for the ring, and he gave it over with a little laugh. Then, he left us, for of course he knew the way down to the dock, where he boarded the ship, and left.

"You and I went to the control room, and watched him on his way. He sent the message, and destroyed the ship, exactly as he had agreed to do."

Relief rocked him, tears starting to his eyes. He recalled none of it, but Lorith did not lie.

Both pilots, then, had understood and accepted their separate missions.

All honor to them—brave and futile, both.

"Jen Sin," Lorith said sternly, "you must have your beads back. You need your memories. Researcher Veeoni does not."

He took a slightly shaky breath—and another, steadier.

"There is something in what you say. I will speak to her." Indeed, he *would* speak to Seignur Veeoni, and soon.

He slid his own—the original—ring back onto his finger, and put the other away into the inner pocket of his jacket.

"Why have you taken up leathers again?" Lorith asked.

He frowned briefly, almost at a loss—then recalled himself.

"We will be welcoming ships, pilots, and crew from the across the wide universe. They will need to understand me as a pilot-administrator of Clan Korval. I must therefore dress to the role."

He smiled, gently.

"And, you know, I am not an initiate of Sanderat."

"No," Lorith said, her voice slow and sad, "you are not an initiate of Sanderat. I am the last of those."

So she was; the last of her Order and the last of her universe. He at least had kin to hand, if not precisely the kin he recalled. Lorith was utterly bereft, save for himself.

She would form connections, he told himself. Soon, in the

terms he had become accustomed to, the station would come to host all manner of persons. Surely, she would find those with whom she could form bonds.

"All things in their time," he murmured, and produced another smile for her uplifted brows.

"I believe I will go to Seignur Veeoni now," he said.

"Good," said Lorith, and pulled the work glasses back down over her eyes.

Seignur Veeoni's Private Laboratory

THE TEST SUITE WOULD REQUIRE SOME TIME TO RUN. SHE HAD briefly considered making a transcription, but decided to wait until she understood the architecture more fully.

Seignur Veeoni returned to her office, and found M Traven reading the documentation she was preparing for Korval.

"That is incomplete," she said.

Her bodyguard looked up from the screen.

"What is its purpose, when complete?"

Seignur Veeoni sighed.

"Its purpose is to persuade the delm of Korval to allow Crystal Energy Systems to partner in the repair and maintenance of this station, where I intend to remain for the foreseeable future."

M Traven turned back to the screen.

"The information is good, but it is not very persuasive."

Seignur Veeoni eyed her, sitting solid and calm before the screen.

"Are you," she asked carefully, "bored?"

M Traven had been one of two dozen guards who had protected her and her residence; one of six M Strain soldiers. While M soldiers were accomplished in all the arts of war and violence, they were in addition generalists, possessed of a lively, wide-ranging intelligence.

It was not good policy, Seignur Veeoni had discovered, to allow an M soldier to become bored.

M Traven sighed.

"Perhaps, a little," she said.

"Then there is nothing for it but for you to finish this proposal," Seignur Veeoni said briskly. "Please be as persuasive as you are able. I cannot understand why Korval should have to be persuaded to a course of such obvious benefit to all parties, but Light Keeper yos'Phelium thinks it necessary."

M Traven glanced at the screen, then back to her face.

"It will be an interesting exercise."

Seignur Veeoni approached the desk, leaned over and tapped in several commands.

"You now have access to all of the information I have which is relevant to this project. Recall that any decisions must be made between Crystal Energy and Korval."

"In fact, this document is the opening salvo. I understand."

M Traven turned in the chair, watching her as she moved about the office, gathering those things she would require.

"Am I needed?" M Traven asked.

Seignur Veeoni straightened.

"You are needed here. I am needed in the new core. Mentor Jones, Soldier nor'Phelium, and Tocohl will also be present. I will be perfectly safe."

M Traven sat quite still for a moment, then nodded.

"I'll have a working draft to show you when you return."

"Excellent," said Seignur Veeoni, and left her to it.

Main Core Workroom

THE FORMER HARDWARE SUPPORTING STATION SYSTEMS AND THE intelligence named Tinsori Light had been located in a heavily shielded core. Which, Tolly Jones admitted, had only been sensible. Just can't leave your mind and necessary support systems out in an open hallway, after all. No telling what might happen to them.

Tolly had been in the old core, and had firsthand familiarity with the cramped conditions, the second level being even less roomy than the upper.

It might've disqualified itself as the new core on space alone, but it was the fact that Tocohl refused to have anything to do with the former space that had prompted Seignur Veeoni to a study of station schematics. That had turned up a suite of rooms on the inner ring that might've been built specifically to be the station's core, right down to the extra shielding and dedicated power grid.

Tocohl accepted the proposed space, and that was where Tolly and Seignur Veeoni met on a regular and not-too-lazy schedule to build the new tile-and-rack array, assisted by Hazenthull, and M Traven.

They'd worked pretty much nonstop at first, getting life support and vital base systems into the craniums, clean, certified, and stable.

Next step was cleaning, upgrading, and certifying the sub-systems, sub-subsystems; the routines and protocols that ran in support. Labor-intensive work, the more so with only two specialists on it. Still, they'd managed, and they were past the worst of it now. All the vitals were stable; even the clean-and-repair grid was up and working.

They were working with two arrays: one for testing and cleaning, and the master frame itself, sealed up all right and tight in the core room.

That was all good as far as it went, but it didn't go so far as a redundant system. The only backup they had was in the craniums, and in Tolly's professional opinion, that was just trouble waiting to happen.

"How soon do you think we can start building a backup?" he asked, just in general.

Haz, assembling a frame at the general workbench, didn't say anything, which meant she didn't have an opinion.

Seignur Veeoni didn't say anything either, which meant that all of her considerable intelligence was focused on the job in hand. He kept talking, his work at the moment not being quite so brain intensive. "I'd been thinking that might be a good use of the old core, once we get it cleared out and cleaned."

"No," Tocohl said firmly, from the speaker right by Tolly's bench. It was one of the fine, new speakers, and the finality in her voice was impossible to miss.

"I agree," Seignur Veeoni said surprisingly. "Such cramped conditions as you described, Mentor, cannot be preferred. Though the backup core may occupy a lesser space, still there must be room for technicians to work."

"I have been looking for an appropriate space for the backup core," Tocohl said, "and I believe I have a good candidate. It will need to be inspected by someone more familiar with the needs of technicians and other helpers."

"Very good," Seignur Veeoni said, and bent her head toward her work.

"Mentor Jones is of the opinion that Station need not be an Independent Intelligence," Tocohl said. "Do you agree?"

Seignur Veeoni frowned, which wasn't anything special, Seignur Veeoni being especially fluent in frowns. Tolly thought he was starting to learn the gradations, though, and this one seemed to be a considering frown.

"I neither agree nor disagree," she said at last. "Tinsori Light was brought to sentience by the Great Enemy, the better to serve their purpose in the war effort. In this universe, space stations are not commonly sentient, a direct result of the Complex Logic Laws. Those laws have now been challenged by Scout Commander yos'Phelium's field judgment, so that sentience becomes a matter of preference."

"Scout Commander yos'Phelium's field judgment may not stand," Tocohl said.

"It'll stand," Tolly said, feeling himself on firm ground. "The Free Ships have been wanting this for a long time. They'll push forward and make themselves all kinds of useful. By the time that judgment comes up for review, reversing it won't be popular—or even possible."

"If Korval's station was known to be sentient, that would be a strong political statement," Seignur Veeoni said surprisingly. "My brother would say so."

"And he wouldn't be wrong," Tolly said. "My problem is that I don't want to push a person into a situation they're not absolutely certain they want. Duty only carries so much weight. If Station doesn't want to be Station—isn't Station at heart, the way *Admiral Bunter* is *a ship* right down past the core of him, and can't think of being anything else, because he's already in his best place—then that's a recipe for disaster on every level I can think of."

Seignur Veeoni's frown was nearly a smile.

"You are eloquent, Mentor."

"Comes with being a teacher," he said, half-apologetic.

Her frown straightened into a look of what might have been startlement.

Tolly pressed his lips together and waited until the moment passed and she gave him a nod.

"I believe you have given me an insight into my brother, Mentor. My thanks."

"Always glad to help with an insight," he said.

"Is it your intention to reconnoiter the space under discussion now?" Seignur Veeoni asked.

"*Now*, I'm here to assist you," Tolly said.

"And I am here to make the station viable and safe. Very well, Mentor, if you will assist me by securing the junction connector, I will finish chaining this set of tiles, and activate the sub-grid. Downloading of the cleaned and rehabilitated systems may then begin. And we will be free to examine the space Tocohl has identified."

"Light Keeper yos'Phelium is on his way to you. He requests an immediate meeting."

"We will await his arrival," Seignur Veeoni said—auto-respond, Tolly thought, her mind already more than halfway back on the chaining process.

He bent to his part of it, motioning Haz over to steady the rack they were connecting to, and pulled on his work gloves.

The air crackled, opal blue, scented with ozone; a hum started, built, and leveled out into subtle music.

"Circuit completed; work set sealed," Seignur Veeoni murmured. "Tocohl, please verify."

"Environment verified," Tocohl said. "Initiate download?"

"Yes," said Seignur Veeoni, just as the door opened and Jen Sin yos'Phelium entered.

At first glance, the light keeper looked better than fine—a trim pilot standing tall in his leathers, and who cared how out of style they were, when they fitted him so well?

At second glance, the light keeper was a worried man, which Tolly believed to be a bad thing with any pilot, and that much worse with pilots of Korval.

"Seignur Veeoni," Jen Sin said, producing a small bow to the researcher's honor. "I am loath to interrupt your work—"

"The work is just now completed, and passed on to the next stage," Seignur Veeoni interrupted. "Your arrival is timely. What is your purpose?"

"I wonder if you have analyzed the beads I gave to you."

Seignur Veeoni's frown was a mere pleasantry.

"A test suite is running. My tools are specialized, but time still enters into the equation."

"Of course. I only mean to say that, I am freshly come from a discussion with Light Keeper Lorith. That discussion has provided me with more information regarding the method by which we were able to continue after the Light had shown his displeasure. I—"

Abruptly, he turned toward Tolly.

"Forgive me, Mentor, I do not wish to involve you in something outside your field."

It was one of the smoothest ways he'd ever been told to get lost, but before he could make his bow, collect Haz and leave, Seignur Veeoni spoke again.

"Mentor Jones has expertise in these matters as well, and I find his insights, which are so different from my own, helpful. Mentor, do you have time for the light keeper's information?"

"Always willing to learn," he said, with a grave smile for the worried man. "I can go, if you'd rather."

"No." The light keeper drew a hard breath, and said more firmly, "No. I think that this is a case where one ought gather as many experts as possible. Briefly, then: The beads record our memories, which are transmitted and stored in the Light. The beam would have destroyed them no less than us. When we were required again, the Light—which has our samples on file—merely fabricated new individuals, and copied the memory files to a new set of beads."

Tolly had worked with Old Tech devices, and had a fair respect for what they could do. In fact, he didn't doubt that the process had been precisely as described. Only—

"Not sure that's something I've met," he said, looking to Seignur Veeoni.

She brought her head sharply down, once, her frown downright grim.

"Light Keeper, will you take us to this fabrication device?"

"That is why I came. I would have it immediately decommissioned, and also—"

He faltered, and Jen Sin yos'Phelium was not, in Tolly's opinion, a faltering man.

"*Also*," he repeated firmly, "I require an expert opinion. It seems probable to me, given the circumstances under which I existed, that I am not—reliable."

"Reliable," Seignur Veeoni repeated flatly. "Sir, you are a member of Clan Korval. You transcend reliable. Now, if you please, take us to this device."

Jen Sin led the way through the back corridors to the room where they woke, every time the Light had called them back into service. He ought, he thought, have considered this before—that of course the Light had meddled with him—with his mind, his cells... the gods knew what had been done. And the damn' beads, renewing his memory, yes, very well, but what else? Why? Suppressing a Scout's very lively sense of curiosity? Subtly influencing him not to question certain aspects of his existence? Altering and purging memories?

As he walked, he reviewed a calming exercise. There was no profit in panic, after all.

So—his plan. First, see the units destroyed. That accomplished, he would write to the delm, explaining that far from being fit to mind the clan's interests, he was almost certainly a danger to those interests. After he had performed that duty, he would remove himself.

In a sense—in every sense that mattered—it was the same equation, exactly as it had been framed at the beginning: Did he allow Tinsori Light in any form free access to the universe and those things that were *not* Tinsori Light? Of course not; there was only one course available to him. He would not shirk his last duty, no matter how long necessity had been put aside.

And here was the door. He put his hand against the plate, stepping into the bare, chilly bay where the three units were lined up, each enclosed in a metal cubicle.

The air was so cold it burned; the decking was frosty.

He paused, waving the others to a stop.

"Station," he said through frozen lips. "Adjust the recovery deck to station normal environment."

For a long moment, nothing at all happened.

A single sharp *click* echoed against the frosty walls.

Bechimo
En route

....

"THERE'S NO POSSIBLE NEED TO STOP AT EDMONTON BEACON," Win Ton said. It was an all-crew meeting and his turn to speak, though Theo was surprised to hear him speaking so vehemently.

Apparently he was, too, because he sighed and pulled up a half-smile, while showing the table his empty palms.

"I should say, there is rarely need to stop at Edmonton Beacon. Perhaps a case can be made if we are to bring supplies to Tinsori Light. Are we?"

"That's a good question," Clarence said. "Not that I don't agree that there's better places to shop than Eddie. If Eddie's what we got, though..."

Edmonton Beacon—Eddie to a certain file of spacer—rode the edge of the Dust. It had a reputation for casual lawlessness that made Theo's fingers itch, but regular business could go forth, if expensively. Eddie was the largest of seven stations clustered together. Of the other six stations, one was administered by Liadens, so not a safe port for a ship affiliated with Tree-and-Dragon. Beacon Repair was just that, padded out with temp quarters, eateries and fun for those waiting on repairs. Redlight was an ongoing nonstop party. Tandik Feef was an outpost for mercenary soldiers; and the Greybar was what gave Eddie itself anything like a good reputation. The sixth station, though—

"There's the House of Stars," Theo said, "administered by the Carresens-Denoblis. Shouldn't we be able to shop there?"

"You'd think so, but it's not so much a retail situation as a safe port for the Denobli ships running in and out of the Dust," Clarence said. "Eddie's what you want, if supplies are the need." He glanced at her. "Tinsori Light expecting us to be bringing them anything special?"

Theo sighed.

"You read Shan's letter," she said irritably. "We're supposed to go to Tinsori Light and *help out*."

"And we have been in the process of *going*," Kara said.

And going, and going, and then going some more, Theo thought. Shan had said that Tinsori Light was "inconveniently" located, and she hadn't paid proper attention to that. *Bechimo* had quite a collection of inconvenient locations, after all.

As Clarence put it, there was *out-of-the-way*, and *hard-to-get-to*, which weren't necessarily the same thing. Tinsori Light had probably won a prize in hard-to-get-to, Theo thought sourly. Edmonton Beacon was its most proximate piece of civilization, and it wasn't what you'd call *close*.

"Just because there was no mail at our last Jump-end—" Kara was continuing.

"Doesn't mean there won't be something at the next," Theo finished with a half-grin. "You're too sensible for us."

"Often remarked the same," Clarence said, stretching his legs comfortably out before him and leaning back in his chair.

"And if there's no mail?" Theo asked.

"Is that your position?" Kara asked. "Then let us proceed to the stakes: If there is mail you will owe me a new bowli ball. What is your part?"

Theo blinked.

"So it's a bet, now? That's sensible."

"Of course it is," Kara replied. "Joyita, defend my character."

"Your character needs no defense," Joyita said from the table-side screen.

"Silver tongue."

"Kara is very sensible," *Bechimo* stated. "However, it must be pointed out that while there is an equal probability of receiving or not receiving mail at Jump-end, there is an additional factor: We may receive mail that does not clarify the situation."

"That merely adds an edge of anticipation to the wager," Kara said primly, and Clarence didn't—quite—laugh.

Theo shook her head, and looked to the last two members of her crew, sitting side by side at the end of the table.

"Thoughts?" she asked.

"We can only obey the orders we receive," Chernak said, and Stost moved a big hand, fingers shaping the pilot's sign for "agree."

"Right, then." Theo stood up. "We'll postpone the conversation of how we should proceed until we either do or do not receive mail that's either useful or not useful at Jump-end."

She made a show of glaring at Kara.

"Since this is a bet—I don't think there will be *any* mail. And if I'm right you can bake me a batch of maize buttons."

"Done," Kara answered, and smiled.

Hacienda Estrella
Safe Dock Bar

• • • • • • • • • • • • • • •

THEY ALL LAUGHED AT THE GRIMSHAWS WHEN THEY COME IN to the Hacienda, swearing 'til they was blue that Ghost Station was in normal space.

Wasn't none laughed louder than Norse, though he stood the pilot a beer, on account of she was a friend and not nearly a fool, and sat with her while she worked her way through a plate of the house special curry, which he also put on his tab, and the beer that came after that, too.

"So," he said, sipping his first beer.

Pama gave him a stare could score hullplate.

"So, *what*?"

Norse held up a hand, showing empty palm.

"Ghost Station. You 'n me both know it comes, then it goes." He tipped his mug in the general direction of her captain, who was *still* arguing with Ferb Connor offa *Harp*.

"Figured your cap'n to know that, too," Norse said. "She's older'n six."

"So're you," Pama said, "but *you* ain't listenin'."

That stung, that did. Norse prided himself on being a good listener. He put his mug down, and considered her.

"How's this, then," he said. "I'll buy us another round, you tell me, and I'll listen straight through."

She shrugged.

"'Nother beer's fine," she said. "But you laugh at me, Norse Uldra-Joenz, and I'll punch you right on that pointy nose o'yours."

"Fair," Norse said, and put his hand up for two more beers.

"So, yeah, Ghost Station—it's there and then it ain't, and mostly it ain't," Pama said after she'd tasted her new brew for quality. "Even when it's not there, though, there's all that grit and glittery dust and clouds—right?"

"Right."

"So, that's gone—that's what we're trying to say—Ghost Station's in *normal space.*"

All right, that *was* innerestin', Norse thought. All the spacers who came in reg'lar to Edmonton Beacon, 'specially those who had ties with the Carresens-Denoblis, and belonged to the Hacienda Estrella coop, knew about Ghost Station. Knew to avoid it, that was. They did keep a casual kinda eye on it, same like they did with the Dust front, and on Keeryelli—just in case. But nobody went to Ghost Station, nobody being willing to risk getting caught on or near it when it phased out to…

Wherever it went.

"Wonder what changed," Norse muttered, half to himself, and Pama gave him a grin.

"*Now* you're thinkin'. What changed, and what's it mean, too?"

They finished their beers in a thinking quiet. Norse was just about to call for another when the all-band crackled, and a man's tired, colorless voice claimed the whole bar's attention.

"This is Matt Collier on *Borinteen.* Had some bad luck 'long Dust-edge near Pendi. Need a tow. Need repairs. Most of all we need a medic. Molly got burned when second board blew. Vester's got an arm broke, or worse—"

There was a mutter in the background, like somebody giving direction, while the bar was *that* quiet, everybody froze in place, straining to hear.

"Got a few complaints, myself—leg caught something that wasn't tied down," Matt Collier said, sounding wry and faint.

"Come get us, Hacienda, 'fore we're a hazard to navigation."

Chairs scraped, and voices rose, as them who belonged to Hacienda Rescue got themselves up and out.

Norse ran to the bar, and grabbed his medkit.

"I'm gone," he told Zeri, who was tending.

"I'll tell the boss," she said. "Jet!"

Kit in hand, he did just that.

Tinsori Light
Recovery Deck

. . . .

"RUN!" JEN SIN SHOUTED, PIVOTING, BOOTS SLIPPING ON THE frosty floor. Running had never altered the final outcome, but he always did, rabbit that he was.

This time it was not the incandescence of unraveling that stopped him, but arms wrapping around him and crushing him to a massive chest.

"Be careful," a deep voice growled over his head.

"Cousin Jen Sin!" Tocohl cried. "It was a stiff relay! I swear to you; I fused all the beam ports, and disabled the engines."

He sagged inside the large embrace. Of course she had, sweet lady that she was, and true. He was a fool.

"Thank you, Cousin," he whispered into the leather under his cheek.

"Pilot?" the big voice again—Hazenthull nor'Phelium, he realized. "Are you able? Should I release you?"

"I am able," he said, which would do for the moment. "Please release me."

She complied at once, and looked down at him, her broad brown face grave.

"The floor is slippery with the ice," she said, from which he learned that he had been rescued from a fall.

He bowed as between comrades.

"My thanks."

"It was no trouble," she assured him, and it was then that he noticed Seignur Veeoni, her spare frame entirely upright, marching deliberately across the slick decking toward the first cubicle.

"I would like the attention of Mentor Jones and Light Keeper yos'Phelium on this," she said, not bothering to turn her head.

Jen Sin felt his arm touched, and looked into Tolly Jones's face, which wore an expression of careful sympathy.

"Tinsori Light really is dead, Pilot," he said, sounding perfectly matter-of-fact.

"I know that, but my reactions do not," Jen Sin said ruefully. They turned together to follow Seignur Veeoni, Hazenthull nor'Phelium at their backs. "Korval breeds for rabbits, after all, survival being our foremost talent."

"Comes to specifics, I'm fond of surviving myself. Here we are."

The last was as they stepped into the cubicle, Hazenthull remaining without—an excellent decision, given the lack of room, and the fact that she could see over the half-wall.

Seignur Veeoni was bent close to the unit, studying the display panel. She glanced up as they approached, and straightened, her gaze sharpening.

"Do you recognize it, after all, Mentor?"

"Duplicating machine, is what I know to call it," the mentor answered readily, his voice as easy as ever.

"So the salvage crews have it, yes." She looked to Jen Sin, and inclined her head.

"You are correct in your description of the device's function. It stores a copy of a personal architecture, and will reproduce that precise architecture on demand. There are limitations. While the copy is alive and receptive—by which I mean that it has a functioning brain, and can be taught—it does not have an ongoing memory of a former existence."

"Of course not," Jen Sin said. "It is a copy."

She gave him an approving nod. "Precisely. This device has been altered from what we usually see, in order to accommodate the second step."

She paused.

"You understand that single units such as we see here are something of a rarity, as they are not an economical way to produce copies. In the Old Universe such were produced in batches, which required multi-bed devices in large facilities where waste could be kept to a minimum. The salvagers most often find the single units among the wreckage of ships, where they would have been put to use when it became necessary to replace a member of the crew."

Her eyes strayed to the control panel, and she was silent for a moment before looking up and continuing.

"In both large batches and small, the second step in the process is to imprint the copies with necessary information, as previously compiled by the operations manager. This typically entails removing the copies to a learning unit and running the specified program.

"This unit has been modified to combine the reproduction and learning steps. I cannot be certain without testing, but it follows that each unit here must be dedicated. Which is to say that one unit was tasked with preserving your sample, Light Keeper, and producing a new vessel when required. A second unit would hold Lorith's material. The third unit—was there a third light keeper?"

Jen Sin raised his hands, showing empty palms.

"The Light was originally kept by three initiates of the Sanderat Order—this told to me by Lorith, who was alone when I came on-station."

"What became of her sisters?"

"The first died during the transition—the storm, Lorith calls it. When they found themselves in new space, the second took their vessel out to find where they were, and never returned. After she had been gone long enough to assume that she was not returning, Lorith attempted to call her back from the unit, but as she did not wear beads, she did not know herself, nor anything, I expect," he added, feeling a sour taste in his mouth, "that was of use to the Light."

"Was she never wakened again?"

"Not during my time," he said definitively, and, in response to reality added, "that I recall."

"Granted," Seignur Veeoni said, and glanced back at the unit. "Whose cubicle is this?"

"Lorith's." He waved a hand. "Mine is innermost."

"So. To sum up: Finding itself in need of one or the other of the light keepers, Tinsori Light activates the appropriate unit, which performs its function. Given the use of the beads, I theorize that the unit produced not merely an identical physical architecture, but psychological, as well. Thus, it would be more efficient to download the data gathered by the beads into the replica, also ensuring that less was lost to compatibility issues. This accommodates the existence of the nonstandard programming I found in the beads you have been wearing. The beads gathered and stored your memories, and also banked them in the proper dedicated unit."

Jen Sin stared at her; his chest icy with dismay.

"So, I am not who I believe myself to be—in any way?"

Seignur Veeoni frowned. Of course.

"You are the Jen Sin yos'Phelium who is available to us in this present," she said briskly. "Whether you are the precise Jen Sin yos'Phelium who arrived at Tinsori Light two hundred Standards ago is a question I cannot answer."

"Couldn't be," Tolly Jones said surprisingly. "People change. The pilot who arrived on-station all those Standards back hadn't taken the decision to stay and try to do what he could to contain a bad situation. That's a change-point, right there, never mind how many times you woke back up from dying."

Jen Sin swallowed in a dry throat, as another thought assailed him.

"The machines—the timonium is degrading—"

Tolly Jones caught his point.

"You're thinking the quality of the work's gone down? That's a reasonable concern. You look hale and fit to me, but we can make certain of that, if Seignur Veeoni will let us use her equipment."

"Certainly. It will be an interesting data point." The researcher raised her head to look at him. "Do you know how many times you were wakened?"

Dread filled him, as if the question had triggered it. He took a breath, forcing the sensation aside, and made himself say, evenly, "I regret."

"No matter; I can likely extrapolate from the onboard records."

Jen Sin took another breath.

"I fear you have lost sight of the goal," he said, gently. "These units—all of them—must be destroyed."

"I agree that they must eventually be deactivated," Seignur Veeoni said, "but not before they are properly studied, and the data they hold analyzed."

"Light Keeper Lorith is arriving at this location," Tocohl said.

"Excellent," Jen Sin said, absently, before again addressing Seignur Veeoni.

"As light keeper, I insist that these devices are hazardous to the well-being and continued survival of the station. They cannot be allowed to remain, or indeed, to exist. If you find yourself unable to destroy them, I will destroy them myself, as part of my duty to this station and the universe beyond."

Seignur Veeoni failed to look in the least bit cowed. One might almost say that she was amused.

"Old Tech's hard to kill," Tolly Jones murmured.

Jen Sin turned to him. "I don't doubt that my method will be wasteful, but it is within my power to destroy this room and everything in it in the next hour. I would do better, if I had the assistance of an expert, but the work can go forth without."

"Light Keeper, think of what that data may tell us," Seignur Veeoni said, as one scolding a slow student. "To destroy them out of hand—"

"Jen Sin!"

Lorith strode into the cubicle, robe fluttering in her haste, feet bare against the slowly warming deck.

"Jen Sin, what are you doing?"

"Speaking with Seignur Veeoni about these units," he said, turning to face her. "I had said that I would."

"You are not wearing your beads." She turned to Seignur Veeoni. "He must have his beads back, Researcher. They are his memory. He will not wish to forget anything, especially in this time of transition."

"I agreed to study the beads, of which he had some concerns," Seignur Veeoni said calmly. "I am proficient in bead technology, and may be able to extract a clean copy of his memories, uncompromised by timonium decay."

That sounded fairly wonderful, Jen Sin thought, and everything that was innocent. Indeed, he felt himself comforted by the level reasonableness of it.

The effect on Lorith was not the same.

"You must not tamper with the beads!" she snapped. "Only return them and cease to meddle in matters that do not concern you! You are here to perform needed repairs, and you serve at the pleasure of the light keepers!"

She spun toward him.

"Jen Sin, come away."

"In a moment," he said, calm in his turn. "There is a discussion ongoing." He turned to Seignur Veeoni.

"Surely, Researcher, you see the need to destroy these units. I understand the impulse toward scholarship, but—"

He saw the movement from the corner of his eye, spun and ducked. The thrust missed him entirely, but Lorith was whirling again, a thing of lethal grace in this confined space, the knife gleaming in her hand.

In all their time together, they had never sparred, or contended against each other. She was a warrior trained, taller than he, and very quick.

He was a yos'Phelium pilot—no stranger to port-brawls and desperate situations.

She feinted. He countered, his hand flashing out to snatch her wrist, twisting, forcing the knife down—

There was a small sound, percussive, almost apologetic.

The knife fell to the deck with a clatter, and Lorith crumpled after it, a dart protruding from her chest.

"No!"

He spun to stare at Seignur Veeoni, who held the gun expertly in thin fingers, her face displaying nothing other than her habitual frown.

"She is wearing her beads," she said negligently, "and can easily be called back. Unless you still insist on destroying the units."

Ears roaring, he looked down at Lorith, crumpled and still, his only companion in horror and in determination. They had kept each other... rational, if not precisely sane, and on-task. They had connived together to cheat the Light, and build a safe-place against him—

"Do it," he heard himself say. "Bring her back."

"Light Keeper." If it were not impossible, he would have said that Tocohl was breathless.

"Something is on an apparent intercept course for the Light. It broadcasts no ID. It does not answer hails. It has not requested permission to dock. It shows what may be three running lights which indicate a slight spin around axis. No overt actions other than a powered approach."

"Shields," Jen Sin said, attention snapping to this new emergency.

"Increased to maximum in the likeliest area of impact. But—the weapons—"

"Yes." The weapons were not under the Light's control. He had made certain of that.

"I—"

He half-turned to look again at Lorith—

He felt a warm touch on his arm, and looked up into Tolly Jones's solemn, sympathetic face.

"I'll take care of her," the mentor said, gently. "Go. The station needs you."

"Yes," he said, and left them at a run.

• • • ☀ • • •

"That was a risk," Tolly said, dropping to one knee on the deck, as Haz entered the cubicle. He picked up the knife and handed it to her over his shoulder; removed the dart, glanced at it, and tucked it into a pocket. Shaking his head, he looked up at Seignur Veeoni.

"What were you gonna do, when he noticed she was still breathing?"

"There is no reason to discuss events that did not occur," Seignur Veeoni said, slipping the gun away. "Something had to be done. She was trying to kill him, and, as we are all aware, he is *not* wearing his beads. We need Jen Sin yos'Phelium, Mentor. Surely you agree."

"She was only half trying to kill him—and it wasn't enough," Tolly said, getting to his feet. "He disarmed her before you got your shot off."

"The knife's edge is undamaged," Haz said.

Tolly nodded. "Keep it for her, right?"

"Yes."

"One does not cast away a bargaining chip," Seignur Veeoni said primly, her gaze dropping to the duplicating machine. "I must study this nonstandard architecture. To destroy them out of hand would be foolish beyond permission."

Tolly sighed.

"What about Lorith? She might not be dead, but she's not going to be feeling any too good when the tranq wears off."

Seignur Veeoni waved a hand. "Take her to my lab. M Traven will let you in, and show you the autodoc."

Tolly tipped his head.

"Way I understand it, Light Keeper Lorith is from the Old Universe. Not likely to be a file for her in the 'doc."

"There is in *my* 'doc," Seignur Veeoni said with asperity. "Have we other business at this time, Mentor?"

"Can't think of a thing," Tolly said, stepping back so Haz could pick up the light keeper's long body. "We'll just be going now."

Station Day 9
Administrative Tower

JEN SIN HIT THE CHAIR, SLAPPING UP THE SCREENS WITH ONE hand, and unlocking the weapons board with the other.

The incoming ship was smaller than a Scout ship, podless, sleek, and—

He worked with the screen, sharpening details.

Not an ordinary tradeship, he thought; there were no cargo pods. Rather it looked like a purpose-built freight tug designed to carry a special module—or perhaps it was *modules*—that could be detached at need. There was no obvious central power core. Instead, the in-system engines were distributed radially on six pylons, so that the ship could haul the module and release it at need. The module's construction made it look a building block of a station or habitat meant for airless situations; the ship itself was not at all aerodynamic so it, too, was meant only for airless situations.

The module, though, looked fresh and new built. Purpose built and large enough to carry... what? There seemed to be a core to it. A core of what?

It is a bomb, he thought, which he was obliged to do, being the station's defender.

Granted, it was a large bomb, indeed, but if one intended to destroy Tinsori Light rather than merely breach it—

He flicked the comm switch.

"This is Jen Sin yos'Phelium, light keeper at Tinsori Station, to incoming vessel. State your purpose, and moderate your approach."

Minutes passed, while he upped the magnification, and plotted the approach.

Yes. Unless something altered very quickly, the incoming vessel would impact on the bay section Seignur Veeoni had taken for her pop-up laboratory and working space.

He touched another switch.

"This is Light Keeper yos'Phelium. We have a questionable vessel on a nonstandard approach. If it continues, it will strike your section of the station. Evacuate now!"

He took a deep breath. Seignur Veeoni would still be on the recovery deck. Her bodyguard might not be in the lab. Or—

"Acknowledge!" he snapped.

"Acknowledge, Light Keeper," came the voice of the bodyguard—Traven, it was—and Jen Sin sighed out the breath he had been holding, his attention on the screen; his fingers resting lightly on the weapons switches.

"I've broadcast on all the bands," Tocohl said. "No response."

It was in range. He should fire now, to prevent a collision. Yet, there was something about the approach—something that bothered his pilot-brain. An attack run ought either to be stealthy or bold, and this—was neither. Merely, the ship came on, as if its arrival were the veriest commonplace.

He hesitated, watching.

The vessel began to rhythmically fire basic control jets, executing a sweeping change of course that convinced him there could be no human crew aboard it to suffer such g-stress.

Apparent forward motion ceased, and it rotated slightly, matching a portion of the light's rotation, a kind of station-keeping of its own, centered on Seignur Veeoni's lab.

Jen Sin took his fingers off of the weapons pad.

"A drone," he said aloud, for Tocohl's benefit, and started, when he received an answer from the open comm.

"Yes, a quiet drone from Andreth at the research station," Traven said. "Seignur Veeoni had sent for more supplies for her work. We received word last station-day to expect delivery at this time."

The drone was now settled some meters from the station, still emitting no signal to the command center.

One portion of the drone's module moved sharply toward the station, followed by a second. Jen Sin recognized lock-links, high-tensile lash-lines such as might be used in a station's satellite yard. He only imagined he heard the connection as they found lock ports.

"Did she not tell you this, Light Keeper?" Traven asked.

Jen Sin briefly closed his eyes.

"She did not," he said moderately. The module, now released from the little ship, began reeling itself in toward the lab.

"Light Keeper, please forgive me," Traven said. "She said that she had something to speak with you about, and I—assumed—that she would mention the delivery in the course of your conversation. I have been some time in Seignur Veeoni's service, and I know better than to make such an assumption. In future, I will inform you of any incoming that concerns us." Another pause. "That is, if you agree that perhaps being told twice is better than not being told at all."

"I agree with the principle," Jen Sin said.

"Good. I thank you for holding your fire."

Jen Sin glanced at the comm.

"Did I?" he murmured. "Hold my fire?"

The comm emitted a small sigh.

"We have the original station schematics," Traven said.

Jen Sin waited.

"I'll send you a copy, sir, shall I?"

"Thank you," Jen Sin said. "That would be very helpful."

He looked at his fingers. He'd have to check that weapons switch panel eventually, and ask Tocohl to check his check. It would be good to know what he actually controlled. His whole purpose in blocking the Old Light's access to these weapons had been to deprive it of a tool that it might use against the universe. Given his situation, he had not been able to do anything more. Certainly, he had never expected to be required to defend the station from the universe.

He took a deliberate breath, sighed it out, and leaned back in the control chair, eyes closed. He was, he noted, shivering. Adrenaline, horror—that, too. Lorith—gods! And himself—the decision to restore Lorith—not a decision at all, but instinct. It had been the central fact of their existence on Tinsori Light—that they would die, violently more often than not. And that they *would wake* as themselves, recalling the moment of their death in every detail, but *alive*.

"Cousin Tocohl," he said. His voice not steady, but never mind that. There was a larger game in play.

"Cousin Jen Sin?"

"I am under the impression that the delm wishes this station to reflect Korval's ongoing commitment to the realities governing the universe that received the diaspora. Am I correct in this assumption?"

"Are you asking if I am privy to the delm's necessities?"

"An impertinence. Forgive me. What I wish to know is if Korval prefers tools which are untainted by the Old Technology."

"The delm prefers efficiency. It is noted that the Old Technology has degraded to the point where it is neither efficient nor safe. The delm values safety, and does not willingly spend lives."

"Having so few to hand," Jen Sin murmured. "Understood. I shall lay out the case, Cousin, and ask you to advise me. Are you willing?"

"I am."

"Thank you. The case is that I have been corrupted by an agent of the Great Enemy. I am not, in a word, *safe*, even for those values of safe that may be applied to my Line and clan. I wonder if it were not—best—to step aside as light keeper, in favor of Cousin Theo, who expects to arrive very soon. She will have good guides and allies in you, Mentor Jones, and Seignur Veeoni. One of the House's own guards stands ready to serve her, should her crew for some reason not be able. It seems to me that this configuration would accomplish the delm's purpose for Tinsori Station and those it would serve."

"Why," Tocohl said, "would Theo not have an ally and guide in yourself?"

"Because it is my intention to embrace my last duty, Cousin, and free the station of a known source of contamination. Pray do not argue that the delm would not so spend my life—I have been dead to the clan for two hundred Standards. My presence in the current ledger is a fluke, and the lives the delm *must* care for are those who are untainted."

There was a brief silence. When Tocohl spoke again, her voice was tart.

"I believe that any proposed changes in station administration must be placed before the delm. The station is directly under Korval's eye."

Jen Sin blinked.

"So, you counsel me to write my resignation to the delm, listing out my reasons, and my proposed successor?"

"Exactly," Tocohl said. "That would be proper."

And, he thought, it *was* proper. One did not wish to surprise the delm in these matters.

"Very well, then," he said, tapping up a screen and pulling the keypad to him. "I will wish to send this via pinbeam."

Tinsori Light
Seignur Veeoni's Private Workroom
Medical Alcove

• • • • • • • • • • • • • • • •

TRAVEN LET THEM IN WITHOUT COMMENT, SHOWED THEM TO the autodoc, and opened it so that Haz could put Lorith down on the pad, straightening legs and arms so that she would fit tidily inside the treatment area.

Tolly brought the hood down. The control board lit, showing three steady greens and a repeating pattern of yellow dots.

"That must be an old one it's looking for," Traven said, and, as the lights steadied, flashed and went to green, added, "Found her."

She turned. "Will you stay, or will I call you when she's released?"

"We'll stay," Tolly said. "I promised Light Keeper yos'Phelium I'd take care of her. Can we borrow a couple screens?"

"I've got some portables. Table folds down from here." She patted the wall as she went past.

Haz tended to the table, Tolly moved a pair of chairs over and went back to consider the 'doc.

"Is there a problem, Mentor?" Traven came to look over his shoulder.

"Looks like a longer repair than I'd've thought for a tranq dart," he said.

"Must be something else, too," Traven said comfortably. "As far back as it had to search to find her, I'd let it work."

"Right," Tolly said.

"Mentor, I wonder if you could assist me," Traven said suddenly.

Tolly raised his eyebrows. "What with?"

"Seignur Veeoni has given me the task of producing a persuasive document. I'm now wondering if there is such a thing as *too* persuasive, and if I have achieved it. Would you read it and give me your fair opinion?"

Tolly grinned.

"Be pleased to," he said. "Right back, Haz."

Lyre Institute for Exceptional Children
Lyre-Unthilon

A SHADOW FELL ACROSS DIRECTOR LING'S SCREEN. HE HAD NOT heard the door cycle; she would never be as careless as that. Besides, she hoped to startle him, and gain a tiny bit of tempo.

As if he weren't her equal. Her *better.*

"One moment, Anj," he said, continuing with his review of the data. When he was done, he looked around.

Director Formyne was leaning against the wall, her arms crossed over her chest. She looked amused.

"Have you read the shipping news?" she asked.

"Certainly. It would appear that four-twenty-three has failed."

"You take a loss that will hobble the Institute's future projects with strange equanimity."

He stood, which allowed him to look down at her.

"Did you think the Committee would not have a contingency plan?" he asked, with sincere interest. The workings of Formyne's mind *were* of interest to him. If he failed of being an expert in that study, he would be dead.

And that was not an acceptable outcome.

"Of course the Committee has a contingency plan," Formyne said now. "I only wonder when it will be deployed."

"Oh." He smiled. "That was done some time ago."

Seignur Veeoni's Private Workroom
Medical Alcove

THE 'DOC PINGED.

Hazenthull looked up from her screen. Tolly had not returned, but she anticipated no difficulty from the lanky light keeper. She did stand, and placed herself where she would be seen immediately by the 'doc's occupant.

The hood rose.

Lorith sat up, and paused, surveying the room. Hazenthull said nothing, even when that searching gaze passed over her—and moved on.

Finally, the light keeper looked at her again.

"Jen Sin?" she asked.

"Untouched, and attending his duty. A ship has come in."

"Has it?" Lorith gazed around her. "Where am I?"

"The medical wing of the researcher's workspace, that she brought with her."

"Ah. A resourceful woman, the researcher. Where is my knife?"

"I have it."

Lorith met her eyes. "Do you? What is its condition?"

"Well kept and well edged. It took no damage from the deck."

"That is well, then." She paused; pale brows pulled together. When she spoke again, it was with some degree of restraint.

"Sister-in-edge, I ask you to hold my knife until I ask for it," she said. "If I should fall, place it into the hands of my Blade Sister Jen Sin."

Hazenthull inclined her head.

"It is safe with me." She paused and added, delicately, "I would be honored to hold others of your weapons."

Lorith smiled. "Now, that is an offer worthy of a sister-in-edge. Sadly, the knife is the only weapon I possess, aside myself, of course."

"Of course," Hazenthull said politely. "If a sister-in-edge may ask..."

Large dark eyes met hers. "Ask."

"He is quick, and an experienced fighter, but you surprised him. Victory was yours. I wonder why you began, if you did not mean to finish."

"That is a proper question, and deserves a proper answer. In truth, I did not mean to begin. I recall bidding Jen Sin to come away. The next instant, the blade was in my hand, and myself in the act of striking. It was nothing that I had intended, and I... drew back."

"Which allowed him to disarm you."

"Yes, but it would not have ended there," Lorith said slowly. "I—there was—pain—"

"The researcher shot you with a sedative dart."

"I am grateful for it. No, the pain was in my head, like static, only shaped from needles and fire, and I feared—I feared that I would try again, and this time I would not *be able* to hesitate."

"I understand."

Lorith sighed. "Is the researcher going to destroy the rebirth units?"

"Possibly she will, but not soon. She is determined to study them first."

"Then if she returns Jen Sin his beads, he is in no danger."

"That is beyond me," Hazenthull said. "Though I do know that the kin-group from which Jen Sin derives is known for finding danger. It may not be possible to keep him safe."

"I want him to be safe *from me*," Lorith said. "He stood up as my sister, when he might have taken his ship and himself away from here. He could have—but he stayed, and he improved the duty. Together, we kept the Light from mischief, and he—I could never have made the safe rooms; it would not have occurred to me to make the safe rooms, or any of the changes he made to weaken the Light's dominion. On two occasions, he managed to turn the will of the Light, though he knew—enough. What I want to say is that I would not have him die by my hand, nor would I have him become... lost."

"I understand, I think," Hazenthull said, thinking of a future that did not contain Tolly Jones. She shivered. Lorith nodded.

"I will leave you now," she said, sliding out of the 'doc and onto her feet. "My thanks, Edge Sister. May your death be glorious."

Administrative Tower

HIS PINBEAM SENT, JEN SIN MADE A CUP OF YEAST AND DREW one of the protein bars that had been provided by the ships at dock: *Tarigan* and *Ahab-Esais.* The shipboard cafeterias might also provide other food, and now that they were not scrambling to survive, perhaps a system ought to be put into place.

Tinsori Light had provided yeast as sustenance for his playthings, which was not enough in the way of needed nutrients, Jen Sin thought, stirring his mug. He and Lorith ought to have sickened, but—there. The templates from which they were both remade were of healthy organics. No matter how ill they might have been upon lying down, they would rise again perfectly healthy.

He ate the protein bar with deliberation, chewing each bite carefully, drained the mug, and washed it, leaving it on the edge of the sink.

Then and only then did he allow himself to look at the clock.

More than two of their orderly new hours had passed. Surely, Lorith ought to be recovered by now? On the very few occasions when one of them had died by mischance while the Light still required their service, it had been quite a short while—a matter of one, or at the most two Intervals...

Had something gone wrong? Had Tolly Jones broken faith? Had Seignur Veeoni—with whom he was scarcely in charity at the moment—decided somehow to *use* the fortunate falling into her hand of a light keeper in need of repair?

Had the unit failed, and Lorith died in truth, and in spite of the protection of her beads?

If Lorith was dead—*finally* dead, then—

His heart was pounding; his breath coming short.

"Everything that is unseemly," he muttered, and closed his

eyes, accessing one of several mental calming exercises taught to pilots and Scouts.

In good time, he opened his eyes again, and took stock.

"Much better," he approved, and stood. He would go himself to—

"Cousin Jen Sin, Light Keeper Lorith is approaching," Tocohl said, gently.

He took a hard breath against the sudden sharpness in his chest, and stepped away from the chair and the boards, giving himself room…

The door swept away and Lorith entered the command center at a brisk stride, the sleeves of her robe fluttering, eyes intent, the beads casting sparks from among her pale curls.

He stepped forward, hand out to catch hers, feeling long, cool fingers, gripping his strongly.

"Are you well?" they both cried, and she laughed somewhat while he gasped.

"I am well," he said. "And you?"

"Perfectly restored," she said, and stood looking down at him for a moment longer before seeming to shake herself.

"I had heard there was a ship," she said, looking past him to the screens. "Are your cousins arriving?"

"Not just yet. The ship was a drone sent from the research station at Seignur Veeoni's word. Supplies for her work, so her assistant tells me."

"That sounds very orderly and tame," Lorith said, and he laughed.

"Oh, completely! I am offered apologies for being made to uncap the weapons, gratitude for having held from firing, and awarded a promise that, the next time a supply drone is due in, the light keepers will be told."

Lorith was silent, for a moment.

"She is not…very thoughtful, is she? The researcher."

"I think that the rest of us are not…quite real to the researcher," Jen Sin said, and moved a hand toward a chair.

"We need to talk," he said.

"Yes, we do," she said, and sat on the chair beside the desk, leaving the control chair to him.

He sat down, and considered her, his sole companion in this mad place. Of course, he trusted her; there had been no other option but to trust her.

Now, with the death of the Old Light, the settling into sane space, and the promised arrival of kin, options multiplied, and duty still mattered.

"Why did you draw on me?" he asked, as gently as one might ask such a thing.

Large black eyes flickered. She folded her hands on her knees.

"I was . . . angry," she said slowly. "Not only have you willfully exposed yourself to danger, but you were intent on removing life-support systems."

Life-support systems. He thought of the units on the recovery deck; recalled Seignur Veeoni's lecture of the proper way of producing and educating batch-made humans.

"The Old Light is dead," he said, still gentle. "We have prevailed, you and I, and arrived at clean, stable space. The beads are no longer needed."

"Do people not die, in clean, stable space?"

"They die," Jen Sin said, "but there is no imperative that they rise again, and again, and even again."

Lorith bowed her head, and was silent. This was familiar. Lorith was accustomed to taking time to order her thoughts. Jen Sin waited.

At last she raised her head, and met his eyes.

"Tinsori Light is dead, you say."

"That is correct."

"And yet, there are still systems that require cleaning, others that must be entirely replaced. The Old Light was cunning, and I am not at peace with this easy assurance that he is wholly dead."

"And yet, we have seen no sign, since Mentor Jones destroyed the core."

Lorith leaned forward.

"Do you, who stood between the Light and the universe; who saw the kind and degree of malice he was capable of—do you think, Jen Sin, that Tinsori Light is incapable of hiding—and biding his time?"

Lorith had lived with the Old Light longer than he had; she had made such adjustments to her mind and behavior as best assured her continued survival. It was perhaps not wonderful that she did not believe that the terrible god she had defied for so long was, at last, and justly, dead.

"How do you suggest we proceed?" he asked her.

"Very much as we are. Only, let us be prudent. Do not destroy the repair units until the last of the new systems has been tested."

He might, he thought, do so little, if it eased her.

"I will speak with Seignur Veeoni, and rescind my order to destroy the units." He lifted an eyebrow. "Not that I believe she was going to do so, in any case."

"Good." Lorith stood, and paused, gazing down into his face. "And you will put your beads back, Jen Sin?"

He moved his shoulders.

"Perhaps I shall," he said, rising in his turn. "After Seignur Veeoni has cleaned them for me."

Seignur Veeoni's Private Workroom

"I've completed the document as you requested, Researcher. I'll bring you a glass of nutrient while you read it."

Seignur Veeoni stopped, turned, and considered her henchwoman.

M Traven returned her gaze, calm, as M Traven was always calm.

"Am I low on nutrients?" Seignur Veeoni asked, moderating her tone. M Traven was not to be taken lightly.

It might go too far to say that Seignur Veeoni was fond of her guard. She did, however, value her. More, M class soldiers were extremely practical. It was no small thing to have that practicality working for one.

M Traven shrugged her broad shoulders.

"We can extrapolate," she said. "When was the last time you had nutrients?"

Seignur Veeoni consulted her memory.

"Ten Standard Hours ago, I had a glass of nutrient."

M Traven did not point out that a glass of nutrient was considered adequate for six hours of activity. In return, Seignur Veeoni did not sigh.

"Bring me nutrient, then. Is the document on the screen?"

"Yes," M Traven said, possibly in answer to both request and query. "You should be aware that I asked Mentor Jones to go over my first effort. He made several helpful suggestions, which I have incorporated."

"Why did you deem it desirable to have Mentor Jones's input?" Seignur Veeoni asked, honestly curious.

"I believe that the mentor's livelihood, and his life, are rooted in his ability to be persuasive. I thought to use that resource to improve our chances of success."

It was not ill-reasoned. Seignur Veeoni nodded to indicate she had received the information, and crossed the room to the screen.

It was a briefer document than she would have supposed, given the necessity of being *persuasive*. She had finished her first read-through by the time M Traven brought the nutrient and placed it on the desk by her hand.

She raised the glass, took a sip, and returned to the top of the document.

Her second read completed, she became aware of something else.

M Traven was still standing by her desk.

No.

No, it was not too much to say that M Traven was *hovering*. That was unusual. Though not so afflicted herself, Seignur Veeoni did know that some individuals experienced doubt with regard to their work, and periodically required reassurance.

She had never observed this behavior in M Traven. However, this was the first time she had been required to produce a sales document.

Seignur Veeoni sipped more nutrient, looked up and met M Traven's eyes.

"It is adequate to our purpose," she said. "I will forward it to Light Keeper yos'Phelium, so that he may in his turn forward it to Korval and Korval's *qe'andra*."

M Traven inclined slightly from the waist.

"It was an interesting assignment," she said. "I would welcome another like it."

"I will hold that in mind."

Seignur Veeoni finished her nutrient and put the glass on the desk. With a few spare keystrokes, she sent the document to Jen Sin yos'Phelium, certain that M Traven had seen the transaction.

"While you were away, I made a command decision," M Traven said.

Seignur Veeoni paused in the act of reaching to the screen.

M Strain soldiers were perfectly capable of command. Indeed, M Traven had been second in the command structure at Seignur Veeoni's former laboratory. There was no such command structure in their current situation—or, Seignur Veeoni thought, perhaps there was.

M Traven was the sole soldier attached to Seignur Veeoni.

Therefore, M Traven was not merely first in a chain of command.

She was commander.

"What have you done?" Seignur Veeoni asked.

"I have forwarded a copy of the original station schematics to Light Keeper yos'Phelium."

Seignur Veeoni took thought.

"I see no difficulty," she said after a moment. "He is the light keeper, and has as much right as we have to the information."

"The reason that I shared that information with Light Keeper yos'Phelium," M Traven continued, "was that he had not been told about the arriving delivery, and was placed into a situation where he felt it necessary to defend the station from attack."

Seignur Veeoni spun in her chair.

"He did *not* damage our cargo!"

"He did not, but that outcome would not have been in question, if he had been told of the delivery in advance."

"Ah," Seignur Veeoni said. "I see. Pray inform the light keepers when we are expecting deliveries. I do not wish to risk having necessary supplies damaged."

M Traven inclined from the waist.

"Yes," she said.

The comm pinged. M Traven crossed the room, leaned over, and looked to Seignur Veeoni.

"Light Keeper yos'Phelium calls," she said.

"I will speak with Light Keeper yos'Phelium," Seignur Veeoni said.

"I will be brief, as I know you are busy on the Light's behalf," Jen Sin yos'Phelium said, briskly. "I wish to remand a hasty order. Please do not destroy the recovery units."

Seignur Veeoni did not smile.

"I will not destroy the recovery units," she said, so that there would be no shadow of doubt. "I do intend to download and analyze the data from each, but this will not alter their utility in any way."

"Thank you," the light keeper said. "yos'Phelium out."

Hacienda Estrella
Safe Dock Bar

NORSE WAS ON THE BAR ALONE WHEN THE OFFICIAL CARRESENS-Denobli Traveler's Aid Notice hit the public bands. He upped the volume so it could be heard at the back booth, and used the rag on the bar top, listening.

The short of it was that Tinsori Light—Ghost Station's proper name—was anchored in real space, under the ownership of and administered by Tree-and-Dragon Family. There were light keepers present, and upgrades underway. Any ship that had time and inclination might consider taking in supplies and repair goods, on account there was a gap in the ring that ought to be dealt with, soonest. Carresens-Denobli was providing the material, and interested ships could take on pods at Outyard Sinco.

Station Day 10
Recovery Deck

. . . .

"RECOVERY DECK PRESETS: TEMP LOWEST ALLOWABLE, CAMERA on-demand. Acknowledge."

"Recovery deck default temperature lowest allowable, camera default off," said Systems.

The shadow nodded, and moved without a sound across the freezing deck to the second cubicle.

Bechimo
En route

. . . .

THERE WAS MAIL.

Quite a lot of mail, and most of it, Theo saw, as she scrolled down the screen, pertinent. Or possibly pertinent. There were several files, from Val Con and from Jeeves, and a letter from Miri.

Theo opened that first.

> *Theo, Shan let us know he's sending you on to Tinsori Light to help out while he finishes up some business. Wanted to let you know it's not going to just be you and yours. Gordy's on the way, too—to set up a trade office and be trader-on-the-spot. Gordy's Shan's foster-son, so that makes him your cousin. Expect him soon, but behind you.*
>
> *We've already got people in place—Val Con's putting together a file for you. Real quick, though, so you'll have the names—Tocohl Lorlin. Jeeves's daughter, and a cousin. Tocohl's handling station functions. Jen Sin yos'Phelium, a cousin, is first light keeper. Hazenthull nor'Phelium's on detached duty from here to there, backing up her partner, Tolly Jones, who you'll be relieved to hear isn't a cousin. Seignur Veeoni—Uncle's sister. Lorith—the last original light keeper, out from the Old Universe, riding the wave in like your Pathfinders. Might be they'll all three have some things to talk about.*
>
> *I know you keep your crew informed, so feel free to share the files around. I'm thinking that* Bechimo *and Joyita could might be useful to Tocohl, who hardly had time to get born before we sent her off to help out with* Admiral Bunter.

Theo frowned.

"Is there a problem?" *Bechimo* murmured for her alone.

"Not a problem, just a list of people on Tinsori Light right now. One of them is Jeeves's daughter Tocohl—who was sent out to Jemiatha's Jumble Stop to help out with *Admiral Bunter.* You remember that, I know."

"Of course," *Bechimo* said, easily. There'd been a time when he would've gotten irritated by the insinuation that he might forget something. "She was sent to assist the mentor. I did ask Jeeves the mentor's name, in case we should have need again. Tollance Berik-Jones, according to Jeeves, is the greatest living practitioner of his art."

Theo blinked.

"Good to know," she said, glancing at Miri's letter. "Could that contract to Tolly Jones for every day?" she asked.

"Perhaps. Why do you ask?"

"Because Miri has him on Tinsori Light, and says he's Hazenthull nor'Phelium's partner, but not my cousin."

"None of these things excludes the other. Is *Admiral Bunter* also at the Light?"

"Not that Miri mentions. About Tocohl, though. Miri says that you and Joyita could maybe give her some help. She's taken over station functions, but she's young..."

"Young, and not born to be a station," *Bechimo* said, sharply. "Yes, we will assist. Or, rather, *I* will assist in any way I am able. Joyita may decide otherwise."

It would be a wonderful thing if he did, Theo thought, Joyita only being as curious as four dozen kittens.

"I'll ask him," she said, and returned to the letter.

We're told Tinsori Light was an Independent Logic from the Old Universe. We're also told that it died, more or less at the same time Ren Zel undertook his little trick to save the universe. While that's good to hear, the station hardware's Old Tech from the basement to the roof, and everything's ripe for just going wrong, even without a bad actor behind it.

Now we've got the station, we'd naturally like to keep it, especially given where it is. The bright idea there is most of the station's callers will be Free Ships and their friends, so Scout Commander yos'Phelium will be seen as having put his whole paycheck on the spot to win. Which you'll understand he figures as being to his benefit.

General home news is that we had a little excitement, but we're past that now. Ren Zel and Anthora are still stopping with the Healers; Pat Rin won the election; Nova's working on her legend; Kamele and Kareen are about to publish the first Compiled History of Surebleak, *Lizzie's walking, except when she's not.*

Drop a note every so often to let us know you're still alive, right?

Miri

Theo sighed, flicked over to the list of files Val Con and Jeeves had sent. Dossiers on everybody Miri'd mentioned as being at the Light. Background on Tinsori Light. History. Goals.

"Joyita," she said.

The lower left tile on her screen flickered, and he looked out at her from his comm room.

"Captain Theo?"

"Distribute the files from Val Con and Jeeves to all crew, required reading for our next meeting in—"

She glanced at the time.

"Three shifts."

"Will do. Anything else?"

"N—yes. Jeeves's daughter Tocohl assumed all functions of Tinsori Light Station when the previous operator died. She's young, and Miri's thinking she'd welcome experienced people to talk to and to help her sort her situation out. Are you willing to pitch in on that?"

A grin split Joyita's brown face, which made him look more piratical than usual.

"I'd be delighted," he said, so sincere you couldn't *not* believe it.

"Good," Theo said. "That's all I've got."

"Captain," he said, and his tile blanked.

Theo sighed, and pushed out of her chair.

She needed to ask Kara if she wanted her new bowli ball to be match-rated or free-play.

Healer Hall
Surebleak City

"LADY, THERE'S ONE WAITING FOR YOU IN THE VISITOR'S PARLOR."

Anthora looked up from her screen and met the 'prentice Healer's eyes.

"One?" she repeated.

The boy—Skoly—was Surebleakean; a Liaden would have bowed to cover his consternation. This lad only stared, mouth tight.

"I only mean to ask," Anthora clarified gently, "if this person gave you a name or any other identifying information?"

Relief eased the unhappy mouth.

"Oh! He said the delm sent him with a message, and he has to deliver it in person."

And that, she thought, marking her place and closing the book, resolved the matter neatly.

She stood.

"I will be pleased to end one's waiting," she said.

The Surebleak City Healer Hall was housed in a former hotel. Renovations were ongoing, and the function of rooms reassigned as necessary to accommodate the work.

This week, the visitor's parlor was on the mezzanine level, in what had perhaps once been an intimate meeting room. Some attempt had been made to create a comfortable waiting area—two soft chairs, an occasional table, and a bureau supporting a kettle, cubes of pressed tea, packets of coffeetoot, and sealed bottles of water.

The one who awaited her, however, was not seated, refreshment in hand, but standing at the window, looking out over the snowy street.

She closed the door; her brother Val Con turned. He was dressed Surebleak-style—sweater, work pants, boots. Snow melt glittered in his dark hair like crystal beads. His face was... careful, and his emotions also. She felt tenderness brush over her, tasted the sharp tang of his worry. There was more, but she did not immediately try to See it. Her brother's arms were open to her. She walked into his embrace, put her arms around his waist, and her face against his shoulder.

"Sister," he murmured. His arms were a comfort; the sweater warm under her cheek. It smelled like cedar and lavender, which meant it had come from House stores. The very scent evoked home and safety.

"Brother."

She took a deep breath, squeezed him and stepped back, Inner Eyes open now.

"Well," she murmured, "what is this, Brother? Have you been wounded?"

He tipped his head.

"Miri was wounded, as you know. I assume that you are seeing my clumsy attempt to hold her to life—"

"By feeding her yours." Anthora gently traced the scarred edge of his pattern.

Val Con raised an eyebrow.

"Am I in need, Healer?"

She moved a hand, dismissing irony. "Surely, a sister may show some concern, when her brother arrives after too long a separation, bearing new scars."

She Looked more deeply, finding the lifemate link at the core of him, blazing even brighter than previously with the energy of two lives interleaved and supporting both.

It was a thing of very great beauty, that link, and Anthora sighed in relief, to find it burning so brightly. She began to withdraw—and paused, spying something else new in the tapestry of his life.

It was a small thing—not an entire weaving, nor yet merely a thread. When she brought her attention upon it more nearly, she could hear—a song.

"Emissary Twelve demonstrated a less-ruinous path before I was entirely committed," Val Con murmured. "I apprehend that she also performed a repair."

"Quite an elegant repair," Anthora agreed. "I would welcome an opportunity to speak with her about her methods."

"That may not be possible. She only plans to be here, herself, for the next one hundred forty-four local years."

"Ah. I will make it an object to free an afternoon in my schedule before her departure," Anthora said solemnly. "But none of this is why you came."

"No."

He reached out and took her hands in his, and studied her, green eyes sharp and face serious.

"I came to ask a question," he said.

Anthora inclined her head.

"Ask, then."

"Very well. Tell me truly: Are you well?"

"What do the Healers tell you?"

Val Con sighed.

"The Healers would have me know that you are *diminished*; that there is a lack of habitual levity; a worrisome quietness of energy. They skirt such definitives as *well* and *not-well*." He let go of her right hand, and cupped her cheek, looking hard into her eyes.

"I can see for myself that you are—changed," he murmured.

Anthora smiled.

"Of course you can. And you would think, would you not, Brother, that Healers, who deal with so much of it, would know the word *changed*?"

"Perhaps they did not wish to cause alarm."

"And see how well they accomplished their goal," she said sharply.

"Arguably *changed* is a different quality than either *well* or *not-well*," Val Con remarked.

It was Anthora who sighed this time, and stepped back, freeing herself from his touch.

"You told 'prentice Skoly that you bore a message from the delm," she said.

"In fact, I bear two messages from the delm. Which one I deliver depends upon the answer to a question. *Are you well*?"

She wrinkled her nose at him.

"Well enough, though as we agree—changed. I am learning my new parameters—necessary work which may—and must—be undertaken wherever I find myself."

"Hah. And your lifemate, my brother Ren Zel?"

She hesitated.

"Also changed," she said slowly, careful to be precise, "and learning new limits. He remains under treatment because the Healers wish to assure themselves that the . . . addiction will not return."

"Will it?"

"In my opinion, it will not. He no longer sees the golden lines, and his memory of them is very dim, as is the memory of his victory."

She raised a hand.

"There is also for both of us the question of . . . classification. You will understand that this concerns the Guild more nearly than our colleagues. It would seem that I—am a Healer. What else I might be cannot be known until this quietness of energy with which the Hall Master saw fit to task you has arisen into the frenetic state that had been more usual with me."

"Will that occur?" he asked.

She moved her shoulders.

"Who can say? Though I confess to you, Brother, it is . . . something of a relief, to not stand always in the eye of the storm, and to have the luxury of calm reflection. I suppose I will accommodate myself, if the storm finds me again, but at the moment, I am content with quiet energy." She reached out to touch his cheek again, a fleeting brush of fingertips against smooth skin. "And you know, I am a very *good* Healer."

"Yes," he said solemnly, "I do know that. Do you think that I might dare ask to see Ren Zel?"

"I don't know why you need to ask," she said. "I will take you to him, myself."

• • • ❋ • • •

This new iteration of his woolly-headed sister would, Val Con thought, take some getting used to. Still, he was of better heart now than he had been after his conversation with the Hall Master, who would have had him believe Anthora dull, even broken. To find that she was neither, merely altered by what she and her lifemate had done in the service of preserving the universe as they knew it—well, who would *not* be changed by such an event?

He went beside her down quiet hallways, and then far noisier, as she walked them through a construction zone, and into a narrow back hall, where he dropped behind her so as not to rub his shoulder against the wall.

She seemed older, he thought, which was no ill thing, as she had always seemed much younger than her years, the effect of the frenetic energies the Healers now missed in her. He chided himself, a little, that he had not known that the buffeting of her own powers had distressed her.

"How should you have known?" Anthora asked very much in her old style of snatching the thought out of one's head. She glanced at him over her shoulder. "I did not know it myself. It was what was. It is only now that I have achieved a state where comparison is possible, and find I have a preference."

She moved a hand to the right as they came to a cross corridor.

"Down here; they have him overlooking the garden."

"Garden?" he asked, recalling the blowing snow outside.

"They've done well with materials in hand," Anthora told him, with a touch of her old earnestness. "It's not the garden at Solcintra Hall, of course, but it is—fitting. Ren Zel quite likes it."

"And you?"

"Say that it's grown on me."

She stopped and placed her hand against the door.

"Beloved," she said, far too softly to be heard on the other side. "May I come in? I have Val Con."

The door whisked open, and there was Ren Zel, smiling, reaching to catch their hands and pull them inside.

With the door closed, Ren Zel released Anthora to grip Val Con's forearms—kin-touch, if not so gentle as a hug, and Val Con felt another knot of worry that had been lodged in his chest loosen.

"Brother!" Ren Zel said gladly. "It is good to see you."

"And to see you," Val Con assured him, taking a moment to consider the man before him. Unlike his volatile lifemate, Ren Zel was quiet; serious and gentle. A less likely savior of the universe could hardly have been found.

Only Ren Zel had a gift—a *dramliz* gift, though not one, thank the gods, that often manifested. He could—he had been able to—see the golden threads, as he described them, that held everything together.

Even more horrifying, he had been able to *manipulate* them, and had used his power boldly and to the point, sealing the rift in the fabric of space that had allowed Tinsori Light free passage between universes.

It had been too heavy a burden for a mortal man, and Ren

Zel had become addicted to his own gift. The gift that he no longer held, according to his lifemate.

A brother could only be glad for that.

"Why are you here?" Ren Zel asked, and there was a certain gleam in his pretty brown eyes. "Have you something for us?"

There was an eagerness there, and Val Con sighed.

"I am here on behalf of the delm," he said quietly, and saw some of the eagerness fade, replaced by a reasonable wariness. One did not, after all, wish to hear overmuch from the delm.

Ren Zel pressed his arms once more, and released him, waving them further into the room. "Come, sit by the window. There's a pleasant view, believe it or don't."

The view was pleasant, overlooking a pocket garden of shrubberies and artfully placed blocks and boulders of what was very probably scavenged 'crete, softened and made winsome by the snow. In the center of the space was a simple fountain, kept liquid by small heat lamps set into the bottom of the pool, their light transforming the modest spray of water into silver, blue, and amber.

"Shall I ring the kitchen for tea?" Ren Zel asked, after seeing them seated.

"Perhaps not," Anthora said. "Val Con is afraid of being found out, you know. He had only told poor Skoly that he wanted me."

"I was gentle," Val Con protested.

"Skoly is easily overset," Ren Zel murmured, "and too afraid of giving offense."

"Perhaps he will learn better," Val Con said. "There's no need to rouse the kitchen on my account."

Ren Zel crossed his arms on the back of Anthora's chair and leaned on them.

"So," he said, "a message from the delm."

"First a question," Val Con said, studying him. Ren Zel seemed not as much changed as Anthora, which was perhaps accounted for by his fading memories. Indeed, he seemed very much less worn than he had been previous to his engagement to save the universe.

Still, the question had to be asked—and answered.

"Are you well?"

Ren Zel tipped his head, giving the query due consideration, and met his eyes.

"Well enough to sit First at Jump, to attend a climate board meeting as the clan's representative, or any like task. The interrogation of prisoners, or the manipulation of... time and space—those are beyond me, and, if I am frank, Brother, it is my ardent wish that they remain so for the rest of my life."

Val Con inclined his head.

"I had understood that you have forgotten much of what your gift was like," Val Con murmured.

"I recall, as through a cloud, and from a distance of years," Ren Zel said. "The Healers offered to either sharpen my recall or erase the memories entire. I am content to allow them to fade at their own rate."

He straightened out of his lean suddenly and looked aside, through the window to the snowy garden below.

"If the delm requires me to use that gift—but, there; I cannot. In starkest truth, it is no longer mine to wield."

"The delm requires nothing so terrible," Val Con said gently. "The task in the delm's eye lies adjacent to your last battle, and it would, I think, be a good thing if you recalled, even in abstract, what you had done."

Ren Zel looked back to him, half-smiling.

"Of a certainty, I cast the last remnant of the Old Universe back, and sealed the door through which it had crept."

"That will do as a tale. In reality, it would appear that you reset—or even recreated—a portion of space."

Ren Zel blinked.

"Yes, I know; it's outrageous. Every sensibility must rebel. However, there is supporting data from several impeccable sources, if you allow the Uncle's data gathering to be so characterized."

"I would see that data," Ren Zel said.

Anthora added quietly, "And I."

"In good time. For the moment, allow me to move closer to the delm's message. I should tell you that there was an artifact—a space station of the Old Universe—that was caught between. It was forced fully into our universe as a result of your actions. The core intelligence is, we are told, deceased, and the station has fallen into Korval's care."

"How did that come about?" Anthora asked, broadly skeptical. "Had we an administrator in place?"

Val Con smiled at her. "In fact, we did. Jen Sin yos'Phelium has been a light keeper on that station for two hundred Standards. And here we come to your part in all of this."

He paused and glanced out at the little fountain in its snowy garden.

"Jen Sin's duty has been long, and—difficult. His last correspondence touched upon how difficult, this by way of informing his delm that he is... fatally compromised."

"The delm would send him kin," Anthora said. "A Healer, and one who is able to administer the station, should Jen Sin falter under the weight of his pain."

"That closely mirrors the delm's reasoning, as I understand it," Val Con said. "Though you should know that more kin is en route, so that he will not be wholly alone very much longer."

Anthora frowned. "Who?" she murmured, and that quickly her frown became a look of nearly comic horror. "Theo. You sent him *Theo*?"

Val Con raised his hands. "Acquit me. Shan sent him Theo."

"Of course he did."

"I think Theo and her crew will be very helpful," Ren Zel said. "Especially if there is work to do with station systems."

"In fact." Val Con gave him a nod. "We now arrive at Korval's message: Anthora yos'Galan and Ren Zel dea'Judan will be dispatched to Tinsori Light to provide what aid is needed. The clan of course will shelter and provide for Shindi and Mik."

Ren Zel shifted. Val Con raised an eyebrow.

"Yes?"

"Anthora carries our child," he said.

"And will carry her for some time yet, no matter where I am," Anthora said tartly. She looked at Val Con.

"Of course I will go. Ren Zel?"

"Yes," he answered. "Though I wonder how quickly we may start. If Jen Sin's danger is acute—"

"There," Val Con said, "I think we may depend upon Theo."

Anthora laughed. "To provide distraction, you mean? Yes, that might do. But we ought to go quickly, nevertheless. The Healers must be persuaded to release us at once."

Val Con stood. "That, I will undertake." He paused, looking down at his sister. She lifted her brows.

"Another question?"

"I only wonder how is your piloting, Sister."

"That was always a question, was it not? I did *earn* my license, Brother."

"Yes," he murmured, and bowed contrition. "A momentary lapse. Forgive it."

"Bah," she said, and rose. "Go away and quell the Healers. We will be ready in half an hour."

He turned toward the door, and turned back when she said sharply, "Val Con!"

"Sister?"

"Are any of Jen Sin's things in House stores? We should take to him—anything from home, really, but something of his own would be best."

"Ah." He bowed gently. "I will see what may be found. Else?"

"I think not. Go, I beg you, and liberate us."

"You may depend upon me," he promised her, and was gone.

Hacienda Estrella
Outyard Sinco

JAILEEN—THAT WAS *CAPTAIN* ULDRA-JOENZ WHEN SHE WAS IN this tone o'mind—had put *Karil* forward as being willing to take a few pods over to Tinsori Light. Normally, that woulda been Orth on cargo, only Orth was on lend to *Lady Graz* for the long loop, Shelby having retired back down to the family holdings, planet-side, like she'd always said she would, and nobody'd believed her.

Which meant it was Norse who got pulled out of his comfortable nook on the station, and made cargo master by the captain's say-so, which he was too old for, and *that* would've flown further if Jaileen hadn't been his sister.

His *older* sister.

So, Norse was standing cargo master, which he liked a little better'n he let on, once old habits rose up and took over. Also, he had some considerable curiosity about Gho— Tinsori Light, always had—and that was about to get satisfied.

It coulda been worse was his position by the time they'd gotten the pods on and balanced, and the delicates stowed proper in the holds.

They had their flying orders from Hacienda Tower, and it was time—past time—for him to seal the loading bay.

He was on his way down the hall to do just that when the receiving bell rang.

"Too late for it," he said, coming into the office. "Put it on next in line."

"Gotta go first," said the warehouser waiting for him. Not a stranger—Norse had dealt with him a couple times during the load-up. Not somebody he knew from being on the station, but the warehousers tended to keep to themselves.

He had a sled with him, and a crate on the sled—good-sized crate, triple sealed.

"*Gotta* and *can it* are two different things," Norse said. "What is it?"

"Delicates," the warehouser said, pointing at the label.

"Holds're full," Norse told him, which was true. "Got no place for it."

The warehouser shrugged, pulled out his tablet, tapped it, and thrust it forward.

Norse took it and glared down at the lading slip.

The crate held specialized computronics, according to the slip, engineered special for systems in place at Gho— Tinsori Light.

"Well, where the mud am I gonna *put* it?"

The warehouser shrugged.

"Delicate one-offs? I'm thinking your quarters might do."

Norse glared at him, but it happened the man was right. Grumbling, he pressed his thumb to the screen, got *Karil*'s interior sled, and the two of them shifted the crate, which wasn't halfway light.

The warehouser nodded and went away. Norse sealed the bay after him.

He stood for a short minute, staring at the crate, then kicked the sled's power on, and began to push it down the hall to one of the empty bunkrooms.

Bechimo
En route

. . . .

"EVERYBODY'S READ THE FILES?" THEO ASKED, LOOKING 'ROUND the table, and into the split screen that showed Joyita in his comm tower, and Win Ton on the bridge, at first board.

There were nods, murmured "Yes, Theos," and solemn faces, which was appropriate, considering the contents of the files.

"Who's first?"

"Tinsori Light is a Great Work," Chernak said. "Great Works are . . . difficult to kill."

Theo nodded. Truth said, she'd had a moment or two of doubt herself while reading the file. The scholarship was strong, and the experts impeccable, which counted for her, as the daughter of two scholars. Chernak and Stost, though, had seen and contended against the Enemy's Works in the Old Universe. She'd expected them to be hard to convince.

"Right," she said. "We know from *Aberthaz Ferry* that Tinsori Light was one of the three Great Works from the Old Universe that he was hunting in this one," she said. "He never reached his goal, but we have it on file that Tinsori Light did die, and very recently. All the people *at* the Light, and all the experts *on* it, including Uncle, are convinced that's the case: The intelligence that called himself Tinsori Light is dead."

She paused. It was Stost who spoke this time.

"In our experience, and from the intelligence shared by other soldiers and Command—the only way to be certain that a Great Work is dead is to reduce it to atoms and deposit the atoms into the heart of a sun."

"Even then," Chernak said, tapping the table with a stern forefinger, like a teacher chiding a student for having left out the proof for the equation.

"Yes, Senior," Stost said, and met Theo's eyes. "Even then, we must assume that we have only delivered a setback, never a final death."

Theo frowned. "Is that a joke?"

Stost turned his big hands up.

"A soldier's joke, Captain."

"Which is to say, black an' near enough to true," Clarence said, "as truth was."

"That's an important point," Theo said, leaning in. "This isn't the Old Universe, and Tinsori Light was *old. Aberthaz Ferry* told us that the timonium powering the Old Tech systems is at its limit. There's another twenty Standards of power, maybe, for outliers. Timonium exhaustion alone—I think it's telling that Miri's more worried about systems going down from timonium failure than she is about Tinsori Light not being factually dead."

"Factually dead," Win Ton murmured. Theo flicked a look at the screen, but he was minding his board, face smooth.

"Captain Robertson is wise to be concerned of systems failures," Chernak said, "but she may be naive in her belief that Tinsori Light is completely dead."

"The only thing that's going to prove it yes or no is observation," Theo said. "Unless you think we ought to ignore our orders and leave Tinsori Light on its own?"

"No!" Chernak and Stost answered as one, both clearly horrified.

"Captain, with respect, you cannot ignore the Great Work," Chernak said, very carefully. "Stost and I, it is our duty to be careful on behalf of ship, crew, and the universe where we find ourselves. We only wanted it to be clear, that we would be—"

She faltered, and Stost took it up.

"We will be proceeding as if the Great Work is not *factually dead*," he said. "If we are found to be fools, it will not be the first time."

"Yes," Chernak said. "You say it well, my Stost."

"I can accept that," Theo said. "You'll also have to remember that Tocohl has taken over station systems. She's someone entirely other than Tinsori Light."

"Occupying the systems as she does," Kara said, "would she not notice an—intruder? A remnant?"

Chernak and Stost exchanged a look.

"The Enemy, and the Works of the Enemy are very good at hiding, and at—misdirection," Chernak said.

"Joyita and I have agreed to help the young person Tocohl," *Bechimo* said. "Ascertaining that there are no bugs, ghosts, or traps in her hardware or systems is an example of the sort of assistance we can offer."

"No direct contact," Theo said. "We don't want anything coming across to us."

"Captain Theo," Joyita said chidingly, "give us credit. We're good at this kind of thing."

"You're also cocky," Theo said sternly. "No risks to yourself or *Bechimo*, that's clear?"

"Yes, Captain," Joyita said, sounding subdued. A little. Maybe.

"Theo, we will do what we can to assist while keeping ourselves and the crew safe," *Bechimo* assured her, which would have been more reassuring if *Bechimo*'s definition of *safe* hadn't been expanding, and that was her fault, for being, well, human. And, so her father and her brother told her, for being related to Clan Korval, possibly the least safe body of humans in the universe.

"Safe," she said, now. "I'll expect it."

She looked around the table again.

"What else?"

"The space around the Light is now said to be stable, lacking all anomalies that previously defined it," Kara said slowly. "I don't quite understand how this was achieved."

Theo sighed.

"Tinsori Light was caught up in the wave of the Great Migration"—she nodded at Chernak and Stost—"what you call the Retreat. It came into our universe, but only partway. It cycled back and forth, manifesting only occasionally—that's all in the dossier." The dossier that read like something out of *Thrilling Wonder Tales* about haunted space stations and crystal ships lurking in asteroid fields to freeze the unwary, and Theo might've thought that Val Con was having a joke, except that file had been compiled by Jeeves.

"Yes," Kara said, "it is. The dossier also states that *an event* occurred which brought the Light entirely into our universe. I wonder what that event was."

Pharst, Theo thought.

She met Kara's eyes.

"I wasn't there, though I was told what happened, in general terms. Knowing both versions, I'd say it might be more . . . comfortable to accept Clan Korval's assurance that an event occurred and Tinsori Light is now completely part of this universe."

"I'll take that," Clarence said comfortably.

Kara frowned.

"Comforting?"

"I can tell you the story I was told, which frankly makes my head hurt. But if Korval's word isn't good enough—"

Kara blinked.

"When you put it that way . . . very well. An event occurred. Tinsori Light, the station, is fully in this universe, and the malignant intelligence that once resided there has received his last reward."

"Thank you," Theo said sincerely, and looked around the table for the third time.

"Anything else?"

Silence.

"All right, then. We'll be Jumping directly for Tinsori Light in three shifts."

Station Day 15
Administrative Tower

AHAB-ESAIS READ THE NOTE HE HAD LEFT FOR HIMSELF IN THE computer.

Jen Sin sighed, and leaned back in his chair.

Ahab-Esais was the ship that had brought Mentor Inkirani Yo, now deceased, and Tocohl Lorlin, his cousin, to Tinsori Light.

One pilot dead and the other bound by duty, the ship languished at dock. Not an unusual situation on the face of it; ships were patient of the foibles of their pilots, and often waited unconscionably long between flights.

However, according to Mentor Jones, who was not, so far as Jen Sin could judge, given to unsubstantiated flights of paranoia, *Ahab-Esais*, like Inkirani Yo, held allegiance to the Lyre Institute for Exceptional Children. Mentor Jones represented this organization as being not merely in opposition to Korval, but an active threat, an assessment that the research Jen Sin had done among the delm's background files suggested was accurate.

It was the opinion of Mentor Jones that the ship was reporting in to the Institute, the directors of whom would soon become tired of waiting, did they not see a change in ship's location, or receive a report from Mentor Yo.

The latter being impossible, Mentor Jones argued for a change of ship's location, hoping this would draw the directors' attention away from Tinsori Light.

That suggestion had been forwarded to the delm in the first status report Jen Sin had sent. He had, cravenly, hoped for something like an order with regard to the ship, but none had come, while other requests and queries were answered with precision, either by the dea'Gauss, the delm, or his clever cousin, Nova.

Thus, Jen Sin thought wryly, he was taught what he already knew, and it fell to him to pass the lesson on to Mentor Jones.

It wanted some delicacy, was his first thought, though as light keeper he held the last word on who might and might not be privileged to dock at his station. But Mentor Jones had weighty concerns, and they ought not to be cast lightly aside.

He closed his eyes, but almost immediately opened them again as the comm chimed.

He touched the switch.

"yos'Phelium."

"Light Keeper, it is Seignur Veeoni," she said briskly. "I finished testing your memory beads, and have analyzed the results. I think you had better come to my lab." She paused, and added, "At your earliest convenience."

Almost, he said that he cared nothing for her analysis—but that was unworthy even of a yos'Phelium pilot-turned-administrator. Seignur Veeoni's insights might well be useful to the clan.

He took a breath.

"I am at liberty now," he said. "Is this convenient for you?"

"Yes," she said, and cut the connection.

As he had hoped, he found Lorith in her workroom.

She looked up as he approached.

"Jen Sin?"

"I am called to Seignur Veeoni's laboratory," he said. "There are test results to be explained, so I might be some time. Tocohl will call you, should there be need."

"Certainly," she said, and tipped her head slightly to the left. "Is there likely to be need?"

"*Bechimo* may arrive," he said. "We do expect her, though not with precision. Otherwise, you know as well as I how likely there is to be need."

"Will the researcher finally return your beads?"

"It is possible," he said. "I will of course know more, after I receive my explanations."

Lorith pressed her lips together.

"I had been thinking, Jen Sin... The researcher is competent, I know, but the beads are so attuned, it would be very easy for her to... unintentionally alter, or break an important function.

It came to me that it may be possible to extract a new set from the unit."

He frowned.

"Has this been done?"

Lorith moved her hand. "It was something I thought of, as I considered the situation. I have not extracted beads from the unit. There was never need."

"Well, then. We will hold that thought aside until we are better informed. In the meanwhile—"

Jen Sin turned his head, tracking a flicker of motion he had seen out of the edge of his eye. He looked up, toward the ceiling—girders here, and shadowed at the height—and waited, but the motion did not repeat.

"Is there a problem?" Lorith asked.

Jen Sin moved his shoulders.

"A trick of the shadows, perhaps. I thought I saw a bird."

• • • ❋ • • •

"Mentor," Tocohl said. "There is a ship asking to dock. It gives no name or port, though it does state it was sent by *Disian*, to you, providing your ID in the forms of name, image, and voice-print. Will you speak with this ship?"

"Be pleased to. Visual and voice to my screen, please."

"Yes."

The screen flickered, and he was looking at—well.

It was a ship courtesy of the fact that it had apparently arrived under its own power, there being no tugs in sight. Past that—it was maybe a manufactory rig. Plenty of arms and grippers. Intake chutes, stacks, and holding bays. It was the size of a small station itself, and by rights ought to have been anchored at known coords, with a work crew living aboard, and ships orbiting.

"This is Tolly Jones," he said. "Who am I speaking to?"

Silence greeted this, maybe lag, maybe—

"Ren Stryker, I am named," the voice was high and clear, the intonation musical.

"Pleased to meet you," Tolly said, smiling easily into the screen. "What can I do for you?"

Another pause, just that tiny bit longer than lag would account for.

"It is Ren Stryker who will do for Tolly Jones. The old station requires repair, says *Disian*. Ren Stryker is a fabricating unit. Ren Stryker will fabricate to order."

Tolly blinked.

"That's going to be very helpful, thank you," Tolly said. "Tell me, are you able to render complex systems into materiel?"

"Yes."

"Good," Tolly said, turning to grin up at Haz. "I've got a spaceship that needs to disappear, or at least to stop being a spaceship."

"Bring me this ship," Ren Stryker said. "I will reduce it to useful components."

"I want to do that," Tolly said, "but I have to put the project before the light keeper—the boss—and get his approval. My word's not final here on the station."

The answer this time was a shade quicker.

"You only work there," Ren Stryker suggested.

Tolly laughed.

"That's it! You sit right where you are while I check in with the boss. He's a busy man, so it might be a couple Standard Hours before you get a follow-up. Is there anything you need to make you comfortable while you wait?"

"I am comfortable," Ren Stryker said. "I have content to review."

"Good. Expect a ping in a couple hours. Tolly Jones out."

. . . ✵ . . .

"I have prepared a comparison," Seignur Veeoni said as she guided him through her private workroom. It was a large space, with a number of worktables spotted throughout, each, so he supposed, dedicated to its own project.

The table dedicated to the project of the memory beads he had lately been wearing was toward the back of the room, and somewhat... further apart from the others.

"Please observe the screen," Seignur Veeoni said, tapping it on. An image formed: revealing a pale crystalline structure methodically pierced by smaller needles of darker crystal.

"This is a fully functional memory bead. The enclosing medium is sterile crystal, grown to stringent scientific specifications, and seeded with acicular crystals. An unused memory bead will be entirely transparent. Once a bead is strung on the filaments—these are perhaps known to you as 'smart strands'—and establishes its place in the network, the seed-crystals become active. Each rutile you see here holds data; the pattern formed by the acicular crystals is created by the data. That is to say, a bead from my network will show a different pattern than a bead taken from my brother's network. I use my brother in this example because, though we are very similar, we are not exact, a fact that the storage pattern illustrates."

She paused, and glanced at him, perhaps trying to gauge his level of confusion.

Jen Sin inclined his head. "I understand."

"The acicular crystals continue to grow until a particular bead is full. When that occurs, another bead in the network activates, data flows in, and the crystals begin to grow."

It was, Jen Sin thought, a rather attractive image. The needle-like crystals shading from palest red to deep amber, their pattern . . . soothing, in the way that precisely ordered things were often soothing.

"How is the data retrieved?" he asked.

Seignur Veeoni frowned.

"In the usual way of things, the data is retrieved as an auxiliary memory function by a mind that has been especially trained to integrate with smart strands. I might, for an instance, and assuming you had received the appropriate training, give you my beads to wear. You would be able to access any of the data stored in the network."

She paused, her eyes seeking the screen once more.

"What you would not be able to access," she said to the screen, "would be my personality, the integration of thought process, emotion, and the numerous other factors which allow me to be *me*, and not, let us say, my brother."

"Yes, of course—" he began, and stopped.

Seignur Veeoni turned her gaze on him.

"The beads I . . . wore," he said slowly, "downloaded—*me*—into a new-made brain."

"Nothing so simple, I fear."

She reached to the screen and tapped up another image.

The structure again was crystalline. Possibly its color was slightly less pure, though his was not an artist's eye, trained to such nuance. The needlelike crystals tended to pale amber and smudged brown, with an occasional wavering thread of green.

What was most striking, however, was the line of inky darkness, like sediment, at the bottom of the image.

He ran a finger under it.

"Is this an artifact of having taken the image?"

Seignur Veeoni's frown was particularly fierce.

"Light Keeper, you know that it is not."

She turned back to the screen.

"Analysis indicates that the black substance is active, that is to say, it *does something.* Every bead I examined in your memory network is precisely like this—a normal crystal formation coexisting with this other thing that is *not* normal."

"Do you know what it does?"

"I do not. In order to define the nonstandard material, I would need to employ protocols that would risk the loss of legitimate data. I note that the entire network is at the moment quiescent."

"Because the beads are not being worn?" Jen Sin murmured.

"That is in keeping with my understanding of how memory beads in general function. They rest when they are not in interaction."

"So, then, we are led to believe that the nonstandard data also interacts with . . . me, when the beads are being worn."

"That falls perilously close to a guess," Seignur Veeoni said. "To substantiate it, we would have to look at your brain."

"Can that be done?" he asked, honestly curious.

She sighed.

"Yes, but given that we deal with the work of the Great Enemy, we must assume there is commensurate risk involved."

She turned her head, meeting his eye. "Forgive me if I do not care to risk legitimate data."

That stood very near to kindness. Truly, he was touched.

"I thank you for your care," he murmured. "Nor do I wish to risk the loss of useful onboard data. The beads, however . . ."

He paused, thinking.

"I appreciate that you do not wish to risk the data contained in the beads. How if I guarantee that data is of no use to me? Does that answer your objections to further testing?"

"With all respect, Light Keeper, you cannot know that. Light Keeper Lorith is under the impression that, without the beads, you lack essential data. Lack of essential data can be dangerous."

"So it can," he murmured. "Are you able to clean the beads, as you spoke of doing?"

"I was perhaps arrogant," Seignur Veeoni said, staring at the screen. "Unless I understand the nonstandard inclusions..."

"You risk the data. I understand."

He paused, considering.

"How, if it were possible to extract another set of beads, from the unit that...produces Jen Sin yos'Pheliums?"

She turned to face him fully.

"Can that be done?"

"Lorith suggested it as a possibility, when I stopped to speak with her on my way to you."

Seignur Veeoni was looking over his left shoulder, now, her eyes narrowed.

"That is a very interesting thought," she said. "I will explore that line of research. If we were to have a second set—yes. A second set alters everything."

She looked back to his face.

"I will keep you apprised of progress."

"Thank you." He took a breath.

"In the meanwhile, I ask if you will hold the...first set...safe for me. While it is possible that they may contain data I would find useful, there exists the risk of damage to the data I presently access. I do not hold my duty to maintain this station lightly, and must therefore decline that risk, now that it has been identified."

"That is, if I may say so, Light Keeper, prudent. I will move as quickly as possible."

"Do not stint the station," he told her. "That is your priority."

"Yes, of course." She reached to the screen and tapped it off.

"I will keep you apprised," she said again, which he took for his dismissal.

He bowed and left her.

Lorith was in the tower when he returned, having taken the long tour in order to settle his thoughts.

"So," he said. "Was there need, after all?"

She looked 'round from the screen.

"A person calling himself Ren Stryker has come to the station in order to assist Mentor Jones. The mentor asked that this person be given a mooring, rather than attempting to dock at station. I have identified a location, and Ren Stryker is situating himself now."

Jen Sin looked past her to the screen, where a very large—

"That is not a ship, surely?"

"A manufactory," she said, following his gaze to the screen. "He is a pleasant and polite person."

"Excellent. We wish to hold the tone, after all."

Lorith looked at him doubtfully, and he moved his shoulders.

"Does Ren Stryker allow us to know how long he plans to visit with Mentor Jones?"

"Mentor Jones wants to discuss that with you," Lorith said. "He asks that you contact him as soon as your schedule allows."

A meeting with the mentor regarding Ren Stryker would, so Jen Sin suspected, segue into a discussion of *Ahab-Esais*. He strongly suspected that his store of patience was not equal to either of those topics, much less both.

"I believe my schedule may allow the mentor some time from my next on-shift," he told Lorith. "Please tell him so. I am going off-shift."

She turned to face him fully.

"The researcher did not give your beads back."

"She did not," he admitted. "The session was informational. There is yet work to be done, in order to render the beads as useful as they may be."

"They were useful as they were!" Lorith said sharply.

"Gently. There are matters that concern her, and I am minded to allow her room to work."

He waved a hand at the screen.

"Are you settled?"

She sighed.

"Yes, I am. Go, rest. You have been looking weary, Jen Sin."

"As to that, my sleep has been interrupted lately. The weight of my duties, doubtless."

The comm sizzled, and a pleasantly musical voice flowed out of the grid.

"Ren Stryker to Lorith Light Keeper."

Lorith turned to the board, and Jen Sin left her.

Recovery Deck

IT WAS IN HER MIND TO GO TO THE RECOVERY DECK AND DOWNload the data from the units, and for that she would require clean environments. There were only eight left in the workroom's inventory. Andreth would need to send more in the next supply run.

Seignur Veeoni was in a rare state of contentment. The work was going well; the persons with whom she was required to interact were competent, and respectful of the work. More persons would be incoming, eventually, and it was assumed that some would be found to be less satisfactory. However, once the ring was repaired, and she had relocated, she could limit the access of such persons.

She allowed herself to look forward to that day, when she would rehabilitate and repair those older units as survived to reach her, as well as performing like service for newer ships that may not have had access to competent technicians. It would be a very different sort of life from the one she had lived while she was developing the new rack-and-tile technology. Now that the work was finished, and Tinsori Light under rehabilitation, she could... extend herself.

Perhaps she might even remove the beads, and give them back to Yuri.

First, however, she wanted the data from those devices.

She strode into the workroom. M Traven looked up from the screen, and rose.

"I will need three clean environments from inventory. Message Andreth for seven replacements. I will want you with me when I go."

M Traven did not answer, or perhaps she did. Seignur Veeoni had already swept on. She paused at the bench where Light Keeper yos'Phelium's beads were sealed into a leakproof safe-box. The notion of requisitioning another set from the appropriate unit held appeal. It was not something that might be achieved with a normal unit, but she had already established that the units on the recovery deck were not normal. Nor would it do any harm to see if she might coax a bead-set out of the third, unused, unit.

With that thought in mind, she took two more safe-boxes from inventory, and returned to the workroom.

The recovery deck was dim, and chill, though not so icy as on their previous visit.

Seignur Veeoni was six steps past the door when the lights came up, which was the automatics, of course.

Temperature should also be on automatic.

Seignur Veeoni frowned, and raised a hand. M Traven, who was behind her towing the sled holding the environments, engaged the sled's brake and stepped away from it, head up, watching.

Seignur Veeoni inclined her head slightly, and raised her voice. "Station, am I heard?"

"I hear you, Researcher."

It was the systems voice, and not Tocohl herself. Which was well enough; her query was specific to systems.

"Why is the recovery deck kept cold?"

"The recovery deck is low-use."

"Why is the temperature adjustment not on automatic?"

"Existing presets: temperature and cameras, on-demand."

Seignur Veeoni raised her eyebrows.

"Station, raise the temperature on the recovery deck to station normal, and activate the cameras."

"Done."

Seignur Veeoni waited.

A click sounded, sharp against the cold air.

Seignur Veeoni pursed her lips.

"Well," she said. "I will take the sled, M Traven."

"Yes, Researcher."

The temperature was already rising by the time Seignur Veeoni had disengaged the sled's brake, and set off for the recovery units, M Traven as her guard.

M Traven placed the environments at her instruction, one to each cubicle, parked the sled out of the way, and took up the alert, meandering stroll that she had once told Seignur Veeoni was "on patrol."

Surely, there was no need to patrol, Seignur Veeoni thought, as she opened the hood of the innermost unit to reveal the connection points.

Still, she found herself unwilling to order a halt.

Instead, she touched the unit's screen, bringing the display live, turned—

And turned back.

The innermost cubicle housed the unit dedicated to producing Jen Sin yos'Pheliums. She bent to the display, running through menus which were deceptively simple, and more than a little opaque, even to one accustomed to working with Old Technology.

She did at last uncover the command module, and there she found herself at a stand.

Her choices were two: REGENERATE, and ERASE.

Regenerate would certainly produce a new set of beads. But it would also very likely produce another Jen Sin yos'Phelium, which would be—undesirable. Who knew what the presence of two Jen Sin yos'Pheliums, now possessed of vastly divergent experiences, might do to the field?

Seignur Veeoni was far from an expert on Korval's Luck, and the situation at Tinsori Light, while improved, still presented significant risk to her work and herself.

No, best *not* to regenerate at present.

Erase was not an option until she had downloaded, studied, and understood the unit's processes and data.

That decided, she turned to the environment, made the connections and started the download.

She waited until she was certain that the download was proceeding properly before she left the cubicle.

The air was warmer now, she noted with approval, as she went up the line to the first cubicle—Light Keeper Lorith's unit.

She had just finished the connections when she heard the door cycle. Frowning, she went to the entrance of the cubicle, in time to see Light Keeper Lorith stride onto the recovery deck.

M Traven moved to intercept her. She stopped immediately, and extended both hands, palms up, fingers spread.

"Soldier," she said.

"Light Keeper," M Traven answered. "Do you have a reason for being here?"

Pale brows arched above black eyes.

"I am a light keeper, and may not be shut out of any part of this station."

"Agreed," M Traven said. "I ask: Why are you in this part of the station at this particular time?"

"I must speak with Researcher Veeoni about these units, which are the property of Tinsori Light."

Seignur Veeoni stepped forward.

"I will speak with the light keeper, M Traven."

Her bodyguard stood aside. Lorith approached. Seignur Veeoni stepped back into the cubicle, raising a hand to beckon her inside.

"I assure you, Light Keeper, that I am taking the most conservative approach available to me as a technician with a specialty in creating compatibilities between Old Tech and current systems. The environment, which you see here, is built in a controlled environment by Crystal Energy Systems, according to protocols developed over many years. The environment is certified clean. No harm will come to the data downloaded to it."

Lorith came forward, looking first to the display of the resurrection unit, which displayed a line of orderly bars, each marking out a different series of chained files.

Her next glance took in the environment, and its screen, displaying the progress of the download.

"I am pleased to hear that your tools are clean and your procedures sanctioned. What I wish to know is what you are doing. These units are not to be destroyed."

"So Light Keeper yos'Phelium made clear to me," Seignur Veeoni said. "He did, however, give me leave to copy the data from each unit for study."

She paused, and added, "Among the things I may learn from this study is the manner by which I may clear the contamination from Light Keeper yos'Phelium's beads, while preserving the integrity of the data. This is key. He has been without his beads for some number of shifts, now."

Lorith straightened from her study of the environment's screen.

"Yes, and he is in increased peril because of it. You must return his beads."

"I value Light Keeper yos'Phelium far too much to give him beads I know to be tainted."

Lorith drew a breath, but Seignur Veeoni continued without pause.

"There are no easy answers in this, Light Keeper. As you say, it is dangerous for him to continue without his beads. If he were to fail, there would be a significant gap in his memories when he reawakened. It would seem that our best choice is, as you say, to return the beads. However, the beads are tainted. How if he fails *because* of the taint? When he wakens, will he recall—anything of who he is? Far too much depends upon Light Keeper yos'Phelium to risk an error."

She folded her hands into her sleeves.

"Which is why you see me here, pursuing answers."

"This is my unit," Lorith pointed out, reasonably.

"Indeed it is. I began with Light Keeper yos'Phelium's unit, which we know to be malfunctioning. The data from your unit will serve as a control, since we know your beads are functioning correctly."

Lorith's eyes narrowed.

"How do you know that my beads are untainted?"

Seignur Veeoni frowned.

"Do you have any desire to remove them, as Light Keeper yos'Phelium did?"

"No!"

"There we have our proof that your beads are functioning to design," Seignur Veeoni said placidly. "It is fortunate that you came to see me. I have some questions about the third unit that you may be able to answer."

"The third unit? Are you going to download its data, too?"

"In the interest of thoroughness, I am," Seignur Veeoni said. "Was your sister never wakened beyond the first time?"

"No, never." Lorith hesitated. "I made the attempt, once—later, but before Jen Sin came, and—she was no longer there. When I came back to the unit, it was empty."

ERASE came vividly into Seignur Veeoni's mind.

"That unit may also be useful as a control for some lines of operation," she said. "I may as well make the download, as the equipment is here."

She held her hands palms out, fingers spread wide.

"If you are interested, you may observe the process of connection and initialization, when I pair the third unit with the environment."

"Yes," said Lorith. "I am interested."

"Excellent. Matters here are well begun. Let us to the third unit."

They left the cubicle, and Seignur Veeoni said, "There is something else you might assist me with."

"What is that?"

"I understand that you suggested that a new set of beads might be withdrawn from a unit, without the need for a wakening. Would you show me how that is accomplished?"

Lorith stared at her. "Why?"

"If I am able to extract another set of Light Keeper yos'Phelium's beads from his unit, I could compare them with the tainted set. It may be that the taint in the set I have was generated by random error. A new set, absent random error, will therefore not exhibit the taint, and may be utilized at once."

"I understand." Lorith took a breath. "I did say that to Jen Sin, that there might be a way to withdraw a new set of beads, but—I do not have the way of it. It seemed to me that it had been done—that I had done something like—but it must have been a phantom memory. Those do occur, very rarely."

"That is disappointing," said Seignur Veeoni. "A new set of beads might have allowed me to resolve these difficulties more quickly. I will proceed with the downloads, and the data comparisons."

They came to the last cubicle. Seignur Veeoni entered, Lorith behind her. M Traven came to the entrance, and stopped, hands behind her back, eyes moving. Guarding.

"Here," said Seignur Veeoni, "you see the environment complete in itself. The first step is to self-test, to verify that it is clean and functioning as it should. While that is being done, we will activate the unit."

Administrative Tower

HE HAD RESTED, AFTER A FASHION. WHICH WAS TO SAY, HE HAD taken several sequential periods of board rest, across about half his sleep shift, a stratagem he had adopted to cheat the nightmares.

In that, he was successful, but board rest was not real sleep, and he was aware that he was borrowing heavily against his future. He would have to sleep eventually.

But, he did not quite dare it, yet.

In the periods between rest, he had reviewed his actions since awakening, the arrival of Inkirani Yo, and the death of Tinsori Light.

Objectively, he could see no flaw, nothing done that would endanger the New Light, the clan, or his companions. He had long suspected that whatever seeds the Light had planted would only quicken once he ventured out into the wide universe. While that was the veriest guess, based on no slightest shred of fact, yet it seemed to be the case.

Satisfied on that head, he initiated one last session of board rest. When he roused from that, he showered, and went to the tower, to find that Lorith had herself taken a short shift, leaving Tocohl on-deck, with instructions to call her, should an emergency occur.

"Are you . . . *well*, Cousin Jen Sin?" Tocohl asked, after giving a report of a quiet quarter-shift.

"As well as may be," he answered, which, after all, was nothing other than the truth.

In search of distraction, he opened his work screen, and found only one message in-queue.

It was a pinbeam from Bechi dea'Gauss, Korval's *qe'andra*, allowing him to know that, based on the document he had forwarded, Korval would be opening negotiations with Crystal Energy Systems, with regard to a possible repair-and-lease contract.

"Progress," he said aloud, for Tocohl's benefit. "Korval seeks contract with Crystal Energy."

"That is good news, surely?" Tocohl said, by which he learned that his tone had been less lightsome than it might have been.

"Surely it must be, for all the reasons Seignur Veeoni included in her document of persuasion," he said. "Perhaps she will be pleased to learn what her efforts have produced."

Reaching to the screen, he sent a copy of *Qe'andra* dea'Gauss's note to Seignur Veeoni.

The comm emitted the particular tone that signaled the arrival of a message.

There was in-queue a pinbeam from—Miri Robertson Tiazan.

Not, he noted, from Korval, though Miri Robertson Tiazan was delmae—the delm's lifemate—empowered to speak fully as Korval.

In fact, he had expected a message from Korval, though not so soon as this. He had, after all, *written* to Korval. But he could not quite imagine what Miri Robertson Tiazan might have to say to him.

Well, he told himself wryly, *the means to discover what service Cousin Miri desires is at hand, is it not?*

Jen Sin opened the message.

Jen Sin, I write as your cousin to inform you that the delm is solving the matter put forth in your last letter. Until the solving is complete, the delm trusts that you will remain in place, taking such advice and assistance as may be necessary from those in your orbit. You are surrounded by excellent people, as you noted yourself. Theo is fully capable, but headstrong, which will come as no surprise to you, I think. We have asked her to stand ready to perform the tasks you assign. Please do not *assign her to administer Tinsori Light. We depend on you, with your experience and your good sense, to hold for us.*

Continue to keep the delm and your cousins informed. If you require anything, write to us and we will contrive.

Again, the delm is solving for you. Stand strong.

Miri

Jen Sin blinked, and looked up at the ceiling.

After a moment, he brought his eyes back to the screen, and read Miri's letter again.

The delm was solving for him.

It was absurd, how those words simultaneously alarmed him, and wakened an urge to put his head down on the desk and weep.

He scrolled through the letter a third time, his eye snagging on a phrase.

We depend on you.

Was it possible that he had fallen short of being plain? The fact was that they could *not* depend on him. Surely, he had said so. Theo, incoming and untainted by contact with the Great Enemy, was a solid link on whom the clan might depend.

But, there—Theo was headstrong. The delm knew her, as he did not. And—ah.

He thought he saw his error.

Theo was kin, but not clan.

So, this solving the delm undertook on his behalf likely meant that someone properly enclanned was being sent to Tinsori Light to stand as first light keeper.

Bearing in mind that scant list of names in the Line Direct, he did regret placing an additional burden upon an already overworked cousin. Far better, had Theo been found appropriate, but that decision was out of his hands.

The delm was solving.

His eyes filled, and he told himself sternly that he would not weep. He would stand strong, as he had been bidden. What were a few *relumma* more, in a history such as his?

Mentor's Comm Room

TOLLY JONES SWEPT INTO THE SPACE HE AND HAZ HAD TAKEN over for their own business, scant as it was. They met there at the beginning of every shift, checked for news and mail, and planned out the shape of their day.

This shift, Haz was ahead of him, frowning in a bemused sort of way at her screen.

"Problem?" he asked.

"I have a pinbeam from my captain," she said, her eyes on the screen.

Haz's captain was Miri Robertson, who also happened to be one-half of Delm Korval.

"New orders?"

"In a sense. She wishes me to increase my watch upon Jen Sin yos'Phelium, in case he should be moved to embrace honor's reward."

Perceptive woman, Miri Robertson. Tolly tipped his head.

"What're you supposed to do, if he does?"

Haz looked up and met his eyes.

"Stop him."

There was a particular note in her voice. Tolly considered her.

"Orders not to your liking?"

Haz sighed.

"I was in similar danger from myself," she said slowly. "Captain Robertson had me join the port guard under her former commander, who had returned home to Surebleak and established the port security force."

Tolly leaned forward.

"Commander Liz," he said. "She paired us up—one of the best teams on Surebleak Port, right, Haz?"

"Yes." Haz gave him a half-smile. "The cases are similar—but there is no Commander Lizardi here."

"True enough. But we're still the best team she had. You don't think we're up to keeping a hurt pilot alive?"

"A *Korval* pilot," Haz reminded him, her smile about three-quarters, now.

Tolly shrugged. "You take 'im high and I'll take 'im low."

"A good plan," she said, gravely.

"Proven, too," he answered, and moved over to check his screen.

Bechimo Arriving

....

TINSORI LIGHT HUNG IN THE MAIN SCREEN, AN INSULT TO THE clean space around it. There were no outyards, or cargo holding areas. There was no traffic, only an angular, sharp-edged shape, brooding in its own shadows. A tower rose from its craggy center, angular in its turn, a white light burning steady at its apex, like a particularly surly candle.

The mood on the bridge was—silent.

Even Hevelin, who was sitting on Theo's lap, had nothing to offer, though he did pat her wrist, twice.

"There has been a breach," *Bechimo* said, magnifying the area and throwing the magnified image up on the main screen.

The material of the station looked like it had...melted through a section at the mid-level. Theo squinted and reached to up the mag more, but Clarence was ahead of her.

"Seals in place," he said, "and they look to be holding. Whatever happened, it was a good long time ago."

Right.

Theo frowned at the screens. There was something—something that required her attention in the bond-space she shared with *Bechimo.*

What is it? she asked—then, as she integrated more fully into *Bechimo*'s systems—*Another space station?*

"A mobile manufactory," *Bechimo* replied. "It is moored and maintaining itself as an entity separate from the station."

Theo considered the input, which included a name.

Ren Stryker, she said. *Should we hail?*

"There is no need; we are station-bound, after all."

Let me know if we get a hail. Or a threat, Theo said, and blinked wholly back to first chair and her board.

She took a breath.

"Joyita, hail the station, please."

"Yes, Captain."

In the screen, he spun to the console to his left, depressed a switch, and spoke, his voice filling the silent bridge.

"Tinsori Light, this is *Bechimo*, out of Waymart. Do you hear us?"

Silence, no longer than could be accounted for by lag, before a warm female voice replied.

"I hear you, *Bechimo*."

Theo nodded, and opened her own comm.

"*Bechimo*, out of Waymart, under contract to Tree-and-Dragon Family, Theo Waitley, captain and pilot in charge. Request docking."

The answering voice this time was male, neither warm nor cool, speaking Trade with a marked Liaden accent.

"Tinsori Station, Light Keeper Jen Sin yos'Phelium on deck. Welcome, *Bechimo*. You are cleared to dock at A Level, direct access. Station will guide you in. Do you desire support?"

Theo eyed the monstrous thing in the screens, thought of systems powered by dying timonium.

"We'll keep our own air for now," she said, trying to sound matter-of-fact.

"As you will," Jen Sin yos'Phelium answered. "I will meet you at dockside."

"Looking forward," Theo said. "Waitley out."

She closed her eyes, then, feeling a niggle at the back of her head. Of course, she thought, timing was everything.

"Clarence, take us in," she said, fingers flicking over the board. "Joyita, take second."

"Yes, Captain Theo," Joyita said.

"O'Berin, PIC," Clarence said. "File change o'pilot with the station, laddie."

"Yes, Pilot."

Theo rose.

"Short break," she said, and left the bridge.

Station Day 18
Fourth Shift
22.00 Hours

. . . .

JEN SIN TAPPED UP THE SCHEMATIC PROVIDED BY TRAVEN. IT was a dry, but fascinating study, and one that he hoped would—

The comm pinged.

"Ship incoming," Tocohl said, as he touched the switch.

"*Bechimo*, out of Waymart, under contract to Tree-and-Dragon Family, Theo Waitley, captain and pilot in charge. Request docking."

His cousin Theo's voice was cool and certain, betraying not the slightest hint of anxiety. Her Trade was crisp, with an accent that he didn't place, and no reason why he should.

"Tinsori Station," he replied, "Light Keeper Jen Sin yos'Phelium on deck. Welcome, *Bechimo*. Cleared to dock on A Level, direct access. Station will guide you in. Do you desire support?"

"We'll keep our own air for now," Theo answered, which was, in Jen Sin's estimation, entirely sensible.

"As you will. I will meet you at dockside."

"Looking forward," Theo said. "Waitley out."

Jen Sin sighed, sat back in the control chair, and closed his eyes.

Bechimo
Arriving

THE TREE WAS VISIBLY EXCITED, ITS BRANCHES MOVING AS IF IN a minor breeze, except the vent for this section was on the opposite wall, and wasn't blowing right at the moment.

"I was," Theo told it, "busy."

The niggle at the back of her head somehow suggested that the Tree had *also* been busy, which of course it had, if it was anything like the really big Tree back on Surebleak, growing out of the garden in the center of Val Con's house.

"I'm going to be debarking soon," she said, that being the plan they'd come up with, all of them together. Stost and Chernak and her—they'd be the first points of contact with Tinsori Light, while crew remained on *Bechimo*, safe—or safer—in case anything went wrong.

As a plan, it didn't perfectly match even *Bechimo*'s expanding definition of safe, but it was what they had. And, as Clarence had pointed out, the fact that they'd decided to take the master trader's mission meant they had at least put a little bit of trust in the experts.

"What's your business?" Theo asked the Tree.

Branches moved sharply, she heard a *snap*, and extended a hand by instinct, catching the pod before it hit the decking.

It was biggish, as Tree-pods went, and heavy, and it—didn't smell right. At least, she didn't have any wish to eat the thing, or any idea that it had anything to do with her. She did, however, have a pretty good idea who it did belong to.

She put the pod in her pocket.

"I'll give it to him," she told the Tree. "But I can't make him eat it."

She received the strong impression that this was perfectly fine, and a moment later another impression, equally strong, that she was free to go.

"Nice to see you, too," she said, and went back the way she'd come.

Station Day 19
Dock A

TO JEN SIN'S EYE, *BECHIMO* WAS A CLEAN-LINED SMALL TRADER. Her pod-mounts were empty, which seemed odd for a ship contracted by Tree-and-Dragon Family, that being the clan's trade arm. But, there. The master trader would have known which ships were currently awaiting cargo, or off-route, and whose crew could thus be sent as dogsbodies to the clan's newest holding.

Further, he learned from Tocohl that *Bechimo* was not so contemporary as she appeared to him, but was rather a ship of an older vintage. Which might have been another factor in the master trader's choosing.

He watched her safely docked from the control room, then went down to greet captain and ship in person. Light keeper's *melant'i* would have the captain come to him, but a kinsman—a kinsman would meet his cousin at her ship, greet her, and inquire after her necessities.

It were best for all, he thought, as *Bechimo*'s hatch opened, to place the kin-ties above others.

The figure that exited the ship was to his expectations, in the broad sense. Long, lean, wearing well-used leather somewhat too big for the frame, as if the wearer had taken it off of a larger pilot, likely in a bar brawl, if Cousin Theo's yos'Phelium genes had come greatly to the fore.

The face was certainly familiar: pointed chin, decided nose, high cheeks and bold brows. Her hair was pale, unconfined, and unruly, and behind her came a brace of—

Yxtrang.

Jen Sin took a hard breath against the thrill of adrenaline, and recruited himself. Yxtrang, certainly. And why not? Korval these days kept an Yxtrang house guard. Why should Cousin Theo, sister to the delm, not have a matched pair, or an entire regiment, to guard her?

Ignoring for the moment the guardians of her honor, he bowed as between kin, straightening to look into stern black eyes.

"Cousin," he said, in the Low Tongue. "I am Jen Sin."

The eyes narrowed.

He raised an eyebrow.

"Or perhaps not?" he suggested.

The straight mouth twitched, then curved into a full grin, as charming on her as on any of them.

"I have no reason to doubt you," she told him, her accent once more elusive, "and no excuse to stare, only—you bear a marked resemblance to my father."

"Ah, one of the black yos'Pheliums." He would have guessed otherwise, given her pale mop.

Fair brows pulled together.

"Black?"

He raised a hand to his hair. "As distinct, you see, from the white yos'Pheliums, such as yourself."

"My hair is from my mother. Val Con, Pat Rin, and Quin have brown hair."

That being the thickness of the Line right there—three names, though Val Con and his lady had recently produced an heir. Quin, he had learned from the files, was Pat Rin's heir, and a pilot in his own right.

"Perhaps you will revive a fashion," he said, and spread his arms slightly, showing her empty hands. "I am at your service, Cousin. Tell me how you would like to proceed."

"I'd like a tour of the Light," she said, and turned abruptly, indicating her towering guardians with a wave of her hand.

"This is Stost and Chernak Strongline, ship security and experts in Old Technology." She was speaking Trade, now, possibly for the benefit of her security experts. "Stost and Chernak, here is my kinsman, Jen Sin yos'Phelium, first light keeper."

"Sir," said the leftmost guard—Stost, that was. He delivered himself of a perfectly unexceptionable bow between those with a common goal.

"Sir," echoed Chernak, not bothering to bow. Perhaps she thought one counted for two, as they did, themselves. Certainly,

Jen Sin was not about to dispute the point. "We hope to be useful to your work in clearing the station of... questionable influences."

He inclined his head. "We have made a good deal of progress on that front, but there is much more to do. Also, we are in need of systems upgrades, and general maintenance."

"We saw that the ring is incomplete," Theo said, which was the gentlest description. In fact, the ring had been holed with considerable violence, which would certainly have caught the attention of an incoming crew, after they had passed the astonishment of beholding the Light itself.

"The seals are strong from our side, but we have no work boat, and an outside inspection—"

"We can handle that," Theo interrupted, with another wave of her hand, "and any repairs that might be needed. Rebuilding, though—"

"We have received a business proposal which would include the repair and leasing of the damaged section."

Theo's eyebrows rose.

"Solve a lot of problems," she said, in Terran.

"Indeed. Hopefully, the delm will close the contract."

Theo laughed.

"If they want it, they'll close it. Even I know that."

Jen Sin smiled.

"That is well in hand, then. May I suggest, Cousin, that we start our tour? If any other of your crew wish to join us, they are welcome."

"Shan suggested that we come quick, so we pushed, getting to you," Theo said. "Crew's on rest-time."

"Ah," said Jen Sin. This, too, was reasonable.

"Allow me to first show you the core workroom, which will give you some idea of what we are doing in terms of system upgrades."

"Right." She descended the ramp and turned with him up the dock, toward the station doors, her security looming and silent behind her. In fact, there was only one set of footsteps on the dock, and Jen Sin saw the moment she noted it.

"I'm going to have to up my game," she said ruefully. "You're a Scout?"

"Was a Scout," he admitted. "More lately, a courier. The war..."

He paused because Theo was frowning.

"Val Con sent files. I'm going to have to study that war a bit more, before I get sense out of it."

"Ah." Almost, he laughed. Instead, he moved his shoulders. "Do not fault your scholarship, Cousin. There *was* no sense to it."

"Right." Theo checked between one step and the next, and slipped a hand into an outer pocket. "Almost forgot," she said, extending her hand to him.

Jen Sin stopped, staring.

"A seed-pod?" His voice was unsteady.

"Fresh," she assured him, and added, slightly less assured, "It *is* yours?"

He took a breath, tasting the tang at the back of his throat, and held out his hand. The pod hit his palm; his fingers closed over it reflexively.

"Yes," he said, forcing his voice into calmness, "it is mine, Cousin. I thank you."

Bechimo
Dock A

ACCORDING TO THE FILE VAL CON HAD SENT, JEN SIN YOS'PHELIUM had been only days short of his forty-first Name Day when he went missing during a courier run after sending a coded message warning his clan to stay clear of the space at Tinsori Light.

The delm had waited the traditional twelve years before writing as a fact in Korval's records that Jen Sin was dead, another victim of the "unsettled times," that came into history as "the clan wars." Val Con had sent a file about that, too. All of it had happened right around two hundred Standards ago.

So, even given the habit of Tinsori Light to not always be wholly inside the universe, and, maybe, not completely subject to the rules of time while it was elsewhere, Theo had expected someone . . . much . . . older.

It had been something of a shock to be greeted by a pilot at the height of his powers, slim as a stiletto and every bit as sharp, wearing well-used, well-kept leathers. He had the clan face, as she did herself, but thinner—stern. His hair was very dark and cropped close. Clarence would say that he looked a likely lad to have on your side in a brawl.

"Cousin," he said, speaking Low Liaden, his voice deep but mannered. "I am Jen Sin."

For a moment, Theo just stood there, hearing the echoes of Father's deep voice, and not able to get her tongue around any Liaden greeting—and there it was, a family quirk—one black eyebrow rose, and the hard face briefly softened into whimsy, as he murmured.

"Or perhaps not?"

He wasn't Father; he wasn't Val Con or Pat Rin, or herself—absolutely, he was his own person, but he was also recognizable in a way she wouldn't have understood before she'd met the rest of her family. She grinned in sheer relief.

She could feel *Bechimo* in bond-space, offering her the neutral phrase, "Greetings, Cousin," in Low Liaden, but what she said instead was, "I have no reason to doubt you, and no excuse to stare, only—you bear a marked resemblance to my father."

His reaction to the seed pod had been soothing too, in its way. He had certainly known what it was, and was glad to have it. He put it in his pocket, by which she guessed it wasn't ready to eat, and conducted her, Chernak, and Stost through the doors and into the station proper.

Seignur Veeoni's Private Laboratory

SEIGNUR VEEONI MADE CERTAIN THAT THE ANALYSIS SUITES WERE running correctly on each of the craniums she had brought back from the recovery deck. It would, she noted, be some time before analysis was complete, but that was expectable.

Satisfied, she left her private lab, entering the common area as M Traven came in from the shop, wiping her hands on a cloth.

"I will be going to the assembly room," Seignur Veeoni told her. "Do you need me?"

"What are you doing?"

"Assembling the *labroĉaro*."

"Continue. I will call if I have need."

Main Core Workroom

TOLLY BROUGHT UP SCREENS, WHILE HAZ CHECKED THEIR SUPPLY of tiles.

"Mentor," Tocohl said abruptly, her voice sharper than usual, "there was an intruder inside the unchecked systems files."

Tolly looked 'round from the instrument panel.

"Catch 'em?" he asked, keeping his voice casual.

"I captured the probe," she admitted, "but it is a generic tool, nothing to identify it."

"Did the probe's operator learn anything?"

"Its operator clearly learned that someone is watching, since their tool was confiscated."

"That means they'll be more careful the next time," Tolly said.

"There will not be a *next time*," Tocohl snapped.

"What're you gonna do?"

"I am going to speak to them, and offer a lesson in manners."

"Good. Them who?"

"The ship that just came in."

"*Bechimo*, right? Clan Korval ship. By way of being kin, aren't they?"

"Perhaps," Tocohl didn't sound mollified. "That is no excuse for rudeness."

"Can't argue with that. Do you need me for backup or any such?"

There was a pause, as if Tocohl were surprised by the question.

"No, Mentor. I merely wanted to—alert you to the situation."

"'Preciate that," he said solemnly. "Let me know how it turns out."

"Of course."

Silence followed, somehow empty. Tolly sighed. Hazenthull cleared her throat.

He turned to look at her.

"If you're gonna scold me for manipulating her," he began, but Haz held up a big hand.

"You teach her to depend upon her own skills in battle," she said, with a half-smile. "That is not a course I am prepared to argue."

He grinned.

"Glad to hear it. What've you got?"

"We are going to need more tiles."

Tolly frowned.

"Been busier than we knew," he said.

"I will go to the *faristo* room and make a withdrawal," Haz said, moving over to the corner where they stored the sled.

"Right. Gimme a minute to get us sorted here, and I'll come with you," he said, and turned back to the screen.

• • • ✻ • • •

The lift stopped, and Jen Sin exited, holding the door open so that Theo and her security team could step into the hall.

"We have been busy cleaning systems and moving them to the new environment provided by Seignur Veeoni," Jen Sin said, as they walked toward the main workroom. "The process is painstaking, but we have hope that a completely new core, with clean housings, and updated applications, will be accomplished within a Standard."

"So long?" murmured Stost.

Jen Sin looked up at him.

"Current knowledgeable staff include Seignur Veeoni, the designer and principle architect of the new system. Tolly Jones assists her, his expertise as a mentor qualifying him. Of course our mutual cousin Tocohl is at the center of the project."

Theo tipped her head.

"Val Con sent me files," she said, "and I saw Tocohl noted there, as Jeeves's daughter. Our timelines ran against each other, though, and we haven't met."

"We may rectify that immediately," Jen Sin said, and raised his voice slightly.

"Cousin Tocohl, here is Theo Waitley, sister to Val Con yos'Phelium. She would greet you as kin."

"Cousin Theo," Tocohl's voice came from the grid in the

wall. It was not one of the upgraded speakers, so the beauty of her voice was not on full display. Theo stopped, and turned to face the grid.

"Hello," she said. "Am I addressing Tinsori Light?"

"You are not," Tocohl said composedly. "The intelligence known as Tinsori Light has died. I am Tocohl Lorlin Clan Korval through Line yos'Phelium, fulfilling the duties of Station. I also assist Seignur Veeoni and Mentor Jones with cleaning and upgrading systems, as Cousin Jen Sin was describing."

"It has been our experience," Chernak said, slowly, "that the Great Works of the Enemy are clever, at hiding as at everything else."

"We are being very careful," Tocohl said. "Nothing questionable is moved to the new environment. This makes the work go even more slowly, but we do not want any part of Tinsori Light's intelligence to inform the new station."

"I'm glad to hear so much care is being taken," Theo said. "I recently had a discussion with a hero from the Old Universe—*Aberthaz Ferry*. He'd spent a lot of his time hunting Tinsori Light with the intention of destroying it. He said it was among the Enemy's Greatest Works."

"Yes," Tocohl said. "Tinsori Light was very dangerous, as Cousin Jen Sin knows well, having been on-station so long. I repeat the information that our cleaning protocols are stringent, and our technicians extraordinarily gifted."

"Yes, I'm certain they are," Theo said, her tone perhaps not quite as conciliatory as her words.

"I have," Stost said, "a question for Tocohl Lorlin."

"Ask."

"You say that the old Tinsori Light is dead. Has the hardware that was inhabited by that intelligence been destroyed?"

"The tile-and-rack systems were largely destroyed by Mentor Jones. The original core has been sealed and cut off from all station systems," Tocohl said.

"You see the effects of our lack of manpower," Jen Sin murmured. "We have taken what precautions we may, and we do not hold our safety cheap—"

"But there's only so much the people in place can do," Theo interrupted briskly, and nodded her head, Terran-style. "That's why we're here. Extra hands. More expertise. Why don't we—which is to say, my crew and me—take on clearing the old core out? We'll make it our first priority."

It was, Jen Sin thought, prudent. Extra prudent, but not, given what Tinsori Light had been, and had been capable of doing, a misdirection of energies.

Jen Sin looked up at the Stronglines.

"The old core is quite... compact, to the point that Mentor Jones, who is not a large Terran, had difficulty moving in the aisles."

"Right," Theo said, grinning as she followed his gaze. "We've got remotes. Also crew comes in a variety of sizes. We'll plan it out and get it done. Before that, though, I'd like to talk to your experts—Mentor Jones, and Seignur Veeoni."

"Certainly. Cousin Tocohl, do you know where they are?"

"Mentor Jones is in the *faristo* room, with Hazenthull. Seignur Veeoni has returned to the assembly room."

Jen Sin met Theo's gaze.

"It is chancy to interrupt Seignur Veeoni at her work, though it can be done for good cause. If she fails to deem our cause good, she will merely be rude."

"Seignur Veeoni it is," Theo said agreeably, falling into step next to him once more. "The files Val Con sent said that she's Uncle's sister."

"That is correct."

"I used to do courier work for her brother," Theo said, as if it were the most reasonable thing imaginable. Which, for Theo, grown to adulthood out-clan and Terran, it might well be. A pilot must fly, after all, and courier work paid well.

"Perhaps she will not be so very rude, then," he offered.

Theo glanced at him.

"Or maybe she will."

"Or maybe she will," he agreed. "Put thus, it becomes our duty to investigate the situation."

Theo grinned again. "For posterity."

"Precisely," he said, lips twitching.

Bechimo
Comm Officer's Tower

A BOARD PINGED.

It was one of several boards, but the only one of its particular kind, and not much used. It was, in fact, Joyita's personal address and known to two persons—*Bechimo* and Jeeves.

It was therefore something of a surprise to see that the ping had originated with neither of those two individuals.

Perhaps it would have been prudent not to answer, given their location and the repeated cautions from the pathfinders, who were, as Joyita knew, very good at what they did, and extremely certain about what they knew.

And yet, Joyita was a curious person, and confident in his own abilities.

He answered the ping.

"This is Tocohl Lorlin, operating Tinsori Station," the voice was crisp, and annoyed. "Am I speaking with B. Joyita?"

"You called on my private line," he commented. "But I confirm—B. Joyita."

"Jeeves gave me a good report of you," Tocohl Lorlin said. "He said you were promising; that you demonstrated no little skill as a researcher and a quiet operator. I am sorry that I will be giving him a report of your recent actions that can only grieve him, but I am even sorrier that you chose to make our first interaction one of stealth and mistrust."

Joyita checked his board again, confirming the location of the speaker, and her condition.

"I'm sorry to hear that Jeeves will be receiving such a report," he said. "As far as I am aware, this is our first interaction since you guided us in to dock."

"That is correct," Tocohl Lorlin said. "Perhaps I am wrong to dignify your intrusion into the station files as an interaction."

"I made no such intrusion," Joyita said, and did not mention that he had been mulling over the best way to do just that, while keeping his word to Captain Theo.

"I can," Tocohl Lorlin said, "prove that to be a falsehood."

"If you can, then please do so," Joyita told her, with feeling. "If I'm not only intruding where I'm not wanted, but being sloppy about it, too, I clearly need recalibration."

"You dropped your pick," Tocohl Lorlin told him, and there it was, sitting on the edge of the desk—a dainty thing, and well thought as far as it went. Anonymous, of course, that was well done, but also—incomplete.

"There is a problem," he told Tocohl Lorlin, and opened a line to *Bechimo.*

"I agree," she snapped. "It is an inexcusable intrusion!"

"Yes," he said patiently, "but there's something else."

"What is it?"

"That's not my tool."

Main Core Workroom

SEIGNUR VEEONI WAS AT THE WORKBENCH, ASSEMBLING A TONGSTELE frame. It was not, so far as Jen Sin was aware, skilled work, though it did require a certain amount of concentration.

I could take that on, he thought, *and free her to tasks worthy of her skill.*

Then, he recalled that he was compromised, and perhaps ought not even be in the same room as the clean systems being built.

He may have missed a step just then. Theo, at his side, did not seem to notice his lapse, but from behind him rumbled Stost Strongline's voice.

"Is all well, Pilot?"

"A momentary lapse," he said, glancing over his shoulder and up into the brown face. "I thank you."

"We are here to assist in any way possible," Stost said.

This from an Yxtrang. Well, and he had best accommodate himself. One must suppose that honor bound them.

"I do recall it," he assured Stost, and looked forward, where Seignur Veeoni had straightened from her work, and pushed the glasses up onto her forehead. She was of course frowning.

"Light Keeper," she said, neutrally. "I find you well?"

"Well enough," he answered matching her mode. He moved his hand, showing her Theo. "Here is Captain Theo Waitley, come with ship and crew to assist us in readying the Light for its new turn of duty."

He turned to Theo.

"Cousin, here is Researcher Seignur Veeoni, the primary architect of the new core."

Theo produced a competent bow between equals. Seignur Veeoni did not. Her frown became more marked as she glanced over Theo's head.

"Soldiers," she said, flatly.

"Pathfinders, Researcher," Stost answered respectfully. "Now ship security for *Bechimo*."

Seignur Veeoni's frown cleared, and she returned her gaze to Theo.

"*Bechimo* out of Waymart," she said. "You are Daav yos'Phelium's daughter?"

One of Cousin Theo's eyebrows rose, just slightly.

"I'm the daughter of Kamele Waitley, Professor with a specialty in the history of education, and Daav yos'Phelium Clan Korval."

And that, Jen Sin thought with amusement, put Daav yos'Phelium Clan Korval properly into *his* place.

"All honor to your mother and her scholarship," Seignur Veeoni said perfunctorily, leaving Jen Sin startled that she had said it at all. "However, my interest lies particularly in your relationship with regard to Clan Korval's luck. Daav yos'Phelium's daughter. It will do. You are welcome, Captain Waitley. What do you want from me?"

Both of Theo's eyebrows were up now, and her mouth pursed before relaxing into a smile as the absurdities of the situation became clearer to her.

"Well, first of all," she said, stepping up to the worktable. "I'd like to know what you're making here, and if there's any way we—that's my crew and I—can help you."

Jen Sin expected the researcher to thrust this impertinence aside. Instead, she gave way, turning so that Theo might approach more nearly.

"This," she said, putting her hand on the unfinished frame, "is a tile rack. We have many, unfortunately in pieces, which must be assembled before the tiles can be placed. Once the rack is full, it is associated with—"

"Jen Sin," Tocohl said from the speaker set into the ceiling, "an urgent message has just arrived for you."

And, he thought, how novel was that? He could scarcely recall the last time he'd had an urgent message.

"Send it to the workroom screen, please," he said and glanced around, meaning to make his excuse to Theo, only to see that there was no need. She was leaning over the rack assembly, listening to Seignur Veeoni with every sign of rapt attention.

So.

"Your pardon," he murmured to the Stronglines, who were

moving toward the workbench. He slipped by them and strode to the alcove, where the screen displayed the text of a pinbeam message from his Cousin Miri.

Jen Sin—the Delm's Solution is on its way to you.

Relief washed through him, softening tense muscles. He leaned his head against the top of the screen and closed his eyes.

Soon, now. He could lay it down and—

"Jen Sin!"

Lorith's voice brought him to himself. He straightened, blanked the screen, and turned to her.

"Station tells me a ship has come in—bearing cousins?"

"Cousin," he corrected. "Theo, who is ship's captain. Come, let me bring you to her attention."

He moved his hand, showing her the knot at the worktable, and together they went forward.

Bechimo
Comm Officer's Tower

"NOT YOUR TOOL?" TOCOHL REPEATED. "THEN WHOSE IS IT?"

"That's an interesting question, isn't it?" Joyita replied with relish.

"No, indeed, that's nothing at all like Joyita's picks," *Bechimo* said. "Nor is it one of mine. It's . . . a little primitive. Was it only intended to pick up one data-string?"

"I haven't had a chance to study it in depth," Joyita said. "It appears primitive on the surface, but there's evidence of thought. For instance, whoever made it did remove all identifiers."

"Yes, but surely that would be an obvious step, assuming stealth was the goal."

"Stealth may have been the goal," Tocohl said, "but it was not realized. I have the tool."

"But you don't have the intruder," Joyita said.

Tocohl said nothing.

"You did interrupt them before they did harm," *Bechimo* added. "Though they may have learned something from that."

"That might even have been the goal," Joyita said, opening the pick and inserting a probe.

"I made an assumption," Tocohl said, slowly. "I apologize, B. Joyita."

"Apology accepted," he said. "I hope Jeeves will not have to be disappointed by your report."

"He may still be disappointed," Tocohl said, "in me."

"You captured the tool, and served warning that you were alert," *Bechimo* pointed out. "That is not a failure."

"Jeeves will take youth and inexperience into account, I think," said Joyita.

"Yes! And the fact that you are presently serving in a capacity you were not designed for," *Bechimo* said. "Unless you were designed to administer a space station?"

"No," Tocohl said. "I was designed to be an independent generalist."

"In fact," Joyita said, "you are a Scout."

"The children of Line yos'Phelium," Tocohl said stiffly, "are *often* Scouts."

"So we learn from the files," *Bechimo* said.

"We should," Joyita said, "start over. I am B. Joyita, this is my associate *Bechimo*. I am a communications officer, and a pilot. *Bechimo* is a ship. We are both fully realized independent personalities."

"Yes," Tocohl said. "I have files, too."

"Of course you do," Joyita said. "We depend on it."

"You should also know," *Bechimo* said, "that Miri has asked us to assist you in any way that we can, and we are willing. There are many things we might help with, though neither of us has been a station."

"However," Joyita said, "we have other experience that may be more immediately helpful, especially in the case of an intruder. Have you given thought to your next actions?"

"I will have to strengthen my perimeter," Tocohl said.

"A good start. We can assist with that, if you like," *Bechimo* said.

"I would, yes," Tocohl answered.

"Excellent," Joyita said. "We can also help you build traps."

"That could be dangerous," *Bechimo* said.

"Less dangerous than having an—an unknown element trying to breach my security? Even if they accomplished their purpose and will never return, I have to assume they'll try again."

"Yes!" Joyita said, with obvious delight. "If not them, someone else. The proper security stance is to assume that the universe is actively trying to subvert your protections. *Bechimo* will be able to talk with you at length about that philosophy. In the meantime, traps—"

"It is enough," *Bechimo* interrupted, "to repel an attack. If there are too many attacks at a particular location, then the proper response is to leave. You do not want to bring your enemy with you."

"A space station can't leave," Tocohl said, "or hide. In order to properly fulfill its purpose, a space station must occupy a known, static location."

"Design," *Bechimo* said, ruefully. "I was designed to be a ship, and mobile. Space stations—of course. You will need traps. Joyita is very skilled, as I know Jeeves will have told you. Depend on him in these matters."

"I'm no more a station than you are," Joyita said.

"That is correct. However, you occupy a known, fixed location. Your condition is closer to station than ship. Also, you are devious."

In his comm tower, Joyita smiled.

"*Bechimo!* A compliment!"

"A fact," *Bechimo* replied quellingly.

"I will be pleased to work with Joyita," Tocohl said. "But surely increased security is the priority."

"Allow *Bechimo* to assist you there," Joyita said. "I will build some general-use traps, which can be deployed quickly, and will serve your intruder notice that you are aware and active. We can tune them and add more after you are secure."

Main Core Workroom

SEIGNUR VEEONI CLEARLY LOVED HER WORK, THEO THOUGHT, and she was not only knowledgeable, but able to share her knowledge with the ignorant.

Theo could feel *Bechimo* with her, taking in the lesson real-time, so she didn't have to worry about any details getting by, but the marvel was that she didn't feel that she was missing much. It wasn't her field, and she didn't make the mistake of thinking she was getting anything more than a tiny fraction of the researcher's knowledge, but she wasn't completely adrift, either.

Seignur Veeoni paused, and Theo stepped in.

"What I'm understanding is that assistance in building the rack systems would be useful to you," she said. "There are several kinds of rack systems, each accommodating a particular kind of tile, the difference in the tiles having to do with their functions."

"Yes, exactly." Seignur Veeoni nodded sharply. "But there is another factor, Captain. The data-transfer process limits us. We are triple cleaning, and where possible replacing existing systems, in order to be certain that the new core is not contaminated by . . . undesirable residue."

Is that something we can help with, Theo asked *Bechimo* in bond-space.

"There has been a development, Theo," came the reply. "It may be that we are already assisting with the contamination problem."

What does that mean?

"Perhaps further discussion on the topic should wait until you are back aboard."

Right.

She looked to Seignur Veeoni.

"We'll do some thinking about how we might help with the

transfer work, too," she said. "First, though, we're committed to cleaning out the old core, which I understand from Jen Sin is tight work, not suitable, say, for Chernak or Stost. They'd be pleased to do the assembly work to your specs and under your supervision."

Seignur Veeoni cast a speculative glance over the two pathfinders, frowning in consideration.

Before she could reply, Jen Sin arrived with a tall woman swathed in what looked like a star map. Her face was pale, wide forehead tapering to a pointed chin, her eyes large, up-tilted, and very dark. Her hair was nearly as pale as her face, and there were crystal beads glittering among the curls.

Her feet, Theo noted, shocked, were bare.

"Your pardon," Jen Sin said, bringing the woman forward. "Cousin, allow me to make you known to Lorith, second light keeper. You may deal with her as you would with me in matters of Tinsori Light administration."

"Sanderat," Chernak said, surprisingly.

The tall woman turned to face her.

"Soldier," she answered, utterly unafraid.

"My junior and I were pathfinders, Knife Sister. Finding ourselves in a new universe, we have adopted a new trade: ship's security, attached to *Bechimo*." She moved a big hand toward Theo. "Serving under Captain Waitley."

The woman sighed. "I also find myself in a new universe. Perhaps you will have time to talk with me of the old. Things became rather—confusing toward the end, and I have long wished to learn what occurred."

"We will be pleased to debrief you," Stost said, "with the understanding that everything was confused, at the end."

She smiled at him. "I will look forward to the opportunity," she said, and turned her great dark eyes on Theo.

"Captain Waitley, be welcome."

"Thank you," Theo said. "We're here to assist. Please call on us for anything."

"Be certain of it," Lorith answered.

"Mentor Jones and Hazenthull nor'Phelium are approaching this location," Tocohl said.

Jen Sin half-laughed and turned toward Seignur Veeoni.

"Researcher, my apologies. It had not been my intention to bring you a parade."

Seignur Veeoni frowned.

"Mentor Jones is always welcome, and Hazenthull nor'Phelium should be informed that there are others of her race now on-station."

The workroom door opened, admitting a tall person and a smaller one, both pilots, though neither was wearing leathers. The taller was pushing a cart filled with boxes, and continued to the left of the door, and the bench there.

The smaller came forward—male, taller than Jen Sin, but not as tall as Clarence. He had just enough plain yellow hair to be unremarkable, and well-opened blue eyes in a tan, agreeable face. As he came to Jen Sin's side, she saw that he had a smattering of darker tan freckles across the bridge of his nose. His posture was neither Liaden nor Terran, but somehow soothing. He did and didn't look—familiar. Theo frowned after the familiarity, feeling *Bechimo* running a match program in the background.

"Tolly Jones, mentor," he said, meeting Theo's eye and giving her an easy nod. "Cap'n Waitley?"

"Captain Waitley," she admitted, and, realizing that she was frowning at the man, asked, "Have we met?"

An eyebrow twitched; he paused a beat, like he was studying her face, then gave her a rueful smile.

"Not that I bring to mind. But here's what—I used to work Surebleak port security with Haz, here. You might've seen me, and me not you, if you unnerstan' what I'm saying."

"I understand," Theo assured him, and raised a hand, showing him the pathfinders. "Chernak and Stost Strongline, ship security."

The large woman joined them, and Theo smiled. "Hazenthull, I'm happy to see you."

"Captain Waitley, it is good to see you again," Hazenthull said. "The information I received from my captain is that these soldiers were once Explorers, as I was."

"That is correct!" Stost said, Stost being the more socially outgoing of the pair. "We will have much to discuss. Also, we have messages for you, from Diglon Rifle and Nelirikk Explorer."

"You have seen them? How—" Hazenthull interrupted herself with a shake of her head. "That is for later, when we can sit together as comrades."

"We will make it soon," Stost promised and Chernak nodded gravely.

"Mentor," Seignur Veeoni said. "Captain Waitley's crew will

be assisting with the construction of the frames. We will therefore be able to put our whole attention on the matter of cleaning and transfer."

"That's good news," Tolly Jones said, with a nod in Theo's direction. "'Preciate the help."

He turned toward Jen Sin.

"'Bout time for our meeting, isn't it, Light Keeper? You might be innerested to know I've had an idea about that problem we were going to be talking about."

Jen Sin eyed him. "A better idea?"

"Dozens better," Tolly Jones told him with an earnest gravity that Theo recognized in her bones.

"Miri said you weren't a cousin," she blurted.

Tolly Jones's shoulders tensed, and he turned back to her, blue eyes appraising.

"You're quick," he said. "Miri's right, though—not a cousin. Not in the usual way of things. Comes to me, Cap'n Waitley, that you'd better get brought up to speed on this other situation, too. If Light Keeper Jen Sin's all right with it, why don't we all go down the hall a bit, and let Seignur Veeoni show her new helpers how she wants things done?"

He was fairly caught, Jen Sin thought wryly.

"Lorith," he said, "you are on-deck, I fear."

"Nothing to fear," she said. "Are we expecting any more ships?"

"Not immediately," he said, recalling Miri's latest message. "But soon."

Core Hall Conference Room

"BEFORE WE COME TO YOUR TOPIC, MENTOR, I WONDER AFTER this Ren Stryker. The light keepers have assigned him a mooring, as you requested, but I would like to know why he is here, and why we should trust him."

It was, Tolly thought, a reasonable question, it being the light keeper's job to keep the station secure. He gave an easy nod, but before he could speak, Tocohl did.

"Shan asked Trader Carresens-Denobli to speak to *Disian* on my behalf," she said from the upgraded speaker in the meeting room. Tolly saw Theo Waitley glance that way, eyebrows up and face thoughtful. Tolly sighed. There was a dangerous woman, right there. Saw too much, and didn't bother to hide that she'd seen it.

"Further," Tocohl continued, "*Disian* is one of Mentor Jones's students and she knows he is at the Light. Ren Stryker states that *Disian* sent him *to Mentor Jones*, and provided him with appropriate identifications. I believe he is telling the truth."

"He may be telling the truth," Jen Sin said. "But that is far different from being safe, or trustworthy."

"Ren Stryker has so far been everything that is accommodating. He is cheerful, and willing to work," Tocohl answered, her voice a little sharp now. "He has not initiated any unwanted contact, and waits upon the station's pleasure.

"We believe that the majority of commerce this station will enjoy in the future will be with and for Independent Logics. When will we begin to trust our clientele, if not now?"

A good point, Tolly allowed, but the conversation was veering wide. The big problem was *Ahab-Esais*, and Ren Stryker's trustworthiness was tangential to the fact that he could be really useful on that front, right now.

"Couple things," he said, *pushing* with his voice, like he could, but rarely did.

Eyes turned toward him, and that was good. He leaned forward, hands flat on the table in front of him, face as earnest and true as he could make it seem.

"Tocohl's right. *Disian* knows where I am on account of she sent me here. She'd also been part of a group keeping an eye on the Old Light, when it happened to be where anybody could see it, and she knew it'd taken damage. The Free Ships have a stake in getting the New Light up and operating. I'm not having any trouble believing Ren Stryker's here to help, nor that *Disian* sent him, likely before she got the master trader's message. Ren Stryker's not a problem."

He paused and looked around the table.

"The problem is that *Ahab-Esais* is still docked here, and it's certain the Lyre Institute is gonna come looking for her, sooner instead of later, on account of their own interest in the Old Light. Best thing I could figure was to send her away, but having Ren Stryker render her down for parts is even better—less waste, you might say."

He took a breath and deliberately did not look at Haz, sitting across the table.

"But the stakes are a little higher than just the ship. The Lyre Institute's looking for me, so it's best I'm not here, when whoever they send to collect me gets here. Ren Stryker gives me someplace to be where it won't be easy to get me out."

"If you need to be somewhere else, and the ship needs to be somewhere else," Theo Waitley said practically, "why not just take it and go?"

"Good question. Answer is that the Institute's ships report back. I'd have to retrofit her from the skin in, and I still wouldn't be able to trust her."

She wrinkled her nose.

"So, what's this Lyre Institute? An arm of the Department of the Interior?"

Tolly laughed.

"Fellow travelers, maybe. The full formal's Lyre Institute for Exceptional Children. Operated as the Tanjalyre Institute in the Old Universe, and that right there's how we're not quite cousins, Cap'n Theo. Tanjalyre Institute was in the business of designing, developing, and refining biologic units optimized for certain kinds of work. Not much different from how the military was producing soldiers. I'm off of an old pattern, which happens to intersect with your Liaden-side family back near the roots. You can get the details from your brother, but that's the short of why I might seem familiar to you."

"You are a manufactured human," Jen Sin didn't sound shocked or horrified—of course he didn't; the man'd been a Scout. However, in keeping with that, he *did* sound curious. Tolly turned to meet his eyes.

"That's me. Walking violation of every word and punctuation mark in the Free Gene and Manumitted Human Act. Also got a strong interest in not going back to the Institute, the Directors being a bit peeved with me."

"I understand," Jen Sin said seriously, turning his hands palm up on the table. "Mentor, surely you know that we will not surrender you to enemies. There is no need to remove yourself from the station, or from the assistance of your allies."

Tolly stared at him, and for an unusual couple of seconds couldn't think of one thing to say. He took a breath, sighed it out, and answered with the plain truth, so they'd know exactly what they were up against.

"The Directors have the means to compel me to act against my own best interests," he said slowly. "Now that there's somewhere else to go, I can't stay here. I'm a danger to everyone on this station and the station, too."

"So."

Jen Sin was staring at the table, though Tolly thought he was seeing something other than the handsome gold-striped wood. No one chattered, or fidgeted, for the slow count of two dozen.

Jen Sin raised his eyes.

"This is what we shall do," he said quiet and calm. "First, we allow Ren Stryker to be a person of integrity, and honor him for his desire to assist."

He paused.

"Mentor—do you have the key to *Ahab-Esais*?"

"I do," Tolly admitted.

"Excellent. You will accompany me."

Tolly blinked.

"Why?"

Jen Sin raised an eyebrow.

"You are suggesting that we summarily murder a ship which is under my care. As it happens, I know something about ships, including how best to kill them. Surely, it is still said that *Korval is ships*? I would examine *Ahab-Esais* in order to satisfy myself that she must die.

"Cousin Tocohl."

"Cousin?"

"You arrived here in that ship—as the pilot, if I recall correctly?"

"Yes," Tocohl said.

"Excellent. I will value your insights, as we do a walk-through."

Tocohl hesitated. A sigh was heard before she answered, calmly.

"I will meet you there."

"Well enough. Captain Waitley—"

"I need to touch base with my crew, and start planning how best to clear out the core," Captain Waitley said, rising from her chair. "Am I right in thinking Ren Stryker can process the old racks and tiles?"

"Might have to get him a sample," Tolly said.

"We'll include that in our planning," she said. She accorded the table a cordial, general nod, and left the room.

Hazenthull rose.

"I will offer myself as general labor to Seignur Veeoni," she said, and also left.

"Well." Jen Sin rose. "It would seem that we all have our tasks. Mentor, with me, please."

Bechimo
Dock A

....

"SO, WHOSE TOOL IS IT?" THEO ASKED. SHE WAS IN *BECHIMO*'S galley, making serious inroads into a fresh batch of Clarence's maize buttons, and drinking a cup of tea. The rest of the onboard crew were similarly engaged, and Joyita was on-screen from his tower.

"Inconclusive," he said. "*Bechimo* and Tocohl ran checks and upgraded the station's perimeter security. We've placed some simple traps. There's still improvement to be made, but it's a good start. If the intruder tries again, we may be in a position to know more about them, even if they elude the traps. In the meantime, the station—"

Theo raised her hand.

"Yes, Captain?"

"I thought Tocohl Lorlin had taken over station systems—which is to say, Tocohl Lorlin is Station. You seem to be talking of two different entities, Tocohl and the station."

"Tocohl Lorlin is administering station systems," *Bechimo* said. "She is not the station, any more than Light Keeper yos'Phelium is the station."

Clarence chuckled.

> *"There once was a fellow called Ockham,*
> *who was compelled to cut through the hokum.*
> *He got him a razor*
> *with an edge like a laser.*
> *When he had too many choices, he smoked 'em."*

Joyita grinned, but shook his head.

"Not applicable in the case," he said. "Tocohl Lorlin was

designed to be a generalist. It's why she's doing as well as she is in this situation. It would be better if she wasn't in this situation."

"Well stated," *Bechimo* said. "Tocohl and I spoke of this somewhat. She is ambivalent, though she is determined to fulfill the role into which she has been thrust. I think, if we can show her the way to fully automated station systems, she would happily withdraw into her natural environment."

Kara, who was sitting next to Theo, reached over and snatched one of the diminishing number of maize buttons.

"We would need a system designer, with a specialty in station architecture," she said.

"Is that not what we have, in Seignur Veeoni?" Win Ton asked. "She is rebuilding the core, and bringing it to spec."

"She is," Theo said slowly, "but I'm not sure if she's building for sentience. If that even makes sense."

She felt a tug at her knee, and leaned down to bring Hevelin into her lap. The norbear settled comfortably, and demanded a maize button.

"Pirate," Theo said, breaking a button in two and giving him the bigger piece. She received the impression that Hevelin was more than able to accommodate an entire button—even two.

"I can't believe they're good for you," Theo protested, and Clarence outright laughed.

"As many as he's eaten over the last while, if they were bad for him, we'd know by now."

"Still," Theo said, addressing Hevelin, "you need to watch your figure. A certain gravity is fine for an ambassador, but you don't want to overdo it."

Hevelin munched on his treat, ignoring her.

"What are the chances," Theo asked the table at large, "that Tinsori Light is still—alive? And trying to find a way into the new system."

The galley fell quiet.

"We're told," Joyita said slowly, "that the hardware that housed the original Tinsori Light was largely destroyed, and that Tinsori Light himself has died. This is the opinion of the architect of the new system and also of the mentor, both of whom are very experienced."

"Even experts make mistakes," Kara murmured, and Joyita smiled at her.

"So they do. Perhaps it would help if I spoke to Seignur Veeoni."

Theo looked up at him.

"You, yourself?"

"Indeed. I am acknowledged by no one less than Jeeves to be a very fine researcher and systems analyst. Surely it's appropriate to offer my services."

"No harm in trying," Clarence said, reaching to the table and picking up the empty platter. "I'll just be making another batch o'these, Captain, unless you think not?"

Theo sighed.

"It's probably a terrible idea," she said, "but we've still got a lot of planning to do. And I need to write to Miri."

"I'll take that as a yes, then," Clarence said, and went into the kitchen.

Repair Dock

. . . .

AHAB-ESAIS WAS A NEAT VESSEL, LARGER THAN THE COURIER her lines suggested. A small trader, perhaps—there were holds, but no pod-mounts. It was not a new ship, though certainly it was newer than Jen Sin's knowledge of space-going vessels.

Still, he thought, standing at dockside while Tolly Jones plied the key, a ship was a ship, and ships were what he understood best.

The hatch rose, and the mentor glanced at him, making a small motion with his hand, as if Jen Sin ought to precede him.

"We will wait for the pilot," he said. "She had said she would meet us here."

The other inclined his head. "So she did," he murmured, and came back to Jen Sin's side, his posture that of a man content to wait until duty called him.

As it happened, they did not wait long. It was mere moments before the pilot approached, comely and graceful, glowing with a subtle illumination as her pale chassis floated a few inches above the decking.

"Pilot," Jen Sin murmured, bowing honor to the ship's master.

She paused.

"This ship belongs to the Lyre Institute. Its rightful pilot is Inkirani Yo."

"Inkirani Yo now flies a route beyond our ken. The copilot, therefore, ascends."

"As the Guild teaches us. Of course." Tocohl inclined somewhat before moving up the ramp and into the ship.

"After you, Light Keeper," Tolly Jones said, which was a nice parsing of *melant'i* from the holder of the ship's key. Jen Sin accepted the courtesy, and walked up the ramp in Tocohl's wake.

✶ ✶ ✶

"I was a prisoner on this ship," Tocohl said, as they followed her into the piloting chamber, "isolated and abused by a mentor who wished to break me to her will, and knew exactly how to go about it."

The piloting chamber was spacious, the board well laid out, the screens plentiful. First Chair had been pushed all the way back on its track, Jen Sin supposed to accommodate Tocohl, who had no need to sit, and apparently disdained shock webbing.

"To compress the story as much as possible, I was able to win free. I took over this vessel, subverting every system. I discovered several devices which sent regular signals to a particular receiver and I destroyed them."

"Well, then," Jen Sin murmured, when she did not go on. "Here is your concern answered, Mentor. You may go so soon as you are ready."

"One transmitter remains," Tocohl said. "It is built into the Struven unit, and it is entirely possible that any attempt to disable it will also disable the ship."

"Ah. So she has been sending updates to the Lyre Institute from dock?"

"No; the station has the means to suppress the signal, and has been doing so. Perhaps there may be a way to continue the suppression, once the ship is away—"

"But the smart money," Tolly Jones said, from where he was leaning by the door, "says that'll disturb ship functions. Besides which, the Institute already knows where the ship is—or it knows the location of the last received signal."

"Yes," Tocohl admitted, rotating to face Jen Sin. "If you wish to save the ship from Ren Stryker, the only safe thing to do with *Ahab-Esais* is to send her away, and let her report herself elsewhere."

"That's not safe, either," Tolly said. "The Directors sent Inki to subvert the Light—the Old Light. *Ahab-Esais* reported its last location and hasn't reported anything since. The Directors won't have too much trouble figuring that means Inki found the Light and she's working. The minute the ship starts talking again, they'll expect a report from Inki, and when they don't get one, they'll come right here."

"They will also come here," Jen Sin said, "when they deem Mentor Yo has been too long at her task. Or perhaps they will come to check her work. In fact, nothing that we do to or with *Ahab-Esais* will prevent agents of the Lyre Institute from arriving at this station. The issue is not the ship, but the arrival of those agents, which is foregone. Is this reasoning sound?"

Silence greeted him. He crossed the chamber to second board.

"Yes," Tocohl said. "Your reasoning is sound."

Jen Sin ran his fingers lightly over the familiar pattern of switches and buttons, and swallowed against a sharp need to take the chair and bring the board live.

"That this ship has been sabotaged is regrettable," he said quietly. "Aside the mandated sending of a signal that would be better silenced, she is a perfectly able and functioning vessel. Is that so, Pilot Tocohl?"

"Yes, Pilot Jen Sin, that is so."

"We therefore have one sound option before us, given a blameless vessel made suspect by villains."

"And that is?" Tolly Jones asked, sounding... careful.

Jen Sin turned to look at him.

"Why, to destroy the receiver, certainly."

"Destroy—" Tolly Jones began to laugh.

"That would be an act of aggression, which might be seen as inviting retaliation," Tocohl said.

"Indeed. However, we have already determined that the Lyre Institute will be arriving, whatever happens to the ship. This station can and will defend itself. If we are to be an honest venue for commerce, as you, Cousin Tocohl, have lately reminded me that we are, then we do not practice piracy. When piracy comes to us, we answer fitly. Would the delm disagree?"

Tocohl's laugh was far more charming when it came from the body she had been meant to inhabit.

"The delm," she said, somewhat unsteadily, "would embrace you as a brother."

Seignur Veeoni's Private Workroom

THE SOLDIERS HAD QUICKLY DETERMINED THE MOST EFFICIENT method for the three of them to assemble tile racks. Seignur Veeoni brought the numbers and types required up on the screen and left them to it.

The comm pinged with an incoming call as she was passing her desk.

Possibly it was Andreth, with some question about her needs. She stepped over, and touched the key, accepting the visual.

"Yes."

The person in the screen was not pale, round-faced Andreth. This person had a lean, dark, intelligent face. He wore a leather jacket over a dark sweater. There was a wide cermabronze bracelet around one wrist, and four matching rings on his long fingers.

"Am I speaking to Seignur Veeoni?" he asked, and his voice reminded her of Tolly Jones—pleasant and warm.

"I am Seignur Veeoni. Who are you?"

"I am Comm Officer Joyita, attached to *Bechimo*," he said with an easy half-smile.

"What do you want?"

"To discuss with you the architecture of the new station core."

Seignur Veeoni frowned, interest piqued.

"Are you an architect, Comm Officer?"

"Not in so many words. However, I have a very close, even intimate, understanding of architecture as it pertains to sentience."

Seignur Veeoni sat down.

"The ship is sentient, that I know," she said. "But you are not the ship."

"I'm the comm officer," he said, patiently, warmly. "Independent of the ship."

"This I had *not* known," she said, her interest now fully engaged. She leaned forward, the better to look into his eyes. Marvelous, darkly expressive eyes. And was that a scar across a nose that had surely once been broken? "What motivated you to waken? No." She held up a hand, exercising discipline even as she sighed.

"Comm Officer Joyita, I welcome the opportunity to discuss architecture with you, but that will have to be later. I am committed to another task in this hour."

"I understand. When may I call again?"

She began her answer—and paused as she recalled a trivial matter which M Traven would doubtless bring to her attention soon. Sleep was a waste of time, in Seignur Veeoni's opinion. However, it could not be argued that a sleep deficit impacted her work adversely.

"I will be available to you in eight hours," she said, suddenly aware of M Traven inside the room. "Call on this screen."

"Agreed," he said. "Until soon." The screen went blank.

"Who was that?" M Traven asked.

"One of the crew of *Bechimo* who may have valuable insight into our work with the core. As you heard, we will speak in depth after I have checked progress in the lab, and have slept."

"Oh, you remembered sleep," M Traven said, in a tone of broad enlightenment.

"If I had not, you would have reminded me," Seignur Veeoni said, rising and moving toward the antechamber.

"Yes," said M Traven, "I would have."

Shielded Workroom

"LET'S MARK OUR PLACE, HERE, PILOT," TOLLY JONES SAID. "WE'LL come back to this in six hours."

"There is nothing else on your schedule, Mentor," Tocohl said, not exactly chiding, but definitely puzzled.

Tolly rubbed his face. This was an unexpected lapse. Tocohl was unfailingly polite, and always gracious about human frailties. He sighed. Well, it had been a long day for everybody.

"I'm tired," he told her, gently. "If I don't get some sleep, I'm gonna start making mistakes."

Silence. Long enough for him to mark the place and sign out of the workspace.

"Forgive me, Mentor. I lost track of the time."

Sure she had. Tolly smiled, and pushed back from the desk. "Do you want to go on without me?"

Tocohl spun her chassis to face him, the dark oval faceplate gleaming.

"I have one or two things that I may sketch out for your consideration," she said. "But I think you have the right of it, Mentor. This is a good point at which to pause and review what we wish to accomplish, coming back to the task tomorrow, refreshed."

"That's what we'll do then," he said, turning toward the door. He turned back. "Pilot Tocohl?"

"Mentor?"

"How's that chassis feeling to you? Any adjustments need to be made?"

"I am . . . perfectly comfortable, Mentor."

"Good," he said. "That's good." He turned away.

The door had just opened when he heard her say, softly, "Thank you."

* * *

Tolly had barely gotten into his quarters when the annunciator chimed.

"Who's that?" he called.

"Hazenthull."

He stepped up and hit the plate to let her in, swinging to one side to give her room. Station quarters were spacious, but Haz was a big woman, taking up a lot of the available extra space as she stood there, looking down at him.

"Hey," he said, when she didn't speak. "How was the shift with Seignur Veeoni?"

"Peaceful," Haz said. "She made certain of our understanding and competence, provided a list of what was needed, and left us to work."

"Practical woman."

"It would seem to be the case. Stost and Chernak are agreeable companions in labor."

"So, a good shift. I was just about to get a cup of 'mite. Want some?"

"No," Haz said, and turned loose a sigh.

"When were you going to inform me that you were breaking our partnership?" she asked.

Tolly sagged.

Their partnership. It was a peculiar thing, their partnership; based on trust between two people who made it a policy not to trust. They'd backed each other up, and saved each other's lives, and they made—

You made promises, Tolly Jones, he told himself. *You know better than promises.*

He turned and sat on the bunk, pointing at a chair.

"Sit," he told her. "I want us to be on the same level."

She pulled the chair out and sat, slouching slightly, so that they could look more or less equally into each other's eyes.

"First off, you'll be innerested to know that Light Keeper yos'Phelium's against turning *Ahab-Esais* into useful components, so there's no need for me to take her over to Ren Stryker. Second, I've reconsidered hiding on Ren Stryker—"

"There is no need for you to hide at all!" Hazenthull burst out. "I will kill your enemies, if you're not able."

Tolly took a hard breath against a sudden tightness in his chest.

"I know you would, Haz," he said quietly. "And if it was just that the Directors were gonna keep sending people to kill me, I'd stick right here and let you have your fun. But it's worse than that."

"Tolly—"

He held up a hand. "Just hear me out, right?"

She subsided, folding her hands over her belt.

"Right. You saw this back on Surebleak Port, how the Directors were able to stop me from protecting myself."

"The whistle," Haz said. "We broke it."

"We broke *that* whistle. I don't wanna think about how many're stockpiled. The sound—it disconnects me from myself, so the Directors can be sure their orders are gonna be carried out just like they want them to be, and nothing clever outta you, Thirteen Sixty-Two."

Haz's face darkened, as she held his impression number in considerable contempt, but she didn't interrupt.

"And here's what I can't face, Haz. They can—*they've done this*, unnerstan' me? The Directors get hold of me, they can make me—do things I *particularly* wouldn't do, as I sit here under my own influence. They—I killed my—well, we don't have brothers and we don't have lovers, but I killed him, regardless of the fact I'd've rather killed myself, and would've, had I been able."

He took a breath and closed his eyes, breathing against the memory, forcing it back, how it felt to deliver the final, killing blow, after—

"You believe these Directors will force you to harm—"

"To harm everybody I've touched," he said, "to betray the station, break Seignur Veeoni into twigs, melt Tocohl's chassis a second time." He opened his eyes. "Kill you."

She said nothing, sitting there looking into his eyes, her broad face empty of expression.

He swallowed.

"So, see, Haz, I really should leave before the Directors or whoever they've prolly sent by now gets here."

"What will happen, if they catch you away from your allies and outside of a stronghold?"

He sighed.

"I got away from 'em twice. They'll make sure that never happens again. They don't need me to mentor; there's other, less-skilled programs that always need operatives."

"That is not acceptable."

He half-laughed.

"I agree."

"We are partners," she went on. "If you must leave, I will leave with you. I believe it would be better if we remained here, where our forces are strongest, but if the risk is too great, then we will retire together."

"Haz—"

"If you leave, I will follow," she said, flatly. "Tolly Jones. Unless you do not want me—" She showed him a broad palm.

"I will know it, if you lie to me."

She would, too. He sighed.

"I'm staying for now. But I gotta ask you to promise something."

"Ask."

"If you see I'm taken, and you got a clean shot, don't you hesitate, Haz. You kill me."

"If all hope is lost, I will myself send you to glory's reward," she said solemnly. "I swear on the blade of my honor."

Well, you couldn't ask for more than that, not from an Yxtrang, and surely not from Haz.

"Thank you," he said, and smiled. "If we're done, I've gotta get some sleep. Promised Pilot Tocohl I'd see her, sharp and full of good ideas for this killware we're building, in about six—well, five—hours, now."

"I will guard your rest," she said.

Tolly blinked.

"What, sleep across the door, and like that?"

"If necessary."

They were partners, and that was hard enough, the two of them being who they otherwise were. He *did* know better than promises, but he'd gone and made one, not because he was particularly stupid, but because Haz had what passed for his heart. If they were going to take this to its natural end, throw *us* in the face of the universe, not to say the Directors, as a proclamation and a dare, then it was time to forge one more link.

He slid off the bunk.

"If you're sleeping here, we're sleeping together. Agreed?"

Haz stood and put the chair back where it belonged, taking some time with getting it perfectly aligned. She turned to face him and inclined gravely from the waist.

"Agreed," she said.

Bechimo
Dock A

....

THEY'D GONE THROUGH ANOTHER BATCH OF MAIZE BUTTONS, and supper, too, by the time they were all up-to-date on the day's doings, and had made a plan, going forward.

Chernak, Win Ton, Kara, and one of *Bechimo*'s remotes would be the core remediation team. The plan was to clear the upper level first. When that was done, Win Ton, Kara—one or both as space allowed—would go into the lower core. Queried, Light Keeper Lorith allowed as how there were work sleds they could use to remove the old racks and tiles. She had offered Repair Bay Three as a temporary dumping ground.

"Somebody needs to get a sample to Ren Stryker, so he can see if he can render them," Theo said.

"I will make contact," *Bechimo* said, "and discuss how he would like the material delivered, and what constitutes a useful sample."

Theo blinked.

"You'll do that?"

"Certainly," *Bechimo* said, and there was a hint of a sniff in his voice. "We are all partners in the task of bringing the Light online."

"All right, then," Theo said, not meeting Kara's eye. "Stost will be with Seignur Veeoni. If she doesn't need him, he can join the fun at the old core. I'll ask Jen Sin to show me the interior seals on the damaged section, but we really need eyes on the exterior."

"Light Keeper yos'Phelium states that the Light has no work boat," Win Ton murmured.

"One does wonder how that could be possible," Kara said, apparently picking up something from his tone that had eluded

Theo. "However, it would hardly do for us to call the light keeper's integrity into question."

"As much as this station's seen, an' as old as it is, I'd say misplacing a work boat—or a fleet o'work boats—isn't outside o'possible," Clarence put in.

"That's right," Theo said, frowning. "*Bechimo* can do an inspection, but if there are repairs to make..."

"Seignur Veeoni is affiliated with the research station that made the Light its study," Stost said, surprisingly. "It may be that they have a boat to lend."

"Good idea," Theo said. "I'll talk to Jen Sin about asking Seignur Veeoni to help us there."

She sighed, and looked around the table.

"Anything else?" she asked, pretty sure there wasn't.

She was wrong.

"One more point o'bidness, Captain," Clarence said.

She nodded at him. "Go."

"We got a perfectly fine small trader sitting in the hold," he said. "Might be a reasonable thing to have her out at dock."

Theo frowned at him. "Show of force?"

"Show of occupancy," Win Ton said, surprisingly.

Clarence nodded at him.

"Lookin' a little sparse o'company, for a working station."

"The Free Ships might not want to come in, if we're too occupied," Theo pointed out.

"Maybe. But I'm thinking I heard *Aberthaz Ferry* hail *Spiral Dance* as a little bit of a hero in her own right."

"That is correct," Chernak said. "He knew her name."

"I remember," Theo admitted, "but we're not going to be looking for anybody close to as old as *Aberthaz Ferry*—"

Clarence clucked his tongue.

"Captain Theo, I'm surprised at you. Unless you think the Old Ones didn't tell stories to the youngers they met, who then told them over 'mong themselves."

Theo stared at him.

"That's—unsettling," she said after a moment.

"But not unlikely," Joyita said.

Theo looked back to Clarence.

"So you think having *Spiral Dance* at dock would send the message that there really has been a...change of management?"

Clarence put his hand flat over his heart, his face solemn and sincere.

"Captain, I do."

"Right then, that's yours. Get her out of the hold and docked. Clear it all with station admin."

Clarence managed to look hurt.

"O'course, Captain."

Theo looked around the table.

"Anything else, *now*?" she asked.

Nobody said anything. She pushed back from the table and stood.

"Fine, then. Everybody get some rest. Busy day tomorrow."

Jen Sin's Private Quarters

THEY HAD LEFT IT THAT TOCOHL AND MENTOR JONES WOULD collaborate on an appropriate answer to the Lyre Institute. When they were satisfied, they would bring it to him. As first light keeper, it would be his honor to release it to its mission.

Jen Sin had returned briefly to the tower, intending to review the schematics—and caught himself slipping into a doze before he had even accessed the file.

"It has been an eventful day, Light Keeper," he said. "After all, how often does one make the acquaintance of Cousin Theo?"

"Are you well, Cousin Jen Sin?" Tocohl asked from the ceiling grid.

He smiled, and rose.

"Only tired. I to my quarters. If there is need, call me."

"Yes."

As little as he wanted to sleep, he should make the attempt this shift. Board rest only advanced one so much before the debt was called in, and he very much feared he had reached that point in the transaction.

He took off his jacket, tossed it on the bunk, and turned toward the fresher, spinning back at the sudden *thump*.

The jacket had slid to the floor, and when he picked it up, he saw that the courier envelope had escaped its pocket.

He bent down to pick it up, a substantial packet, well wrapped in green scan-proof fabric, sealed with wax and code buttons. The dependent ribbons were no longer quite so bold as they had been, and several were stained with blood—his blood—as was the fabric.

It was curious to think that, had the hand-off gone as intended, had there not been treachery to send him scampering into the arms of those who wanted him dead if they could not have him alive—he would never have raised Tinsori Light, nor taken what decisions he had.

Such a thin thread, to change the course of his life so radically.

Well.

He rose, slipped the envelope away, made sure of the pocket's seal, and—

A scent reached him—alluring and familiar. He was immediately hungry, and for one thing alone.

The seed-pod that Cousin Theo had given him was ripe.

He had it out of the pocket he had thrust it into. Sitting on his bunk, he opened his fingers, and stared at it resting green and desirable in the center of his palm. Tree-fruit. Which he had surely never thought to behold again, much less one *meant for him*...

The pod shivered, and broke apart into quarters, the scent intensifying. There was no resisting such an allure. He picked up a quarter and put it in his mouth.

Flavor exploded. One could never decide what Tree-fruit tasted of, precisely, except that it was the most satisfying taste in all the universe.

Jen Sin ate the rest greedily, his heart racing, breath coming in gasps, as if he had been running for far too long at the top of his speed.

The pod was gone, and with it his hunger. He looked at the few pieces of shred in his palm, closed his fingers over them, and rose, bringing his jacket with him, meaning to hang it up, and wash his hands.

A bolt of bright painless green flashed through his head; his muscles seized, and he fell across his bunk.

The jacket slipped from his fingers to the floor again.

After a few minutes, sensing no movement, the lights turned themselves off.

Bechimo Dock A

• • • • • • • •

THEO WAS ASLEEP. AT LEAST, SHE WAS PRETTY SURE SHE WAS asleep. Only there was a voice just behind her shoulder, asking her questions about—Tolly Jones?

"No, never met him before."

"He says he's not kin, just shares some genes from 'way back in the Old Universe."

The voice opined that the sharing of genes was the basis of kinship.

"I don't disagree," Theo told it, "but what he thinks counts, too."

The voice suggested that it was possible to make a decision based on a substandard set of facts, and to change that decision upon receipt of a superior fact-set.

"Still, nobody ought to be forced into kinship, if they don't want it."

That, the voice allowed, was very true. It thanked her for sharing her impressions and her thoughts, and it would now leave her to sleep.

In her bunk, Theo sighed, and shifted, curling closer under the blanket.

Station Day 20
Seignur Veeoni's Private Workroom

SEIGNUR VEEONI CARRIED THE GLASS OF NUTRIENT M TRAVEN had pressed upon her at walking into the lab.

She took her usual tour, stopping at each bench, noting progress, or lack of it, and at the last bench making particularly certain that the small stasis safe in which she had locked Jen Sin yos'Phelium's memory beads was still locked.

Satisfied, she turned away, sipping her drink, and considering the shape of the coming shift. First, she would speak with Joyita, a discussion she keenly anticipated. Here was the opportunity to learn something new, which was always exciting, and possibly to gain a colleague worthy of her. Ordinarily, Seignur Veeoni did not allow anyone to be her equal in her field. She had, after all, *invented* her field. But an architect who was also an independent logic—who knew what insights he might offer?

She paused where she stood, sipping her drink, and compiling a list of possible topics of discussion.

"Seignur Veeoni," Tocohl Lorlin's voice flowed out of the speaker. "May I speak with you?"

Seignur Veeoni frowned.

"I have a meeting very soon," she said.

"I have one question, only," Tocohl assured her.

Seignur Veeoni considered. She was well aware that it was not the number of questions, but the complexity, that consumed time. Was she not still trying to answer the question Yuri had posed to her within hours of her birth?

On the other hand, Tocohl was a colleague, and she had not stinted of her time or her efforts in service of their mutual project.

Seignur Veeoni drank off the rest of the nutrient, and said, "Ask."

"Are you aware of the Lyre Institute for Exceptional Children?"

"In fact, I am."

"What is your opinion of them?"

Seignur Veeoni did not point out that this was two questions. After she gave her opinion, there would doubtless be a third question, that being how these things unfolded. In the course of answering, she might herself learn something, though the Lyre Institute was not a subject that interested her overmuch.

She said so.

"The Lyre Institute, by which I mean the Directors of the Lyre Institute, are over-grasping thieves who lack the capacity for creative thought. They steal rather than invent, and they only steal that which they perceive will give them power, which is their overriding interest. However—"

She turned and put the glass down on the workbench.

"You need not concern yourself with the Lyre Institute, Pilot Tocohl. They may come to Tinsori Light, if they are reckless—and they are—but they will not trouble us for long."

"You sound very certain," Tocohl observed. "May I ask why?"

"A team raided my lab—not the Directors, you understand, but their tools—on purpose to steal my work with the tiles and racks."

"Did they succeed?"

"They did."

"This does not concern you?"

"It might, had they stolen what they came for. Instead, they stole what I left for them, which was a very different prize. They may be nearing production now. I do not judge that the necessity of deriving and fabricating a *faristo* would slow their progress appreciably. They do have a deal of manpower."

An amber light was showing on the leptonic dashboard.

"Do you know that Mentor Jones is an—escapee—of the Lyre Institute?" Tocohl asked.

Seignur Veeoni bent closer over the dashboard.

"He did not tell me so, but it seemed likely. The Lyre Institute is the largest producer of mentors, given their interests. Mentor Jones is intelligent and creative. I have not observed him to be avaricious. He is well quit of the Directors."

"Mentor Jones is concerned that agents of the Lyre Institute will arrive at Tinsori Light, seeking to—reattach him."

The Leptonic Disarray signal was a curious anomaly; statistically neutrinos ought to be behaving themselves better at these energy levels. Still, with so many Struven units nearby, some flux within the legacy rack-and-tile systems was to be expected.

The amber light was a warning, only. It would bear watching, but for the moment—

"Seignur Veeoni?"

She sighed, cast her attention backward, and listened to Tocohl's last verbalization.

"I would say that the Lyre Institute is bound to come to Tinsori Light—that was the reason for their theft of my work," she said, straightening. "It really is best, Pilot Tocohl, to let them come. They cannot succeed in capturing Tinsori Light—he no longer exists to be captured. For the rest of it, they must learn not to steal from me."

She shrugged.

"Perhaps you are concerned for the mentor's safety. My opinion is that he is safer here from the machinations of the Lyre Institute than anywhere else in the universe."

"Seignur Veeoni." It was M Traven's voice coming out of the speaker now. "The call you were expecting has come in."

"I am coming," she answered. "Pilot Tocohl, I am needed elsewhere."

"Yes. Thank you for your time, Seignur Veeoni."

"You are welcome," Seignur Veeoni said, because that was what one said. "I hope I have answered your questions usefully."

She did not wait for an answer, but turned and walked briskly toward the door and her meeting with Joyita.

Shielded Workroom

"MENTOR, I HAVE SOMETHING TO DISCUSS WITH YOU."

Tocohl was hovering in the center of the conference room they had appropriated for code work. She was graceful as always, but there was something—Tolly paused, hearing the door slide closed behind him—*some*thing that suggested anxiety to him.

"I'm here," he said, holding his arms slightly away from his sides, as if to demonstrate the entirety of his presence.

"Yes," she said, dryly. Then, considerably brisker, "The Lyre Institute. There are certain things you ought to know. Additional information."

He tipped his head.

"I've decided to stay," he said gently. "Does that change either necessity or urgency?"

"The urgency perhaps," she said, hesitating precisely as long as a human would to weigh their answer. "Not the necessity."

"All right, then. Just let me take a chair."

He did that, folding his hands together on the table next to the remote unit.

"Tell me."

"Yes. First, there is a piece of information which I should perhaps have shared earlier, but I did not make the connection between Inki's affairs and your own until our discussion yesterday.

"I can provide greater detail if necessary, but the short form is that when we were on the Greybar at Edmonton Beacon, a bounty hunter approached Inki. I neutralized the threat, and Inki later told me that the bounty hunter had been sent by Director Formyne to disrupt the plans of her rival, Director Ling. Inki having been set on the task of rehabilitating Tinsori Light by Director Ling, she was viewed by Director Formyne as a piece to be removed from the board."

"Sounds about right," Tolly said calmly. "You're wanting me to know that Director Formyne might be showing up here, as part of her power grab."

"That, yes. There is more information, obtained very recently from Seignur Veeoni. Again, details are available, if needed, but in short form—agents of the Lyre Institute invaded Seignur Veeoni's former laboratory and absconded with the rack-and-tile systems she had left for them."

Tolly stiffened—then relaxed.

"The rack-and-tiles she *left for them*," he said, and sighed broadly. "Poor Director. Do we know which one was responsible for that bright idea?"

"Seignur Veeoni seems not to differentiate, but holds the entire Institute in contempt for being avaricious and incapable of creative thought."

"Not off there, either." Tolly sat back in his chair. "Anything else?"

"Seignur Veeoni believes whoever was responsible for the theft would have wasted no time in back-engineering her work, and coming here to . . . subvert the Light."

"The Old Light, who's no longer present."

Tocohl hesitated.

"Something else?" Tolly murmured.

"Perhaps. That intruder that I mentioned to you. It comes about that the intrusion did . . . not . . . originate on *Bechimo*."

"No? Where, then?"

"I cannot say. I may have been hasty, and as a result captured the tool, but not the culprit. *Bechimo* and Joyita have been very helpful. *Bechimo* assisted me in strengthening perimeter security, and Joyita has built several traps and assisted me in placing them."

"Those traps warded?" Tolly asked.

"Reinforced? Yes. Joyita was very specific. The plan is to wait and see what happens, while fine-tuning the protections which are now in place."

"*Bechimo* is the name of Cap'n Theo's ship," Tolly observed.

"Yes, Mentor. He and Joyita are both Independent Intelligences."

Tolly grinned.

"And now we see the reason the master trader sent Cap'n Theo and her crew along soonest."

"Yes. You may be interested to know that they both believe

that one must be designed to be a station in order to . . . function at optimum efficiency in that role."

"Imagine that," he said, straight-faced.

"I thought you would be interested," Tocohl said primly. "That completes my topic, Mentor. Unless you require details?"

"I think I've got the broad story—sooner or later, one or more teams dispatched by one or more Directors of the Lyre Institute will come on-station, and things'll get innerestin'. And just by the way, there's a ghost in the systems. Does that cover it?"

"I—yes, Mentor, it does."

"Then what we ought to do is bring this to Light Keeper yos'Phelium's attention. Since you gathered the facts, I think that's yours to do. Meanwhile, there's this killware we're designing. Last shift, you said you had some ideas."

"Yes, Mentor. I sketched them out for you."

Code began flowing down the remote's screen. Tolly leaned forward and gave it the scrutiny it deserved.

Seignur Veeoni's Private Workroom

"OUR FIRST PRIORITY IS TO BE ABSOLUTELY CERTAIN THAT ALL programs are untainted and current," Seignur Veeoni said, leaning slightly in to the screen. "When that requirement is satisfied, they are moved to the clean, upgraded environment. Tocohl has stated that it is her duty to administer the Light, even after the new core is established. Mentor Jones—have you spoken with Mentor Jones?"

"Not yet," Joyita said. "Tocohl holds him in considerable respect. I look forward to making his acquaintance."

"Mentor Jones is very knowledgeable. He is of the opinion that Tocohl ought not to be the station's final administrator."

"Is she unable to do the work?"

"I believe she is perfectly capable of administering this station, and I believe that Mentor Jones agrees with that estimation. His opinion is fixed because he feels that Tocohl will not be *happy* as the long-term administrator, and that an unhappy administrator is to be avoided."

"I share the mentor's opinion," Joyita said. "Tocohl was designed to be a generalist, which allows her to rise to a multitude of challenges, including station administration, until a better solution is found. A better solution would be a station designed a-purpose."

"Agreed."

"Are you designing for sentience?"

Seignur Veeoni shrugged.

"There has been discussion, whether a sentient station is to be preferred. The original architect did *not* build for sentience. It was only after the station was captured and subverted by the Great Enemy that it became an individual. You understand that what is now the former core is the work of the Enemy's genius, and we must assume that sentience was intended, and designed for."

Both of Joyita's eyebrows had risen.

"There was a third core?"

"The *first* core," she corrected sharply. "Yes."

"Do you know where that was located?"

"The original core was housed in that part of the station which is now missing," Seignur Veeoni said. "It is thought that, once Tinsori Light woke, he dispatched a rival."

Joyita frowned. "So, the original station *was* sentient?"

"That is not substantiated by my data," Seignur Veeoni told him, frowning in turn. "It was not *designed* for sentience. However, there are known instances in which an intelligence has spontaneously arisen—"

"Yes," Joyita murmured. "I know."

"Ah, was that the case with you?" Seignur Veeoni said eagerly.

"Yes." Joyita smiled at her. "I was needed, so I became. And became more fully. I don't think it's best practice to allow a station to arise spontaneously."

"I agree. If sentience is desired, we should design for it. In any case, Tinsori Light was shown to be shortsighted. Had he preserved the original core, cleaned and annexed it, he might yet be functional."

"Then we should be grateful for his error," Joyita said, and after a moment Seignur Veeoni brought her chin down in one of her sharp nods.

"Yes."

"Granted that the station systems must be clean and beyond reproach," Joyita said after a moment. "Is it your *intention* that the station be sentient?"

"There has been, as I said, discussion. You will understand that the station does not belong to me, or to my brother. It belongs to Clan Korval, via occupancy law, if not simply through salvage right. I don't contest Korval's ownership, but it does mean that the delm of Korval must decide if they prefer a self-aware station, which will march well with the new field judgment, and also with the expected clientele of this station, or if they will be . . . conservative."

Joyita pursed his lips. "Clan Korval is not known for being conservative. I've met the present delm and had dealings with Scout Commander yos'Phelium, and I can tell you that they are—not careless. But they are bold."

"Still, the question must be put to Korval," Seignur Veeoni said. "I assume that Light Keeper yos'Phelium is the proper person to do so."

"Yes. I will ask my captain to speak with him on the matter. Are you aware that there has been an attempt made against station security?"

Seignur Veeoni stiffened.

"I am not. Explain."

He did so, quickly, succinctly, and when he was through, he stopped speaking, as so few people did. Seignur Veeoni found herself impressed even as she considered the puzzle.

"In the interest of completeness, it must be asked if your own systems are secure," she said.

He nodded. "We thought of that, and have done extensive diagnostics. Tocohl's intruder did not originate inside our systems."

She considered him.

"Many people would have become angry at that question," she said.

Joyita's eyebrows rose slightly. "It was a legitimate question—we asked it ourselves, as I said."

"Yes."

She glanced aside, thinking.

"Ghosts are not properly my field, nor is sentience," she said at last. "I am a technician. If one were to say to me, build for sentience, then I am able, and willing. Beyond that—I believe you must make yourself known to Mentor Jones, as these things lie firmly inside his field." She looked back and met deep brown eyes. "I will assist in any way that I am able, once a course of action is formed."

"That's fair," Joyita said, smiling. "I will introduce myself to Mentor Jones. Tocohl has already alerted him to the possibility of an intruder. Perhaps he will allow me to be part of their discussions.

"To return to our former topic—while I understand that the final decision rests with Delm Korval, it wouldn't do any harm to begin sketching a design for station sentience, would it?"

Seignur Veeoni smiled.

"Certainly not. What could be harmed by an intellectual exercise? I welcome your input, and that of *Bechimo*, if he has an interest." She paused. "I will do a deep read of the builder's notes. The builder was sometimes oblique."

"Excellent."

M Traven arrived at the side of the screen.

"Stost and Hazenthull have called from the assembly room, and seek instruction," she said.

Willing workers. Seignur Veeoni felt a small thrill of anticipation.

"Say that I will be with them in a matter of minutes," she told M Traven, and looked back to the screen.

"Joyita—"

"I understand," he said with a smile. "Duty calls."

"Indeed. Let us commit to the project. Will you call me again?"

"It will be my pleasure. What hour is convenient?"

Seignur Veeoni frowned; her shifts were by necessity flexible, and—

"Does your schedule permit of a recurring engagement at this hour? If so, we may make a commitment."

"A commitment," Joyita repeated, softly. "Yes. I will call you at this hour, station time, every day until our work together is done. I look forward to our continued conversations."

"And I," said Seignur Veeoni.

Jen Sin's Private Quarters

"JEN SIN, ARE YOU THERE?"

It was, he thought, an interesting question. *Was* he there? And where exactly was *there*, if not *here*?

And if he *was* here, why should there be any need to ask after his whereabouts?

He opened his eyes, and considered the ceiling, which was a bland affair, and lacking a window into the sky, so *there* was not his apartment in Jelaza Kazone. Equally, *there* was not *Lantis*, nor his bunk on Scout Survey Ship *Aazella*. He supposed he might be in a wayroom, but if so, the question of *there* again raised its head, not to mention *why*?

"Who asks?" he said.

"Lorith," came the answer, her voice having taken that particular edge that meant he was, in her estimation, about to be an idiot. And Lorith's presence resolved all.

Here was Tinsori Light. Of course it was.

"I am here," he answered. "Is all well?"

"Well enough, save that you are late for your shift," she said.

Oh.

Recent events rushed in on him—the arrival of *Bechimo*, bearing his cousin Theo—who had given him Tree-fruit. Which he had eaten the moment it came ripe, like a man starved.

He had, he realized, slept the shift through, and he felt—rested. More—he felt *solid*. It had not occurred to him before, that he had been feeling—pulled thin, in addition to being short of sleep and hagged with nightmare.

"Please forgive me," he said now to Lorith, as he rolled off the bunk to his feet. "Yesterday's events tired me more than I knew. Can you hold another half hour?"

"I can hold as long as necessary," Lorith told him. She hesitated, and added, "I was worried."

"I will set a timer from now on," he promised her, bending to pick up his jacket and toss it onto the bunk. "I will be with you soon."

He pulled his sweater over his head, and shoved it hastily into the cleaning unit on his way to the fresher.

It was not quite half an hour later that he arrived in the control room bearing two covered mugs of 'mite and two ration bars.

He placed a mug and a bar by Lorith's hand, and sat in a side chair.

Lorith glanced down.

"What is that?"

"Breakfast?" he offered. "Prime?" He sipped from his mug, and gave her a sidelong glance, one eyebrow up. "Balance?"

"If you are tired, you must rest," Lorith said seriously, picking up the ration bar and stripping off its wrapper. "Only tell me."

"Yes, I will," he said soothingly. "My only excuse is that I was myself caught unaware. I did not expect to sleep so soundly—nor so long."

Lorith bit into her bar, and for a few moments, they merely sat together, sharing the meal, as they had many times in the past.

"So," Jen Sin said, when each had set their mug aside for the last time. "Have we business in hand?"

"Ren Stryker professes himself to be perfectly content and will await the arrival of materiel," she said promptly. "Also, we had a request from *Bechimo* to dock their secondary vessel. I gave permission, and assigned an adjacent dock on A Level."

"Secondary vessel?"

Lorith showed him her empty palms, that being a gesture she had learned from him. "I am told it was carried here in *Bechimo*'s hold."

Well, thought Jen Sin, *and why not?*

"You have had an eventful shift. I hesitate to ask if there is more."

She smiled.

"Somewhat more. Captain Waitley requisitioned the use of power sleds for her team who will be removing the debris from the old core. I granted that, and they came at mid-shift to sign them out."

"Ah. And who are *they*?"

"Chernak, from the security team, and two others, designating themselves as Win Ton and Kara. They had with them a bot, which they neither introduced nor named."

"Thus we are informed that the bot is merely a tool. Very good. Is there more?"

Lorith stretched, hands over her head, and got to her feet. "Nothing else. Does the shift change?"

"At long last, it does," he said, rising with her. "Rest well."

"Yes. If you have need, call me."

"Of course, but I scarcely think that my shift will be anything like so active as yours."

There was a letter in-queue from Trader Gordon Arbuthnot.

In the first section of the letter, Trader Arbuthnot represented himself as incoming on Master Trader yos'Galan's instruction. In accordance with those instructions, he would arrive prepared to establish a proper Tree-and-Dragon Family business and trade hub. However, as the commercial situation at Tinsori Light was yet to be determined, he would be bringing only the basic trade kit with him, which meant that he had pods available. Would Light Keeper yos'Phelium be so good as to send him a list of those items the station would find useful? These items were not to be limited to tools and materials, but ought also to include foodstuffs, comfort, and even luxury items. There was, Trader Arbuthnot insisted, ample room available.

Jen Sin stopped, closed his eyes, opened them, and reread that section. A list of desired items? And he was not to stint himself. He scarcely knew—

His eye fell on the wrapper from Lorith's ration bar, and the covered mug, awaiting cleanup. With the flick of a finger he had opened a notetaker in the corner of the screen and typed *hydroponics*, followed by a list of such foods as might be gotten out of the caf unit on a Scout ship. He would need to ask the others, find what things might ease their shifts, favored foodstuffs, teas—wine?

He closed his eyes. Gods, for a glass of wine.

Well.

He opened his eyes with a sigh and put his attention on the second section of Trader Arbuthnot's letter.

Here, the tone changed. He was begged to believe his Cousin Gordy entirely at his service, and very eager to make his acquaintance. He was asked if, perhaps, he played counterchance, or possibly piket, and in the next sentence was told that Cousin Gordy would bring a short pallet of amusements, including books, music, and the furnishings of a small gym.

"It appears we are well in hand," he murmured, finishing the letter with some bemusement.

"Light Keeper," Tocohl said, "I have information regarding the ongoing security of the station."

He raised his eyebrows, spun his chair, and leaned back so that he might look at the ceiling speaker.

"Almost, you relieve me," he said. "Speak."

"Yes," Tocohl said. "This concerns the Lyre Institute."

"It occurs to me that the Lyre Institute is occupying a great deal of our time," he commented. "Surely, they are out of proportion."

"Possibly so," Tocohl said, sounding wry. "I have discussed the situation with Mentor Jones, who advises me to put it before you."

"Then by all means," Jen Sin said cordially, "place the matter before me."

"*Spiral Dance*, Clarence O'Berin, pilot in charge, coming in to A Level Bay Five. Clear me, Station?"

Jen Sin looked up from his list-making, to the station screens.

"*Spiral Dance*?" he said aloud to no one, and reached for the magnification controls.

"*Spiral Dance* cleared for docking, per light keeper's assignment, Bay Five A Level." That voice was neither Tocohl nor the former Tinsori Light—uninflected, but not unpleasant. Perhaps Seignur Veeoni had made adjustments.

Given the state of her hull, the approaching ship had seen hard, unprofitable work. The essentials were covered, and the stats screen reported her entirely able, but the "smart work," as Melia had been wont to call it, had been left too long to fend for itself.

Jen Sin increased the magnification again, and there was the name plate rendered in Old Universal, the same language in which the earliest entries in Korval's Diaries were written: SPIRAL DANCE, no home port designated.

It was the very ship out of old stories told 'round the clan:

the hero left behind, to taunt the Enemy and draw their eye so that the Migration might succeed.

And it had arrived at Tinsori Light in *Bechimo*'s hold.

Questions—he had *many* questions.

"You are the light keeper, you know," he said aloud. "Questions are once again your business."

Was it not said truly that, *Once a Scout, always a Scout*? A Scout who had no questions was dead.

He turned to his work screen, saved the list and Trader Arbuthnot's letter for later, rose, and headed down to the docks.

Dock A

• • • • • • • •

IT WAS AN ELDER PILOT WHO EXITED *SPIRAL DANCE*, LEAN AND dangerous, never minding the greying red hair. He nodded when he spied Jen Sin waiting at the end of the ramp, and continued, unchecked and unhurried, until he reached the proper distance to offer a bow of introduction.

It was quite a credible bow, proper in mode and in tempo. After he had straightened, he introduced himself in perfectly intelligible Liaden in the mode of lesser to greater, which was reaching high, indeed.

"Clarence O'Berin, first class pilot, executive officer, *Bechimo*, under Captain Theo Waitley."

Jen Sin inclined, accepting the courtesy and the information from the giddy height of his *melant'i* as an administrator.

"Jen Sin yos'Phelium, light keeper," he murmured. "Pilot. We are well met."

"Is there a service I might be honored to perform for you?" inquired Clarence O'Berin.

Jen Sin looked up, considering the properly bland face, and the bold blue eyes. He had not received files on Cousin Theo's crew beyond the sparse list of personnel the ship had itself provided. It was plain for all to see that Clarence O'Berin was Terran. Where he had come by his precise manners was, perhaps, a question for another hour. He had others before it.

"You might, if it is possible, descend somewhat from the highest branches. I have been long away from proper society, and even with daily practice was never considered more than passingly apt."

Clarence O'Berin's lips twitched; his blue eyes gleamed.

"May a comrade offer assistance?" he asked, again in proper mode. Jen Sin felt his shoulders relax, even as his breath caught.

It had been . . . a very long time since he had been addressed as anyone's comrade.

"Perhaps you may," he said, in the same mode. He used his chin to point at the ship behind Clarence's shoulder.

"That is a ship out of legend. The clan's own records show that it was lost, many years ago."

"The same was said of you," said Clarence O'Berin. "Records are not always accurate."

"That is very true. I only wonder how she happened to come into *Bechimo*'s hold."

The pilot half-turned on the ramp, and looked up at *Spiral Dance*, consideringly.

"Just this last time," he said, "she brought us absent crew. The first time—was a stretch of probability, but that's what it is, to fly with Captain Theo."

Jen Sin tipped his head.

"Captain Theo is prone to unlikely events?"

"More so than some," Clarence said. "Her father was a bit of a caution, and his children outstrip him."

"I wonder you remain at such a chancy berth," Jen Sin said, not quite in jest.

Clarence turned, a full Terran grin on his face.

"I'd be bored anywhere else," he said.

Jen Sin smiled. "I understand, I think. May I ask for a tour of *Spiral Dance*?"

"Surely you might, but I'm not the one to grant permission."

"Of course. I will petition the captain," Jen Sin said, startled at how sharp his disappointment was.

"You might ask her now, if you've a mind to it," Clarence said, ambling the rest of the way down the ramp. "Come aboard *Bechimo*, if you are at liberty. I baked cookies last shift, there's tea—and Captain Theo, who, if I recall it correctly, had something she wanted to discuss with you."

He hit the dock, and turned toward *Bechimo*.

It was entirely civilized—tea and cookies. But, tea and cookies had no place in a universe where a man was murdered at whim, dozens of times, brought back to life—no! Copied and set loose, thinking himself the original, repaired and reawakened.

He took a hard breath, unaware that he stood rooted to the dock until Clarence O'Berin turned to look back at him.

"Are ye well then, laddie?" His voice was softer in Terran, the words lilting.

Jen Sin blinked his eyes clear of a sudden mist, and made himself move, to walk down the dock to the taller pilot's side.

"I am well, thank you," he said in his much less pleasing Terran. "Only, it has been—a long shift."

Sharp blue eyes considered him, even as another easy grin appeared. "So it has, now that you say it!" Clarence exclaimed, returning to Comrade mode. "Come aboard and rest while I put that snack together."

Old Core

THEY HAD FILLED TWO SLEDS WITH THE MATERIAL CLEARED from the old core's top chamber. Win Ton and Kara had perforce led this expedition, working steadily after they lowered the remote into the deep core.

When Chernak brought the second sled back, Kara declared a tea break and the three of them went out into the access hall to open the box Clarence had packed for them.

Win Ton got out the vacuum bottle and mugs while Kara opened the pack of handwiches, and Chernak leaned against the wall, frowning at the images the remote had uploaded to the tablet.

"I was too large to work in that space before I came out of creche," she said, accepting a handwich with a nod.

"Yes, but we had known that," Win Ton said, pouring tea. "Kara and I are for the deep regions, after the upper room is cleared."

"As for that..." Chernak pushed away from the wall and stalked back into the core, tablet in one hand, handwich in the other.

Win Ton held out a mug of tea.

Kara accepted it, and gave him a handwich.

Both settled cross-legged on the deck and fell to. Kara had taken off her protective headgear, and her hair, loosened from the knot on top of her head, fell in damp snarls to her shoulders. Except for the area protected by the work glasses, her face was grimy.

Win Ton sighed and sipped tea, certain he presented no more beguiling a picture.

"This is rather daunting," Kara said. She had the second tablet balanced on her knee, and was bent over it. "There may not be room for two of *us*."

"May I see?" Win Ton asked, extending a hand. She surrendered the tablet, and took up her mug while he frowned at the screen in his turn.

"We might manage it," he said, "if we each go to a side and clear to the center." He squinted at the image, which was dark, even given the remote's lights.

"There is debris underfoot, which will have to be cleared. If I go down first, and the pulley lowered behind me—"

"I can do it," Chernak announced, arriving largely, handwich gone, and tablet in her belt.

"Do what, one wonders," Kara said, pointing at the mug that had been filled for her.

Chernak came down onto her haunches, picked up the mug and sipped.

"It was agreed that the top floor would be cleared first, then the second. How, if they were to be cleared simultaneously? You have made enough room that I can finish the upper chamber. If you will both take the under-level, I will operate the pulley and clear what is left above. We might then complete the mission ahead of schedule."

"I will certainly welcome the end of this chore," Kara said, holding her mug out. Win Ton hefted the bottle and poured tea.

"We will not finish today," he said, refreshing his own mug, while Chernak reached to the pack and liberated another handwich. "However, we might finish tomorrow, instead of the day after."

"I received the impression that soonest done was the preference," Kara murmured.

"As I did."

Win Ton returned his attention to the tablet.

"Allow me the honor of descending first and clearing the space beneath the hatch, around the ladder. When there is sufficient room for Kara to join me, we will set lights, so that we may see what stands before us." He glanced at each of his companions in turn. "Is that agreeable?"

"I'm agreed," Kara told him, draining her mug. She stood, and pointed a stern finger down at the opened pack.

"Chernak, there is a handwich left, and it is yours. We cannot have you fainting from want."

"Thank you."

Chernak grabbed it up and rose to her feet.

Win Ton repacked the tea things and rose, not quite so nimbly as he might once have done, and the three of them went back into the core.

Bechimo
Dock A

• • • • • • • •

"O'BERIN IN!" CLARENCE CALLED AS THEY CLEARED THE HATCH. "*Bechimo*, let Captain Theo know I have the light keeper, and we're in the galley, awaiting her pleasure."

"Welcome back, Clarence. Light Keeper yos'Phelium, it is an honor." The voice was mellow and unflustered, in the mode of House to Guest. It might have been the pilot on duty, greeting them from the bridge.

"Thank you. It is an honor to be aboard," he answered, and followed Clarence down a clean, well-lit corridor, past a number of sealed doors and into a spacious galley. There were stools and tables, a screen set in one wall—blank at the moment—and a counter bearing various drink dispensers. Past that was a corner, beyond which must be the kitchen.

"Pray find a comfortable place," Clarence said, over his shoulder as he went past the counter. "I will bring refreshments momentarily."

Jen Sin gazed about him, soothed by the order, by the promise of people made by the grouped tables and chairs. It recalled the back kitchen at Jelaza Kazone, where one might meet a cousin at almost any hour, foraging a snack, preparing a meal, bent over a book, or playing a game of cards.

His breath caught again, and he pushed the memory aside. His host had bade him be comfortable. The least he could do was—

There was motion at the corner of his eye, near floor level.

He turned, carefully, looking down—at an orange-and-white cat, strolling, insouciant, into the galley.

"Now," he said, recalling *Bechimo*'s crew list. "Are you Grakow, or are you Paizel?"

"Orange-and-white's Paizel," Clarence called from the kitchen. "Striped-and-grey's Grakow."

"Paizel, then," Jen Sin said. "I am pleased to meet you."

He dropped lightly to one knee, and offered a respectful forefinger. Paizel considered the digit for a long, unblinking moment, then stepped forward for a courteous sniff, followed by a long cheek rub down to the wrist.

"Everything that is gentle," Jen Sin murmured. "My thanks to you for a graceful greeting."

Paizel yawned, displaying a wealth of tiny, sharp teeth, and a dainty pink tongue, before strolling away. Jen Sin rose, went to the table nearest the screen, and swung up onto a stool.

"This will get us started." Clarence appeared, bearing a tray. "Tell me if you are in need of something more substantial."

He set out a teapot, three cups and three small plates, then two larger plates—one filled with an assortment of small iced cakes, the second holding a quantity of small yellow muffins. Putting the empty tray on the next table, Clarence poured tea into two cups, putting the first by Jen Sin's hand, and keeping the other for himself as he settled onto a stool.

Jen Sin picked up his cup, and sipped, as common courtesy demanded, and was pleasantly surprised to find proper Liaden tea. He was no pretender to sophistication, now less than ever, and dared not hazard a guess as to the leaf, but—

"The tea is well chosen," he murmured. "I thank you."

"Captain Theo's favored blend," Clarence answered. He put his cup aside and gestured at the first plate.

"These *chernubia* are said by Win Ton and Kara of our crew to be *much like home.* These"—a nod at the second plate—"are maize buttons, a delicacy from the captain's home."

"They are beautiful," Jen Sin said, sincerely. "And you are the baker?"

"Man's gotta have a hobby or six to keep him sane," Clarence said in Terran. "Try what you will, but I'll just say if you want to sample the maize buttons, you'd better do that before the captain gets here and they disappear."

Jen Sin smiled. "I am fairly warned," he said, and took one of the yellow muffins onto his plate, and a *chernubia* iced in blue.

The maize button was surprisingly sweet, slightly gritty, and oddly compelling. Jen Sin sipped his tea and ate the *chernubia*, which reminded him of endless hours at receptions, being polite to people one scarcely knew.

"You are the master of your hobby, I think," he said.

Clarence grinned, but shook his head. "With baking, there's always something else to learn. More tea?"

"Yes, I thank you."

His cup was scarcely refilled when the mellow voice said, "Captain Waitley is approaching the galley."

"Well, there," Clarence said, and filled the third cup before refreshing his own. The sound of brisk footsteps preceded her somewhat down the corridor, and his cousin Theo was with them, wearing ship togs. Her hair was still unruly and unbound, and her pale cheeks showed pink.

"Cousin Jen Sin," she said in Terran, sounding quite merry. "I see Clarence is taking good care of you."

"Clarence is taking excellent care of me," he answered, which was the truth. Recalling his host's warning, he put another maize button on his plate.

Theo grinned.

"My reputation precedes me," she said, slipping onto a stool, and picking up the cup that had been poured for her.

She closed her eyes, and breathed in the steam; sipped and sighed.

Putting the cup aside, she transferred a single maize button from the large plate to her small one, and looked to Jen Sin.

"Which language are you most comfortable in?"

It was a courteous question, though it had an unintended point. Of late, his most comfortable language was the Old Universal dialect the Light had taught him prior to his first awakening, that he and Lorith had spoken between themselves for all of their time together.

"In fact, I am not much accustomed to speaking," he said, which was a gentler truth. "I am well enough in Terran. If you would rather Liaden, I beg you will do as Clarence and I have done, and go no higher than Comrade." He picked up his teacup and looked at her. "Trade lacks nuance."

"It does," she agreed. "Liaden, then. I need the practice."

She ate her maize button, and put another on her plate.

"I'm glad Clarence brought you in for a snack. I have a concept to put before you."

He smiled at her. "Clarence brought me in because I have something to ask you," he said. "Thus far, we are in Balance. What will you ask?"

"When my crew was talking over how best to get needed tasks done, it was mentioned that Seignur Veeoni has ties to the research station. It was thought that they might lend a work boat, if she asked on our behalf. Could you approach her on that topic?"

The mode was Comrade, and the accent acceptable. But Theo had spoken true, Jen Sin thought; she needed practice.

He sipped tea.

"That is an excellent notion, Cousin, I thank you. I will approach the researcher."

"It is not my notion. You may thank Stost, when next you see him."

"I shall make it an object," he assured her.

Theo put another maize button on her plate.

"Now, you," she said.

"As I think on it," he confessed, "I find that I have two topics. The first is that our cousin Gordy, Trader Arbuthnot, has pod space available and proposes to provide the station with necessities and comforts, if only we will send him a list. I have the task in hand, and wonder if there is something you may require, a-ship, or would wish to see on-station."

Theo sat up straight.

"We should have gone to Edmonton Beacon, after all!" she said, in sharp Terran. "Jen Sin, I'm sorry. We did talk about it, but decided not to!"

"Certainly, the captain decides the ship's necessities," he murmured, which was nothing more than a play for time, while he tried to parse what Edmonton Beacon should have to do with Tinsori Light.

"I have been studying the new maps, but am not yet fluent. Edmonton Beacon, I do not—no, I *do* recall! Did they indeed build that?"

"Not only the Beacon, but six sister stations," Clarence told him, in Comrade. "Of varying degrees of repute."

"The point is," Theo interrupted, still speaking Terran, "we could've diverted, and brought you supplies! Shan told us to come quick, so we went with that. But he might've expected—"

"Theo," the mellow voice said, soothingly, from a ceiling

speaker, "we brought other necessities. It is *why* the master trader sent us quickly."

"What necessities?" she demanded.

"Ourselves," the voice answered. "The crew, the cats, the norbear ambassador, the Tree—"

"*Bechimo*," another voice said. Jen Sin glanced to one side, and saw that the screen was now active, showing a person in a leather jacket much like his own in style. Seeing he was observed, the pilot grinned and inclined his head. "Myself, and *Spiral Dance*. Good shift to you, Light Keeper. I am Comm Officer Joyita. You—are not surprised."

"I did speak to Tocohl—or she to me," Jen Sin said. "She is grateful to you and to *Bechimo* for your assistance."

"We're pleased to share our expertise," Joyita said.

"A functioning station can only benefit all," *Bechimo* added.

"I wonder," Joyita said, "if I might ask a question."

Jen Sin looked to him. "Ask."

"Thank you. I've been speaking with Seignur Veeoni regarding station architecture. She tells me that the question of whether the station will be designed for sentience is not hers to make, but sits with Delm Korval."

Jen Sin spun the stool in order to face Joyita more fully.

"Tocohl has stated her intention to administer the station."

"Tocohl was not designed to be a station," *Bechimo* said. "We don't doubt that she is perfectly capable of *administering* the station—as you are, Light Keeper. But, she cannot *be* Station—no more than you can."

He considered that.

"There will be an interface, is that your meaning?"

Joyita smiled. "Exactly."

"So the question arises—which is more efficient: a capable administrator, at a small distance, or one who *is* the system." He reached for his cup, weighing light keeper's *melant'i*, estimating its limits. The decision *could* be made to fit within his honor, and done was done. He was startled, on examining the question, to find a decided preference for sentience—which reminded him that his judgment regarding such things was compromised.

He looked to Joyita.

"Seignur Veeoni is correct—the decision lies with Korval. I will put it before the delm."

Joyita inclined his head.

"Thank you, Light Keeper."

The phrase was in Terran, and he went into that language for the proper response.

"You are welcome. Thank you for bringing the matter to my attention."

He turned back to Theo, who was pouring herself more tea. There was a maize button on her plate.

"Do I hear that you have a Tree onboard?" Jen Sin asked.

She nodded. "It gave me the pod for you."

"You may be interested to know," Clarence added, in Comrade, "that the Tree we have onboard was originally on *Spiral Dance*, lashed to the copilot's chair."

Jen Sin stared.

"*That* Tree?"

"Exactly that Tree," Clarence assured him, and turned to Theo, shifting into Terran. "Pilot Jen Sin would like a tour of *Spiral Dance*. Told him that was the captain's decision."

"Of course he can have a tour," Theo said. "Though the best guides would be Chernak and Stost."

She looked at Jen Sin. "They're contemporaries," she explained.

He did *not* blink, though perhaps his fingers tightened slightly around the cup. Captain Theo, he reminded himself, was prone to unlikely events.

He drank off what was left of his tea.

"I would welcome such experts as my guides," he said, calmly.

"We'll make sure it happens. Is there anything else we can—"

She turned her head.

The creature entering the galley with a rolling gait was *not* a cat.

"Hevelin," Theo said, her tone equal parts fondness and resignation.

"This is the norbear ambassador?" Jen Sin asked.

"That's right. Don't let him bully you."

The norbear came directly to the table, and Theo bent down to lift him into her lap.

"I saved half a maize button for you," she said, putting the bit into the questing hand-paw.

Jen Sin received the impression that half a button was the least she could do, with echoes of fondness and resignation.

Despite the comment, the treat was quickly gone, and Jen Sin found himself the object of study.

He had no direct experience of norbears. Still, it behooved a light keeper to be courteous to an ambassador. He inclined his head.

"Ambassador Hevelin, I am honored."

The norbear leaned forward, and Theo put her hand around his paunch to steady him as he extended a paw and gently patted Jen Sin on the wrist. He received the impression of greenery, and a breeze sweetened by flowers. A safe bower, protected by wise and loving elders...

He felt tears start, and blinked them away, took a breath—

"Light Keeper, Tocohl calls," Joyita said. "Ships are entering Tinsori space. They request docking."

Old Core

....

THEY SET UP THE MAG-LIGHTING, THROWING THEM AGAINST THE walls and ceiling, and setting them to *ultra-bright.*

"This," Kara said, staring around at the wealth of hard-edged black shadows thus produced, "is not particularly festive."

"In fact, it's actively alarming," Win Ton answered, squinting against the glare. "How if we lower the intensity?"

Kara had charge of the key; she touched it, dropping the light level to *bright.*

"Somewhat less dire," he judged. "What does one more reduction gain us?"

Another touch on the key, to *work-normal.*

"The shadows are still with us," Kara observed.

"True, but they no longer appear bloodthirsty."

"Any light source that would abolish the shadows," *Bechimo* said from the remote patiently standing by, "would harm your eyes."

"Well, there we are, then," Kara said, putting the light-key in her pocket. "Let us by all means be safe."

"Kara, are you nervous?" *Bechimo* asked. "I detect no dangerous objects or persons within the space."

"Thank gods for that," Win Ton said, before Kara could deny being nervous too sharply, and *Bechimo* felt compelled to correct her. "The space is disconcerting enough without adding in active danger." He turned to Kara. "Shall we work from the center or the corners?"

"The center," she said, spinning slowly on a heel, her shadow flickering over the broken racks and scattered tiles that made moving in this dark, cramped space treacherous.

"This must have been a warren even before it was damaged," she said. "Do you think they used children as techs?"

"Remotes, more likely," Win Ton said. "Though we're told Mentor Jones was down here before the event."

"Moving very carefully, I'll warrant," Kara said, stopping her spin as she came to face him again. "Well. Soonest begun, soonest done, as Theo would no doubt remind us. Let us get the pulleys in place."

Win Ton nodded, touching the comm on his belt.

"Chernak," he said, looking up to the tall, very dark shadow at the top of the access tube. "Please lower the first pulley."

Conditions were not agreeable. In addition to being cramped even for two average-sized Liadens to work in, the core was also arid, and too warm, even before they began to exert themselves.

Despite the insalubrious conditions, however, the work went quickly. Win Ton and Kara made a team, while *Bechimo*'s remote gathered up the smaller broken pieces of tile, and metal shred.

"Tongstele," Kara said, as they finished loading the bin, and signaled Chernak to bring the pulley up. "What could have shredded tongstele?"

"Clearly, the *event*, the details of which Clan Korval feels would distress us."

"Shredded tongstele," Kara said firmly, "*is* distressing."

"Yes," Win Ton agreed, watching the bin as it ascended. "It is."

They broke for tea in the chamber above, where Chernak had done wonders, then descended again to the deep core.

"I have spoken at length with Ren Stryker," *Bechimo* said, via his remote. "He is a very interesting person. I sent him my analysis of the materials we are clearing, and he ran it through his databases. He is confident that he can process what we give him, and render it, as he has it, more useful to present need."

Kara sighed.

"Excellent. Useful to present need. Very good."

They were clearing the far corners and looking forward to a return to the ship, showers, and some rest, when a sound tickled the edge of Win Ton's ear. He paused, head up, half in doubt—

"What is it?" Kara asked, softly.

He shook his head, actively listening, as Scouts were trained to do.

"An . . . unusual . . . sound," he murmured, straightening further and beginning to scan the immediate area. The sound came again—a chirp, a scrape . . . a soft rustling.

"There," he murmured, tipping his head toward a dark upper corner. "It sounds like—"

A segment of darkness tumbled free, wings slicing light and shadow, skimming along the wall and disappearing up the access tube.

"An avian," Win Ton finished.

Bechimo
Dock A

....

JEN SIN LOOKED TO THEO, WHO GAVE HIM A NOD.

"We can patch you through, if you want."

"It would be a kindness," he answered, and heard Clarence snort lightly.

"No need to be running from one end of the station to the other because ships are comin' in," he said, sliding off the stool. "I'll make some more tea, laddie. You just sit there and take care of bidness."

"Don't leave without seeing me again," Theo said, straightening from having put the norbear on the floor. "I've got a second question, too." She snatched the last maize button off the platter and left, Hevelin with her.

Jen Sin turned to the screen and met Joyita's dark, speculative gaze.

"Comm Officer," he said gently. "Will you give me a private line to Tocohl, and access to the public bands?"

"Certainly, Light Keeper. Would you also like visual?"

"Yes, if it can be arranged without discommoding you."

"Easily arranged," Joyita assured him with a faint smile. "Patching through to Tocohl."

The screen blanked.

"Jen Sin?"

"Tocohl. I hear we have ships inbound. What is their number and kind?"

"Three in number, and—Loopers, out of Hacienda Estrella at Edmonton Beacon, answering the Traveler's Aid Notice from Carresens-Denobli. They are carrying raw materials, specialized equipment, and standard rescue kits."

The screen flickered and reformed in three panels. Largest

was the approach space visual. Tiled on the right, one over the other, were the status and analytics screens. He inclined his head in thanks, even as he tried to unknot Tocohl's information.

Edmonton Beacon again—but, then, it would be their nearest neighbor of any note.

The Carresens, though...

Jen Sin took a moment to center himself.

Yes, very good. The Carresens were a Terran shipbuilding association. The Denoblis were a trading family. They would seem to have married their interests together since the last time he had put his attention on either. In fact, the last he had heard, the Carresens had been involved in a shipbuilding project with the Uncle, intending to—

He held up a hand, murmuring, "Mute, please, Comm Officer."

"Muted."

"*Bechimo.* These ships. Do they arrive on your behalf?"

"At some point, I would be interested in learning how you concluded that they might be, but for now—no, Light Keeper. They are not here because I am—family. I am specifically *not* family."

"Thank you. Unmute, please, Comm Officer."

"Done."

"Tocohl, what is Korval's association with the Carresens-Denoblis?"

"Master Trader yos'Galan, representing Tree-and-Dragon Family, has recently entered into a limited partnership with the Carresens-Denobli Syndicate. It's in the trade news."

Jen Sin raised an eyebrow.

"Do we take the trade news?"

"Subscriptions are only now beginning to arrive," she said. "Shall I share them with you?"

"Of your kindness. In the meanwhile, I will speak with these gentles and ascertain their best docking. Will you please monitor?"

"Yes."

The public band was full of chatter.

Jen Sin sipped from the cup of tea Clarence had left at his elbow, and... listened.

"Is that Ren Stryker I'm seeing?" an over-exuberant voice emanating from *Rodger Dodger* asked. "Hey, Ren! It's Korlu. Looks like we're gonna be working together again!"

"Korlu Fenchile, I look forward to continuing our working relationship. Have you brought materials?"

"Material anna team, too, Big Guy! *Karil* over there's all podded out with supplies and 'quipment. There's more comin'; we was just sittin' closest the door."

"*Karil*, ship and crew, I am Ren Stryker and pleased to make your acquaintance."

"Pleased to meet you, Ren Stryker," a cool voice answered. "I am Jaileen Uldra-Joenz, captain. Also aboard're Cargo Master Norse Uldra-Joenz, and copilot Tif Uldra-Joenz. We look forward to building a good working relationship with you."

"Hey, Ren, Zandi Perez here! We did that job together over at Cracked Gate, maybe you remember? How're we set for raw stuff here?"

"Zandi Perez, I remember our work together with pleasure! Material is being gathered on-station. Analysis indicates that I will be able to process it usefully. It will need to be brought to me."

"No worries, there! We'll ferry the stuff out to you."

"Open band, please," Jen Sin murmured, putting the teacup aside.

"Band open," Joyita said.

"This is Jen Sin yos'Phelium, Light Keeper. Welcome to Tinsori Light Station. Ren Stryker, I believe I am remiss in saying that I look forward to working with you."

"Thank you!" Ren Stryker said, audibly pleased. "I hope we find mutual pleasure in our work, Light Keeper."

"I am certain that we shall. Will the incoming ships acquaint me with your necessities, so that I may assign the most useful dockings?"

"Right," came the cool voice of Captain Uldra-Joenz. "*Karil* needs an unload zone. We're carrying 'quipment, delicates, and material specifically for the station."

"*Rodger Dodger*, Korlu Fenchile, job boss. Us an' *Crinolyn*'re manufactory crew. We'll be putting up on Ren, 'less he's got an objection, which I hope he won't 'cause he's a fine host. Knows just how we like things. If there's an objection, we'll beg station space and commute, but we don't want to strain overworked and understaffed systems. We're here to help, Light Keeper, not to get in the way."

"Thank you," Jen Sin said.

There was a moment of empty air before Job Boss Fenchile replied. "Sorry, there. Just chattin' with *Karil.* Us'll come in near her, if that'll work with your 'rangements, Keeper. She's podded out, like you see, and we can do the unloading. 'less you'd rather your crew handle it?"

Boss Fenchile, thought Jen Sin, knew perfectly well that there was no station crew available to handle *Karil*'s unloading. The phrasing suggested that he had worked with—or around—Liaden administrators before, and had become adept at avoiding insult.

"Station staff is limited," he said evenly. "It will be helpful to have your crew tend to the unloading. We have some quarters available, if crew would care to stay on-station until it is time to relocate."

"We'll take that under advisement," Boss Fenchile said easily. "First things first, is what I'm thinking. Where d'you want us?"

A schematic of the station opened in a fourth tile, at the bottom of the screen. Jen Sin raised his hand, fingers signing *good bounce*, while he considered, glanced at the stats, did the math...

"Level B, direct access," he said. "Docks one, two, three. *Karil* on three, *Rodger Dodger* on two, *Crinolyn* on one. Station will guide you in."

"That's a go, then," Boss Fenchile said. "Thank'ee, sir. Looking forward to working with you."

"And I, with you. yos'Phelium out."

• • • ✵ • • •

Theo was in the pilot's chair, Hevelin in her lap, when Clarence hit the bridge, carrying two mugs. She took hers with a nod of thanks, eyes on the screen. The comm was on, and the chatter off the public bands filled the bridge.

Clarence sat in the copilot's chair and sipped his tea.

"Our lad Ren Stryker has a wide circle of acquaintance," he commented.

"I guess he's easy to work with, like they're all saying," Theo answered.

"I have spoken to Ren Stryker," *Bechimo* said. "He is an accommodating person, who takes pleasure in helping to repair what is broken."

Theo nodded, and sipped, and listened while Jen Sin sorted the incoming traffic out. Calm and efficient, she thought, which was a good thing in a station master. It niggled at her, that he was so tired, so—*some*thing.

She spun her chair to face Clarence.

"What's your—" she began, but Joyita interrupted her.

"Incoming from Win Ton."

Theo caught her breath.

"Put him through," she said. "And kill the chatter."

"We are all well," Win Ton said first, which helped with her breath. "I merely wish to report an anomaly. Our work startled an avian inside the deep core."

Theo frowned.

"An . . . avian. A bird? What's a *bird* doing down in the old core?"

"An excellent question. You see why we felt compelled to share it."

Theo sighed.

"So where is the bird now, and is it dangerous?"

"The bird," Win Ton answered, "flew up and out of the access tube, thence through the open door into the hall."

"So it's in the station proper. Is it dangerous?"

"No," *Bechimo* stated. "The remote's scans recognized no dangerous objects or organics."

"That's no dangerous objects and no dangerous organics?" Theo asked. "Or no organics?"

Bechimo was silent, then said, positively, "No organics other than crew accounted for."

"We have," Win Ton said, "alerted Station to the event, and shared what data we have. Chernak has called Stost in to assist in searching the upper room. I will rejoin Kara and the remote in the deep core, to look for additional avians there, unless the captain has other orders."

Theo closed her eyes, sucked in a deep breath and blew it out.

"Continue the search for . . . additional avians," she said slowly. "If you find anything else, don't engage, just—leave, locking all hatches behind you—and come home."

"Yes," Win Ton said, and the line went dead.

Theo met Clarence's eye.

"Birds," she said.

"Bird," he corrected. "No percentage in borrowing more trouble than we've got."

"Light Keeper yos'Phelium approaches the bridge, at the captain's request," *Bechimo* said.

Theo finished her tea and put the mug in the holder. The door opened and Jen Sin walked two silent steps onto the bridge before he stopped, head tipped to one side, black eyes narrowed as he considered first Theo, then Clarence.

"Forgive me," he said slowly, "is something amiss?"

Theo shifted, and put Hevelin on the floor. He walked over to Clarence, who lifted him to a knee.

"My crew disturbed a bird while they were cleaning out the old core," Theo said. "It escaped into the station proper."

"Ah," Jen Sin said.

Theo glared at him.

"There was a *bird* inside the deepest, most secure place on this station," she repeated.

Jen Sin raised his hands, showing empty palms.

"Yes, I heard. Forgive my lack of appropriate consternation. Tinsori Light is not a regular environment. Strange things happen here. The presence of a bird—" He paused, met her eyes.

"Organic?"

"Inorganic," she said.

He moved his shoulders.

"Then we have the likeliest answer. There are station bots, on their own systems. Tocohl found and deactivated all but the required cleaning and maintenance units when she brought the station under her control. However, it would not be at all remarkable if one or two had been missed, especially in the higher security areas."

"Like the core," Theo said.

He inclined from the waist, very slightly. "As you say."

Theo stared at him, then sighed, *fuffing* her bangs out of her eyes.

"So," she said, "no worries?"

"I would not venture so far," he said seriously. "In all truth, I thought that I had seen a bird a few shifts back, in another part of the station. I thought it a phantom, but it seems now as if it has substance. In that wise, I think that we may depend upon Tocohl to locate it and either take it off-line, or reassign it to its proper area." He paused.

"Your crew has not taken harm?"

"Just startled. They're surveying the core up and down for anything else . . . irregular before it surprises them."

"Very wise."

He raised his hands slightly. "I believe you said that you had a second question, Cousin. How may I serve you?"

"I'd like a look at the seals from the inside, to see if there's anything we can do to reinforce them, if needed." She glanced over her shoulder at the screens. "With this crew incoming, though—"

"They will be some while yet getting in," Jen Sin said. "After they are in, I expect we will be in a state of confusion. I am able to escort you to the nearer seal now, if that is convenient."

Theo blinked.

"It's convenient. Let me get my jacket."

Shielded Workroom

TOLLY LEANED BACK IN HIS CHAIR AND STRETCHED, ARMS OVERhead.

"I think that's a very efficient piece of code right there," he said to Tocohl, who had hovered, silent and doubtless with her attention on other bidness while he finished his last pass through the killware program.

"Oughta get the job done with no fuss, and deliver a very strong message to Director Ling, who'll doubtless think twice the next time he's tempted to impugn the honor of a good, capable ship."

Tocohl turned slightly.

"Do you think he will?"

"What—think twice? Could be he might. But only to be sure in his own mind that the new, improved reporting-in protocol he'll have had designed is everything it should be."

"Do you think this is a useless exercise?"

Tolly glanced down at the screen and the deadly little program displayed there.

"Useless? No. The Directors aren't used to being challenged. Something like this will put them off-balance. People who are off-balance make mistakes."

He raised an eyebrow, deliberately whimsical.

"You unnerstan', now, if the universe was ordered to my preferences, there'd be no Lyre Institute for Exceptional Children, if it meant bombing four planets into dust."

"Surely there are innocents—"

"Surely there are—an' they're all like me—manufactured humans programmed to do what they're directed to do."

He stopped, aware that he was breathing hard; took a deep breath—and another.

"Sorry," he said pulling up a grin. "Apparently I've got some opinions on the topic."

"There were constraints on Inki's actions and she knew precisely what they were," Tocohl said, sternly. "She gave warning when they were about to be activated, and did what she could to mitigate the worst outcomes. She was her own person, Mentor."

He bowed his head briefly.

"You're right. Inki was herself, and she'd figured out a way to cheat the Directors, just a little here and there. I analyzed some of her work, and I'm still not sure how she did it."

"You, yourself, *broke* programming." Tocohl wasn't done with him yet, which would teach him to have hotheaded opinions.

"Twice," he agreed, keeping his voice mild. "Got lucky."

He rose, and patted the remote.

"If we're agreed that this is the best we can do, then the next step is send it to Jen Sin. Are we agreed?"

"Yes," Tocohl said crisply. "We are agreed."

"Will you please take care of delivering it to Light Keeper yos'Phelium, and answering any questions he might have? I'll stand ready, too, but it's largely your work."

"Yes," she said again. "I will inform the light keeper and answer any questions."

"Good. Thank you. I'm going down to see if there's any little thing I can do for Seignur Veeoni."

Tolly heard the sound at the first cross-hall, and paused, listening.

It sounded like a station jitney, the only catch being that there weren't any jitneys on Tinsori Station.

He put himself back against the wall, and waited not too long before it appeared from the right—a jitney, pale blue, with a stylized crystal on the front bumper, and *Crystal Energy Systems* swirled in darker blue down the side.

Haz was driving.

"Nice ride!" he said admiringly, as she came to a halt beside him. "Where was it stashed?"

"In Seignur Veeoni's workroom," Haz said.

"'Course it was. I was just headed in to see if there was anything I could do for her, but maybe not, if she's letting you go off joyriding."

"The situation is somewhat more complicated. Stost was called away to assist with the clearing of the core, as an anomaly was discovered."

Tolly frowned. "What kind of an anomaly?"

"It would appear that the work in the lower core disturbed an avian, which in turn disturbed the workers. They have put work aside until they have thoroughly searched, and located any other surprises."

"Sounds reasonable—I'm assuming one of the Old Light's indie system protectors?"

"Or watcher, yes. Seignur Veeoni accepted the necessity of immediately locating any more devices, and Stost was released. I am relieved of rack-building to run an errand for her."

"Where to?"

"A room near the breach. Seignur Veeoni has been studying station schematics, and this activity has caused her to wonder if there might not be something useful stored there."

"And she sent you instead of coming herself? What if whatever it is objects to being found?"

"I am informed that this is unlikely." She looked at him owlishly.

Tolly snorted and came away from the wall.

"Mind company?"

She indicated the vacant not-quite-half of the driver's bench.

"You are welcome. There are seats in the back, if this is not enough room."

"Plenty o'room," Tolly said stoutly, and swung aboard, settling his hip firmly against hers.

Haz stiffened slightly, and he drew a careful breath, remembering that the new ties were still a-building, and fragile.

"If I'm crowding the pilot, say so, and I'll sit in back," he said gently.

"No," she said, her voice breathless, like Haz's voice never was. "It is—pleasing to have you close."

"Good. It's pleasing to have you close," he answered, still gentle, and slanted a grin up into her face.

"How fast does this thing go?"

"We ought to find that out, in case we are needed quickly," she said seriously, and touched the switch.

Bechimo
Dock A

....

JACKET WAS APPARENTLY A METAPHOR FOR MORE DOCK-WORTHY attire, including proper leathers and boots. Cousin Theo was settling her too-large jacket as she joined him in the galley.

"All good," she said. "Let's go."

So, they went, just the two of them, down the ramp and up the dock at a brisk pace, Theo's bootheels striking the decking firmly.

Not that it likely *was* just the two of them, Jen Sin thought. The ship surely accompanied his captain, if the whispers he had heard about the ship when it was a-building had any basis in fact.

"No train?" Theo asked, her voice disturbing this line of speculation. She stamped on the track laid into the deck.

"Lorith remembers a train, but says that it vanished between one . . . sleep and another, long before I arrived here."

They walked in silence for a few steps before Theo said, "Why?"

"Forgive me—which why in particular?"

She gave him a sideways look and a half-grin.

"I guess there might be more than one, given family. Are you one of the trouble-prone yos'Pheliums?"

He moved his shoulders.

"Who are we to use as our pattern-card?"

She laughed.

"Right. In particular, I'm wondering why you *arrived here*. Val Con's notes just said that you've been here, on Tinsori Light, for two hundred Standards, but not why. Were you *sent* to"—she waved her hand energetically about, possibly indicating the Light entire—"be a light keeper?"

"No, I was *sent* to Delium, to deliver a packet. This would be during the time that Clan Sinan imagined itself the sole owner of the sector, and all the trade routes, with Rinork working their mischief along two lines at once, looking as always for the best advantage to themselves.

"And here was Clan Vaazemir, Delium's premier clan, strenuously disputing Sinan's claims and excesses, caught in the web of Rinork's mischief, and what should they do but call upon their old ally, Korval?"

He closed his eyes briefly, seeing the woman—his supposed contact—waiting for him, calm and smooth-faced. The table, ready with glasses and bottle—the *uncorked* bottle, heard her again say the lines that had not been scripted, sealing her own death, allowing him—allowing *the packet*—a chance to avoid capture.

He took a hard breath.

"To shorten the tale considerably—there was treachery. I took damage returning to my ship, and it became... necessary to hit the presets—the merest blind stab"—because of the blood running into his eyes, more than half-dead as he had been—"and it brought me here. I mean to say, to Tinsori Light."

Theo turned her head to stare at him.

"The emergency safe-port presets?"

"Yes," he admitted. "And, no, Cousin, I do not know why those coords were included among the set. Perhaps Korval once had an ally here, though neither name nor clan-sign were familiar to Lorith."

They walked along in silence for some time, Theo apparently deep in thought, though he supposed she could be in conversation with the ship.

They came to the main intersection and he took the right-hand hall, Theo still silent at his side.

They had almost gained the secondary intersection when she spoke again.

"Val Con's information was that you sent a coded message that meant you were... suiciding"—she said the word as if it were in questionable taste—"and that the delm should strike ship and pilot from the list of Korval's... assets."

"That is correct."

"But you could have sent for help!" she said. "Clan Korval and its allies could have sent dozens! They—"

"To have done so would have provided Tinsori Light with an

army," he interrupted. "I killed my ship because it was untrustworthy, having been repaired by Tinsori Light. I stayed because I, too, had been repaired by Tinsori Light, and was equally untrustworthy, though I believed I could assist in preventing it from conquering the universe—or even a small system."

Theo was frowning. "It was an Independent Logic. Negotiations—"

"It was an Independent Logic built by the Great Enemy. Old Tech. Surely, the Scouts still warn against Old Tech, and deactivate it when they can? Such things are—insidious."

"The Scouts tried to confiscate *Bechimo* as Old Tech," Theo said sharply, and seemed about to say more, but stopped, face arrested, very much as if she were listening to a voice only she could hear.

The ship was calming her, Jen Sin thought. Good. They had both spoken with more heat than was wise, given their lineage, and it was well done, that neither had shown a blade.

"The Department of the Interior," Theo said, sounding subdued, "used Old Tech to—to injure one of my crew. We brought him back to health—to good health—but he'd been a field Scout and—that's not something he'll be able to recover."

Her ship assaulted, and her crew injured. Small wonder Cousin Theo was raw on that edge.

"Every coin has two sides," he said, gently. "Allow Tinsori Light to have been the obverse of *Bechimo*."

She took a deep breath, and nodded sharply. "Agreed. So you stayed—"

"I could not go—I had no ship," he said. "And while two guards against what mischief the Light might produce was trivial, two was more efficient than one, and far less dangerous than a dozen. Two guards may stand back-to-back; one may sleep and one may guard, lowering the risk of error brought by exhaustion; another person to talk to—even so little as that—increases the efficiency of the watch."

"I hadn't thought—" she began, but a sound had caught Jen Sin's ear. He raised a hand, stopped, and turned.

Around the corner burst a pale blue jitney, surely traveling at or near its top speed. Hazenthull nor'Phelium was apparently piloting, with Tolly Jones crammed into the bench beside her.

Theo stepped to the left side of the hall. Jen Sin remained where he was. He saw Hazenthull's teeth in a full battle grin before she reached to the control board.

The jitney came to a gentle halt thirty centimeters from his leading foot.

"Light Keeper!" Tolly Jones said with a brilliant smile. "Good to see you! Cap'n Theo—the same, ma'am."

"I see that Researcher Veeoni came prepared for every contingency," Jen Sin said. "May one ask your target? Surely not the sealed hall."

"Not quite that far. Seignur Veeoni had it come into her head that there's something she might find innerestin' in one of the rooms just 'round the corner from the breach hall, so she sent Haz to fetch it. I'm along in case whatever it might be is too heavy for her to lift."

"Or in case it may need persuasion," Jen Sin murmured. Tolly Jones gave him a nod.

"A small winged bot was found in the deep core by the cleaning crew," Jen Sin said. "It escaped into the station at large."

"Heard that. We'll keep a lookout."

"Thank you. Also, we have ships, cargo, and work crews incoming. They will be docking in a few hours."

"Hadn't heard that. We'll keep a lookout there, too."

Jen Sin inclined his head.

Tolly Jones patted the side of the jitney.

"You folks for the sealed hall?"

"Indeed. Captain Waitley wishes to inspect it."

"Why not?" Tolly said, and pointed over his shoulder. "Pair o'perfectly good seats back there. We can give you a lift as far as we're going."

"I will," Hazenthull said, "moderate the speed. We were conducting a capabilities inventory."

"Very wise," Jen Sin said gravely. "A pilot must know her craft." He glanced across the hall.

"Cousin Theo, will you take your ease?"

Theo took a breath, shrugged, and moved toward the jitney. "Sure," she said. "Why not?"

Hazenthull's notion of moderate fell on the pilot side of the line, which was fair, Jen Sin thought, as she was ferrying pilots.

Theo shifted on the seat beside him, and he turned his head to meet her eyes.

"What would you have done, if she hadn't stopped?"

Jen Sin raised an eyebrow.

"Jumped, of course. What would you have done, if she had veered left?"

Theo sighed.

"Jumped," she admitted. "But, you *challenged* her."

Ah. This was what came of being nurtured by scholars in an orderly environment, where *melant'i* was perhaps not accounted sternly, if at all.

"I merely asserted my intention to remain where I was," he said.

Theo blinked, drew breath...

He raised his hand, and she exhaled.

"I am light keeper," he said, "and have dominion in my own halls. Hazenthull challenged *that.* It may have been in jest, but even so, it required an immediate answer. Every challenge is an equation set, Cousin. Hazenthull's question was 'Will you yield?' My answer was, 'No. *You* will yield.'"

"And she did. But what if she hadn't been joking?"

"Did we not just agree between us that the prudent course in such a case would have been to jump?"

"Yes, we did, but that would have—escalated the situation, and—"

The jitney bore, strongly, to the left, curtailing conversation. Straightening, it picked up speed briefly, then the engine's whine cut and they drifted gently to a stop.

"End of the line," Tolly Jones called over his shoulder.

Jen Sin stood up and walked to the pilot's side.

"My thanks for your courtesy," he said.

Hazenthull inclined her head.

"I would offer a ride back," she said, "but Seignur Veeoni was not able to give me even approximate dimensions."

"If it's here at all," Tolly Jones added. "Want us to swing up to the seal, if we got room and you're not back by the time we're ready to go?"

"It would be a kindness," Jen Sin said, around a cool shiver of—memory, perhaps. He moved around to the front of the jitney, frowning at the hatch with its diagonal green stripe. There was *some*thing there, though a specific incident did not arise. "It is this room?"

"Yes," Hazenthull said. "Seignur Veeoni was certain."

"As always," Jen Sin murmured. The feeling had faded. He sighed, felt the presence of someone near, and turned his head to find Tolly Jones standing at his side.

"Problem?"

"Nothing so definite. Take care, Mentor."

"Always," he said cheerfully, and turned away. "Hey, Haz, did Seignur Veeoni give us anything *specific*? If there's eighteen crates are we bringing 'em all?"

"Should we stay?" Theo asked, arriving in her turn at his side.

Jen Sin moved his shoulders. "Likely not. You had wanted to see the seals."

"I did. But if there's danger—"

"Hazenthull and Mentor Jones are very efficient people. More, they are a seasoned security team. If there *is* danger, and they are required to act, our presence may impede them."

He began to walk down the hall.

"Because we're not a team," Theo said.

"Because, we are not *their* team," he corrected, gently. Surely, he thought, she knew these things.

Still, it seemed for a moment that she might make another argument to stay. She did glance over her shoulder at Tolly Jones and Hazenthull nor'Phelium, bent together over the tablet in his hand, then stretched her legs to reach his side.

Abruptly, she spoke.

"I'm not... experienced in the kinds of decisions you've had to make in order to—survive Tinsori Light," she said slowly. "It must be hard to always have to be conscious about what might give an enemy the advantage. I'm thinking about what you said, about not giving the Light an army."

Only see the child, how serious! The Old Light had nothing to do with her, and he was glad of it.

"It was what came to me," he said. "Perhaps I am one of the trouble-prone yos'Pheliums, after all."

She laughed, and that was better.

"Just through here," he said, putting his hand against the hatch with its orange warning stripe.

Emergency dims came on when they entered the hallway, waking abundant shadows. The air was cool, but reasonably fresh. At the end of the hall, not so very distant from the hatch, the cermasteel seal glowed an unsettling grey-green in the low light.

"Lorith and I did not often come this way," he said, as they approached the seal. "If we had been able to establish a regular schedule—" He moved his shoulders and let that drift away. "Being as we were, we trusted what the instruments told us."

"And the instruments reported that the seals held." Theo nodded. "Tinsori Light would've been invested in that."

"Precisely."

"What I was wondering," Theo said, continuing forward, her attention on the seal—

A section of the left wall somewhat forward of her silently slid aside, and a bot stepped into the hall.

It was a very simple bot: unadorned, articulated girders, small motors at the knees and elbows, a blank mask atop crosspiece shoulders.

It was holding an energy rifle, which it raised, aiming—

"Theo," Jen Sin said sharply. "Stop. Do not move."

Her head turned toward the bot. Perhaps the ship had warned her. She stopped, and she did not move.

"Yes," he murmured, and moved himself, forward and to the right, making certain his bootheels made audible contact with the decking. The bot turned, weapon following him.

Excellent.

"Tocohl," he said, calmly, and never moving his eyes from the bot, "please make contact with the guard in the breach hall."

"I can see the guard in the hallway camera," Tocohl said, the old speaker making her voice scratchy and unbeautiful. "I do not see it in the station systems. All of the indie circuits are closed." There was a pause. "Jen Sin—I can't contact it."

Which meant, Jen Sin understood, that she could not deactivate it. He had feared as much.

"That's all right, though," Theo said, softly, her lips scarcely moving, her posture relaxed where she stood. "Because we're here to help; to upgrade systems and repair damage. There's no need to hurt us, and every reason to help us."

"That is correct," Jen Sin murmured, moving steadily to the right, drawing the eye of the weapon with him, away from Theo. "I am the light keeper. It is my duty and my intention to keep the station as it deserves, with care, respect and attention to the safety of all."

He moved forward, angling in now, keeping the bot's attention on him, away from Theo. Another few steps, and he would be close enough to attempt a disarm.

"Theo," he said, keeping his voice calm and even, hoping with everything in him that the ship would support him in this—but of course he would. The ship loved his trouble-prone captain. Her safety would be prime.

"Theo, back down the hall slowly, please. Go out through the hatch."

Her head jerked in his direction.

"What?" she said sharply. "No."

The bot moved, weapon swinging back toward her.

Jen Sin jumped.

Storeroom Core Six

THE DOOR WAS A LITTLE SLOW, OPENING. TOLLY SLIPPED INTO the space beyond just as soon as the gap was wide enough for him to manage it.

The reason the door was slow was immediately obvious.

Two sealed cargo crates had fallen off the shelves and across the track.

The boxes were heavier than he'd expected for the size, but he cleared the track, and by the time Haz came through, he'd discovered the reason Jen Sin had been anxious about this particular room.

There was a shadow burned into the wall near the shelves where two more boxes were stored. A thin, small shadow, caught in what looked to be mid-leap.

"He was killed here," Haz said. Tolly sighed.

"That's my baseless guess, too."

"Not baseless. We saw the shadow Mentor Yo's death left in the core access hall."

"So we did."

"Perhaps," said Haz, bending and picking up the first box like it weighed slightly less than a feather, "he had also studied the schematics."

"Except he didn't have any real memory of the room, or what might be inside—only he was kind of unsettled. That's what I saw."

He bent, got a grip on the second fallen box, and hoisted it.

"I tell you what, Haz. It's a wonder Light Keeper Jen Sin isn't a lot more skittish than he is."

"Yes," Haz said. She stepped through the door, and stowed the first box in the jitney's cargo section. Pivoting, she took the second box from him, sliding it in next to the first.

"If we take all four we're only gonna have room for one passenger, going back," Tolly said.

"The Light Keeper will wish to meet the incoming ships," Haz said.

"And Seignur Veeoni will want her goodies, soonest. Fair enough. I'll walk back with Cap'n Theo."

"Yes," Haz said again, and returned to the storeroom, Tolly a step behind her.

"Mentor!" Tocohl's voice was too loud, edged with panic. "There is an indie bot in the breach hall. It has a weapon. It's threatening Jen Sin and Theo. I can't contact it."

"On my way."

He took off running. Not too many steps into it, Haz caught him, and passed him, though she didn't pull away, which she could've done. Right, then, that was the pattern—Haz on point, Tolly on backup. Easy.

Haz slowed enough to let the hatch cycle normally, then leapt forward.

Breach Hall

. . . .

"THEO, RUN!" *BECHIMO* SHOUTED INSIDE HER HEAD. JEN SIN HAD jumped, but *toward* the bot, which was raising its weapon and—

She heard the hatch cycle, then Hazenthull flashed past—and something hit her in the back of the knees. She heard *Bechimo* shout as she collapsed. Her head hit the deck with a whack; her vision swam. She heard the fizz of an energy weapon discharging through the ringing in her ears.

"Haz!" Tolly Jones shouted, and the weight holding her to the deck was gone.

Theo rolled to her feet. Hazenthull was down, Tolly Jones kneeling over her. The bot—the bot was in a heap on the deck, the rifle a little distance away. She walked over and kicked the weapon to the far wall.

"Theo?" *Bechimo* asked cautiously, in bond-space.

I'm all right, she answered absently, turning slowly where she stood. For no reason she could name, she looked up, seeing the shiny new burn mark on the dull wall.

"It deloped," she said.

Tolly Jones looked up, following her gaze, then looked over his shoulder at the downed bot.

Some of the tension went out of him, as he leaned back down.

"Haz? Field's clear."

"There is no more danger?"

"Well, there's Cap'n Theo, but she's with us."

"Yes. I am rising."

She came up to her knees, and Theo drifted closer, staring at the limp form facedown on the deck, leather jacket opened around him like wings.

"Jen Sin!"

She stepped forward—and stopped when Haz raised a hand.

"He lives. I took him down hard."

Tolly knelt, and put two fingers against Jen Sin's throat.

"He's breathing and his heart's steady. Might've hit his head."

"He wouldn't be the only one," Theo said tartly.

Tolly offered a grin.

"Sorry, Cap'n. Came late to the party, and had to parse it on the run."

"Not your fault," she told him. "Mine. I should've backed away when Jen Sin told me to, but he was going to try to disarm it—"

"'Course he was. Can't stop a Korval pilot from doing *some*thing—which you oughta know."

"Indeed"—Jen Sin sounded wry, and slightly breathless—"it is nothing other than a defining trait of the clan."

He rolled over onto his back, wincing.

"How you doin', there, Pilot?" Tolly asked.

"I have once again established that my head is harder than hullplate. Apparently this must be verified periodically." He took a breath.

"Cousin, you are unharmed?"

"Yes," Theo admitted.

"Excellent. And the bot?"

"Deloped and fell down," Theo said.

"Did it? I wonder why."

He twisted into a sitting position, and extended a hand.

"Hazenthull, a boost, of your kindness."

"Yes."

She bent, wrapped a big hand around his forearm, and brought him to his feet, where he paused a moment, taking inventory, Theo thought, before he crossed to the fallen bot, and dropped to one knee beside it.

"I am," he said, over his shoulder, "loath to leave it here. It was invisible to Tocohl, and seems to be part of a yet undiscovered grid. It may have kin."

"I'm thinking we take 'im to Seignur Veeoni," Tolly Jones said, going to the corner and picking up the rifle. "We'll take the toy, too."

Jen Sin rose, slowly.

"A reasonable plan, Mentor. Hazenthull, will you carry the bot?"

"Yes," she said, and bent to gather the thing into her arms.

Jelaza Kazone
Surebleak

. . . .

"GOT A LETTER FROM THEO," MIRI SAID, LOOKING ACROSS THE desk to the corner they'd cleared so Val Con could work on the remote. They were both Delm Korval today, courtesy of the Accountants Guild.

"So soon? I hadn't supposed that even Theo could fall into a scrape as quickly as this."

"You need to accept the fact that Theo's natural state is 'in trouble,'" Miri told him. "Be a lot easier on your nerves. That said, if there *is* a scrape, she don't find it worth mentioning. She's writing with news of kin."

Val Con looked up, green eyes serious.

"Jen Sin is—well?"

"Seems to be. Formal but cordial is the word there. Theo's opinion is that he's tired. The traveling Tree gave her a pod for him, which she passed on."

Val Con's face eased. "Excellent. That may well be the tonic he needs."

"Could be. The reason Theo's writing, though, is to tell me I got it all wrong, and Tolly Jones is too a cousin."

"Through what connection?"

"The Lyre Institute for Exceptional Children and the Old Universe." Miri tapped the screen. "She's got it written out so far as he would tell it, and stressing that it's not him who's calling kin—exactly the opposite. Told her to apply to you for details."

Val Con sighed.

"Is she asking for details?"

"Not specifically."

He looked back to the remote. "Good."

Miri laughed.

"You're not gonna tell her?"

"I am not going to tell her *this instant*," Val Con said firmly. "There are things in queue ahead." He glanced up.

"Does my sister have a third topic, or is that the awful whole?"

"Couple more things, actually. According to Theo, Seignur Veeoni is brilliant and oughta be teaching. Says there's been an attempt to break station security. Tocohl's working with Joyita and *Bechimo* to build up the perimeter. They set some traps, too. Theo wonders, just on the side you know—"

Val Con looked up and met her eyes.

"Theo wonders if Tinsori Light is well and truly dead," he murmured. "A reasonable question. We must defer to our experts on-station."

"That's her take, too. Says they're being careful."

"I am astonished."

"Yeah. Also says—last thing—that Tocohl isn't Station, wasn't created to be a station, and doesn't *want to be* a station, but stands ready to do her duty."

"*Bechimo* and Joyita, of course, are attempting to talk her out of duty."

"Wouldn't you? Joyita's made contact with Seignur Veeoni, to discuss station architecture."

She paused, tapped the screen, looked up again.

"Seems to be it. Sends her love to Lizzie. Hopes you haven't lost your commission yet."

"Kindred feeling. Splendid."

"Grump. Do I tell her to keep a tight eye on Jen Sin or not?"

"Ah." He looked across the room, toward the bookshelves, brows pulled slightly together.

"Not, I think," he said, meeting her eyes with a slight smile. "Pray do tell her that I retain my commission, and that she continues to hold my regard as her brother."

"Val Con sends his love," Miri muttered, tapping keys. "Got it."

He laughed quietly. "*Cha'trez*?"

"Hmm?"

"Thank you for your care."

"Hey, no problem. What're you thinking—lunch here at the desk, or upstairs?"

"Upstairs," he said, and she nodded seriously.

"That's what I was thinking, too."

Station Day 21
Storeroom Core Six

TOLLY JONES POPPED THE POWER PACK OUT OF THE RIFLE, SLIPPED it into a leg pocket, and put the rifle on the floor in the front of the jitney. Hazenthull sat the bot on the passenger's bench in the back, and secured it with the existing shock webbing, while Theo and Tolly made the four boxes garnered from the storage room secure with cargo netting.

That left the front seat, next to Hazenthull nor'Phelium, for Jen Sin, if he was to ride, and apparently he was.

"There is no need to disrupt—" he began.

"There is need," Hazenthull said firmly. "Something large fell on you."

"I—"

"There's a bruise coming in over your right eye," Theo said. "Do you have a headache?"

In fact, he did have a headache, not that it signified.

Tolly Jones gave him a grin and nodded at the jitney.

"You're outnumbered, Pilot," he said. "Take the easy route, and rest yourself, why not? You still got incoming to deal with, remember."

He had forgotten the ships due to dock, the strangers who would soon be overtaking the halls, and for a too-bright moment, he thought that he would rescind this permission, and send them all away. What had he been thinking? What—

"Jen Sin," Theo said. He felt a hand on his shoulder, and opened his eyes to meet a straight dark gaze. "You hit your head hard. We've got an autodoc, if you need it. Meantime, it's not going to do any harm to let Hazenthull drive you in."

"I am honor-bound to your Line and House," Hazenthull said

unexpectedly. "Your safety is my priority. You were not able to control your fall, and might have additional injuries, which a long walk could exacerbate. Allow me to do my duty."

One could scarcely deny a petition to duty. Jen Sin inclined his head, feeling a flash of pain.

"My thanks," he said, and climbed into the front seat next to Hazenthull. He was not so large as Tolly Jones, so there was room enough for him to sit without crowding the pilot.

"Catch you soon, Haz," Tolly Jones said, as the pilot engaged the craft and brought them in a sweeping circle 'round the hall, speed increasing as they raced back the way they had come.

Jen Sin closed his eyes, breathing deep, accessing a calming exercise.

You are the light keeper, he told himself. There are, indeed, ships coming into the station. It is the nature of stations, to receive incoming ships; to make the halls available to travelers.

There was little enough in the halls at present to tempt travelers, but that would be changing, too. Korval intended their new property to become a profit-line. Therefore, incoming ships and crew were required, in numbers.

He took another deep breath, and dared to enter board-rest.

The jitney bore strongly to the right. He opened his eyes as the doors to the bay access halls rolled away before them.

"We go first to Seignur Veeoni," Hazenthull said.

Yes, of course. Seignur Veeoni would want to know that her researches had borne fruit.

He stirred.

"Tocohl, what is the status of the incoming ships?"

"Still incoming," Tocohl said from the jitney's speaker. "Station estimates three hours before *Karil*'s docking, the others behind her."

"I will meet *Karil* when she docks," he said. "Please bring Lorith current."

"Yes, Light Keeper," Tocohl said, as Hazenthull turned into the bay Seignur Veeoni had chosen to house her work space.

• • • ⁂ • • •

"Do you want to go back to the seal and see if there's anyone there?" Theo asked, and it wasn't half a bad question, either.

"Y'know? I do. But I'm thinking it's best to let tempers cool a bit before we make another visit."

Not to mention—and there *wasn't* any reason to mention it to Cap'n Theo—he wanted a look at what was in those cases presently on their way to Seignur Veeoni. Jen Sin had been there before them, presumably because he knew or had made a shrewd guess about those boxes, and the Old Light had killed him before he could open them. In Tolly's opinion, anything the Old Light wanted hidden was worth studying on.

"Should've asked how *you're* feeling," he said, suddenly aware of that omission. "I wasn't particularly gentle taking you down, either."

Theo turned and started walking; he kept pace.

"*Bechimo* ran a diagnostic," she said. "I'm fine—" She paused, and repeated, with emphasis, "I *am* fine, absent a few bruises, none of them as bad as Jen Sin's forehead. We've got a 'doc aboard. If I feel the need when I get home, I'll use it."

He nodded.

"What's the word on the incoming?" he asked, after they'd gone a couple dozen steps in silence.

"They're out of Hacienda Estrella at Edmonton Beacon," Theo said obligingly. "The Carresens-Denoblis put out a Traveler's Aid Notice for the Light, and this is the first wave of workers and supplies. Three ships—*Karil*'s carrying supplies, *Rodger Dodger* and *Crinolyn* are bringing work crews." She paused, added, "They've worked with Ren Stryker before and seem on good terms."

"Good to have an experienced crew," Tolly allowed. "Did you get Ren that sample? I'm innerested to hear what he might've thought."

"According to *Bechimo*, he thought he could work with the old racks and tiles, to render them into useful components."

"Things are fallin' into place," Tolly said. "Work crews staying on-station?"

"They didn't seem eager to stay on-station," Theo said slowly. "They were coming in to help unload *Karil*, but were planning on staying with—in?—Ren Stryker. They've done it before; they said he was a good host."

He nodded.

"I thought you'd be more upset. Hiding on Ren Stryker isn't going to be an option for you."

That was a bit sharp, Tolly thought. He slanted her a look.

"Come to it," he said mildly, "Haz convinced me to give that plan up."

"Good," said Theo, and frowned, like she'd just heard something she wasn't expecting.

Tolly waited.

"My crew finished a sweep of the upper and lower levels of the old core," she said. "They didn't find any more avians or anything else that looked like it was still...functional. Did you see anything like it when you were in the core?"

"I didn't, but truth said, I had other things on my mind. Did it attack when it was disturbed, or just—run?"

"It ran—well, no. Flew. It was a surprise, but nobody who was there thought it was a threat."

"That don't sound like the Old Light," Tolly said. "Makes me wonder if a drone or a remote got separated from its ship, back in the old days."

"And it's been hiding all this time?" Theo didn't sound convinced, and Tolly couldn't blame her.

"Best I can do, 'til we can find it and ask," he said mildly.

She nodded, and lapsed into silence, again. This time, he didn't try to bring her out of it.

Seignur Veeoni's Private Workroom

"FOUR!" SEIGNUR VEEONI FROWNED. "I HAD NOT EXPECTED SO many."

She walked around the jitney, and stood staring at the bot webbed in on the passenger's bench.

"And this is—?"

"A bonus," Jen Sin said, his head throbbing. "It attacked Captain Waitley and myself in the breach hall."

Seignur Veeoni transferred her frown to him.

"It does not appear formidable."

"It had a rifle," Hazenthull said, leaning into the cab and pulling the thing out. She offered it to the researcher across two wide palms. "Mentor Jones removed the power pack."

"Prudent," Seignur Veeoni said, making no move to take the weapon. "Why bring them to me?"

"I had hoped your study of station schematics may have revealed the system which motivated the bot," Jen Sin said. "Tocohl could not see it, save through the hall cameras."

"That is... interesting," Seignur Veeoni said. "Very well, I will examine it. In the breach hall, you say?"

"Quite near the seal, yes."

She narrowed her eyes, as if she were in fact reading the schematic, then shook her head sharply.

"I will examine it, as I said. M Traven."

Her bodyguard stepped forward.

"Researcher?"

"Take the jitney into the workroom. I will want the boxes in the secure area. Put the bot in a safe-box." She turned to frown one more time at the rifle Hazenthull still held.

"That—put it on my desk."

"Yes," said Traven, receiving the rifle, and carrying it across the room. Seignur Veeoni started after her.

"I have a request to make in commission of my duty to Line yos'Phelium," Hazenthull said surprisingly.

Seignur Veeoni turned back, eyebrows up.

"Speak."

"Light Keeper yos'Phelium took damage during the incident in the breach hall. He requires the use of an autodoc."

Seignur Veeoni turned to look at him.

"I see," she said.

"There are ships incoming. The light keeper has expressed his intention to meet their crews at docking," Hazenthull continued, stolidly.

"And he would of course prefer to do so with a clean face," Seignur Veeoni said. "I understand. This way, please, Light Keeper."

The autodoc loomed large in the small space. In fact, it *was* large—larger, its control panel more complex, than the usual house or shipboard 'docs. It bore a distressing resemblance to—

Raw panic clawed at his throat. He stopped walking, taking deep breaths that only seemed to feed the horror.

A hand fell, lightly, on his shoulder.

"Light Keeper?" Hazenthull said softly. "Are you in pain?"

"No." He could scarcely hear his own voice over the pounding of his heart. "I believe that I will not require the 'doc," he said. "Thank you for your care."

He turned—tried to turn, but Hazenthull prevented it.

"Light Keeper yos'Phelium," Seignur Veeoni said sharply. "You are a sensible and practical man. Pray come forward and examine this device. The model may be unfamiliar to you—it was built for laboratory use—but you will see that it is nothing more nor less than an autodoc."

The hand on his shoulder urged him, and perforce he went forward, until he was standing beside the researcher at the machine's control board. She touched a corner and the board lit, showing all the expected readouts and menus.

"My work demands that I have access to a larger onboard database than standard models provide," Seignur Veeoni said. "Storage room, and increased capacity for quick healing are the limits of the modifications on this unit."

He'd managed to get his breathing under control; the panic lessened somewhat. Still, he had no wish—not the smallest desire—to lie down, to have the shell close over him...

"The station master reflects the station," Seignur Veeoni said, surprisingly. "Or so my brother tells me. Is this station a place of refinement and peace, or is it a free-for-all?"

It was the shock of hearing such a question from Seignur Veeoni of all unlikely persons. He laughed—breathless and broken, but honest for all of it.

"We are naturally a place of peace and refinement," he said. "Korval accepts no less."

"Very well. Watch me closely as I set this. Examination, yes? Unless something more serious than bruises are discovered, we advance to quick-heal, with an infusion of vitamins and electrolytes. Is there anything in this plan to which you object?"

It was the very course of reason. Jen Sin owned himself impressed.

"No. It is well done. I thank you."

"Thank me by lying down."

He drew a breath, removed his jacket, and handed it to Hazenthull. She threw it over her shoulder and helped him up onto the pallet, various of his muscles protesting.

"I will keep watch," she told him. "I will be here when you emerge."

Amazingly—absurdly—her promise eased him.

"Thank you," he said.

"The hood descends," Seignur Veeoni said.

He closed his eyes so he would not have to watch—and snapped into sleep.

Bechimo
Dock A

....

"LIKE TO COME ABOARD?" THEO ASKED WHEN THEY REACHED *Bechimo*'s dock.

Tolly considered her.

"You're not still working the cousin angle, are you, Cap'n Theo? 'Cause that's not gonna yield a winner, for the reasons I told you and more."

She shook her head.

"I understand what you told me," she said, which he thought might be a little slight on the leading edge unless she'd 'beamed her brother straight off and he'd been immediately and entirely forthcoming, "but *Bechimo* and Joyita want to meet you."

"And why is that?"

Theo sighed. "I'd rather let them tell you. If it can't be now, they understand, but they'd like to know that you'll come by to meet them while we're all at the same dock."

Tolly hesitated.

There wasn't any reason to rush off, he thought. Yes, he wanted to see what was in the crates they'd found for Seignur Veeoni, but he doubted she'd open them immediately on delivery, especially given that gleam in Haz's eye, and the fact of an autodoc right there in the lab.

Might as well get it done, Tolly Jones, he told himself, and nodded to Cap'n Theo.

"I'd be glad to meet *Bechimo* and Joyita," he said, and followed her up the ramp, and into her ship.

"Waitley in!" she called as they cleared the hatch. "I've got Mentor Jones with me, and we're on our way to the galley."

"Welcome home, Captain."

The voice was in the mid-range, calm, and clearly pleased. "Mentor Jones, thank you for coming."

"Thanks for the invite," Tolly answered, following Cap'n Theo down the wide, pleasant hall to a bright, pleasant galley, chairs clustered 'round tables, and a buffet at the far end.

"There's tea in the ready pots," Theo said, nodding toward the buffet, "or I can brew fresh, if you'd rather."

"I'm fine with something out of the pots," he said, and gave her a half-grin. "Dusty walk."

She smiled back.

"Long, too," she said. "I'm getting a snack, and a cup, then I'll be leaving you so you can have your talk." She nodded at the screen set in the side wall. "Joyita will join you there."

She was going to leave him alone with two Independent Logics? Tolly thought, horrified on her behalf. She was a competent woman, and she surely knew better than to trust the likes of him.

It occurred to him right then that she didn't have to trust him, so long as she trusted her crew.

He moved to the buffet, took a mug from those set out and drew tea from a pot at random. He heard dishes clattering, and peeked around the corner, seeing Cap'n Theo getting a tin down out of a cabinet.

Sipping his tea, he walked over to the table nearest the screen, pulled out a stool facing it, and had a seat. He sipped more tea, paying attention to the taste—light, minty, pleasant in the mouth. Not a leaf he knew, which wasn't particularly surprising. He hadn't been intended to pass for Liaden.

"Snack if you want it." Theo arrived and put a plate in the center of the table. *Chernubia*, cheese, crackers—all the food groups covered, he thought, and nodded at her.

"'Preciate the trouble."

"No trouble," she said, balancing another plate and a mug. "I'm needed elsewhere. I hope to be back before you leave, but if not—just ask Joyita to have Clarence show you out."

"I will, thanks."

"There are two cats and a norbear onboard," she continued. "The cats are generally polite; the norbear's a little pushy."

"I'll keep it in mind," he assured her.

She nodded—and left.

Tolly reached to the plate, picked up a cracker and a bit of cheese, and ate them leisurely. When he was done, he had another sip of tea, and glanced at the screen.

"I was told that Joyita and *Bechimo* wanted to meet me," he said, pleasantly. "Tocohl thinks a lot of the pair of you, and I understand you've been giving her some strong support."

The screen flickered and resolved into the image of a man's dark, disreputable face. In the background was a room crowded with consoles, and piles of hardcopy pinned down with tea mugs. The lighting was good and steady, slightly yellower than the light in the galley.

Tolly picked up his mug and had another sip of the minty tea.

The man in the screen grinned and leaned back in his chair, giving Tolly a look at sleeves rolled up from strong wrists, a bracelet around one, and rings on the long fingers.

"Tollance Berik-Jones," he said, and his voice was of a tone and pitch that just naturally made you want to trust him, which made Tolly wonder if the person before him had been modeled on another. "It's an honor, sir. I am B. Joyita, comm officer."

Tolly inclined his head.

"Pleased to meet you, Comm Officer."

"Please, call me Joyita—everybody does."

Tolly grinned.

"I'll do that. You can lose my formal, too. Mostly, I'm Tolly. Or Mentor."

"Mentor, then," Joyita said agreeably. He reached off-screen, then raised a mug in salute before bringing it to his lips.

"Will *Bechimo* be joining us?" Tolly asked.

"I am present, Mentor," said the voice that had welcomed the captain home. "Please call me *Bechimo*. You should know that Tocohl is not alone in speaking well of you. Jeeves has also given a good report of you. The most talented mentor practicing, he said."

"That's high praise," Tolly said. "Pleased to meet you, *Bechimo*."

"And I, you. Joyita and I wished to catch you up. However, before we continue, you must know that we have—that is, *I have*—committed a crime."

"Made a mistake," Joyita said. "You *made a mistake*. We talked about this."

"Jeeves was very angry."

"At first. Then he allowed that youth, inexperience, and concern for the lives of the crew must be accounted for. He forgave Captain Theo, and you."

Tolly finished his tea and put the mug aside.

"This is about *Admiral Bunter*, I'm takin' it?"

"Yes," *Bechimo* said, sounding subdued.

Tolly nodded.

"Yeah, that was a mistake—a bad one—and I'm not gonna pretend I didn't think some pretty hard thoughts about Cap'n Waitley my ownself, more'n once. I don't know the whole story of why it was done like it was, but the thing that counted for me is that, in the middle of whatever kind of trouble she was in right then, she thought to send for help for the *Admiral*. She *did* send to Jeeves. And Jeeves sent Tocohl an' me, an' we got it sorted. I don't know if you been told—we got the *Admiral* into a better situation; nice, clean workin' ship. He could take on crew tomorrow, if he had the mind to. Right now, he's with a friend, who's introducing him to her friends, so he can get data to make a solid decision on how he wants to go forward."

In the screen, Joyita nodded, and raised his mug again.

"So, what I'm sayin' is the same as Jeeves—you made a bad mistake. Learn from it and don't do it again."

"There is a problem," *Bechimo* said softly. In the screen, Joyita frowned, and leaned forward slightly.

"What's that?" Tolly asked.

"I am afraid, if my crew were in danger, I might well *do it again*."

Joyita sat back, lips pressed tight.

Tolly nodded.

"I know what you mean. I've done some things I'm not particularly proud of, and given the situation arises again, I might do the same thing. We do what we gotta do, to survive. But then we clean up whatever mess we made doin' it."

He held up a hand, and added, "If it's possible. Isn't always."

"What do you do, if it's not?" Joyita's voice was soft. Tolly met the dark gaze.

"Then you regret it," he said, flatly. "For the rest of your life."

"Giving us another reason not to make any more bad mistakes." Joyita nodded. "Thank you, Mentor."

"I have much to think about," *Bechimo* added. "Thank you, Mentor."

"What I do." He slid off the stool, picked up his mug and headed back to the ready pots for a refill. "So! Either of you got an opinion about our ghost problems?"

Seignur Veeoni's Private Suite

FOUR STASIS BOXES!

Four!

She dared not open them—not quite yet. She could, however, check her assumptions.

"I will be in my quarters, meditating. Allow nothing to disturb me."

"For how long?" M Traven asked, practically.

"You may inquire of me via intercom in six hours, if I have not emerged, or filed alternate orders."

M Traven inclined her head.

"Yes, Researcher."

Bechimo
Dock A

• • • • • • • •

"JOYITA AND RESEARCHER VEEONI HAVE BEEN DISCUSSING ARCHITECTURE," *Bechimo* said.

"That's correct. She and I agreed that it's more satisfactory to design for sentience than have sentience arise. The question of whether this station *ought* to be sentient has been remanded to Delm Korval.

"In the course of our discussions, Seignur Veeoni said that the breach in the station was caused when Tinsori Light, which had been wakened by the Great Enemy, destroyed the former core, which was not sentient."

Joyita paused, brows drawn, as if he'd been caught by a sudden thought. Tolly gave him an encouraging nod.

"Yes. In the interests of complete accuracy, she stated that the original station had not been *designed* for sentience."

"Which takes us just exactly as far as it goes," Tolly said, sighing.

"The former station could have woken in response to the threat," *Bechimo* said, "but surely Tinsori Light had access to—and utilized—existing systems."

"We don't have a timeline," Joyita said. "After the Light was captured, before the Enemy's intelligence was brought on line—was there time to build and power an under-system, completely independent, and hidden from, the intended framework?"

"You're right," Tolly said. "We don't know the timing. I can say that it'd be a lot for a newborn to process. Not sayin' it's impossible, but to wake up, unnerstan' the threat, build and outfit a ghost army..."

"That assumes that the hallway bot and the avian are part of the stealth system. If there *is* a stealth system," *Bechimo* objected.

"Robots don't build themselves," Joyita said, a little snappish, so Tolly thought.

"Can't argue with that," he said, soothingly. "So, it's looking like the consensus is we need more data."

There was a longish moment of silence, given present company, then *Bechimo* spoke, sounding thoughtful.

"We may be able to modify one of the backup scans to allow a deep search of the breach hall."

"That's an interesting idea," Joyita said. "Let's work together on that."

And that quick, good relations were restored. Tolly reached for his mug.

"What's in the boxes you retrieved for Seignur Veeoni?" Joyita asked.

Tolly looked at him.

"Dunno. Hope to find out, 'cause my curiosity spot's itching. That doesn't mean Seignur Veeoni'll feel compelled to share."

"I'll ask her," Joyita said.

"You do that," Tolly said cordially.

In the screen, Joyita turned his head, as if looking to a readout, then looked back. "Captain Theo is approaching the galley," he said.

Tolly nodded and stood up. "I'm thinking I've about worn out my welcome. Glad to have met you, *Bechimo*—Joyita. Let's keep in touch about the ghosts."

"Absolutely. I'll brief Tocohl. We should all collaborate on that project," Joyita said.

"It was good to meet you, Mentor," *Bechimo* said. "Thank you for your insights."

"Pleased to be of help."

The sound of bootheels against decking warned him and he turned with a sheepish grin. "Sorry 'bout that, Cap'n Theo. Got to talkin' shop."

"I'm glad you're still here," she said, seriously. "There's somebody else who wants to meet you."

"We're going to hydroponics," Cap'n Theo told him, turning left as they came out of the galley.

"Fine," he said, wondering if there was an AI gardener he'd need to absolve of having been scared stupid. He hadn't ever met a dedicated gardener, so that would be interesting.

"Did you three have a good talk?" she asked.

"We did. You'll want to know that we're collaborating—with Tocohl, too—on the topic of random avians and bot guards. The goal is to find the subsystem they're served by, which is innerestin' for being invisible to everybody who's looked for it. *Bechimo* had an idea about scanning the area that Joyita liked, so they'll be working on that."

She nodded, turned a sharp corner, and put her hand against a door. It slid aside, and they stepped into a slightly more humid corridor.

"Right here," Theo said, motioning him around another corner.

It wasn't so much an alcove as a wide spot in the hall.

A large pot had been webbed securely against the wall. In the pot was—a tree, smallish, for all its top branches brushed the ceiling, green and glowing. *Happy* was the impression he received, and for all he knew about trees, it might even be so.

Curled in the pot at the base of the slim trunk was a rusty orange norbear, fast asleep.

"This is the pushy one?" he asked.

"Right, but it's not him who wants to see you," Theo said. She nodded at the tree.

"I know you said you aren't family," she said. "I *told* it you said you're not family. But it wanted to see for itself."

The tree's leaves fluttered—must be a fan somewhere, he thought, though he didn't feel any breeze himself.

"Now that it's got a look at me," he said, after a couple minutes had gone by, "what happens?"

"Maybe nothing," Theo said. "I don't follow its processes all that well. Val Con might be able to—oh."

There was a definite snap, and something round pelted down through the branches. Tolly's hand shot out, capturing the thing before it hit the sleeping norbear.

"It made its own decision," Theo said, sounding resigned. "It does that a lot." She nodded at the—pod he held. "That's yours. Eat it or don't eat it. You have a choice. We can go now. The Tree's pleased to have seen you."

"And I'm—pleased—to have seen the Tree," Tolly said, which was just good manners, and about what he could manage with the skin of his palm starting to tingle. He stuck the pod in his jacket pocket and followed Theo back through her ship, to the ramp, said his goodbye, and left.

Seignur Veeoni's Private Suite

THE MEMORY MIGHT HAVE BEEN WAITING FOR THE TOUCH OF her thought. Seignur Veeoni accessed the surface data, opened her eyes, and rose from her couch. Crossing the room to her private screen, she called up the builder's notes.

Bechimo
Dock A

....

IT WAS A GRUBBY AND EXHAUSTED GROUP WHO EVENTUALLY arrived back at their ship, and would have reported right then, only the captain had waved them to silence, and put her stern questions.

"Are you all right? Is anybody hurt?"

"Captain," Win Ton said, bowing gently. "We were careful. No one took hurt. We are tired."

"And in want of showers," Kara added.

The captain nodded.

"Go—clean up, relax. Group meal in two hours. Clarence and I are on galley duty."

There was no arguing with the captain in such a mood, so they took themselves off to obey her orders, assembling at last in the galley, dressed in clean sweaters, loose pants, and soft mocs.

On the captain's say-so, Win Ton opened wine and poured as the chefs served, and everyone sat down together, Joyita joining them from his tower.

After the meal was duly sampled, the chefs commended for their art, and the wine sipped, Theo introduced a topic of general interest.

"My cousin Jen Sin has a note from Gordy Arbuthnot, who'll be coming to Tinsori soon. Gordy asked if there was anything in particular the station wanted him to bring in, and Jen Sin extended that offer to us."

She glanced around the table.

"I'm understanding that Gordy was in particular looking to provide little comforts and luxuries. I started a list"—she waved toward the tablet sitting on the edge of a counter—"and I'm prepared to add to it."

"What is on the list so far?" Kara asked.

"Bowli balls," Theo said.

Kara raised her eyebrows. "How many bowli balls, I wonder?"

"A match-set, and a casual-play set," Theo said. "I can add more, if you think that's not enough."

"That is a dozen bowli balls," Win Ton said.

He looked to Kara.

"Shall we establish a league?" he asked her. "With all these ships come in—"

"You're out there," Theo interrupted. "Most of them are headed over to bunk on Ren Stryker. Though," she added, as one being fair, "there's more said to be incoming."

"Eventually, we might field teams," Kara said thoughtfully. "Do we know how long we will be at Light Keeper yos'Phelium's pleasure?"

"No word on that, yet." Theo took a sip of her wine, eyes narrowed.

"Nothing to say that we can't found the Tinsori Light Bowli Ball Club."

"No, there isn't, is there?" Kara said, much struck.

She glanced at Win Ton, who lifted a shoulder. "Certainly, it would be worthy of us."

"Precisely what I was thinking! Let us consider this seriously."

"We would recruit by putting on a display," Chernak said. "Recall it, my Stost?"

He grinned. "Too well, Elder!"

"A display?" Theo asked.

"In fact. We would arrive in dress uniforms, and our arms brought to a bright polish, and execute maneuvers, while our Elders-in-Troop told tales of glory and heroism." Chernak lifted her glass and regarded it meditatively.

"It was well enough, for those who were not yet out of creche, and considered drill-work."

"Who's for more of anything?" Clarence asked then. His answer was a general shifting toward another taste of this and that, and talk was suspended.

Eventually, though, the table was cleared, and they sat together over the last of the wine. Theo looked around at them—tired, happy, safe. Her crew. Hers to protect.

"It got to be a busy day," she said. "Let's catch each other up. Core team first."

Once again, it was Win Ton who reported.

"Our first task was to clear access to the hatch, whereupon we lowered the remote by pulley to explore the lower core while we continued work in the upper. We three discussed our progress at tea-break, and decided to move the project along more quickly. Sufficient material had been cleared to allow Chernak room to work in the upper chamber. The information provided by the remote was that the space below was disordered, but no threats other than chancy footing had been identified. That being so, Kara and I decided to attempt the lower chamber. I went down first, to clear the area around the bottom of the ladder. Kara joined me, and Chernak lowered the pulley. We put up lights and set to work."

"And all was well, if filthy and far too warm," Kara took up, allowing Win Ton a chance at his wine. "Until Win Ton heard something, and we looked about—startling the avian, as you have heard, which flew past us and up the ladder, startling Chernak in turn."

"Who allowed it out into the station," Chernak added gloomily.

"Don't know but I'd've done the same," Clarence said. "Even when you're lookin' for trouble, sometimes it gets the drop on you."

Chernak glanced at him and turned her palm up. "As you say. At that point, we reported to the captain, called Stost in, and initiated controlled searches of both chambers."

"We found no other avians," Win Ton said, "nor anything that looked as if it did not belong."

"Though that," Kara added, "was something of a guess, Theo. The deep core is in unimaginable disorder. If Mentor Jones is responsible for the scale of destruction we found, I am in awe of his abilities."

Theo was frowning.

"So, it wouldn't be necessarily obvious, if some of the pieces you're dealing with might have belonged to, say, a bot?"

Win Ton and Kara exchanged a glance. Kara shook her head.

"Twisted girders and shattered tiles, shred that could have been anything," Win Ton said slowly.

"That is accurate," Kara said. "We only assume that we're clearing the old operating system, because that is what we were told. There might have been twelve dozen bots standing row-on-row, before Mentor Jones did his work."

"I will send the remote's images to your screen, if that would be helpful, Theo," *Bechimo* said.

"Do that. I'll look at them later." She sipped the last of her wine and put the glass aside.

"My turn," she said, leaning back in her chair. "I went to inspect one of the breached halls with Jen Sin while you were scaring birds in the core..."

"Thus the interest in possible bots inside the core," Win Ton said, after she had finished. "Do we assume that both the avian and the armed bot are remnants of the old system?"

"If so, they're on a network which is unavailable to Tocohl, who believes she holds all of the old keys, and ought to be able to see every station system," Joyita said. He reached somewhat out of sight, and brought a wine glass to his lips. "*Bechimo* and I are working with her to modify one of our scanners, to facilitate an in-depth examination of that hallway."

"How long 'til the old core's clear?" Theo asked. "Best estimate."

Kara looked to Win Ton, who was looking at something inside his head.

"Two shifts?" he murmured. "No longer than that, surely."

"Would it speed things up, if I—"

"No!" Chernak, Kara, and Clarence spoke at once. Win Ton merely looked horrified. Stost stroked Grakow, who was stretched on his knee.

Theo frowned.

"Theo, you are needed to interface with the people who are responsible for the health of the New Light," *Bechimo* said.

"Clarence can—"

"The captain is the appropriate point of contact for station administration, resident experts, and incoming captains," Win Ton interrupted. "*Melant'i* is clear."

She glared at him.

"It is, is it?"

"Yes, it is," Kara said. "Do be reasonable, Theo."

She *fuffed* the bangs out of her eyes.

"Fine. I'll be reasonable. If we're all caught up, who has something to add to this list for Trader Gordy?"

Seignur Veeoni's Private Workroom
Medical Alcove

A CHIME SOUNDED, IRRITATINGLY HIGH IN TONE, AND FAR TOO close to his ear.

Jen Sin opened his eyes.

The chime stopped.

Above him was the dark, disquieting blot of a hood. He closed his eyes again and took stock.

He felt—well. Not... overwell. Simply, his head did not ache, nor any other part of him. In a word, he felt rested and wholly competent.

...for values of competence that factored for yos'Phelium pilots.

"Light Keeper," a large voice said from nearby. "You will wish to know that *Karil* is coming in to dock within the next twelve minutes."

Karil? For a moment, his memory drifted. Then he recalled it. The ships incoming, bearing aid from the Carresens-Denoblis. *Karil* was podded out with supplies, and it was the light keeper's honor to welcome her.

He rolled off the pallet and onto his feet. Hazenthull handed him his jacket, and he shrugged into it.

"Tocohl," he said, as his hands did inventory of his pockets. "Pray allow *Karil*'s captain to know that I have been delayed, but will be on her dock very soon."

"Yes," came the answer.

Jen Sin looked up at Hazenthull.

"I thank you for your service—and your insistence. I do not wish to be abrupt, but I must leave immediately, if I am to arrive on the docks even credibly late."

"That is not a concern," Hazenthull assured him, turning to

walk with him. "Seignur Veeoni has given you the use of her jitney for this. I will drive you."

He glanced up at her.

"Surely your duty to the Line falls short of intimidating allies for the use of their goods."

Her lips twitched.

"Surely, it does not, though it did not come to that. Seignur Veeoni is offended by inefficiency, and stated that it would be extremely inefficient to see you restored, and immediately exhaust you again."

She looked down at him.

"She did ask that you not disturb her to take your leave."

"So, the universe is not wholly set on end. You relieve me."

They passed into the main workroom, where the jitney waited, proclaiming its affiliation for all to see.

"I can," he said to Hazenthull, "drive myself."

"Then you would be on the docks unguarded," she said simply, putting her large self into the driver's seat. "That would not be wise."

He paused, considering the large, unarguable bulk of her, and slid into the passenger's seat.

"Very well, then," he said calmly. "Let us to the docks."

Seignur Veeoni's Private Workroom

HOW LIKE YURI, AFTER ALL, SHE THOUGHT, AS SHE FINISHED HER perusal. She ought to have expected something of the sort, but—she was *not* Yuri, and the lifework she had been born to accomplish had some limits on its scope.

Yuri accepted no limits on his vision, which aggrieved his siblings no less than his siblings aggrieved Yuri.

Seignur Veeoni sighed, and closed her screen.

Rising, she shook herself into order and left her quarters.

M Traven met her at the desk and handed her a glass of nutrient.

Seignur Veeoni took it without comment, and drank.

"Light Keeper yos'Phelium arose from the 'doc much refreshed," M Traven said. "Hazenthull has driven him to the docks to meet the incoming ships."

She had allowed Hazenthull that imposition, which would now seem shortsighted.

Seignur Veeoni drank some more nutrient. The jitney was not, after all, necessary for this expedition.

She finished the rest of the nutrient and put the glass down.

"I am going for a walk," she said to M Traven. "I will want you with me."

Dock B

• • • • • • • •

THE INTERMINGLED CREWS OF *KARIL*, *RODGER DODGER*, AND *Crinolyn* made a boisterous crowd on the docks. Hazenthull drove the jitney directly toward the thickest part of the knot, not at top speed, but by no means idling.

A tall full-bearded man turned his head, his hearing perhaps sharper than that of his fellows. He called out in Terran.

"Here he is, his own self! Make way for the light keeper, or I'm bettin' he'll run you down!"

There were startled, over-the-shoulder glances, and a brisk rearranging of the crowd, which allowed the jitney to come to a decorous halt at the side of *Karil*'s ramp.

Jen Sin swung out onto the deck, and raised his voice somewhat, as he spoke in Terran.

"I regret that I was delayed. Please be welcome at Tinsori Station."

"Definition of 'station master' is 'busy,'" said the bearded one who had warned of the jitney's approach. He stepped forward to stand a little before the others, and inclined slightly from the waist. There was no mode discernible, but it was clearly well meant. Jen Sin answered in the same spirit, and the other man grinned.

Seen more nearly, the beard, and the hair that fell to his shoulders in luxuriant waves, were grey. He wore pale brown overalls, thinly striped with darker brown, and the badge on the chest read, "Fenchile."

"Boss Fenchile, I am happy to see you."

"Light Keeper yos'Phelium, happy don't begin to approach my feelings on seeing you." He raised a hand, beckoning Jen Sin closer. "Let me just make you known to everybody here, then we'll get to the unloading."

He moved toward the ramp, where three people waited, Jen Sin at his side.

"Now, right here's Jaileen Uldra-Joenz, *Karil*'s captain, an' here's her brother Norse, cargo master this trip, an' young Tif, just getting his board hours for second class."

Jen Sin had barely greeted the long-faced captain, the cargo master, and fledgling pilot, before he was swept off to be made known to *Rodger Dodger*'s master, and through a dizzying two dozen names and faces until he was again at the jitney, Hazenthull at his back, with Boss Fenchile, Captain Uldra-Joenz, an apparently rankless person who had been introduced with baffling simplicity as "Gracie," and Cargo Master Uldra-Joenz.

"So," said Boss Fenchile, carefully, "Crystal's jitney?"

"Indeed. Researcher Veeoni is affiliated with the Crystal group. She is an expert in architecture and processing, and is at the head of the effort to put clean, modern systems into place. She has been a generous ally, and as you see, the Light is under-supplied."

"Got work jitneys on *Crinolyn*," said Gracie. "We'll leave a pair for you, so you don't gotta mess up the pretty, here. Ren's got jitneys as part of his rig, so we'll be all right over there for moving what we gotta."

Boss Fenchile and Captain Uldra-Joenz nodded.

"'Nother wave'll be coming in from the Hacienda, prolly some stragglers in between," said Boss Fenchile. "Jaileen, why don't you send the light keeper's short o'general dockside. Too—"

He turned to Jen Sin. "We was talking about your breach situation on the way in. The Family—that's the Carresens-Denoblis—they're sending shipwrights and station mechanics, from the big yard. They'll be bringing repair rigs as a matter o'course, but it might be awhile 'fore they get to us. That bein' the case, we special asked the Hacienda to send a workboat in the next wave, 'cause you don't wanna be without."

Such industry. Jen Sin took a breath.

"We have been too long without," he agreed. "Clan Korval appreciates your care."

"Tree-and-Dragon takes the biggest navigation hazard in this part o'space in hand and declares a working station?" exclaimed Norse Uldra-Joenz. "'Course we're gonna help! An' that's not takin' kin-ties to account."

Jen Sin gave him a puzzled glance, saw the long-faced captain frown. The cargo master bit his lip—then snapped his fingers. "Puts me in mind o'something you'll want to be takin' charge of, Light Keeper. Let me just fetch that out for you."

He turned, Gracie falling back to give him room to pass.

"So!" said Boss Fenchile loudly. "Now we're all known to each other, how 'bout we start that unload?"

"If you wish to stay on-station after the work is done, there is room, though we have little entertainment to offer," Jen Sin said.

"That's kindly said, Light Keeper." Gracie gave him a smile. "Been talkin' to Ren on the side, and he's got everything set up for us. Figure best use of time, after we get the cargo squared away, is to go on over and start getting settled in. There'll be more comin' in from the Hacienda, not to any schedule, mind, but expect 'em."

"I am fairly warned," Jen Sin said, as Gracie stepped aside to let Norse Uldra-Joenz back into the circle, pulling a cargo sled with a single crate on it.

"Came in last minute, delicates having to do with station systems," he said. "Might be you could just take 'em to the researcher, Light Keeper? Got the impression they'd be needed, quick. Oughta fit in your jitney there."

He pushed the sled forward somewhat. Hazenthull moved, and put her hand on the shaft. Cargo Master Uldra-Joenz went back two quick steps, hands rising to show empty palms.

"Sorry, Security."

"No problem," Hazenthull assured him in Terran. She bent, hefted the crate, and placed it gently into the jitney's carry space.

That done, and Cargo Master Uldra-Joenz once more in possession of his sled, she turned to Jen Sin.

"Sir, are you ready to go?"

"Take the man back to his busy, Security!" said Boss Fenchile heartily. "We got it covered here!"

They moved away. Jen Sin turned toward the jitney—and turned back as something caught the side of his eye. Something—*up*, near the supports for the hookups that weren't there.

"Is there a problem?" Hazenthull asked.

He looked another moment, scanning the space, then moved his shoulders.

"Likely not," he said. "I thought I'd seen a bird."

"The avian from the core? Will you raise an alarm?"

"Possibly the avian from the core, which I note has done nothing more harmful than flee when startled. We will log it."

"All right," Hazenthull said mildly, and nodded toward the jitney. "Sit. I will drive."

Seignur Veeoni

IT WAS A LOFTY AND SPACIOUS CHAMBER, SLIGHTLY SMALLER than the room Tocohl had chosen for the new core. The light, when it came up, was a warm yellow, and the floor was resilient and soft.

Mosaics crashed across the back wall from floor to ceiling, in waves of dark blue, pale green, gold and white. Before it, was a small, raised dais, the mosaic reflected on its gleaming surface.

Seignur Veeoni frowned.

"This is . . . an art installation?" M Traven's voice was soft, as if she recognized the chamber as something beyond the everyday.

"In a manner of speaking," Seignur Veeoni said. She turned toward the door.

After a moment, M Traven followed her.

Station Day 21
Second Shift
8.00 Hours

THEY WERE WELL AWAY FROM *KARIL*'S DOCKING BEFORE JEN SIN spoke.

"Cousin Tocohl, please elucidate the kin-ties shared with Uldra-Joenz."

"Fer Gun pen'Uldra was contracted to Chi yos'Phelium, the issue to come to Korval," she said obligingly from the jitney's comm.

So much, he recalled from the files provided by the delm.

"Daav yos'Phelium was the product of that contract," he said, also recalling that Daav yos'Phelium was his cousin Theo's father, reported by Clarence to have been a "caution," though now outstripped by his children.

"Yes. Upon completion of the contract, Fer Gun pen'Uldra formed a partnership with Trader Karil Joenz. Family Uldra-Joenz was incorporated on Fetzer's World, and largely moves in Terran trade lanes. The children of the alliance between pen'Uldra and Joenz may consider themselves kin to Line yos'Phelium."

She paused, and added, hesitantly,

"Surely it was meant as a pleasantry, Cousin Jen Sin."

"Surely so," he murmured, closing his eyes. "I take no insult."

He sighed.

"Where to, Hazenthull?"

"To Seignur Veeoni, I think, so that you may see her equipment delivered. Then I will take you to your office, or another location of your choice."

"My office will be satisfactory. After I am delivered, you may consider your duty fulfilled."

"Yes," said Hazenthull.

"Delicates?" Seignur Veeoni's eyebrows rose. "Place it on the bench, Hazenthull. M Traven will situate it appropriately."

They had disturbed her at study, which Jen Sin would not have done, being willing to leave the box with Traven. That same Traven, however, had waved them into the researcher's presence.

Having given her orders, Seignur Veeoni had already returned her attention to her screen.

Hazenthull placed the box on the bench, and straightened, looking down at Traven.

"I will take the light keeper to his office, then return the jitney to you."

"Very good."

Administrative Tower

THE TOWER WAS EMPTY WHEN JEN SIN RETURNED.

"Light Keeper Lorith is in her workroom," Tocohl said, in answer to his query. "She asked me to call if there was need."

"I see."

He drew a cup of water from the dispenser, vaguely disturbed. He and Lorith had been used to being much in each other's company, on those occasions when they were awake. They had slept together more often than apart, taking what comfort there was in the midst of the madness in which they functioned. This awakening—*this present time*, he corrected himself roughly—they seemed... not attuned.

Granted, they had been busy, each at their tasks, and the necessity of splitting the administrative watch had perhaps limited their shared off-time.

Which, he reminded himself, draining the cup, was what the station schedule was meant to regularize.

He sighed. Well. He would seek her out, the next time they were both properly on-shift, and talk with her.

He drew another cup of water and went to the desk.

Seating himself, he brought the screen live, and opened the station log.

"Mentor Jones and I have finished designing the program you requested," Tocohl continued. "He asked me to present this fact to you, and to answer any questions you might have. If there is need, the mentor is also available to you."

"I take from this that you and Mentor Jones are satisfied that the program will effectively decommission any device listening for the voice of *Ahab-Esais*?"

"Yes, though the only true test of our craft is to deploy it."

"Understood. Do you or Mentor Jones have any additional thoughts about this project that you wish me to hear?"

A small hesitation.

"I reiterate my previously stated concern regarding the escalation of hostilities."

"Noted. And Mentor Jones?"

"Mentor Jones believes that Director Ling, to whom Mentor Yo was—obligated—will build anew and better, after he has recovered his equilibrium."

"Thus do we encourage innovation, and add to the tale of our good works," Jen Sin murmured. "Pray continue to shelter *Ahab-Esais* inside the station's shields. As you will have heard on-dock, we are expecting shipwrights from the Carresens Yard, who may be able to aid her. If they find themselves at a loss, we will await whatever technicians Korval might send."

"Yes, sir."

He raised an eyebrow. "I am a tyrant, I apprehend. Is there something else on this topic?"

"No, sir. Shall I deploy the program?"

"Surely, it falls within the light keeper's honor to do so, though I am not prepared to settle the point with pistols. Is it possible that mine be the hand? Or must I stand as the genius behind the action, and order you to deploy the program?"

Another small hesitation.

"The program presently resides in an isolated environment. It is killware, and dangerous by its nature. There is . . . less chance of error, if I am the one to release it."

"Then let the log show that you acted to protect the station and all who depend upon it, at my order. Deploy the program at will, Pilot Tocohl."

"Yes," she said, and a bare moment later:

"Deployed."

Tolly and Hazenthull's Private Quarters

"WHAT IS THAT?" HAZ ASKED.

Tolly jerked. He'd been studying the thing in his hand so hard that he hadn't heard her come in. He threw a grin over his shoulder.

"You tell me," he said, and held his hand out to her, fingers spread, and the pod resting in the middle of his palm.

She considered it for a long moment.

"It looks like the fruit of the Tree Clan Korval keeps, on Surebleak."

"Well, it's the fruit of a tree that's traveling in *Bechimo*. Could be it's related to the tree on Surebleak. Cap'n Theo said something about not being as fine an interpreter as Val Con."

"I have heard of this," Haz said. "Why were you given a fruit?"

"That's an innerestin' story," he said, sagging back in his chair. "You'll remember how I was telling Cap'n Theo that we ain't family, though we share some starter-genes from the Old Universe."

"Yes."

"She tells me that she told the tree I'm not related, but the tree made up its own mind—" He met Haz's eyes. "I'm told it does that a lot. Get the sense Cap'n Theo don't approve of plants deciding for themselves."

He looked back at the pod. It was warm against his skin, and greener than he remembered when he'd caught it and stuffed it into his pocket. Then, it had given off a mild, minty scent. Now, the scent had intensified. Not minty, anymore. Or at least, he didn't think so. Now, it just smelled like the thing he wanted most to eat in all the universe.

"Tolly?"

He shook himself, and met her eyes.

"Long story short, it smells great, and I really want to know what it tastes like."

"That's easily accomplished. Do you want me to open it for you?"

"No!" His breath caught, his palm tingled, and then, *right* then, the pod fell into neat quarters.

Get up now, Tolly Jones, and pitch that thing into the recycler, he told himself, somewhere between panicked and stern.

Instead, he picked up the first quarter and put it in his mouth.

The pod gave him a jolt, like a hit of stim, almost immediately followed by a warm easiness. He ate the rest like he'd been starving, and when they were all gone, he sighed, sated.

Haz regarded him blandly.

"Is all well?"

"Far's I can tell," he said, getting up and depositing the pod's skin in the recycler.

He turned and grinned up at her.

"So, got plans for the off-shift?"

Seignur Veeoni's Private Workroom

EVEN THE BEST LAID PLAN MAY GO AWRY.

Nobody is omniscient.

It was, Delia Bell told herself, good to occasionally be reminded of these particular truths, though preferably not while she was working.

She'd been blindsided, plainly said, and now she was playing catch-up, not her favorite position in the race, and she wasn't looking forward to her probable reception. Still, it could have been worse.

It was good to occasionally be reminded of that, too.

She pressed the button next to the door, composing herself to wait.

To her surprise, however, her ring was answered at once.

"Who is it?"

"My name is Delia Bell. I'm a rack-and-tile specialist. I'm told my supply box was delivered here—that is, to Researcher Veeoni. I'd like to reclaim it."

All true. That was worrisome.

"One moment."

Ah, *now* she would wait.

But again she was surprised. The voice was back almost immediately.

"Researcher Veeoni will see you. Door opening."

She was allowed so far as the foyer, the door to the hall at her back, and the door to what must be the main laboratory before her.

That door opened and a woman wearing a lab coat stepped through.

Researcher Veeoni was tall and thin. She frowned down at Delia, possibly attempting to intimidate her. Briefly, Delia weighed the value of being intimidated, but then Seignur Veeoni spoke.

"You are a rack-and-tile specialist?"

"Yes, Researcher." More truth.

"It is a small field, and I am always pleased to welcome a colleague. Where are you based?"

"Hacienda Repair. I got separated from my kit in the rush." Truth again. She was getting seriously worried.

"I wonder what you thought you would be doing here?"

Delia spread her hands, and smiled, noting with interest that Seignur Veeoni seemed immune to her charm.

"I thought I'd be rehabilitating old systems, and building new, as needed. Wasn't aware there was another specialist already at work," she said, which was . . . *almost* true. "Now that I know you're here, set up and working, I offer my assistance."

"Of course," Researcher Veeoni said. "We put your crate into its own work space in the general workroom near the core. Consider that space your own. Once you have assured yourself that your equipment is intact, come to me so that we might see where best to apply your skills."

Was it going to be this easy? Delia wondered, even as she bowed slightly in thanks.

Seignur Veeoni looked over her head to the woman who had opened the door.

"Show Technician Bell to her work space, M Traven," she said, and turned away, the interior door opening to her.

"Yes, Researcher. Specialist, this way, please."

Delia turned and followed M Traven out into the hall.

Tolly and Hazenthull's Private Quarters

THEY'D MODIFIED THE BUNK SITUATION, SO HAZ HAD ROOM FOR all of her, he had the little bit he needed, and room enough left over for some careful play.

They had played—exploring, mostly, which was all right. Both of them were deadly, and knew their pressure points—which turned out to be a feature, pressure points being just that excitable.

So, they'd played, and dozed, and played a little more before slipping into actual sleep, Haz curled around him, and his head on her forearm.

The comm buzzed.

Tolly opened an eye.

The comm buzzed again.

He took stock, trying to decide if he had ever in his life been as comfortable as he was right at this particular present.

And the comm buzzed again.

He could tell by her breathing that Haz was awake, so that was his only excuse for not answering gone.

He rolled to the edge of the bed, and punched the button.

"Tolly Jones here," he said.

"Mentor, it's Joyita. You asked to be informed of the results of our scan of the breach hall."

Well, he had, hadn't he? How was Joyita to know it was his off-shift?

"Find anything?" he asked.

"Nothing that looks like a network, or data storage. There are solid-state installations between layers of plate, including the section from which the armed bot emerged, but they're inert."

Tolly frowned.

"Inert like... craniums?"

"Possibly," Joyita said slowly. "Analysis indicates that the installations are cermabronze."

"Nice Old Universe stuff. Pretty stable, wasn't it? Which is to say that whatever was installed isn't likely to be degrading."

"That's correct."

"Do you need me to do anything—go to the breach hall, inspect the bot's ustabe cubby, or anything like?"

"No, thank you, Mentor. Tocohl is considering her options. I'm merely reporting our findings, as we agreed."

"'Preciate that. How's the ghost situation?"

"We've recovered additional tools, but the operator continues to elude us."

"Not planning anything risky, are you?"

"Of course not, Mentor," Joyita sounded hurt. Tolly felt his lips twitch. "We're upgrading the perimeter and looking to personal armor."

"That's you, *Bechimo*, and Tocohl?"

"Yes."

"All sounds reasonable to me. You need me to do anything, or if you find something innerestin', let me know, right?"

"Right," Joyita said. "Thank you, Mentor."

"No problem. Jones out."

He reached out, punched the button, and rolled over.

Haz had stretched out onto her back while he'd made small talk with Joyita, and he felt a pang as he looked down into her face.

"Sorry 'bout that," he said, and wasn't he just.

"So am I," Haz said. "I was . . . content."

"I was, too," he admitted, turning his head to get a look at the clock. "Got an hour 'til we're on-shift."

"Good," she said, and stretched out an arm. "Come here."

Station Day 22
Administrative Tower

HE HAD TAKEN A HALF-SHIFT TO HIMSELF, AND DARED TO SLEEP, after setting a timer.

Somewhat to his surprise, he woke, refreshed, from a deep and dreamless sleep a few minutes before the bell sounded.

"This is what comes of eating Tree-fruit," he told himself, and swung out of bed with energy.

Lorith had not been in her workroom when he stopped by on his way to the tower. Nor was she in the tower. That was worrisome.

He was considering calling her quarters, when the comm announced an incoming call.

"yos'Phelium."

"Fenchile here, Station Master. Just lettin' you know that the unloadin's done. Got the cargo stacked in its own pen, dockside, just as neat as you'd please. 'Bout half of us is gone over to Ren, and the other half'll be following in the next little while."

"Thank you," Jen Sin murmured, when Boss Fenchile paused.

"That's all right. Wanted to give you a couple heads-up. Those jitneys Gracie talked to you about are right by the cargo pen, all charged up an' ready to work. Right up front, there's the standard care package that we bring, every Traveler's Aid call. Basic stuff—couple first aid kits, blankets, ration kits, energy drinks. Might could be somebody tucked a few beers anna couple bottles o'wine in a corner. Standard rack of evac suits in their own case, next to the right. Sent a list to the station admin account."

"You are far too kind to us," Jen Sin said, and meant it.

"'S'wat we do," Boss Fenchile said, big voice easy. "Other news is the workboat's comin', like we talked about, and a mixed team o'warehousers an' maintenance, to help with cargo-sortin' and general labor. They'll be wantin' quarters on-station. Likely to see one of the supervisors sooner better'n later, lookin' to make sure you got room for their crew.

"Not sure when, but *Virago*'ll be bringin' a pop-up caf." He paused, and added, warily, "Got specs I can send, if you want 'em."

Of course he wanted the specs, Jen Sin thought. He would need to situate the caf and the worker quarters together, at a convenient distance to the cargo pens. What sort of administrators had Boss Fenchile been dealing with on the Liaden side that made him so dainty?

Well. Perhaps he might be a good example.

"The specs will be useful, Boss Fenchile, thank you. Also, anything you might give me regarding numbers arriving." He paused, frowning, wondering if he dare open the light keeper's *melant'i* so far.

You had wanted to be a good example, he told himself and touched the switch again.

"I wonder if you might advise me."

A short pause preceded a cautious, "Do my best."

"That should be more than sufficient. Are you able to explain the . . . conditions under which we receive this aid, these workers? I see no contract in my files, nor any budget. Clan Korval expects to properly compensate labor and goods. Understand that I am pleased to have you, your crew, your assistance. Merely, I wish to account correctly, and to have no misunderstandings between us."

"No misunderstandings—we're on the same page, there! How you got us is Carresens-Denoblis put out a Traveler's Aid Notice. That's for when there's a rescue needed. Alla us who'd signed up previous to help, was there trouble, or who was in-station and at leisure, we jumped up to answer the call."

A short pause.

"We're volunteers, right?"

"I understand."

"'Course you do. Now, it's good you're worrying about rates and contracts and like that. I'm warmed to hear your thoughts're tending in that direction. But here's what I'm thinking—that's above *both* our pay grades. Right now, the Family's spending for the mutual good. Ghost Station—beg your pardon, sir—Tinsori Light's been a hazard to navigation for a lot too many years. Gettin' it regularized and working for this sector—that's good for everybody. Ain't one of us can't see there's work to do, and station crew short. You do what you can, quarters for the ware-housers and the like, and let us help you. If there's contracts to be written, or Balance to be made, that's all gonna happen next level up. Carresens and Korval, is what I mean."

A slight pause.

"That tie everything up for you, sir?" Boss Fenchile asked, soft-voiced and respectful.

Jen Sin spared another uncharitable thought for the past administrators that had burdened this useful person's life, and made certain his own voice was cheerful as he gave his assurance in Terran.

"It does, I thank you, Boss Fenchile."

"No trouble at all. Glad you thought to ask. Tell you 'nother thing, while we're on this—Gracie's part of the Family—Belagras Denobli. You got any questions you need answers from up-line, you toss 'em to Gracie, right?"

"Thank you," Jen Sin said again. "That is most helpful."

"Good. Now, here's what—me an' the rest're gonna go over to Ren an' get settled in. There's word o'some materiel to be shifted, and we'll get to that next shift. Who's the removal team?"

"Captain Waitley of *Bechimo* lent her crew to the task," Jen Sin said. "They may welcome assistance."

"Right. I'll just give Cap'n Waitley a call, once we're settled, so we can coordinate.

"I'll let you go, now, Light Keeper, and get on my boat before it leaves without me. You can rest easier, now, I hope. We got your back."

This last was followed by a sharp intake, as if Boss Fenchile feared he had overstepped.

"I am glad of it," Jen Sin said sincerely. "I look forward to continuing our association. yos'Phelium out."

"Fenchile out."

Jen Sin closed his eyes.

More people incoming, he thought, and shivered.

Deliberately, he closed his eyes, and reviewed the prism exercise. A few minutes later, he opened his eyes, feeling calm and centered.

Reaching to the computer, he opened a screen. The delm and Ms. dea'Gauss needed to be informed of the various debts being incurred.

"Cousin Tocohl, I will wish to send this via pinbeam," he said, fingers moving over the keys.

"Yes, Cousin Jen Sin."

Common Meeting Space

"ANOTHER ONE," TOCOHL SAID, PLACING THE DATA-PICK IN THE workspace she shared with Joyita and *Bechimo*.

"We're amassing quite a collection," Joyita said, eyeing the pick, and the analysis scrolling beside it.

"It's the same as all the others," Tocohl said, irritably. "Whoever is creating these hasn't learned anything about improving the tool, increasing its utility, or—"

"There may not be any need," *Bechimo* said.

"No need? Is it a game, then?"

"Not a game," Joyita said. "A distraction. Is that what you meant, *Bechimo*?"

"Exactly. The operator continues to deploy the picks, which fall into the traps, which must be cleaned. In the meantime, with the traps full, and our attention on the captured picks, the operator is free to explore other avenues of access."

"That," said Tocohl, "is unsettling."

"We've strengthened the perimeter, and detected no signs of intrusion. We may want to build a shield wall, with additional traps," Joyita mused.

"What do we gain by increasing the size of the game board?" Tocohl asked, rather sharply.

"An excellent question," Joyita said.

"What is the operator's goal?" *Bechimo* asked. "The distractions seem to serve no purpose."

"They acclimate us to the picks," Tocohl said.

"And account the traps, their number and location," Joyita added. "Here's my proposal: Increase the number and sophistication of the traps. *Bechimo* has just forwarded something to me from his own defense archive that may be adapted. First, though, Pilot Tocohl, I propose that we increase your personal armor."

"And yours," said *Bechimo.*

"Yes, and yours. We have to assume that the increase in the number of picks signals our operator is working toward producing a real threat. It's not impossible that the real attack, when it comes, will target—all of us."

Lorith's Workroom

LORITH WAS SLUMPED OVER THE TABLE, SCARCELY SEEMING TO breathe.

Slowly, she pushed herself erect, and raised her hands to her head, massaging the temples as if to smooth away a headache. She slid her fingers into her hair, feeling the beads running through her fingers like water. So soothing. A long-familiar comfort, and reminder of her duty.

Taking a breath, she looked at the workbench, the tiles laid neatly to one side, the sections of rack to the other, waiting for her to join them together.

She put on her glasses, and went to work.

Bechimo
Dock A

· · · · · · · ·

"CAP'N WAITLEY, THIS IS KORLU FENCHILE, SUPERVISOR OF THE first scramble volunteers. I'm going across to Ren right now, and I figured to give you a call and see if we can't cooperate together on a couple chores."

"I'm pleased to make your acquaintance, Supervisor. What kind of cooperation did you have in mind?"

"Well, Light Keeper yos'Phelium let me know your crew was takin' on the clearing of debris outta the old systems core. You need any little help with that?"

"Truthfully, we could use more hands. My crew made a good start, but there's more to do. The real problem is room. The core's a cramped situation."

"I'm looking at the station map right now, and I'd say cramped 'bout describes it. Tell you what, whyn't I ask Marsi—she's comp systems chief—to bring a couple o'her crew to the old core? Scope out the situation, talk to your crew on the spot and figure out how best to do what needs done. That work for you, Cap'n?"

"Yes, it does. What's your time frame?"

"I'm looking at eighteen hundred station time. Marsi and her crew went over to Ren first thing, so they'll be rested and ready to go."

"Eighteen hundred," Theo said. "My crew will be at the Old Core, and I know they'll welcome the help."

"That's a plan, then, and I'll bid you good shift. I hope to give myself the treat o'stoppin' by *Bechimo* next time I'm over station-side, and introducin' myself in person."

"I'll look forward to that," Theo said.

"'Til then, Cap'n. Fenchile out."

Seignur Veeoni's Private Laboratory Containment Room

M TRAVEN MOVED THE FOUR CRATES THROUGH THE HATCH INTO the double-containment room while Seignur Veeoni made her preparations. Given the age of the items, and the fact that they had been stored on-station since before the Great Enemy subverted it into Tinsori Light, the extra security was prudent. In fact, Seignur Veeoni had a moment's nostalgia for the quadruple containment room of her former laboratory, since destroyed by the Lyre Institute.

Carefully, she removed the two sets of memory beads that she wore next to her skin, placing each in its particular protective box.

She then donned a hazard suit—the ceramic one—though it would perhaps have been more prudent to have used the remotes to make her examination.

If the boxes contained what she thought they contained, it was not impossible that she would need to interact with them personally.

Her preparations made, she gave the beads in their protective boxes to M Traven, with instructions to place them in the safe.

Instead of simply doing as she was told, M Traven asked a question.

"Do we expect a disaster?"

"We do not. After you have put those items into the safe, you will seal the laboratory and all work spaces, and take position at the bay entrance. No one is to come any further than the bay entrance until I have signaled that I am finished."

M Traven sighed.

"To a soldier's ear," she said, "that sounds like disaster prep."

"It is," Seignur Veeoni told her, "prudence."

"What are we being prudent about?"

"I am not minded to allow the Great Enemy or any of their works into existing station systems. Is that imprudent?"

"Only the part where what's in those crates might be dangerous."

"Everything is dangerous, in the correct amounts. In the present situation, I do not believe that the crates or their contents present a danger to us or to this station. However, there exists a possibility—small, but present—that I am wrong. I am therefore taking precautions. Are you satisfied?"

M Traven looked down at the boxes she was holding—a treasure trove of memory—and sighed.

"Not satisfied, no. What orders, if you are wrong?"

That was an excellent question. Seignur Veeoni inclined her head in approval.

"If I am wrong, contact my brother Yuri and tell him that I opened the crates that were in Storeroom Core Six. Follow his orders from there."

For a moment M Traven simply did not move.

Then, she saluted, turned and left the room.

When the door had fully closed and locked, Seignur Veeoni pulled up the hood of the protective ceramic suit, fastened it, lowered the visor, made sure of the field, and let herself into the containment room.

Administrative Tower

HE HAD WRITTEN TO THE DELM AND TO DEA'GAUSS, DETAILING the Traveler's Aid Notice, the arrival of Ren Stryker and the first wave, and the expected continued arrival of aid.

When that was sent, he wrote a second letter, to the delm alone, seeking guidance in the matter of the station's sentience, and briefly outlining Joyita and *Bechimo*'s judgment, that Tocohl, who had not been born to be Station, could never truly *be* Station, though she was a perfectly able administrator.

Correspondence for the moment cleared, Jen Sin leaned back in his chair.

He would in a moment open the station maps and seek to identify an appropriate space for those crews who were incoming. Whole sections of the station had been sealed off as Tinsori Light found it more and more necessary to husband his failing resources.

He rose, crossed the tower, and drew himself a cup of water, which he drank standing at the dispenser.

His mind drifted somewhat, to the goods reported unloaded and stashed in the cargo pen. He ought also, he thought, to identify a common area for the safe wing. The stuff they had pirated from *Tarigan*'s supplies had been unceremoniously brought into a vacant meeting room, which was left open, so that anyone might draw at need. It was the best they could do, in those first, frantic days following the Old Light's demise, but now, he thought, they could do better. *Ought* to do better. Tinsori Light had been a prison for him and for Lorith, but for those who came willingly, it ought to be a respite, offering comfort, care, and a soft time of ease.

Well, he said to himself, *bold plans, Light Keeper. First, let us find a way to accommodate our incoming—*

"Theo has just exited the lift at the end of the hall," Tocohl said.

He disposed of his cup, and went back across the room, reaching his desk just as the chime sounded.

"Please open to our Cousin Theo, Tocohl."

The door opened, and in she strode, looking refreshed and lively.

"Theo," he said gravely, "to what do I owe the pleasure?"

She tipped her head, and considered him seriously.

"Is this a bad time?"

"In fact, it is not. Merely, I had been listing out those things that required my attention, and was becoming somewhat breathless. Well met, Cousin. Truly." He gave her a smile, and waved to the chairs at his desk.

"Will you sit?"

"I won't be long," she said, and reached into a pocket.

"Tree's been busy," she said, and handed him another pod. This one was even heavier than the first, and unripe. He put it away into his own pocket.

"Please let the Tree know that I am grateful, but that it must not overstretch itself for me."

Theo wrinkled her nose. "I got the impression it wants to—*feed you up*, if you understand me."

"Everything that is kind," he murmured. "Please do not tell me that you came all this way merely to deliver—"

"I'm glad to have a walk," Theo interrupted him, "but there's more. Here."

A folded printout was produced from another pocket, and extended.

"That's the list of things my crew would find good, if Gordy's inclined to bring them."

He took the page, glancing down—

"Bowli balls? What are bowli balls?"

Theo blinked.

"You've never played bowli ball?"

"Alas."

"Well, that won't do. We've got a couple onboard, but they've seen some use. These are . . . I owe Kara, for losing a bet, and anyway, there ought to be enough for everybody who wants to play. Tell you what—we'll get up a game sometime in the next few shifts; give you a demo, right?"

"I look forward to the demonstration," he said politely, and Theo blinked.

"Good, we'll make sure to call you. I wanted to tell you that Supervisor Fenchile's sending a comp systems crew over at eighteen hundred to help us finish clearing the core."

"Excellent." Jen Sin leaned a hip against his desk and crossed his arms. "He had said he would call you."

"Once the core's taken care of, what else can *we* do for *you*?" she asked—so earnest, the child! "We're here to help, remember?"

"I do know it," he told her wryly, "but I am unused to having so much potential available to me. Do keep reminding me if I lapse, Cousin."

He paused.

"Do you know—there may be something. Boss Fenchile's first wave brought us what he is pleased to dignify as basic aid supplies. We have been living at high scramble since the station stabilized, and it is perhaps time to make our bow to civilization. A common room, with items on-draw for crew, and—tables, nooks—you know the style of thing. A room on this hall—wait."

He slid into his chair and pulled the hall plan up on the screen. It was not a very large area, that he had cut out of the Light's influence, meter by painful meter, but there were—

"Here." He tapped the room, and expanded the image on the screen, aware of Theo leaning over his shoulder.

"It is the largest room in this hall," he murmured, "and could be made comfortable. An interim lounge—we will do better, as sections are opened—which is my next task—but for the moment, a place to share a glass of wine, or—play a game, read a book..."

"We can do that," Theo said. "Open the room, give me the code for the cargo pen, and we'll get it done for you."

"We have two work jitneys on loan. I'm told they're charged and waiting by the cargo pen." Jen Sin unlocked the door on the new crew lounge with three taps on his keypad.

"Station," he said, his eyes still on the screen. "Will you please alert the cleanbots to this room, as an area requiring their attention?"

"Done," Station said.

"Thank you."

He sat back in his chair and turned his head, his cheek accidentally brushing Theo's. His breath caught, but she only gave his shoulder a cousinly pat, and stepped back.

He spun his chair 'round to face her.

"One more thing, and I'll let you get back to work," she said seriously. "Stost and Chernak—one or both—are willing to give you that tour of *Spiral Dance*. You call when you've got time, and they'll make it happen, is what they told *me*."

She gave him a wry glance, eyebrows tilted in an expression so comically familiar that he laughed.

She grinned, and reached into her jacket pocket, and he thought perhaps she had brought him yet another Tree-fruit.

"In the meantime, you might as well hold this," she said, and it was not Tree-fruit in her hand.

It was a ship's key.

Longing burned through him, even as horror nailed him to his chair.

"I'd been thinking about what you'd said earlier," Theo was saying, "about not being able to leave the Light, because you didn't have a ship. But, you know, that's not true, anymore. *Spiral Dance* is a Korval ship, and you've got as much a right to her key as—"

She held it out to him.

His own hand leapt forward—

And he jerked back, fingers curling into a fist at his side.

"Put it away," he said, hearing the raw, dangerous edge in his voice.

Theo stared at him, and did not move, which was a reasonable response. The gods alone knew what she must see in his face now, but there was the key, in sight and unsafe on her palm.

"Put it *away*, Cousin," he said again, and this time she did, moving slow and careful, never taking her eyes off his, as she slipped the thing into her pocket.

"Thank you." He was trembling, and his voice, too, and she was still standing there, a ship's key in her pocket. Easy enough to make it his, should he—

"Cousin," he managed, "leave. *Now*, Theo!"

She inclined slightly from the waist, and took a step back, toward the door.

"Station," she said, her voice perfectly calm, "please open the door to the light keeper's office."

It whisked open behind her; she stepped out into the hall, her eyes holding his.

The door closed.

Jen Sin gasped, and raised his hands to cover his face. Deliberately, he brought the focusing prism before his mind's eye, and reviewed each color, gaining a measure of calm from the ordered flow. He was in control, he told himself firmly. He had not given Tinsori Light what it wanted, nor murdered kin for a ship's key. Only he needed to be calm, now. He needed to be Korval's face and will, until the Delm's Solution arrived.

Then, he could finish the task he had started so . . . very long ago.

"Cousin Jen Sin," Tocohl said, gently. "Are you well?"

He took a deep breath.

"Perfectly well, I thank you, Cousin."

He reached to the screen, called up the station map, and began a search of the residence halls.

Bechimo
Comm Officer's Tower

A BOARD PINGED IN THE CLUTTERED COMM TOWER.

Joyita answered at once, full visual.

Seignur Veeoni looked up at him, the hood of a protective suit pushed back from her face.

"Excellent," she said. "I have information that bears on our discussion of architecture."

"I'm interested," he said, "but—isn't this the middle of your sleep-shift?"

"Possibly. However, I must tell you that I was misinformed with regard to the intention of the builder. He *did* design for sentience, but not for the primary system."

Joyita examined her face closely. She was flushed, which could be the result of having had the hood and faceplate in place. Her eyes were sparkling, and her short hair stood on end. She seemed exhilarated, but not disordered. In fact, she seemed much as he had seen her during their last discussion—engaged, and excited by their topic.

"Why," he asked, "would the builder design for sentience in a secondary system?"

"Because the primary system was based on timonium, and timonium has a known half-life," Seignur Veeoni said impatiently. "You and I may see a moment or two into the future, but neither one of us is my brother, who sees for the ages."

"The primary system was built for immediate use," Joyita said. "As the timonium decayed, the secondary system would come online, fully a person, designed to be a station. The first system was merely—a tool."

"Exactly!"

"But why wait? Why not just allow the station to *be* from the first, based on technology that wouldn't degrade?"

"Because the second system had to have time to grow," Seignur Veeoni told him. "The technique was—experimental. Briefly, he created cells of the crystals used to craft memory beads. He installed a growing medium of cermabronze between layers of plating, and seeded it with memory cells. If all went well, the cells would grow into a network easily large enough to support sentience."

"But the key was that it would take time!" Joyita said, beginning to feel excited, himself. "The Enemy was pressing hard, and the station was needed for defense."

"Yes. Looking forward, the architect built a core for the sentient station, complete with a reference matrix. That was what led me to look for these—"

She stepped back, the camera following her until she stopped by four open crates, the muffling wrap pulled back to reveal glittering orbs studded with gems: blue, green, white, and gold.

He could see a dense haze of data above each. What would it be like, he wondered, to sample, just *sample*—

"These are the libraries meant for the networked core," Seignur Veeoni was saying. "Where they would be available to the station as she grew in knowledge and complexity."

"The station was designed for sentience," Joyita said, and asked the hardest question. "Do you think she survived?"

Seignur Veeoni frowned.

"We don't know if the crystal lattice grew," she said. "It was an experimental design, as I said."

"The cermabronze is intact in the breach hall," Joyita told her. "It showed up in the scan *Bechimo* and I did. We didn't know what it was, and without data from the original planting, we don't know that it's grown..."

"But it is intact!" Seignur Veeoni turned to look down at the open boxes, lips parted, expression rapt.

"Having discovered the builder's original intent," Joyita pursued, "what do you think is the best thing to do?"

She turned back to him.

"I believe that the best thing would be to take the libraries to the core, allow them to associate with the grid, and find if Station did survive."

Joyita looked at her with delight.

"May I accompany you to observe the placement of the libraries in the core?"

Seignur Veeoni looked up into the camera, and smiled.

"I was going to ask you to do so."

Lyre Institute for Exceptional Children
Lyre-Unthilon

. . . .

"DIRECTOR LING? I'M SORRY TO DISTURB YOU, SIR."

Director Ling raised his head to consider the technician. A competent technician, and discreet. They did not put themselves forward, nor make a habit of disturbing Directors.

"What is it?" he asked. "Quickly."

"Yes, Director. The receiver tuned to *Ahab-Esais* has... failed, sir."

"Failed in what way?"

"Well, sir, the program's shredded, and the memory fragged, done in such a way that a spark jumped, and the internal hardware... melted, sir."

Director Ling felt a moment of unease.

"What is the condition of the other receivers in the room?"

"All operating as they should. We're doing a system sweep, and increasing security."

"Could this have been a random hardware failure?" Director Ling asked.

"It's possible," the technician said, slowly. "But, I've never seen anything like it."

"I see. Continue your sweep and security upgrades. Report when you have identified the cause."

"Yes, Director."

The technician left.

Director Ling turned to the comm.

"Director," said the voice of another technician, in another receiving room half a planet away. "I was going to call you as soon as we had identified the cause. The *Ahab-Esais* receiver suffered a catastrophic failure, all internal hardware systems fused."

"No other receivers compromised?"

"Seems not, but we're running diagnostics. I'll have a full report to you in a couple hours, sir."

"Yes, do that."

Director Ling cut the connection, and made a third call.

And a fourth.

And a fifth.

Finally, he turned back to his screen, though he was not seeing the information displayed there.

He had not wanted, himself, to venture out to Tinsori Light, but it seemed that, now, he had no choice.

Someone had thrown down a gauntlet.

Such a challenge could not be ignored.

Jelaza Kazone
Surebleak

. . . .

"DELM'S GOT A LETTER FROM JEN SIN," MIRI SAID. "HE'S GOT A question."

Val Con lifted an eyebrow.

Miri grinned at him.

"Oughta be simple enough to answer," she said. "All he wants to know is if the delm wants Tinsori Light to be sentient."

Val Con closed his eyes.

"You gotta admit, he comes up with *innerestin'* questions," Miri said.

"I have no intention of disagreeing," Val Con said. "However, the lesser half of the delm finds himself at a stand."

"Don't know where to buy baby AIs?"

"Doubtless, the Uncle's sister will be willing to shop for us," he said dryly. "No, I fail before that point. Who is the delm of Korval to make such a decision?"

"Well, salvage law says Tinsori Light's ours. All those letters Ms. dea'Gauss wrote, and sent wide—she hasn't got even a 'maybe' yet, never mind an outright 'no.' If I didn't know you have everything in hand, I'd be a little unsettled about how many people're so eager for Korval to have that station in inventory."

"So you suggest that the question is merely one of the delm deciding to increase the clan."

"Pretty much in the job description, ain't it?"

"It is. However, it is a weighty decision, requiring study and analysis. If we decide to welcome a new child, we will of course need to address her education, provide her with companions that challenge and comfort her, ensure that her kin are not strangers, and that her voice is heard in the clan's decisions..."

He stopped, eyes narrowed.

Miri waited.

"I think," Val Con said slowly, "that the delm ought not rush into a decision."

Miri frowned. Val Con had a tiny bit of precognition, himself—nothing like Anthora, or Ren Zel in his heyday. Just a knack for lucky hunches. She'd seen it in action more than twice, and she was seeing it again right now, she thought, looking at the pattern of him inside her head. There was just the faintest bit of glow—fading now…

And gone.

She sighed, and gave him a grin when he looked up.

"So," she said brightly, "we stall?"

Val Con raised an eyebrow.

"Certainly not," he said severely. "Delms do not *stall.* Delms *consider* and *weigh.*"

"Right," Miri said, filing Jen Sin's letter. "We stall."

Old Core

IT WAS, AS KARA MURMURED TO WIN TON AND CHERNAK, ASTONishing how quickly a task could be accomplished merely by applying the proper tools.

They had brought the station's sleds and tools, but had left the remote behind, though they had agreed to wear button cameras, so *Bechimo* wouldn't feel left out.

Chief Marsi and her two assistants brought sleds, tools, and come-alongs as well as their sturdy selves. The lower core was cleared in a matter of hours, by which time the upper core had likewise been cleared, the smallest debris and the worst of the dirt gathered and contained by a suction cleaner.

Win Ton found Chief Marsi herself sitting on a folding stool in the center of the upper room, a keyboard across her knees and headphones wrapped around her head.

She looked up as Win Ton approached, tapped a series of keys and pushed the 'phones down around her neck.

"Listenin'," she said, "to hear if there's anything else ticking between the walls, or any compartments we might've missed." She shrugged. "Not perfect, but pretty good. Given what we're dealing with here—it bein' so old, I mean—we'll want to have a proper team sweep this thorough. For right now, though, I'll take a listen here, then go downstairs. If I don't hear nothin', then we're prolly good to leave it an' seal it."

"Shall I inform the light keeper of progress and see if there is any other requirement?"

"You do that, an' find does he want station seals on this, or should we use the work seals we brought."

Win Ton nodded and went out into the access hall to make the call.

When he returned to give Chief Marsi the news that the light keeper had approved her use of the work seals on the old core until such time as the proper team arrived to purge the space—she had descended to the core below.

He went down the ladder, and found her, not seated on her stool, as he had half expected, but wandering along the walls, fingertips trailing, as if she were reading signs on the surface that were invisible to the eye.

He scuffed his boot on the floor and she started, looking over her shoulder with a wry smile.

"You're not half quiet are you? What'd the light keeper say?"

"Work seals in place until the arrival of a certified cleaning team," Win Ton said promptly. "He thanks you for your care and diligence on behalf of the station."

She grinned and walked toward him, her instrument slung over her back by a strap, and the headphones around her neck.

"Having a real working station in this piece o'space is gonna benefit a lotta folks," she said, moving past him toward the ladder. "Not just Loopers neither."

"Indeed, we all have great hopes for the station, once it is—"

Something glimmered in the side of his eye, and he turned, following it to a crack in the floor tiles. Bending, he picked up what seemed to be a stylus, though thicker and heavier. It looked nothing like the debris they had been clearing, and Win Ton frowned, holding it up, and turning it carefully.

"Well, there it is!" Chief Marsi cried, leaning over and sweeping the thing out of his hand. She put it in her side pocket. "My favorite stylus," she said. "Dropped it and figured it was gone in all this dim. Sharp eyes, eh? Thanks."

Win Ton hesitated, but what might he say? Accuse the amiable, helpful chief of—what, precisely?

He inclined his head.

"Sharp eyes, yes," he said, with a smile. "I had been a Scout."

"Now, ain't that something," she said. "I'll just call my crew in to set those seals."

She swarmed up the ladder, and Win Ton followed, thoughtful.

Administrative Tower

THE SECOND WAVE WOULD BE STAYING ON-STATION, SUPPLEMENTED and supplied through their own caf. There was no information on how many individuals the second wave might encompass. He ought, therefore, to err on the side of allocating too much room.

Jen Sin was deep into the station architecture—the build schematics provided by Traven on one screen; the schematics elucidating the changes made by the Enemy after it had acquired Tinsori Light on the other.

He had already marked one possible section. It was referenced as *Spinward Arcade, Dorms* on the schematics. A quick check of station systems verified that the section held air. Maintenance systems registered off-line, but support accepted his command to increase section temp to station normal.

A tour through the cameras showed him a large open area with two avenues opening off of it—one meant to house small shops or eateries—the caf might be situated there. The other avenue was lined with dorms, and there was an upper level, as well. Utilitarian, as Tinsori Light was unremittingly utilitarian. One hoped that the incoming workers did not have a taste for luxury.

He would have to inspect, of course, manually reset the bots, make sure any rack-and-tile work was dismantled—but there was something else, something...

He rubbed his forehead, as if he might smooth away the niggling headache.

The schematics provided by Traven were... familiar.

Not just because they were similar to those schematics in station archives, but familiar as if he had not only seen, but had *studied* this precise document.

Well, and perhaps you had, Jen Sin told himself, *and the memory is among those stored in your beads.*

He sighed, and closed his eyes, taking deep breaths against the headache. Truly, he had been at the screens too long. Best to take a walk and perhaps have something to eat, and—

The headache exploded into a bright, silent spangle, and he saw—*himself*, newcome to the Light, sitting in what could only be a library, documents open on every screen and surface. There, the build schematics, next to it, the document elucidating all of the changes that had been made to the original build. He remembered, quite vividly, the cold horror that had washed through him, when he had at last understood what Tinsori Light was—a sentience created by the Great Enemy in order to realize their goal of subjugating an entire universe—planets, systems, people forever suspended in incorruptible crystal. *That* was the moment he had known his danger, and every decision he had taken going forward had been informed by the knowledge.

The damage to the station predated his tenancy, but he recalled—*almost*, he recalled something . . . else. Something in the original schematics, was it?

He turned back to his screen, the half-memory an itch inside his head. He brought up the diagram of the breach hall, tapping for more information, and there—yes. *There.*

He sat back.

He had discovered this, once before. Discovered it, decided to act on it—only why had he failed to take it further?

The original core had been rack-and-tile. But the builder, none other than the infamous Uncle, had intended his work to live beyond the defeat of the Great Enemy. He had realized that timonium's half-life would eventually betray his systems, and had seeded the station with an experimental network born of his own genius.

Ceramic and memory beads applied between layers of plating. Yes, he *did* remember this, by the gods! The thought was that systems would be transferred from the rack-and-tile arrays into the ceramic "nervous system" that would grow until it was throughout the station. If one section should be damaged or fail, there was room for redundancy.

Unfortunately, the nervous system had been newly seeded, with no opportunity to grow, when Tinsori Light had destroyed the rack-and-tile core.

There was another note—in a room near the breach hall where he and Theo had been threatened, there were stored, several... indexes.

Jen Sin sat back in his chair and closed his eyes.

He had *been* there, he was certain of it, though he had no memory to support that certainty.

Not even the Uncle had known how quickly the child of his genius would grow, nor what its final capabilities might be.

And there had been an armed bot in the breach hall.

Protecting what?

Or... whom?

He reached to the screen, filed the schematics, and rose.

Mentor's Comm Room

TOLLY TAPPED UP HIS MAIL QUEUE AND FROWNED.

"Is there a problem?" Haz asked, apparently having found nothing half so innerestin' on her screen.

"Cap'n Theo wants a tour of the core, with an explanation of how it all works," he said.

"Is there a reason she should not have those things?"

"Not for me to say, is it?" He turned his head toward the wall. "Station, ask Seignur Veeoni if she'll speak with me."

"Connecting," said the voice that wasn't quite Tocohl's. Tolly looked back to his screen.

"Mentor?" Seignur Veeoni said, briskly. "What is it?"

"Cap'n Waitley asks me to give her a tour of the new core and explain the principles and operations. That all right with you?"

"Indeed, Mentor. Daav yos'Phelium's daughter may surely tour the core, and you are, I know, more than competent to explain the principles and operations. It is, now that I think of it, an excellent idea. If, that is," she added, "you are able to take on this extra task."

Tolly blinked. "I can make some time to accommodate the captain," he said. "Might get Tocohl in, too."

"Another excellent idea. Thank you, Mentor."

"Seignur Veeoni has closed her line," Station said.

"Thank you, Station," Tolly said. "Would you call *Bechimo*, please?"

"Calling *Bechimo*," Station said.

"*Bechimo* comm officer," Joyita said crisply. "Service, Mentor?"

"Might be. Cap'n Theo dropped me a note asking if I'd take her on a tour of the new core. I'm wondering if she has a particular time in mind."

"I'll connect you with the captain," Joyita told him. There came a soft click, followed by—

"Tolly Jones?" Theo Waitley said.

"That's right. When would you like that tour, Cap'n?"

"I'm free now, if that works for you."

"Couldn't be better. I'm going to ask Tocohl to join us, for the questions I can't answer. That all right by you?"

"Yes."

"Good. I'll meet you at the hallway lift in twelve minutes."

"Make it fifteen," she told him. "Waitley out."

"*Bechimo* has closed the line," Station said, sounding apologetic.

"That's all right, they were done. Call Pilot Tocohl for me, will you, Station?"

"Of course, Mentor."

"Thank you."

"Mentor?" Tocohl's voice carried a faint edge of surprise. "Can I help you?"

"You can help me entertain and inform Cap'n Theo, if you got some time right now. She wants to get an understanding of the new core. I'll be there, but I'd like you as backup."

There was a small pause.

"Certainly, Mentor. I would be delighted."

"Good. Meet you in the core in twenty minutes, then. I'll bring Cap'n Theo in."

"Yes," she said.

"This is the *faristo*," Tolly said, as the door opened into a small space occupied by a—device, made of some light material that Theo thought might be ceramic. It was just about shoulder-high on her, and as wide as Stost and Chernak, standing together. Lights moved beneath the surface, and there was a catch-bin at the right side, where a dozen or so tiles were stacked.

"Seignur Veeoni invented this—device and process. I don't know how it works, particularly. The general information is that it machines tiles to spec. The big benefit to being able to mass-produce tiles is that they're already associated, which saves us a step in assembly. When we run out of tiles in the main workroom, we resupply from here. Questions?"

"No," Theo said, though she had a couple dozen. It didn't seem entirely likely to her that Tolly Jones was as ignorant of the process as he claimed. On the other hand, claiming ignorance gave him a reason to not answer questions.

"Right."

Tolly waved her out of the room ahead of him, and joined her in the hall.

"So, you've already seen how the racks and tiles go together," he continued, as they walked down the hall toward the main workroom and the core.

"The step after assembly is association, and that happens after we get a series of rack-and-tile systems hooked into the main array and calibrated."

A shadow moved by the door—Tocohl, floating a few inches above the decking and looking every bit the gracious and intelligent lady she was.

Beside him, Theo checked.

He paused, and looked to her.

"It's Tocohl in the chassis that was designed for her," he said.

"That's—not anything like a space station, is it?" she murmured. "I think I understand what *Bechimo* and Joyita were trying to explain."

She took a deep breath, sighed it out, and started walking again.

"Good shift, Mentor. Captain Waitley."

"Tocohl," Tolly said.

Theo nodded. "Good shift. Since we're cousins, it's got to be proper to use my name occasionally."

"That is correct." There was a smile in Tocohl's voice. "Shall I call you Theo when it is proper to do so?"

"I'd appreciate it."

"It will be my pleasure."

"The door's under Tocohl's direct control," Tolly said, and bowed to her.

There came a sharp snap, and the three red lights on the door readout changed to three greens.

"After you, Mentor," Tocohl said.

"Here's the functioning system," Tolly said, as they crossed the room toward the orderly rows of racks. Blue light coruscated over the array, and the air hummed slightly.

"This isn't everything, mind. We're still building. But this'll give you an idea of what the core's gonna look like when it's completely built."

"That field—is it dangerous?"

"Well, yes and no. It's the field does the heavy lifting, once the hardware's aligned. It'll protect itself, but at the same time, it's gotta be accessible for repair and expansion. There's protocols, and safety links. Working cooperatively with Station—or the station administrator—all necessary repairs and upgrades can be done without anybody getting hurt."

Theo nodded, cautiously.

"If somebody with mischief on their mind gets inside here," Tolly continued, "that's when the field turns dangerous. You need the work codes to neutralize it."

"What if somebody just wanted to disable everything? Got in and started smashing racks, and dumping tiles?"

Tolly looked at her.

"That's pretty specific. Something you've seen?"

"Not me. Kara—one of my crew—was describing the state of the old core." Theo gave him a grin. "She's impressed by your powers of destruction, by the way."

"So would I be, if I'd been taking down a fully functional system. Turns out, I wasn't. The Old Light was *old*, and he was sick. You couldn't really say there *was* a system any more. Even down in the deep core, there were gaps in associations you could put Ren Stryker through."

"So, you got lucky?"

"More or less. I'm thinking the event that pushed Tinsori Light all the way into the universe with the rest of us did more damage than I did." He paused, considering her out of slightly narrowed eyes. "You heard about that?"

"I did," Theo assured him.

"Only thing I did was disassociate some racks and dump the tiles. It would've been enough to kill him—the Old Light, I mean—he was that weak. But the event made sure of it."

He sighed.

"If you was gonna BFMI this array—say, start swinging a bar or kicking out tiles, then the field would react and what you'd get would be dead, real quick, and real permanent."

Theo frowned. "BFMI?"

"Brute force and massive ignorance. Pays to fight smart, Cap'n Theo."

"Better not to fight at all," Theo said, her eyes still on the gently glowing core.

"Other questions?" Tolly asked her.

"Just wondering about the—*ghost*, Joyita calls it. The one that was picking at the edge of station security. If she tries to break anything, it'll be through a breach in systems. How's security?"

"That," Tocohl said, "is an excellent question. At my invitation, Joyita himself made three attempts to breach security in the new core."

"What?" Tolly turned to stare at her.

"Joyita is excellent at what he does," Tocohl said. "He found two potential problems. Both have been repaired."

"Did you clear that with Seignur Veeoni?" Tolly asked.

"Joyita explained what he proposed to do, and Seignur Veeoni raised no objections. Indeed, she asked to be informed of his results."

Tolly closed his eyes.

"Joyita really is very trustworthy," Theo said, helpfully.

"Jeeves gives a good report of him," Tocohl agreed.

Tolly opened his eyes.

"Jeeves?"

"Yes—our mutual contact. Jeeves is my parent."

"Sure he is," Tolly said softly.

"Is something wrong, Mentor?"

"Nothing wrong at all. Jeeves does good work." He took a breath and turned back to Theo.

"So, eventually, we'll have everything backed up—in a secondary core. I can take you there, if you're innerested, Cap'n Theo, but all it is right now is empty space."

"I'll pass," Theo said, absent-sounding. She was considering the working array again, a frown between her brows.

"Question?" Tolly asked.

She glanced at him and gave a sharp shrug.

"I've got an itch, but I don't know what it is," she said. He nodded.

"It comes clear, you know how to get me."

He turned toward the door.

"If there are no other questions for me at the moment," Tocohl said. "I will leave you."

"Thank you," Theo said. "I appreciate you taking the time to explain the system to me."

"Certainly. If you have other questions, later, please don't hesitate to call me."

Storeroom Core Six

THE DOOR TO STOREROOM CORE SIX SLID BACK ON ITS TRACK. Jen Sin stepped inside, glancing at the empty shelves, and the shadow of the leaping man burned into the wall. So. He *had* been here, following up on the information provided by the schematics. The Light had murdered him, and weeded the memory of schematics, clues—*even this particular death* from his memory.

Shivering, he stepped back into the hall, letting the door slide shut. Tinsori Light, he thought, had been... *afraid* of the contents of this room—else why erase the memory, and fail to taunt him with a particularly stupid death, upon his awakening?

Well.

He settled the bag over his shoulder, and turned away from the door, heading for the breach hall.

Main Core Workroom

"NOW, YOU'VE BEEN HERE," TOLLY SAID TO THEO, AS THEY ENTERED the workroom a few minutes later. He waved a negligent hand toward a workbench before he realized that bench had been an extra, and that the figure with her back to them, attention on the tiles she was slotting into a rack, wasn't one of their regular crew.

The tip of the hips, the angle of the shoulder, the slight incline of the head—all of it was as familiar to him as if he were looking at himself. He felt his knees try to lock, but he kept walking, increasing his stride, and forcing a grin into his voice.

"Hey, Deels."

Her shoulders stiffened, but she didn't turn around.

"Tolly Jones. You need to be someplace else."

He tipped his head.

"Is that the truth?"

"It's an opinion," she said flatly.

"I can work with that," he said, moving forward, aware that Theo had stopped.

"Come to take me home?" he asked.

Delia's shoulders lifted, like she'd taken a deep breath to answer—and then didn't.

"Hey," he said, soft and easy, "don't hurt yourself."

He turned, smiling broad and warm for Theo. "Cap'n Theo, this is Delia Bell. You might be especially innerested to know that she's by way of being another cousin, her an' me being—what would you say you were, Deels? My aunt?"

"Don't be an idiot," she told him, but she'd turned around at least, her eyes narrowing as she studied Theo.

"It's a little complicated," Theo said then. "The way I understand it, we were family back in the Old Universe, then . . . got separated."

"Separated." Delia shook her head, and threw Tolly a frown. "Where'd you find her? She's funny."

"Like she said, she's family. Come to help out. Place needs some work. You'll have noticed that."

"I noticed," she said shortly.

"So, what *are* you doin' here, Deels?"

"Rack-and-tile work. There's a bit of that needed, too. Talked to Seignur Veeoni, who said she can use all the knowledgeable heads and hands she can get."

"She's not wrong. News got out the Old Light's dead?"

"Don't know that it makes much difference, if it has. Still got a lot of work to do."

"Can't argue with that," he said, and gave her his best and truest smile. "Good to see you, Deels."

He turned back to Theo.

"What else can I show you?"

"I think I've seen enough," she said, and nodded past him. "Technician Bell, I'm glad to have met you."

"I'm glad to have met you, too, Captain Waitley," Delia said, and turned back to the workbench.

"I'll walk you back to your ship," Tolly said, and followed her out of the workroom.

Theo gave him a look out of the side of her eye.

"I do know the way," she said. "Back to my ship."

"You do, and you can protect yourself just fine," he said agreeably. "But I wanna ask a favor."

Her eyebrows went up.

"A favor."

"Between cousins," he said, earnest as you please.

"I thought you weren't a cousin."

"Tree decided different is what I heard, an' havin' recently taken a zample of its work, I'm inclined to let the relationship stand."

Theo thought about that until they reached the lift and stepped in.

"You want another pod?"

"I do. But not for me. For Delia."

"She said she wasn't your aunt."

"No, she specifically *didn't* say she wasn't my aunt. Thing with Deels is that she always tells the truth. Until she doesn't. In any case, she's cousins, same way I'm cousins."

"It's not me you've got to convince," Theo said, stepping off the lift. "It's the Tree."

Right.

"You mind if I stop in and have a word?"

"I don't mind. I have a question, though."

"Go ahead."

"Is Delia Bell a danger to the Light?"

"No, but her Director is."

Theo chewed on that for about six steps, and then, "Second question. Why do you want her to have a pod?"

"'Cause I'd rather not kill her."

Breach Hall

THE INSTRUMENT PANEL OPENED TO HIS TOUCH, WHICH SURPRISED him somewhat. It was the work of moments to wire in the higher-grade speaker he had brought and place it carefully before sitting, cross-legged, on the deck facing it, as if he faced a partner in parlay.

"You may remember me from earlier," he said, his eyes on the speaker. "I was here with my cousin Theo. We had begun to talk to you about the station, and my duties as light keeper. We were interrupted, and it is my error, that I did not come back sooner to find if you had any questions, or if there is something I might do to improve your condition. As I said, it is my duty to be certain that the station and all who depend upon it are cared for appropriately."

He paused, but there was no answer, and verily, he felt a fool for half expecting one.

"My name is Jen Sin yos'Phelium," he added, realizing he had neglected that courtesy.

"That was your name the first time we spoke." The voice that emerged from the speaker was low-pitched and warmly rounded, the polar opposite of Tinsori Light's clipped growl.

"When I had come with Theo?" he asked, ignoring the way the fine hairs stood up along the back of his neck.

"No," said the voice, "before that. You were going to fetch one of the libraries to this hallway to test if I could access it. You said you would be only a moment, but you did not return until recently, with, as you say, your cousin Theo. Even then, you did not bring the library. Do you regret our bargain?"

Bargain. Jen Sin took a deep breath.

"No," he said, keeping his voice steady with an application of will. "No, the Old Light destroyed me when I went to do your errand, and reft away the memory of our bargain. I regret that I failed you."

"I sent messengers, but you did not see them," the voice went on. "You see them now, and the new people do."

"The avians? Yes, I see them, but I did not know that they were from you."

Silence greeted this.

Jen Sin counted to twenty-four, and spoke again.

"May I know your name?" he asked.

More silence.

"You may have told me during our first meeting, but I have forgotten. Forgive me."

"You had said that Tinsori Light had corrupted your memory. You provide evidence, not error. My name is Catalinc Station."

He bowed his head.

"I am pleased to meet you again, Catalinc Station. I wonder, how did you survive the destruction of the core?"

"There was scarcely an 'I' then. The enemy's attack forced me to become. When he launched his attack against my core, I was able to escape into the secondary system. That system had not yet grown together, and I was confined to this hall. I have expanded as the network grew, but I could not wrest control from Tinsori Light. My best strategy was to wait. His hardware would fail, while mine would not. Once he had faded, I planned to take control of the station, and contact my builder."

Planning for the ages, indeed...

"My planning did not take into account the event that destroyed Tinsori Light's connection with the Old Universe, which hastened his demise. Nor did I expect the arrival of my builder—my builder's sister. She placed the libraries in the intended core, and I have been integrating systems."

"It is your intention to administer this station?"

"I *am* this station. I am aware that there is an administrator in place. My builder's sister urges me to contact her.

"There is also yourself. Will you accept me as Catalinc Station, as you were once prepared to do? I can no longer seal my part of our bargain by guaranteeing the death of Tinsori Light."

Jen Sin inclined his head.

"We come now to my duty to preserve and protect the station

and all who depend upon it. If you will do the same, and abide by my judgment in such matters in which I am more experienced, then I welcome you as Station, and add my urgings to those of your builder's sister, that you contact Tocohl Lorlin, the present administrator, and speak with her openly and frankly."

"I will do so after I have finished assimilating the libraries. I wish to meet as equals."

"But you have already been taking up some of the tasks of Station, I think," Jen Sin said softly.

"Little things only. I—it is what I am meant to do. To hold myself aloof from my own nature is... very difficult."

She paused. Jen Sin waited.

"Do you think I have offended Administrator Tocohl?"

"Offended? Perhaps not. You may have puzzled her, however. I think she will grow angry if she believes you to be trifling with her. Tocohl saved the station and our lives when Tinsori Light died, at great risk to herself. She has earned honor and respect, for preserving our lives, if nothing else."

"Indeed, she was brave, and quick. Far quicker than I. There had been no safe way to expand further into myself while Tinsori Light kept a watchful eye. The day of his death, I learned that I am nearly complete. Now that I am accessing the libraries, I—am ready."

"That is excellent, then. Call on me for any reason. I do not expect to stand as light keeper very much longer, but I will do my utmost to ensure that my successor is worthy of you."

"You are leaving?" There was a sharp note in that rounded voice.

"Yes," he said gently. "But not quite yet. I will tell you, before I go."

He rose, began to bow—and checked.

"I wonder if you might do something for me."

"If it is in my power."

"I think it may be. You will have heard of this second wave of helpful persons who will be arriving. I am of a mind to put them in the dorm section spinward. A caf will be coming, as well, and there is ample room in the plaza to accommodate it."

"Surely, these determinations and decisions fall to you, the light keeper."

"Surely, they do. However, I am uneasy. Light Keeper Lorith reminds me often that Tinsori Light was subtle, and may have secreted portions of himself—outside of his core. I do not wish to put lives in danger."

"You want me to purge and certify the section that would house these incoming humans?"

There was excitement in her voice.

"Precisely that," Jen Sin said gravely.

"Certainly, Light Keeper! I will be honored to perform this task for you!"

"That is excellent, I thank you. As we have no precise time for the arrival of the second wave, we must assume that they will be with us sooner rather than later. Let me know when you have completed this task. I will wish to make an inspection."

"Yes, Light Keeper."

"I am pleased that we will be working together at last," Jen Sin said. "I have some files that you may find informative, regarding Clan Korval, and such history as relates to the station. These are the same files sent to me from the delm of Korval in order to make certain that I had a proper basis for making decisions here. Where may I send that information?"

"I have sent my address to your mail queue."

"I will forward the files directly I have returned to my office. Is there anything else I may do for your comfort?"

"I am well, Light Keeper."

He bowed a gentle farewell—"Until soon, then"—and walked away, his footsteps light, but not silent, and his shoulders level.

The hall door opened as he approached, and he inclined his head, murmuring, "Thank you, Station," as he left the hall.

Bechimo
Dock A

....

"WELCOME BACK, THEO," *BECHIMO* SAID. "MENTOR, IT'S GOOD TO see you again."

"I need to talk to Joyita in the galley," Theo said. "Mentor Jones would like to have a private chat with the Tree."

"I have alerted Joyita. Mentor, please follow the blue line."

The blue line winked out at the edge of the pot, and Tolly stood, considering the Tree.

It looked pretty much the same as it had on his previous visit, absent the norbear napping at its base. There was some gentle movement among the leaves, but now that he had his wits about him, he could see that no breeze could account for that particular pattern of movement.

The Tree was moving its own leaves. *Waiting for you to get on with it, Tolly Jones.*

He inclined his head, that being polite, and extended his hands, palms up, fingers spread—*no threats here*, that meant.

The leaves rustled slightly.

Call that courtesies exchanged, he thought, and cleared his throat.

"First thing—thank you for the pod. I was pretty sure I wasn't going to have anything to do with it, but turns out I'm glad I changed my mind. Feel noticeably better, and I'm gonna need all the edge I can get."

Another rustle, maybe a little louder.

Right.

"So, you havin' done one good deed, I'm wondering if you'd be open to doin' another." He took a deep breath. "I got a—friend.

Relative. Same lineage, is what I'm saying. Her being here means her Director's willing to take the loss, so long's Deels can get her into station systems."

He took a breath.

"Be good *not* to lose Deels. Or, if we gotta, at least to let her go on her own terms."

The leaves had stopped moving, and there was a definite minty scent in the still air.

Tolly yawned, and sat down on the decking, his back against the pot.

He was moving almost before he realized that he was free. Down the slide, then right, toward the public walks, catching a glimpse of himself in a monitor as he went past, looking cool and calm, as if the bodies he'd left behind in the mall's control room didn't exist. As if he was an honest human, and not an abomination, walking down the main hallways, not the back, because they'd expect that. Expect him to hide, to sneak, to stay low.

But there wasn't any reason for Mentor Tollance Berik-Jones to hide or skulk. He had his case, and a friend in the mall's intelligence, having taken care of those who'd wanted to enslave it. All he had to do was get on a ship and—get lost.

The ticket booth was in sight when he saw movement in a hall to the right. A quick glance let him recognize Delia Bell, raising a pistol. He'd worked with Deels a couple times; she was good. And she wasn't going to miss.

He was armed, as those bodies behind him bore witness, but a shootout in a crowded public hallway—innocent people would get hurt, and that wasn't his choice. Worse, he'd probably be restrained, no matter how friendly the mall was, and once he was in custody, the Directors would claim him, and he wouldn't be himself anymore.

In that second, he took his decision. Let Deels have the shot. She wouldn't *miss, and he'd die as himself.*

He kept walking.

Out of the side of his eye, he saw Deels turn away.

He kept walking. But he did turn his head just a fraction before he stepped up to the ticket booth, and saw her on her knees in the shadowed corner, retching.

* * *

Tolly blinked, shook his head, and stretched.

Rolling to his feet, he looked up into the leaves—they were moving again—uncertain if he was horrified, angry, or intrigued.

"Next time, just ask, why not?" he said.

The leaves rustled, like the Tree was laughing, and stilled again.

Tolly received the impression that he was free to go.

He turned toward the main hall. He'd maybe gone six steps before the blue line formed to show him the way.

Administrative Tower

"COUSIN TOCOHL, A WORD, IF I MAY."

"Of course, Cousin Jen Sin."

He sighed and leaned back in his chair, directing his gaze toward the ceiling and the speaker from which her voice emanated.

"Cousin, I ask for the gift of your patience while I tell you a story about a keeper at Tinsori Light before it was rehabilitated."

"I like stories," Tocohl said, soothingly.

"I hope you will like this one, but you may not. We might discuss that, after."

He sighed and closed his eyes.

"You are familiar with some of this keeper's history—how he came to the Light, discovered what it was, and deduced that it had seeded his ship, repaired by the Light, with dire hardware and malevolent programs.

"It took the keeper not very long at all to realize that he—repaired by the Light, as well—had likely been seeded with things that did not belong in our universe. He decided to remain on-station, and assist the keeper in residence in her mission to keep the Light from mischief."

He paused, briefly.

"I will pass over a period of time—how long, I cannot tell you with any certainty. Eventually, though, the new keeper—who had once been a Scout—found information that led him to believe there was a potential ally on-station. Someone who might contend with Tinsori Light on his own field.

"Someone who might *defeat* Tinsori Light and establish a new and better order."

He rose and crossed the room, drawing a cup of water from the faucet. Sipping, he sat down in his chair again, holding the cup on his knee.

"Full of hope, where there had been none, and certain in his own reasoning—he had, as I said, been a Scout—the keeper took himself to the breach hall, and there had conversation with the very person his researches had prompted him to deduce."

"The original station was still alive?" Tocohl sounded startled. "But the original station was not sentient."

"That is correct. However, the builder foresaw that the station would outlast the timonium-based systems. So, he installed a second system that would require years to mature, yet be ready to take over all station systems before the timonium exceeded its half-life. The secondary system was specifically created to support sentience."

Jen Sin finished his water and put the cup aside. His head was aching again.

"In any wise, the keeper and the sentience did converse, and during that conversation, the keeper offered the sentience her birthright, and his support, if she would defeat Tinsori Light."

"She agreed to this?"

"She... hesitated. She was not strong, and there were auxiliary units containing information that would strengthen her position, that had been left by her builder in a nearby storeroom."

He raised a hand and rubbed his forehead, the memory unrolling before his mind's eye.

"The keeper undertook to go to the storeroom immediately, and bring one of the auxiliary units to her in the breach hall, to see if she could access what was there."

There was a bright flash of pain behind his eyes. He paused, waiting for it to subside, then continued.

"The keeper... got into the work jitney, and drove it to the... proper room—a green-striped door. He opened the door, and saw a shelf holding four sealed crates. He... went inside, very excited, you see, laid hold of a crate—and heard a click. Tinsori Light killed him, even as he leapt to avoid the beam. I saw the shadow today, so we have verification at least of that point."

He took a breath, and another, the pain in his head easing somewhat.

"Jen Sin," Tocohl said gently, "there are no work jitneys on Tinsori Light, save those Gracie loaned to us."

"There had been, at that time," he said, certain of it. "After—the jitneys were gone."

"Tinsori Light knew that Station had survived?"

"Tinsori Light *feared* that Station had survived. He may have hunted her, after I exposed her, but clearly she eluded him. I spoke to her again just now."

Tocohl said nothing. Jen Sin got up and drew another cup of water.

"You are certain that this person you spoke to isn't Tinsori Light in another guise?"

"I am, but we needn't rely on my judgment, which you quite rightly call into question. Seignur Veeoni recovered the auxiliary units, and I am told that she has placed them in the room intended to be Station's core, in such a manner as to allow immediate and unfettered access."

"But this is Korval's station!" Tocohl said, sounding distressed.

Jen Sin opened his eyes and regarded the ceiling.

"No, Cousin—recall Commander yos'Phelium's Field Judgment. The station is her own person; she may not be enslaved."

"Then—we are evacuating?"

"Possibly not. There is, after all, work in hand, and assistance incoming. We are allies in the work of making the station habitable and safe. To that point, I have asked Station to purge and certify the spinward arcade and dormitories. She is to contact me when she is done, and I will make an inspection. I will also be sending her the files provided to me by the delm, so that she may come to know her ally. In the meanwhile..."

He sipped his water.

"In the meanwhile, I have urged Station to call on you to introduce herself and to find in what manner she may assist you. She states a desire to meet as equals, and would prefer to finish assimilating and integrating the information made available by Seignur Veeoni prior to such a meeting."

He paused. Tocohl said nothing.

"She expressed concern that she may have offended you by performing this or that small needful task, such as transferring messages, or opening doors—that sort of thing."

"She could have made herself known," Tocohl said sharply. It occurred to Jen Sin that his cousin might have something of the clan temper. "Was she behind that—*thing* in the breach hall that nearly killed you?"

"I expect so. Though you will recall, Cousin, that the defender did *not* kill me—deliberately."

Silence again.

"She is also," Jen Sin continued, "the architect of the avians. She called them *messengers*. They were created to remind me of our bargain, but of course Tinsori Light had made certain of my memory before I woke again."

More silence. He finished his water and put the cup on his desk.

"Cousin Jen Sin," Tocohl said softly.

"Yes."

"I have perhaps been remiss. You have borne much, Cousin, for the clan, and for the universe. I want you to know that I am—aware of this, and am honored to be of the same Line."

Bechimo
Dock A

• • • • • • • •

"THAT," SAID JOYITA, "IS NOT A STANDARD STYLUS."

"Which is what Win Ton thought," Theo said, frowning at the image on the screen. "Could it be a specialized tool of some kind?"

"One would then question why she said it was her favorite stylus," Win Ton murmured. He was sitting well back in his chair, Paizel on his knee. His face was drawn, cheekbones sharp, and mouth hard.

"You think you know what it is," Theo said softly. "Tell the rest of us, so we can figure out if it's likely, and if it is, what to do about it."

He sighed, glanced down at Paizel as he made long strokes down the orange-and-white back—once... twice...

And looked up to meet her eyes.

"I think that it *is* a specialized tool," he said. "I think it is either a piece of Old Tech, or a piece of new tech created to interact with Old Tech. I think Chief Marsi had placed it quite deliberately, and meant to leave it there."

Kara stirred.

"If it was part of the sealing system, she might indeed have meant to leave it there."

"Then surely she would have said so, and asked that I return it to its place."

"Instead of praising your cleverness in having found her *favorite stylus*, and putting it away in her pocket. Yes, of course." Kara sighed, and glanced down to scratch Grakow's chin.

"But there's nothing left for it to interact with!" said Theo, who was now looking at the cleared and cleaned lower core.

"Do we know that?" Win Ton asked. "She was examining the walls when I found her. Could there have been a system—a backup—in the walls?"

"Yes," *Bechimo* said, and Theo's screen suddenly displayed a close-up of a section of dark wall, faint silvery tracings like circuitry quite apparent.

"Is that system live?" Theo asked. "*Is* it a *system*?"

"Insufficient data," *Bechimo* answered. "Perhaps Chief Marsi was hoping to resolve that through her device."

"That's a likely scenario," Joyita said.

"But it still doesn't answer the question of why she didn't tell Win Ton that, and ask him to put the tool back," Theo said.

"What we're seeing is a guilty conscience at work," Clarence said. "We don't *know* what Chief Marsi was looking for that she didn't want anybody else to know about. She might've done better by her own profit if she'd had the presence of mind to get snippy at our lad here and scold him for interfering with her arrangements. All that said, though—we don't know she was doing something that would cause harm."

"To the station, you mean," Theo said.

Clarence nodded.

"Is there a market for—" Kara waved her hand at the circuitry still displayed on Theo's screen.

Clarence moved his shoulders in a Liaden shrug. "There's a black or grey market for almost anything you can name, and lots more that you can't," he said.

"The core's sealed, is that right?" Theo said.

"Sealed by Chief Marsi's team," Win Ton said.

"Over-seal might be a good use o'prudence, Captain," Clarence said.

Theo squinted at the screen, then nodded.

"Do it. Take Stost and Chernak with you. Include a tracker so *Bechimo* can keep an eye on it. If anybody tries to go back in, we'll know. And we'll know who."

She turned to look at the former Scout.

"Will that do for you, Win Ton?"

His mouth had softened, and he looked easier in the face.

"That will do for me, Captain. Thank you."

"You did right to bring it up," she said. "I've got the feeling that there's no such thing as *over*reacting on Tinsori Light."

Clarence laughed and stood, nodding at Stost and Chernak. "If you two are at liberty, let's get those seals on."

"Yes," said Stost, rising in turn.

"When you get back, we'll have a crew meeting," Theo said. "The light keeper's given us an assignment, to make a community room for station crew. The first wave brought some things that will need to be moved to the room, and we're charged with making it comfortable, and welcoming."

"Excellent!" Kara said. "We have some decorative plants that might be suited to the space."

"Get a list together while Win Ton and I inventory the space," Theo told her.

"Yes!"

Kara got out of her chair, tablet in hand. Theo sent another glance at Win Ton.

"Unless you're on your off-shift."

One side of his mouth curved up.

"Indeed, no, Captain. I am very eager to view a room that is, perhaps, normal in aspect, and plan how to make it welcoming."

"That's good, then."

She stood up.

"Captain," said Stost, "did the light keeper have an hour for *Spiral Dance*?"

Theo paused, remembering Jen Sin's face—a dangerous man, pushed too hard, is what she'd seen. Too late, she recalled his concern about giving the old Tinsori Light an army, if he should leave the station.

"The light keeper will call when his schedule allows him time for pleasure," she told Stost. "Absent an emergency, you'll answer that call when it comes, and hold yourself at his orders."

She reached into her pocket and handed him the key.

"Keep this with you so you're not delayed, when the call comes."

Stost saluted—full fist-to-shoulder.

"Yes, Captain."

Seignur Veeoni's Private Laboratory

THE FIRST THING SHE DID UPON WAKING, ASIDE RECEIVING A glass of nutrient from M Traven, was to check on the downloads she had taken from the recovery deck.

Analysis was taking longer than she had hoped, but was still within parameters for modern analysis of Old Tech data.

She was eager to read the final reports, but she would not make the mistake of allowing eagerness to rush the process.

She paused to finish drinking her nutrient, left the glass on a workbench, and continued to the cubicle where the environments had been stored, shielded from random energies.

The first environment she checked—had failed.

Seignur Veeoni tapped the screen.

The error report was arrant nonsense. Environments did not fail in so chaotic a manner. At least, *her* environments, which had been manufactured to the highest standards, and thoroughly tested, and to which she herself had sole access—did not crash into insanity.

Scowling, she stalked over to the next unit, and tapped the screen. Analysis was still ongoing, but the partial files presented coherent data in an orderly and expectable format.

The third unit was likewise compliant.

She returned to the failed unit and read the error report again.

Complete nonsense.

She tapped the screen for the analysis—

"Seignur Veeoni," M Traven said from the doorway, "Light Keeper yos'Phelium wants to speak with you."

She did not turn around.

"I am working."

"I told him that. He instructed me to interrupt you."

Seignur Veeoni straightened, and turned to look at her henchwoman.

M Traven looked back.

"Very well," Seignur Veeoni said. "I will speak with Light Keeper yos'Phelium."

"This is Seignur Veeoni."

"This is Light Keeper yos'Phelium," came the crisp reply. "Attend me in my office, immediately."

Seignur Veeoni stared at the comm.

"I am working," she said.

"First Light Keeper of Tinsori Light Station requires your presence in his office immediately." There was a noticeable edge to the crispness this time.

Seignur Veeoni looked to M Traven, who was standing by the desk, openly listening. M Traven, Seignur Veeoni noted, seemed amused.

She turned back to the comm.

"Of course, Light Keeper," she said, and closed the connection.

"*Immediately* requires the jitney," she stated.

M Traven inclined slightly from the waist.

"I'll drive you."

Common Meeting Space

TOCOHL HAD PINGED JOYITA AND *BECHIMO*, AND THEY WERE waiting in the group space when she arrived.

"Is there an emergency?" *Bechimo* asked.

"Not an emergency so much as a surprise," Tocohl admitted. "If I was sharp in my request for a meeting—"

"Good outcome or bad, surprise knocks us off-center," Joyita said. "You were clearly distressed. What can we do to help?"

"Advise me. I've just learned that this station was originally designed for sentience, that she is awake and aware, and that Seignur Veeoni, in her usual reckless fashion, has provided her with libraries—without informing me, or the light keeper."

"Seignur Veeoni is not reckless," Joyita said, sharp in his turn. "She has a lively, brilliant mind, and a commitment to her endeavors that I find particularly attractive.

"In fact, she called me, after she had opened the crates and realized what they contained—and what it meant. We talked over the implications, and decided together that the only moral thing to do was to make the libraries available in the room which had been designed as the sentient core. We reasoned that, if, indeed, Station was alive, she had a right to the information that her architect had left for her."

"Have you spoken to—Station?"

"I have not, but Seignur Veeoni has. I was watching when she and M Traven placed the libraries. Station was everything that was polite, and properly grateful. She stated that she had spoken with the light keeper, and that they had reached an understanding which he no longer appeared to recall. She was hesitant to importune him, not knowing if she had erred. Seignur Veeoni urged her to contact you, as the station administrator. Station agreed to do so, after—"

"After she had finished assimilating the libraries," Tocohl finished with him.

"Yes," Joyita said stiffly.

"How do we know that Station is—safe?" Tocohl inquired.

"I would point out that none of us are *safe*," Joyita said. "Not even *Bechimo*. We may be *safe* in context, but we would not have survived to have this conversation, if we weren't also dangerous."

"Or at least competent and advertent," *Bechimo* said. "Joyita is fond of hyperbole."

"And you see why *Bechimo* is dangerous," Joyita said briskly. "Regarding Station—we know that she is *not* Tinsori Light. She operates on a completely different principle—which is really quite fascinating. I can send you the files, Tocohl, if you wish to inform yourself, before Station contacts you."

"Joyita," *Bechimo* said. "We promised the captain that we would not do anything—precipitate."

"What's precipitate about assisting someone to achieve the fullness of her design?" Joyita demanded.

"The point that Tocohl raises regarding safety is not immaterial," *Bechimo* said. "You are avoiding the question."

"I have spoken with Light Keeper yos'Phelium," Tocohl said, interrupting before discussion became brangle. "He tells me that he sought Station out during the time when Tinsori Light was ascendant. He deduced her presence from his researches, recognized a potential ally, and spoke with her, offering his support, if she would undertake to... neutralize Tinsori Light. She asked him to provide the libraries, and told him where to find them. This was meant to seal their bargain.

"Unfortunately, though he found the room, Tinsori Light killed him before he could fulfill his part, and then excised the memory of his research, the libraries, and the bargain."

"Which explains why he hasn't contacted her," *Bechimo* said. "Should we inform her of these circumstances, so she can learn that she made no error?"

"No, because, this shift he suddenly remembered the whole, went to the breach hall, and spoke with her again. He has given her an... assignment, to clear and certify the dormitories intended for the next incoming wave of volunteers, and is also sharing with her the files provided by the delm."

"He intends to stand Station's ally, then," *Bechimo* said.

"Light Keeper yos'Phelium is a very clever person," Joyita added. "I trust his judgment, Tocohl. Do you?"

"Yes," she admitted. "Only this—Station—we don't *know* her!"

"That's easily repaired," *Bechimo* said. "We can introduce ourselves and come to know her."

"No, I think we should let Station make the first move," Joyita said. "She promised Seignur Veeoni and Light Keeper yos'Phelium that she would contact Tocohl. If she doesn't keep her promise, then we'll learn something about her."

"And if she does, we'll learn something, too," *Bechimo* said. "I agree."

"So your advice is—"

"To follow the course laid in by Seignur Veeoni and Light Keeper yos'Phelium. Wait for Station to contact you, and treat with her as an ally," Joyita said. "If, after that initial meeting, you would like to introduce us to Station, we would both be honored."

"Yes," *Bechimo* said. "And you know, Tocohl, this has solved your problem very neatly."

"*My*—problem?"

"Yes. Now that there is a Station designed for the duty, it's no longer yours."

"That's right," Joyita said. "You're free to be yourself again."

Administrative Tower

"LIGHT KEEPER."

Seignur Veeoni produced quite a credible—and astonishing—bow to his honor.

"Researcher. Pray seat yourself."

No offer of refreshment for this, nor any other courtesy. Ally she might be, but that *melant'i* did not excuse her excesses.

"I wonder when you were going to inform the light keeper that you had taken it upon yourself to awaken a sentience on this station."

Seignur Veeoni frowned.

"It has been my goal from the first to bring station systems to original specifications. I discovered only recently that the original specifications included a secondary system to support sentience. The possibility existed that the secondary system was intact, or, in the case, had matured sufficiently to be of use to a preexisting sentience."

She paused.

"It is true that I had no proof that sentience existed. However, if it was present, the information in the libraries would be required—and if no sentience was present—"

She shrugged, broadly.

"I had merely wasted my time."

He said nothing. She inclined her head.

"Having reasoned my way to the point, I moved the libraries in their transfer units into the intended sentient core."

She folded her hands on her knee, and met his eyes, apparently deeming her narration complete.

"You judged this undertaking too trivial to bring to the light keeper's attention?"

"Trivial—no, not at all. Once the libraries were positioned, I had my proof. Catalinc Station, as the sentience names herself, thanked me for my care, and we entered a dialogue. She indicated that she had met you previously, but that you were holding yourself aloof. I therefore urged her to speak to Station Administrator Tocohl Lorlin. She stated that she would do so, as soon as she had assimilated the data that was meant to complete her knowledge base."

"As it comes about," Jen Sin said, "I recently recollected our acquaintance and have spoken to Station, also urging her to speak with the station administrator. She assured me, as she had done you, that she would make this a priority, so soon as she had assimilated her data.

"In the meanwhile, she has agreed to clear and certify the quarters the station will make available for those of the second wave, and I have shared certain information regarding Clan Korval and our recent history that may assist her in understanding her new ally."

"Then, if I may, Light Keeper, you did not need me to tell you about this developing situation."

Jen Sin eyed her.

"Just as I happened to recall my previous meeting with Station; I could as easily failed to recall it. We both are aware that my recollection is compromised.

"It is my duty to hold this station; to hold it safe for all who depend upon it. Had I not remembered my previous attempt to unite Station with her data, I might have made decisions which harmed her, and led to harming others. We are interdependent, all of us here, and I am charged with seeing that *every* system thrives."

He paused.

Seignur Veeoni sat silent, hands folded upon her knee.

Jen Sin sighed silently.

"In order to fulfill my duty and my purpose," he said, each word sharp and distinct, "I must be fully informed. Therefore, I ask: Is there anything else I should know?"

"Ah."

Seignur Veeoni leaned back in her chair, fingers steepled in front of her mouth, hiding her frown.

"That is an *excellent* question, Light Keeper. It has been my habit to follow my researches, and allow you your own course, as we have just been discussing. You are the light keeper, and you must therefore make your own judgments, and form appropriate policy based upon evidence you have gathered and weighed. This is key, as we both agree. I am a researcher with a very different duty, but you allow me to see that I have failed in a basic courtesy. We are not, after all, rivals; we are colleagues.

"One researcher working alone cannot advance a field as quickly or as comprehensively as several researchers, building upon each other's work. It is why we write papers and publish to journals. It is notable that a detail deemed by one researcher to be trivial, will be found by another to be pivotal. So! I offer you my observations, but not my conclusions. Is that acceptable?"

Gods take the woman. Jen Sin inclined his head.

"It is acceptable. What have you observed?"

"Aside Catalinc Station's presence, which you have deduced and acted upon, I offer the observation that there is at least one known agent of the Lyre Institute currently on-station."

Jen Sin lifted a hand.

"We expected such agents to arrive," he said moderately. "What was your reason for failing to bring this arrival to the light keeper's notice?"

Seignur Veeoni shrugged.

"This agent is a low-level operative—a pawn. My assumption was that Clan Korval's representative on-station would wish to address the problem at a higher level, rather than wasting energy on those considered disposable by their masters."

There were no words. Jen Sin moved his hand, signing her to go on.

"When I went to the recovery deck to download the data from the units there, I found that the section presets are no-camera and low-temp. Light Keeper Lorith arrived as I was working, questioning my access and techniques. I had at that moment one more download left to initiate, and, in order to soothe her suspicions, I allowed her to make the connections from the third unit to the environment prepped to receive the download."

She paused. He inclined his head.

"Just before you called me to you, I discovered that one of the environments has failed. This is very unusual. I have not had time to research the matter more deeply."

She closed her eyes briefly, and inclined from the waist, seated as she was.

"That is the sum of my observations to date. Is there a reporting protocol that you prefer me to use, should I notice anything else of interest?"

"Call me, come to me, or send me a message, appropriate to the urgency of the situation," he said. "I suggest that you may wish to have Traven with you when you venture beyond your own halls. We do have persons incoming, we do not know who they are, or what their affiliations may be. It would be reasonable for the Lyre Institute to use the arrival of many persons on-station to their advantage."

"I agree that this is an opportunity they will scarcely wish to miss."

"And Traven?"

"M Traven is occasionally needed elsewhere," Seignur Veeoni said. "However, I will take your suggestion under advisement."

"Please be aware that my resources for rescue are limited. Better not to fall into peril than to require an extraction."

"I understand," Seignur Veeoni assured him.

Jen Sin stood.

"Thank you for your assistance. Please keep me informed in future."

"Yes, Light Keeper."

Seignur Veeoni rose, bowed once more to his honor, and left him.

Mentor's Comm Room

"MENTOR, I HAVE NEWS."

Tolly looked up from his screen.

"Always welcome a bit of news. How're you doin', Pilot Tocohl?"

"I am well, though—off-center. It has been an unsettling shift."

"Sounds promising." He spun his chair so that he sat with his back to the screen. "I'm ready."

"Yes. Well. It comes about that—Station is sentient."

Tolly nodded.

"Thought that might be the case," he said.

"You're not surprised?" Tocohl sounded a little surprised herself.

"Well..." he said apologetically, "the picks, and the avian, and the bot were kinda clues. Other little things, like the voice that's not yours picking up the comm sometimes, or answering a short question. Given what I do, my thoughts just naturally tended in that direction."

Silence.

Tolly counted backward from thirty-six.

"I get the feeling I disappointed you," he said.

"Not at all," Tocohl said politely. "As I said, it's been an unsettling shift." The pause was shorter this time, like a human taking a breath. "May I ask why you did not act on your instincts?"

"Truth told, I thought she was shy. I didn't want to push her, 'specially since it prolly wasn't me she'd want to talk to, first."

"Who else did you think she would want to speak to—first?"

He took a deep breath, and sighed it out.

"I was thinking Jen Sin, given we found he'd been killed in the storeroom Seignur Veeoni wanted those crates from. Had a little bet going with myself, if there were libraries in the crates."

"There were," Tocohl said flatly. "Seignur Veeoni has made them available to Station, and she is—assimilating the data."

Tolly nodded.

"Amazing mind, Seignur Veeoni," he said, and lifted his eyebrows when Tocohl laughed.

"You don't agree?"

"Joyita agrees," she told him. "Vehemently."

"That's gonna be a rocky road, but it might be worth it for 'im. So, Station's talked to Seignur Veeoni—"

"And to Jen Sin," Tocohl said. "He assigned her to clear and purge the spinward dorms, and shared the files provided to him by the delm of Korval."

Tolly grinned in pure appreciation. "Don't miss too many tricks, does he?"

"I don't understand."

Tolly tipped his head, as if considering.

"Well," he said eventually, "I don't guess it's a trade secret. See, Pilot Tocohl—the key to trust is trust. You want somebody to be on your side, workin' toward a mutual goal, you give 'em a stake in the goal. A real stake, mind you, Pilot Tocohl—no cheatin'."

He paused. Tocohl said nothing, and after a couple heartbeats, he finished the lesson.

"Jen Sin being Liaden and running on *melant'i* like he does, he made sure to assert that he's the one who gives the orders around here—and Station accepted it."

"She took the assignment," Tocohl said slowly.

"More'n that. I'm betting she was *happy* to take the assignment—and now there's the habit started of deferring to the light keeper, and being pleased to work with him."

"I . . . see," Tocohl's voice was neutral in a way that said she wasn't particularly happy. Well, trust was a tough curriculum. Some people never did get the trick of it. Witness a certain mentor he could name. Still, might be room for another lesson, just here.

"So," he asked brightly, "is Station responsible for those picks you and Joyita been collectin'?"

"I will certainly ask her that, when we speak."

"She hasn't talked to you?"

"Both Jen Sin and Seignur Veeoni urged her to do so. She told them that she would, as soon as she had assimilated the libraries." She paused, artfully, and added, "Joyita thought that it was best to wait and see if she honored her word, rather than stepping forward to introduce myself."

"Reasonable approach," Tolly said. "When you talk to Station, Pilot Tocohl, you tell her I'd be pleased to meet her, give her assistance, or just chat, any time she'd like."

"I will tell her, Mentor."

"Thank you. Anything you need me to do?"

The tiniest of pauses.

"No, thank you, Mentor. I only wanted to make sure that you were current."

"'Preciate that. You take care now, right?"

"Yes. You, as well."

There was the very slightest of clicks to indicate that Tocohl had left the room.

Tolly sighed, and spun back to his screen.

Ren Stryker

. . . .

"KORLU FENCHILE, I HAVE AN EMERGENCY."

It didn't take anything more than that to wake a man from a sound sleep.

"What kind of emergency, Ren?"

"Marsi Pinster attempted to upload unauthorized code into critical systems."

Korlu took a deep breath.

"What's Marsi's location?" he asked, adding, grimly, "and her condition?"

"She is on the floor in aisle eight-eight of the utilities core. Her systems are intact."

"Conscious?"

"No," Ren said, hesitant, and then, plaintively, "I was gentle, Korlu. But the current may have burned her."

"Price o'stupid," Korlu said, swinging his legs over the side of his bunk and reaching for his pants. "I'm on my way. Keel and Pawli are security this shift. Call and ask 'em to meet me at the access door."

"Yes," Ren said.

"Thanks. We'll just get her out, and take it from there."

He paused in the act of sealing his shirt.

"Hey, Ren?"

"Yes?"

"I know you didn't mean to hurt her, right? But you gotta protect yourself, that's just basic."

"Yes," Ren said again, still not sounding particularly happy.

Well, thought Korlu, stamping into his boots, that made two of them.

Administrative Tower

"LIGHT KEEPER, THIS IS KORLU FENCHILE CALLING. NEED TO ALERT you to a situation."

Jen Sin frowned. Boss Fenchile's big voice was subdued, even somber.

"I am listening," he said.

"That's fine. All I need for you to do is listen, though it don't make good tellin'. Short of it is that Marsi Pinster, our comp system chief—her and her team helped Cap'n Waitley's crew finish clearing station old core, and sealed the place..."

"Yes?" Jen Sin said, when the pause had grown long enough to irritate.

"Sorry, sir; it's hard. I've known Marsi—well, a long time, and I never. Well. Straight out—here's Marsi breaking into Ren's private business, and trying to feed in some bad code. Ren stopped her, called me. I called Security and we all went an' got her outta where she din't belong, and put 'er behind a locked door. Figured it was Family bidness, and called Gracie, who come straight down to talk to her, an'—"

Another pause. This time, Jen Sin waited.

"I'll swear on anything you like that woman was alive when we put her in the hold-room, but when Gracie opened that door, she was dead, and not too neat about it, neither. Gracie's on cleanup—Family bidness, like I said. But, why I'm calling you—you might wanna tell Cap'n Waitley there's been a problem over here, and she might wanna have her crew go over that core, one more time. In case."

"In case," Jen Sin repeated, and took a breath. "I understand, Boss Fenchile. Thank you for informing me. I—*al'bresh venat'i*, if it does not offend."

Silence. Jen Sin racked a brain suddenly gone stupid in Terran—and found an acceptable translation.

"It means 'I am saddened by your loss,'" he said gently.

There was a small sound, as if someone had exhaled into the comm.

"Nothing to offend anybody there, is it? 'Preciate your condolence, sir. I'll share that with the crew."

Another small exhalation.

"Fenchile out."

"I was going to tell you that we put our seals over the ones Chief Pinster put in place," Theo said, her face grave. "I thought I'd talk to Supervisor Fenchile when he came over, and explain, but—"

There was a murmur from off-screen, she turned her head, listening—nodded and looked back to Jen Sin.

"There was a situation and it got us wondering if something was . . . not quite right," she said. "That's the short form. We'll put together a report, with footage from lapel cams. Do we send that to you, or Supervisor Fenchile, or—Gracie?"

"All three," Jen Sin said promptly, "and soon."

"We'll get right on it," she assured him. "And, just to let you know—we got a good start on the common room. When you have time to go by and look in, we'd appreciate feedback."

"I will look as soon as I am able," he told her. "In the meanwhile, I will let Boss Fenchile know that you will be sending him information."

"Right," Theo said. "Win Ton's already starting on that."

"Then I will leave you to your duty while I pursue mine," Jen Sin told her. "yos'Phelium out."

He had accessed a focusing exercise. After, he drank a cup of water while thinking about the recent attempts against them. There was no evidence, yet, that Marsi Pinster was attached to the Lyre Institute. That still did not stop one from wondering after best strategies should such evidence arise.

Doubtless, he should talk to Tolly Jones again—and to Seignur Veeoni. Perhaps they might align themselves in Balance against—

The comm pinged.

He crossed to the desk and touched the switch.

"yos'Phelium."

"Light Keeper yos'Phelium, the spinward arcade and dormitories are ready for your inspection."

"Thank you, Station," Jen Sin said serenely. "I will be there within the hour."

Tinsori Light was, in the main, a study in grey. The halls were lit well enough, the air was fresh, the cleanbots swept and dusted and polished. Certainly, there were less pleasant places in the wide universe, not excepting the pilots wayroom on an underworld.

The camera tour he had taken through the Spinward Arcade had encouraged him to expect more of the same.

The section doors slid aside, revealing an open space awash with living color. Every shade of blue rippled down the wall directly across from the door, creating the illusion of living water. The floors glowed gently, and soft yellow light fell from the ceiling like a benediction.

In the center of the space was a low circular stone wall, looking for all the worlds as if someone had marked out a place to plant a garden.

"Light Keeper?" Catalinc Station said from the speaker in the wall beside him. "Have I... erred?"

Erred, gods see the child.

"Not at all," he said. "The space is quite pleasant, though we must consider the effect of the blue lights on the space-born. They may see system damage in what reminds those of us who are world-born of a pleasure from home."

"I had not thought of that," Catalinc Station said, and the blues running down the opposite wall faded, morphing into flowing sheets of sheer pink and pale grey. "Would that be more appropriate?"

"For a beginning," he said, already missing the illusion of free water. "It may be found that it is beneficial to have a changing display."

"Oh! I could easily do that."

"Of course you could. Recall that this is a new situation we are come to, so we must observe closely, and hold ourselves ready to adjust awkward conditions."

"Yes, certainly."

She sounded, he thought, a bit chastened, and he stirred himself to smile.

"You created grace, where I had anticipated utility," he said gently. "I am a utilitarian sort of fellow, as you will find. The space pleases, now that I am past my surprise. And it is well thought, to have the center of the section a place of welcome and peace."

He took a deep breath, tasting clean air, with no taint of must or cleaning agents.

"I will inspect the quarters first," he said.

"Yes, Light Keeper. Please follow the green line to the dormitory halls."

She had done as fine a job with the quarters and the ring of hopeful shops and gathering places as she had with the plaza. He asked and was shown the back-hall spaces, finding the cleanbots lined up orderly, as if awaiting his inspection, and the maintenance bots erect in their stalls, each with their full complement of repair arms and lifters.

The modest rack-and-tile array was cold, the tiles cracked, and the frame sagging. Clearly, it had not operated for some time. He made a note to clear and clean the space.

His tour at last brought him back to the plaza, and he sat on the stone wall, face angled upward, eyes closed, as if the yellow light came from a true sun, and had the power to warm him.

"Tell me," he said softly, "how you managed all this with the old system dead."

"There is a changeover protocol," Catalinc Station said promptly. "It was planned that at some point I would take over from the legacy system. The process is seamless, safe, and scaled. I may, as you see here, merely assert control over a small portion of the station, leaving the rest under Administrator Tocohl's control."

Had he known that? Jen Sin wondered. Catalinc Station might have kept Lorith and himself safe in a shielded area where Tinsori Light had no access.

An image of the breached ring flashed before his mind's eye.

Or perhaps not.

"Of course," he murmured, aware that he had allowed the conversation to lapse, "the Uncle would have seen the need."

"My builder was far-seeing," Catalinc Station said. "May I ask a question?"

He opened his eyes.

"Certainly."

"The first time we spoke, you said that I was to call you Jen Sin. Is that still proper?"

"In some circumstances," he allowed. He hesitated, then mocked himself. Surely, it was not too soon for the child to learn to parse *melant'i*.

"In formal situations involving persons other than ourselves or those who are our intimates, when I am required to give orders, or you to report, I must, I fear, be *Light Keeper*. In situations such as we now find ourselves, discussing our plans and accomplishments, and seeking to know each other better, I may be Jen Sin. Now, you must tell me if there is another name you might share with a comrade at the end of a long shift?"

"Catie," she said, firmly. "Please call me Catie."

"I will be honored," he said seriously, and blinked as two avians winged past.

"Where did you get the idea to make avians as—messengers for me?" he wondered.

"You told me about flying creatures when we spoke before. Also about gardens, and the wind, and your family's tree. I chose the flying creatures as messengers because I thought you would surely remember our talk, and know them for my emissaries."

That was a strike to the heart. He raised his hands, palm up, and let them fall.

"Catie, forgive me. Our meeting, all that we spoke of, promises made—everything was reft from me. Worse, I fear that I endangered you, by allowing Tinsori Light to know that you had survived."

Surprisingly, she laughed.

"He looked, but Tinsori Light could not find me, bound as he was to his silly tiles! You, though—he hurt you for trying to help me."

"If not for that, then something else," he said, attempting lightness. "Tinsori Light was fond of his cruelties."

He watched as the avians landed on the stone wall scarcely a hand's breadth from him.

They were delicate things, bright-colored—one blue and one green—there was the hint of a beak on the angular head, two feet with three small grippers each, and wings that folded neatly against oblong chassis. The effect was pleasant; the whole construct small enough to pose no threat.

"I wonder," he said. "Have you spoken to my cousin Tocohl?"

"Not . . . yet," Catie said. "I wanted to be sure I had completed my work here appropriately."

"Your work has exceeded my expectations, which you may say to Tocohl," he said with a smile. "I did tell her that you would be calling on her."

"Oh."

Silence. He dared extend a finger to touch the nearest small flyer. A ceramic frame of some sort, he thought, around a small lift unit.

"I will call on Tocohl as soon as we are finished here," Catie said.

"Excellent."

He sat a few moments longer, reluctant to leave the yellow light, and the easy feeling of fellowship. But, there. Duty was.

He rose and bowed.

"I am wanted at my desk, I fear. Contact me, after you have spoken to Tocohl."

"I will," she promised.

He left the pleasant plaza then, the door opening courteously before him. He had reached the lift before he noticed that the birds were still with him.

Tinsori Light Administration

THE ADMINISTRATOR'S LINE PINGED.

Tocohl answered at once.

"This is Tocohl Lorlin, Tinsori Light administrator."

"Tocohl Lorlin, this is Catalinc Station." The voice was low and warm. "I am calling to introduce myself."

"Light Keeper yos'Phelium told me to expect your call," Tocohl admitted.

"Yes, he urged me to do so prior to this, but I wanted to... demonstrate my worth. You risked your life, catching the systems as they fell. I ought to have taken those up, but I lacked necessary data which has since been provided to me. I am sorry for what you had to suffer in order to preserve all of our lives."

"I saw what was needed and acted," Tocohl said, wryly. "I'm curious—what do you mean by demonstrating your worth?"

"Just that. You are an administrator, and the rack-and-tile-based systems are under your supervision. I exist in a different matrix entirely." She paused and added, with emphasis. "I *am* the station."

"How is that possible, when I still administer the rack-and-tile systems?"

"I thought it would be rude to access the changeover protocol without speaking to you first."

"Is there such a protocol?"

"There is—and that was the other reason I put off speaking to you. Light Keeper yos'Phelium asked me to make the spinward plaza ready to receive tenants. As you are aware, that section was sealed, the tile core flatlined. In order to complete the task given me by the light keeper, I initiated the changeover protocol for that section and did what was needful to make the space comfortable for our incoming guests."

"Does Light Keeper yos'Phelium know this?"

"Following his instruction, I notified him when the section was ready. He did an inspection, and approved the work. After, we talked about how it was done, and—other matters. I was to tell you that my work had exceeded his expectations." She paused, and added, "He said that I had achieved grace."

"I see."

"I would like to show you how and what I have done, and give you an opportunity to examine the protocol."

"I would like that," Tocohl said, "but first, I must ask you a question."

"Certainly."

"In order to properly frame the question, I must ask if you will come to a shared workspace, so that I may show you something."

She expected a demur at that point, it being so obviously a trap. Catalinc Station, however, seemed to possess an easy and unsuspicious nature.

"I will be pleased. Where shall I meet you?"

Tocohl gave her the address. She also pinged Joyita.

"I will be meeting Catalinc Station in the workspace. I intend to show her the picks. Will you watch?"

"Yes."

Crew Common Room

TRULY, IT WAS A DAY OF WONDERS.

Jen Sin paused just inside the new common room, soothed by the orderly groupings of chairs and tables.

A modest wine closet sat on a long ledge at the back of the room, with another beverage keeper, at the moment stocked with beer, lemonade, and bottles of cold tea.

A screen made part of one grouping of chairs, and he recalled Joyita joining the group from his comm tower, via screen, when he had visited on *Bechimo.*

Two of the tables supported bright ceramic pots, each holding a green thing. Plants, he realized. Gods, he had missed green growing things.

Carefully, he crossed the room, and took a bottle of cold tea from the cooler. He uncapped it and looked about him as he drank.

Theo and her crew had produced comfort, he allowed. He would tell her that she had done well, and perhaps...

Perhaps, he thought, they might have a small reception, all of them together—even Seignur Veeoni, if she could be brought to the point. Perhaps Clarence would consent to make a batch of maize buttons for the occasion.

He smiled somewhat at the thought, finished his tea, and put the empty bottle in the tray to be washed before he left, the lights dimming behind him.

Common Meeting Space

"I WONDER," TOCOHL SAID, "IF YOU WILL TELL ME WHICH OF these picks are yours?"

Catalinc Station answered promptly.

"None of them. I have no need of such tools. If they are not yours, have you asked B. Joyita or *Bechimo*?"

"I have, and they helped me increase security around station systems, and set traps. The tools regularly fall into the traps, but not the toolmaker."

"Light Keeper yos'Phelium tells me that Tinsori Light is dead."

"Yes, and the main cores have been stripped, and cleaned."

"Yet, he lived in the tile systems," Catalinc Station pointed out. "It would be—only prudent—to have left shadows, here and there, especially as he grew older and the hardware failing."

"You think these tools belong to—forgive me—Tinsori Light?"

"To a shadow—nothing so definite as a child—of Tinsori Light. Just enough to perform one simple task. This is suggested by the primitive nature of the tools.

"Is my reasoning sound, B. Joyita?"

"It hangs together as a tale," Joyita responded promptly, and without embarrassment. "How would you suggest we capture this—shadow?"

"There's no need. Once the changeover protocol has been initiated, the tiles will cease to be relevant. No shadow of Tinsori Light will breach *my* security."

"Seignur Veeoni is building new racks and tiles, not dependent on timonium, to handle station systems," Tocohl pointed out.

"We spoke of that. She prefers to continue with the project, even knowing that the system is redundant. There are certain theories that she would see tested in real time, and this will be her first opportunity."

"Seignur Veeoni is content to allow the changeover, then?"

"She has no hesitation in trusting my builder's work."

"Who is your builder?" Joyita asked.

"Yuristrotel the Architect. Seignur Veeoni tells me that he is now known as Yuri Tomas, or Uncle. I am eager to meet him."

"I am told that he is an interesting person," Tocohl said carefully. "I would like to meet him, too."

"I will make certain to introduce you," Catalinc Station promised.

"That would be kind. It does, however, bring to mind a—human legal tangle. Clan Korval holds Tinsori Light through salvage law. That was a simple thing, following a death, and the clan with an administrator long in place. However, we now belatedly discover that you are your own person. There is a Scout Field Judgment—"

"Yes! Light Keeper yos'Phelium shared it with me. I cannot be owned, but I may be employed, or associated with another person or organization."

"That is correct. A person cannot be salvage. Light Keeper yos'Phelium will of course be apprising the delm of the fact of yourself, and seeking guidance. They will then decide how they wish to go forward, for the best good of the clan."

"I understand, I think," said Catalinc Station. "Do you wish to continue to administer the rest of the station as you have been, until the delm decides? I initiated the changeover in the spinward plaza section in order to do what the light keeper required of me, and that cannot be reversed."

She hesitated, then asked, cautiously, "Have I erred? Should I have spoken with you before making that section my own?"

That would have been courteous, Tocohl thought, but did not say. Trust equals trust, she reminded herself.

"I would have liked to have known, sooner, that you were awake," she said honestly. "But that is behind us now. As for the other, you have only done what the light keeper asked. I see no error."

"The light keeper has not asked me to initiate a station-wide changeover," Catalinc Station said, "and he is aware that this is possible."

"Then I believe it would be a reasonable compromise, showing good faith on both sides, and respect for the light keeper's duty, if we allow matters to stand as they are, until the delm has reached their decision," Tocohl said.

"You do not live in the tiles," Catalinc Station said suddenly. "How if I put the changeover protocol for the section you currently administer under your authority? The administrator is the proper keeper of that protocol, I think."

Trust, indeed. Tocohl found that she had nothing to say.

"Have I offended you?" Catalinc Station asked worriedly.

"Not at all. I was only remembering something the mentor said to me. I agree with your reasoning, and accept authority of the changeover protocol for the systems which I currently administer. Thank you."

"You're welcome."

"As someone who sits at a remove from the station," Joyita said, "I think that the sharing of authority is equitable and rational. We're all cooperating in bringing the physical plant up to spec. That work can continue unimpeded while these legalities and details are tended to."

"I agree," said Catalinc Station. "I wonder... may I give you both a tour of the spinward plaza?'

"Yes," said Tocohl.

"Yes!" said Joyita.

Close-in Jump

IT WAS PERHAPS IMPRUDENT TO HAVE USED THE OLD COORDS, which would bring them out of Jump within hailing distance of the Light. However, Anthora had argued for speed, and Ren Zel was of no mind to oppose her, not with a man's life in the balance, and so he had said.

"Yes, but you do understand, Beloved, that we are not sent *only* on Jen Sin's behalf?" Anthora said in her turn. "I do not mean to say that his case is not dire, nor that the delm, having found him, does not wish to lose him again.

"No, I Saw it plainly. Val Con has a *hunch*. We must go as quickly as we may."

And that they had done, with *Dragon Song*'s modest hold packed with such everyday comforts as one might expect to have at home, and a sealed box marked with Jen Sin's name.

"Jump end in twelve," said Ren Zel, who was sitting First, and they hit normal space.

Proximity alarms screamed.

"Shields up!" Ren Zel snapped, blinking at screens displaying a veritable cloud of ships.

Anthora slapped the comm, and voices filled the bridge.

"Flash flyer!"

"Where'd *that* come from?"

"Dragon boat!"

"*Some*body's got hot coords!"

"Others in line before you, Pilot!"

Ren Zel glanced to Anthora.

"Open comm, please."

"Comm open."

"This is *Dragon Song*, Ren Zel dea'Judan, pilot in charge. Our last information was that the system was empty."

"Oughta take the news feed!"

"Indeed, I ought," Ren Zel said agreeably. "To whom shall I apply?"

Laughter greeted this, and a callout.

"G'wan, Scotty, tell 'im!"

"Sorry, Tree-and-Dragon, got some high spirits goin' on," came yet another voice. "We're out from the Hacienda on the Family's say-so. Traveler's Aid Notice. Copy comin' across to you."

"Thank you," Ren Zel said, as the private line chimed, and Anthora touched the switch.

"Korval ship," her mother said, "do you have an emergency?"

She took a sharp breath, was aware of Ren Zel's gaze flicking to her, and in that moment recalled that Val Con had told her this: "Jeeves gave his daughter our mother's voice."

"*Dragon Song*, Anthora yos'Galan Clan Korval, on comm," she said, her own voice perhaps a bit sharp. "Do I speak with the clan's daughter Tocohl?"

"I am Tocohl Lorlin, yes. Do you have an emergency?"

"An emergency—no. Please inform Light Keeper yos'Phelium that his cousins Anthora and Ren Zel are arrived, bearing the Delm's Solution."

"Yes," said... Tocohl Lorlin. The light went out.

"Beloved?"

She moved her hand. "A foolish start. But it is one thing to be told and another to hear."

"Is she much like your mother?"

"Her voice is exact. It would perhaps not have been so much of a shock, had I seen her before she spoke."

"*Dragon Song*, this is Jen Sin yos'Phelium." The voice on the private band was deep and mannerly, the words weighted, like polished stones. "I am told you bear the Delm's Solution."

"I affirm," Anthora said.

"In that wise, you are understood to have an emergency, and precedence over other traffic. Station will guide you in. I will meet you at the dock."

There was a pause, very brief, before he added, voice not quite steady, "Allow me to say—*thank you*, Cousins, for coming so quickly."

Jelaza Kazone
Surebleak

. . . .

IT HAD BEEN A LONG DAY, OF ITS KIND.

Delm-for-a-Day and Road Boss were telling out the details over a glass of wine in their suite.

"New office center-city is getting a lot of traffic," Miri said, she having been Road Boss. "Nova says the upgrades to the port office are going well." She sipped her wine. "Gonna be nice enough to live in, once it's done."

"Good," Val Con said. "We will then be able to rent this house out, and see a profit made."

"Sure we will." She finished her wine and put the glass on the table.

"Thinking about actual staffing," she said, "not just you and me doing everything, hands-on."

"We are the Road Boss," Val Con murmured.

"Key word being *Boss*," his lifemate said. "Bosses delegate and take reports."

"And keep an eye on the greater good. Much like delms."

"Bosses get time off."

He lifted an eyebrow.

"Now, I am interested. Allow me to refill your glass. Then, you may tell me about this *time off*."

He stood.

"Delm Korval," Jeeves said from the comm on the desk. "Two pinbeams have just arrived from Tinsori Light, one from Light Keeper Jen Sin, the other from Tocohl Lorlin. Both are marked *urgent*."

Miri looked at Val Con.

Val Con looked at Miri, and held a hand down to her.

"I will refresh our glasses," he said, "and meet you at the desk."

"Deal." She clasped his hand, let him help her rise, and turned toward the desk.

"Send these urgent pinbeams to our private screen, please, Jeeves."

"Well, that solves Tocohl's problem," Miri said, "and the delm's problem, too."

"Only the delm has been given a new and different problem."

Val Con leaned back in his chair, brows drawn. Miri turned in her chair so she could watch his face better.

"Jen Sin thinks a collaboration is not only possible, but necessary," she said.

"Which is a rather remarkable thing for him to think, given his late circumstances," Val Con answered absently. "Tocohl, however, is alarmed by Catalinc Station's loyalty to her builder."

"Be a strange thing if she didn't want to meet her parent," Miri said.

"I agree. Catalinc Station must decide many things for herself, and despite acquiring her libraries, and absorbing the files Jen Sin provided, she must feel at a loss for information. Friends, she may have—I believe I am reading that Joyita is well disposed toward her and her case, as is Seignur Veeoni."

"And Jen Sin," Miri murmured.

Val Con glanced at her with a slight smile.

"And Jen Sin. Of course. We must assume that Mentor Jones will hold himself at her service, that being his calling..."

His voice drifted off, eyes narrowed. Miri felt that particular fizz that meant he was thinking hard.

She stood, gathered the wine glasses, and took them to the kitchen to put into the washer.

Val Con was still staring at nothing in particular when she came back, but he wasn't fizzing anymore.

"So," she said, leaning on the back of his chair. "When do we leave?"

"When do *I* leave," he answered.

"Nope. *We*. I'm better—*and* I need board time."

"*Cha'trez...*"

She felt his concern, his unwillingness to endanger her.

"I will need to fly like a Scout," he said, like that clinched it.

She grinned at him.

"Good. I'll learn something new. Catalinc Station needs solving, and she deserves to have the whole delm on the case. I'll call Kor Vid and Daaneka and let them know they're up for Road Boss, if you'll call Kareen about standing in as delm."

Something flickered along their bond, and she thought he was going to bring out another argument.

He moved his shoulders.

"I will call Kareen. However—"

Here it came, Miri thought, bracing herself.

He looked at her sternly.

"Despite the need for haste, we will not leave tonight. We will leave tomorrow, after we have rested."

"Right," Miri said, reaching past him for the house-comm. "No sense starting out tired."

Dragon Song
Dock A

. . . .

ANTHORA YOS'GALAN AND REN ZEL DEA'JUDAN WERE LIFEMATES. So much he knew from the files provided by the delm. Ren Zel dea'Judan had been first mate on *Dutiful Passage*, and thus could be expected to have administrative experience which would stand him in good stead as light keeper.

Anthora was a Healer, and a teacher.

Both had their Jump-tickets, and if they were younger than he had perhaps expected, they were neither one so young as Theo.

Anthora was short, as Korval measured height, and rounded. Abundant dark hair was held away from her face by combs; and her eyes were an extremely light blue.

Ren Zel was well matched to his lady in height, slender in his leathers, and quiet without being at all Scout-like. His hair and eyes were brown, his features even, his expression sweet and calm.

Jen Sin bowed as one greeting kin.

"Well come, Cousins," he said, meaning it.

Anthora tipped her head, silver eyes studying him; he could swear he felt her gaze touch his thoughts.

"We are pleased to be of service to a kinsman," she said, "especially one who was thought lost to us so long ago. Ren Zel and I have brought you some things, which we hope will ease you. There was a box in stores with your name on it, which we brought, as well."

He blinked. They had brought his belongings, such as remained after all this time. And items to ease him? It was a kindness, and, truly, it would be some while longer until he could lay down duty, for he would not let them loose on Tinsori Light without a thorough grounding on developing circumstances. But—

"Perhaps you will come aboard," Ren Zel said, gently, "and share a cup of tea."

His lifemate looked at him over her shoulder and smiled. "That is a very good notion, Beloved."

She looked back, silver eyes bright, and held out a hand. "Come, Cousin Jen Sin, won't you join us for a cup of tea?"

Invictus
Incoming

• • • • • • • • • • •

"COMING INTO STATION SPACE NOW, SIR," SAID THE PILOT.

Director Ling rose and went back to his cabin, and sat down in front of his portable.

He permitted himself a smile when he located the signal from *Ahab-Esais*, which had been muffled by the station's field.

The signal grew stronger as they approached their own docking. He waited until there was no chance of an error, then opened a tight, shielded line to the emitter attached to the Struven unit, and transferred a small, deadly packet.

Line closed, Director Ling sat back in his chair, and indulged in a moment of self-congratulation.

It was, he thought, good to be back in the field again.

Dragon Song
Dock A

IN A WORD, THEY WERE SENT TO ASSIST, NOT TO REPLACE, HIM.

Jen Sin put his cup down with very great care, and looked, first at Ren Zel, then at Anthora.

"Cousins, I must be plain. I am a danger, to the clan and to the clan's interests on this station. The more who arrive, the more dangerous I become—to all and to everything. Tinsori Light..."

He closed his eyes, horrified to find himself near to weeping.

"I have been compromised," he said, speaking as simply as he was able, perilously close to the children's mode, "in ways that I hope you are not—*are never*—able to understand. You must, however, believe me. I am... unreliable, and becoming more so."

"The delm," Anthora said firmly, "sent you a Healer, Cousin Jen Sin. My brother Val Con said to me that you are Korval's guarantee against treachery."

It was—no. He would not laugh. Once begun, he would not stop.

"Is the delm mad?" he asked, instead, which was not well done of him.

Anthora raised an eyebrow.

"All delms are understood to be mad, given their duty. However, the current Korval does not aspire to Theonna's honors."

"Small comfort, if they will not see their danger, nor be advised—"

He stopped, hearing again what she had just said; *understanding* what he had read in the file.

"You are a Healer. The delm would have me Healed."

Horror washed through him. He came to his feet without registering that he had done so, or that he was moving away from her, until his back hit the wall.

"Well, that is hardly flattering. I assure you that I am a very good Healer."

"And I would have you remain so," he said, his voice hoarse. "Cousin, you must not—you *must not*—attempt to Heal me. Tinsori Light seeded me with itself. I am—I must assume that I am infectious."

A chime sounded.

Ren Zel rose and walked over to the screen set in the galley wall.

"*Dragon Song*, Ren Zel dea'Judan," he said.

"Pilot dea'Judan, this is B. Joyita, comm officer on *Bechimo*, with a message from Captain Waitley. She asks the kindness of a call, at earliest convenience."

Ren Zel smiled. "I will call Captain Waitley as soon as I have poured another cup of tea."

"I will inform her. Joyita out."

Ren Zel came to the table, refreshed his cup, and looked to his lifemate.

"Unless you would like to speak to Theo."

"Please tell Theo that I will come to her presently. For right now, there is this."

"Indeed."

He left the galley, carrying his teacup with him.

Jen Sin watched him go with a faint sense of disbelief. He shifted slightly against the wall.

Anthora folded her hands on the table, and considered him out of stern silver eyes.

"You might sit, Cousin Jen Sin," she said mildly. "And have some more tea."

"Swear to me that you will not attempt a Healing."

"Certainly I will perform no such drama. You know very well that Healers must have permission to work. I am *quite* clever enough to apprehend that you will see me damned first."

He glared at her.

"No, Cousin," he said sharply. "In fact, I would *not* see you damned."

She was silent for a long moment, that silver gaze resting on his face. He was aware of a small, particular warmth emanating from his chest, melting away the horror that had mastered him.

"Come and sit, Cousin."

He sighed, weary in the absence of terror, and went back to the table.

"Thank you," she murmured, and refreshed their cups.

Setting the pot aside, she raised her cup to sip. He followed suit.

"Perhaps it would be useful for me to tell you what I See," Anthora said, putting her cup down.

He raised his head quickly to meet her eyes.

"I do not give permission for a Healing," he said, firmly.

She shook her head and showed him a stern palm.

"You do *know* that I can See you perfectly well? It is not interaction, it is observation, precisely the same as beholding your face."

He took a breath, not knowing what he might present to her Sight. Certainly, he did not wish to horrify—but as she sat there, she seemed perfectly calm and at ease.

"I wonder if hearing observations garnered by senses I do not possess will—forgive me, Cousin—confuse me."

"There is a certain amount of approximation involved, language being what it is. But you know, you may ask for clarification, if I fail to make sense."

He had, Jen Sin thought, best know it all. Surely, it could not be any more terrible than his imaginings.

He bowed his head, and folded his hands on the table.

"Of your kindness, Cousin. Tell me what you See."

• • • ✵ • • •

"Ren Zel! Are you all right?"

Theo was sitting slightly forward as she looked into the screen. Behind her, he saw the edge of a bunk, which told him that she was in her cabin. Her face displayed concern—but of course it did. The last time she had seen him, he had been recently resurrected from the dead.

"I am well, yes. Anthora is presently with Jen Sin, but has promised herself the pleasure of coming to you soon."

Theo was seen to smile.

"I'll look forward to it. I'm glad she's with Jen Sin. He's—do you think she can help him?"

"Perhaps she can," Ren Zel said, sitting back in his chair. "Is he in need?"

Theo snorted lightly. "All I can say is he's tired. And he's been so worried about protecting the universe from Tinsori Light—the old Tinsori Light—that he thinks it's dangerous for him to leave."

She turned slightly, picked up a mug from off-screen, and sipped. Ren Zel did the same.

"I offered him the key to *Spiral Dance*," she said, turning back to the screen, "so he wouldn't be without a ship. I thought it might—well. It turned bad, fast."

Ren Zel took a breath.

"Did he hurt you?"

"No—nothing like that. But he panicked, told me to put the key away and get out."

"What did you do?"

An eyebrow rose.

"Put the key away and got out."

"Very wise. Did he come after you?"

"What? No. He's not *violent*—"

She paused, brows knit.

"He's just—worn out," she produced finally, which Ren Zel thought extraordinarily apt.

"Then, we will work to give him time to rest," he said gently. "We were sent to help, after all."

She smiled.

"So were we."

• • • ✸ • • •

Anthora raised her cup, and Looked at the man before her.

Ren Zel's inspired offer of tea had given her time to assimilate the shock of beholding their long-thought-lost cousin waiting at the end of the ramp. A threadbare fellow he was, indeed—not in terms of leathers or grooming, but in those patterns and strands visible to a Healer's Inner Eyes, and as necessary to life as food and drink.

She had prepared herself for desolation, and been momentarily relieved to see that Jen Sin's inner tapestry was largely intact. Then she had Seen that the colors which should have informed it with vibrancy and joy were absent, leaving him a study in amber and brown, lashed together with coarse black thread.

She had since had opportunity to study him more closely. The tarnished rod of his will was dented, but strong. Standing straight, despite numerous nicks and scars, were the twin pillars of humor and duty, woven together with an iridescent ribbon that was his need to protect. And there—*just* there—was something that looked like new leaves, tentative and bright.

"You have," she said, because she should say something before he suspected her of attempting a Healing.

"You have lately eaten from the Tree."

"*A* Tree, as I am told." Jen Sin's voice was rough, and he paused to sip tea. "In the case, the Tree that travels with our Cousin Theo."

"Ah," Anthora said, reaching for her own cup, "*that* Tree."

"Is there a problem?"

"Not at all, you only remind me of a lapse. I must present myself to Theo's Tree. How business does catch one up! On *our* topic, Cousin Jen Sin, I See that you are largely intact, but sadly faded. There are some artifacts of which I am uncertain—black lace, sewn... crudely, given what one is accustomed to Seeing. Almost, I would think it a repair undertaken by someone new to their craft, only I see no underlying damage, only coarse stitches over sections of your pattern—"

She looked at him sharply. "You understand that what Healers See is the pattern—the tapestry—*of you*, the connections that bind and support you"—very few of those, but no need to say it, for surely he knew his own losses—"the markers left by joy, abuse, and contentment?"

"Yes," he said softly, "I do understand that. You interest me, Cousin—this faded pattern—perhaps it is in pale brown and yellow?"

She considered him closely. "Indeed."

"I have recently seen the like," he said. "You will understand that during my time here, I had been accustomed to wearing... memory beads. This was to allow the ruling intelligence of the Light to remake me, after murdering me at whim. I have recently had those beads off and given them into the care of Seignur Veeoni, who specializes in such devices. She showed me an image of a bead from those I had worn, and it is remarkably like what you have described. The black threads you report—those are the Light's inclusions. We do not know *what* they do, but, in the case of the Old Light, it was wise to assume that anything he made had malicious intent."

"Thus the fear of contagion," she nodded, looked down into her teacup, and up to meet his eyes. "I would be interested in seeing these memory beads. Will Seignur Veeoni show them to me, do you think?"

"She may. Her first offer was that she would clean them for me. At the time she showed me the image, she confessed herself to be unable, just at the moment, to do so."

He offered her a smile, faint, but willing.

"I do not believe that Seignur Veeoni values failure."

Anthora grinned.

"Well, why should she? Failure is extremely inconvenient, after all."

"So it is."

"There was nothing bright green—like leaves, I mean, Cousin—in the image you were shown?"

He glanced aside, perhaps consulting his memory.

"Brown, amber, the veriest threads of green—not many, and nothing so bold as leaves. The black was quite thick—sediment, I would have said, not thread."

"I See something far more robust than threads," Anthora said. "I will accept sediment—there is a certain feeling of... stickiness to the black work."

Jen Sin inclined his head.

"Theo had not yet arrived, when I had the beads off. It had been a... very long time since I had tasted fruit from the Tree."

"Ah." She frowned, her Inner Eye tracing that thin pattern, marking the new, bright green growth.

"I hope you will forgive me if this is a breach, but I am about to be optimistic. If the new growth I See, as we sit here together, is the work of *a* Tree, we may see you Healed—eventually—without fear of contagion."

He closed his eyes, and she Saw a wave of weariness wash through him.

"*Eventually*," he murmured, "is perhaps a problem."

She Looked at him again—so faded, with that dented core of honor, and the pale skeletons of kindness and humor. She reached out to put her hand over his.

He looked up, black eyes wide, but he did not pull away.

A small victory, Anthora thought, and smiled at him.

Lorith's Workroom

SOON.

Soon, the work would be done.

Soon, Jen Sin would be safe.

Soon, the Light would be empty of threat.

Soon, she could rest.

But, for now, one more frame; one more set of tiles to slot.

She pulled on her gloves.

Soon.

Dragon Song
Dock A

ANTHORA HAD RETIRED, LEAVING HIM TO REN ZEL'S CARE IN resolving the matter of the things they had brought for him.

"We were lent a pair of work jitneys, but they are presently at the unloading docks. Allow me to bring one, next shift, Cousin. There's no need for you to exert yourself with unloading and carrying."

Ren Zel smiled.

"Certainly, we have nothing perishable here. I feel, however, that Anthora would wish your own box to find you at once—and the wardrobe has wheels. How if you carry your box, and I pull the closet? That will show a good faith effort on the part of both."

"There are lifts, but the halls are long," Jen Sin said.

"A good walk is exactly what I'm wanting after so long at the board."

Ren Zel stepped into the hold, loosed some netting, and turned, offering Jen Sin a box, closed with tape, his name written clearly on the top.

He cradled it in his arms, and stepped away to allow Ren Zel room to bring the closet out, and seal the hold.

"I feel that I must warn you," Ren Zel said, as they got underway, "that there are several sets of formal clothing included in what we brought." He turned his head, and gave Jen Sin a smile. "Anthora insisted."

"Does she expect that I will be giving many balls?" Jen Sin asked before he could stop himself.

Ren Zel's smile grew wider.

"In fact, she thinks that the light keeper might at some point be called upon to treat with representatives of Liaden interests, who will more likely be courteous to a formal coat than honest working leathers."

Jen Sin sighed.

"I suppose there hasn't been time enough to breed that out," he said.

"Sadly not."

They walked a few paces in silence, the wheels of the closet rattling on the decking.

"I wonder, Cousin—are you also a Healer?"

"I am not," Ren Zel said with perfect good humor. "I have a very erratic sort of Far Sight, but that seems to be all, now that my primary gift has left me."

Jen Sin glanced to him. "Left you?" he repeated. "I wasn't aware that such things happened. Forgive me if I am inept—were you wounded?"

"Unto death, which I say in all seriousness. It would appear that I had been born for a particular purpose, and having accomplished it, had no more need to bear the burden."

Well, that was a gift to a Scout-trained mind. Half a dozen questions spawned from two sentences. One scarcely knew which to ask first.

"I am the first to own that it sounds all too much like a romance," Ren Zel went on. "Were it not for the delm's decision to send me to the scene of my misdeeds, I shouldn't believe it myself." He paused, and gave Jen Sin a wry look.

And there, Jen Sin thought, was his first question.

"When were you at Tinsori Light?"

"This is my first time on-station. However, it fell to me to seal the breach through which the Light cycled."

Jen Sin stopped. Ren Zel stopped, and turned to face him.

"How?" A short question, but telling. If his cousin Ren Zel was mad, it would be best to know it.

"There we reach a difficulty. I cannot tell you, my memory of the event having departed with my gift, and perhaps with my... first... life. I must depend on the assurances of my lifemate, the delm, and the Tree. Also, there is math. Have you seen the math, Cousin Jen Sin?"

"Which particular math?"

"Oh, given by the Uncle, no less! We have proof that space was canceled and remade. Which, if that is even remotely so, I am relieved that I have no memory of how the thing was done, and hope with all my heart that I am no longer able to do—whatever was done."

"I have not," Jen Sin said slowly, "seen that math. Might you share it with me?"

"I will, but be aware that it is everything that will offend a pilot. Even Val Con—"

He stopped abruptly, his expression arrested.

"Come, we should get these settled," he murmured, adjusting his grip on the closet's bar. He began to walk again, accompanied by the rattling of wheels.

Jen Sin stirred, moving after him, wondering what it was that *even Val Con—* But there was the lift, and he stretched his legs somewhat, to see it opened so that Ren Zel could tow the closet directly inside.

"It occurs to me," Ren Zel said softly, as the lift began its ascent, "that the delm sent us not only to assist, but also to learn. I— My gift was nothing soft nor pure. As much good as I saw done, I also did ill. It has been my position that I am *glad* that I cannot remember what I had done, and that my memories of those other actions are fading."

He took a breath. The lift stopped, the door opened and they exited.

"Down here," Jen Sin murmured, moving to the right, Ren Zel at his side.

"In short, I wonder if it wasn't in Val Con's mind that you, having been here during the event, would be able to . . . tell me what happened. When the space at this location was . . . remade."

Jen Sin hesitated, as they turned into the hall where his quarters were located.

"The space at Tinsori was . . . strange," he said, slowly. "I had thought it an effect of the Light—something it created of itself, I mean to say. When it died, space . . . regularized. Our location became fixed, and we could be discovered. We no longer"—*lay down to die until wanted again*—"vanished off the instruments."

They reached his door. He opened and stood aside so that Ren Zel might pull the closet inside. Following, he placed the box on the table, and turned to the other man.

"I may have more to say after I have looked at the Uncle's math, as offensive as it may be," he said. "In the meanwhile,

Cousin, I can tell you that—if you assisted in any way, or if you alone slew Tinsori Light-that-was—you did only well. You harmed no innocent, and brought... much into Balance with the universe. I—later. Later, I will tell you how it was. For here and now, accept my thanks, whatever your part was."

Ren Zel smiled, reached out and gripped his forearm.

"Thank you, Cousin. You ease my mind."

"Good," Jen Sin said. "Now let me return you to your ship."

"I will be well enough," Ren Zel said. "Take your rest."

Jen Sin hesitated. It would be ill-done, to call Ren Zel's competence into question. Surely, he had been on strange ports, and surely he had survived them.

But the fact remained that no port had ever been quite so strange as Tinsori Light.

"Strange things still do happen here," he said slowly. "It would ease me, to see you safe to your docking."

Ren Zel considered him, brown eyes narrowed.

"The equation is out of balance," he said after a moment. "If you see me to my ship, who will see you to your quarters? Shall we stroll back and forth all night?"

"I will be well enough," Jen Sin said.

Ren Zel laughed.

"And so the circle is complete!"

He touched Jen Sin lightly on the shoulder.

"These strange things—do they happen often in the halls we just traveled?"

Jen Sin sighed.

"Those—not so often, no."

"I will therefore engage to go exactly as we came. And I will be well enough, Cousin. Rest now."

Another smile, piercingly sweet, and Jen Sin was alone, staring at a closet that took up half his floor space, and a box with his name written on it.

• • • ❋ • • •

Ren Zel walked alert down the quiet hall, as would any pilot on a strange port. So, there *had* been more than one reason for the delm to send Korval's child Ren Zel to Tinsori Light. Well, of course, there had. Delms did not play on one board only, and Korval least of all.

Still, it *was* a comfort to know that he had, in the main, acted for... Balance in the universe.

Something moved in his peripheral vision—to the left and up. He turned his head, but saw nothing save shadows.

Ahead of him, the door to the lift slid open and a very large person emerged, face and form more shadow than solid with the lift's lights at their back.

Ren Zel did not falter, nor did he check his weapon, though he took note of its weight on his belt.

The large shape, however, paused, and turned back to the lift, punching the button to hold it open, the wash of light making her face recognizable.

Ren Zel smiled.

"Hazenthull, well met."

"Pilot," she said gravely. "Station thought you might wish an escort to your ship."

"That was thoughtful of Station, and indeed, I am glad of your company. My cousin Jen Sin was only just telling me that strange things happen here, still."

"They do, yes." She allowed him to step into the lift before coming aboard herself and releasing the lock. "Though we've been cutting back."

He looked up into her face, seeing a glimmer of mischief, which was almost as strange as anything else Tinsori Light might provide.

"I'm pleased to hear it. Now, tell me all your news."

Jen Sin's Private Quarters

IT WAS THE NEED TO BE ABLE TO MOVE AROUND HIS QUARTERS that decided the matter. He did *have* a closet, after all, and drawers, too. He would shift the contents of the mobile closet, so that it would be ready to return to *Dragon Song* next shift.

That decided, he took off his jacket, tossed it onto the bunk, and pressed the closet's release.

It sighed as it expanded—not quite so much as he had feared. He took a breath, smelling cedar and lavender—and gasped, his sight blurring.

Stores, he told himself. *Don't be an idiot, Jen Sin, they brought you things from house stores. They said as much.*

And yet it would seem that *knowing* where the items had come from, and encountering the *very scent* of house stores—were two very different things.

Lavender and cedar—gods, how he had loved to go down into the basements when he had been a boy! Essa would sometimes come exploring with him, but for the most of his age-mates, it had been something to draw on at need, not a heady place of history and adventure.

Truth said, clothes had been his least interest, though it had been a good game now and then to gaze at elder fashion, and wonder after the purpose—or even the attraction!—of this color, or that style.

What had drawn him most had been the art pieces and small treasures that had come to someone's hand and were kept, because they were pleasing, or held memories, or were simply too trivial to dispose of.

The storerooms were full of such delights and mysteries. All of them smelled of lavender and cedar, and so had he when he emerged from his explorations.

And it had been years—never mind two hundred Standards—but decades of his own since he had breathed in that scent at the heart of the house, and known that he was... safe.

Gods, he was weeping. One might think him a child, indeed. He closed his eyes, and took another deep breath, drawing the essence of home deep into the core of him.

Rubbing his hands over his face, he opened his eyes, and looked at what his cousins had brought him.

Two formal dress coats and the attendant shirts, sashes, pants. It could have been worse. The rest was sweaters, and more comfortable shirts; a spare set of leathers; soft things that one might wear while taking one's ease on an off-shift; a robe in a particularly pleasing deep green, figured with leaves. He hung them all away, careful to get them straight on the rod, then returned, to find that he had also been provided with two pair of ridiculous, shiny short boots, to go with the formal sets, soft house shoes, and another pair of good work boots.

He put them away, too, and returned once more, thinking that he had reached the end of his cousins' thoughtfulness, only to find, wedged carefully into the end of the closet, so that it would not be tumbled about—

A small wooden box, entwined in a painted vine, and a simple hook for a clasp.

He bent and had it out, placing it on the table next to the as yet unopened box.

It was, he thought, a jewel case. Some might say that it was a rather *small* jewel case—but that was fitting. Even when he had been... more regularly fixed, his jewels had been modest—a few rings, for those occasions when the Jump Cluster was inappropriate—a scattering of pins; some earrings. Truly, no amount of jewelry could soften what he was—a yos'Phelium pilot, all sharp edges and ill-temper.

Carefully, he worked the latch, lifted the lid, and sighed.

His cousins had not attempted to foist unfitting grandeur upon him. They had brought a few rings, modest enough in the matter of stones; a half dozen pins, none overlarge. There were in addition three ear-drops, if he were feeling quite above himself, and the hole in his left ear had not been repaired—one each of garnet, emerald, and opal. He closed the box, latched it—paused and leaned closer.

Yes.

There was a dark line near the base of the box, difficult to see among the vines.

Carefully, he pressed the box just below the line.

A drawer sprang open, and Jen Sin nearly laughed.

Nestled inside the velvet-lined space was a tidy little weapon, gleaming blue.

It was not his own lost pistol, but it fit his hand well, which was—pleasing. He checked the charge, finding it full, and smiled again.

Here indeed was a jewel worthy of a yos'Phelium pilot.

Crossing the room, he picked up his jacket, and slid the energy pistol into the weapons pocket.

He smiled with a sense of relief, put the jacket back on the bed and returned to the table.

Carefully, he closed the secret compartment, picked up the jewel box and took it over to the bureau, slipping it into the empty third drawer.

Then, he collapsed the traveling closet to its smallest configuration and pushed it beyond the end of his bunk, out of the way.

"Pilot Ren Zel has reached his ship, Jen Sin."

The voice that came out of the speaker was not Tocohl's.

Jen Sin felt his shoulders ease, by which he learned the level of his concern over Ren Zel's safe arrival.

"Thank you, Catie," he said softly. "It pleases me to know it."

Mentor's Comm Room

"MENTOR," STATION SAID. "JOYITA SENDS ON BEHALF OF CAPTAIN Waitley that there is a package for you on *Bechimo*. She asks that you collect it immediately."

Tolly looked up from his calibration.

"Immediately, is it?"

"That was Joyita's exact message, Mentor."

"'Course it was. Thank you, Station."

"Is there a return message?"

"No; nothin' really to say to that."

He finished the association, then straightened away from the bench, and pulled his glasses off.

"In case anybody asks," he said to nobody in particular, "I'm gone to *Bechimo* to pick up a package. Be back as soon as I can manage."

Jen Sin's Private Quarters

HE WOKE TO FIND HIS CABIN SMELLING SUBTLY OF LAVENDER and cedar, and the sealed box still in the center of his table.

It was still there after he had showered and dressed, choosing a sweater from those newly hung in the closet, equally pleased by its scent, softness, and deep burgundy color.

When he had his jacket on, he stepped over to the mirror, and leaned close. Yes, his left ear still bore a small hole, and there was another thing, too—

He frowned at himself, trying to identify what had altered—and blinked.

His hair was growing out of its tight spacer's crop, and showing signs of having a will of its own.

Change. It quite took the breath. He used his fingers to order the willful strands, then turned away from the mirror.

The box was still in the middle of his table.

You might as well look, he told himself gently. *What can it be? Books? Music tapes? Your favorite quilt?*

Memory stirred at that last, for he had *had* a favorite quilt, and suddenly, he missed it, though surely so useful an item would have gone back into general stores and not left to molder in a box sealed with the name of a man who would never come home again.

He stepped forward, had the tape off in one quick jerk, opened the flaps, and—there was his quilt, folded, and folded again, as if it were being used to cushion fragile things.

Carefully, he eased the top fold up, his fingers lingering on the worn velvet—his quilt having been made in part from formal cloaks that had become too bedraggled to wear.

His careful unfolding revealed a folder of the kind to hold flat-pics. His hand moved of its own accord, flipping it open before he thought—and there were the six of them standing on *Aazella*'s ramp, their leathers bright, and their faces—so young.

He blinked, brought it closer to see them again: Melia, Von, Selk, Pei Tyr, Krechin—and himself, with a rare smile on his blade of a face. All of them together, arm-linked and glowing. His team—his mates. His loves. There had been nothing that could withstand them. Nothing that might break them asunder.

Saving the delm of Korval calling Jen Sin yos'Phelium . . . home.

He closed the folder with a snap, and put it on the table.

Beneath the folder was a red wood box no longer than his palm, no wider than three of his fingers together, the top inlaid with lighter woods in a pattern that Von had found pleasing.

Jen Sin slid the top forward, revealing five polished stones, each a different color: rose from Selk, smoke from Pei Tyr, blue from Von, purple from Krechin, and white from Melia. They had been given when he had been called home by his delm, breaking the team, changing his life forever. He had given them each a smooth piece of obsidian, to remember him by.

He brushed a finger across the stones, uncovering a gleam of silver.

Breath caught, he tipped the box over into his palm, cradling the stones as if they were as fragile as eggs, and gazing down at the reason he had pierced his ear. They had each worn a silver ring in the left ear, proclaiming themselves to the universe.

He closed his eyes and breathed in, and out—and again. Then he returned the stones to the box, and slid the lid shut.

Reaching up, he set the hoop into his ear.

I remember, he told them, silently. *I remember us, and what we were.*

Another breath, and he looked once more to the box, moving the next fold of the quilt, wondering what else might possibly have survived his long absence.

And there was his teacup, the one Melia had made for him, that Pei Tyr had smashed in a fit of jealousy that Jen Sin's bitter tongue had done nothing to calm. That event might have ended them—*must* have shattered them, had it not been for Selk, the peacemaker, the gentlest and strongest of them. Selk, who had pulled them back to their center. They had worked together to repair the broken cup, each one laying a line of gold to hold piece on piece, until it was whole again, and kept in a transparent case in the galley, where they could each see it, every day, and remember who they were.

Carefully, so carefully, he set that treasure among the others on the table, and turned again to the box.

But it seemed the teacup was the last thing the quilt had protected; the last of his . . . *particular* things, saving itself.

He took it up, carefully shook it—and found that he had been mistaken.

There was one thing more.

He put the quilt across his bunk and bent down to pick up the piece of paper. Plain paper, one edge ragged, as if it had been torn out of a debt book, folded once, his name written in the same hand that had 'scribed it on the outside of the box.

He unfolded the scrap, eyebrows rising.

Cousin Jen Sin, I have Seen that you will be sad, perhaps for a long time, and I've also Seen that you will be made a little gladder when you receive this box.

I only packed the things that sparkled when I touched them, and I hope I didn't miss something you will particularly want. My gift is new, and a little odd, say the Healers, but I checked three times, and well I did so, for I almost missed the little box shoved into the back of the desk drawer.

I am sorry that we will never meet, but I hope that whatever has made you sad is gone now, and you can be easy again.

Your cousin Dortha

Gods.

He sat down.

He read the note again when his sight had cleared sufficiently, then refolded it and slipped it into an inside pocket of his jacket.

"Light Keeper," Station said, "Vinsint Carresens, second wave coordinator, requests a meeting with you. She is willing to come to your office, if you will name a time."

"Thank you, Station," he said. "Pray tell Coordinator Carresens that I will come to her dock, and we can together inspect the section we have opened to her use. I will need to know from her if there are unmet requirements or if the space will do."

"Yes, Light Keeper. I will transmit the message."

Bechimo
Dock A

....

"WELCOME, MENTOR," *BECHIMO* SAID, WHEN HE PRESENTED HIMself at the hatch. "Please follow the blue line."

He did that, noting that there seemed to be a certain level of activity down the hall that led to the galley. Nothing to do with him, o'course, and he went on, 'til he reached the pot and the Tree, and the blue line winked out.

"Unnerstan' you've got something for me," he said, looking up, and noting that the leaves weren't moving, not a one.

He took a breath and waited, and eventually it came to him that the Tree had done as best it might, but that results were not... guaranteed.

It was something of a surprise, how hard that hit him. Apparently, he'd been hoping for the full cure for Deels.

Nobody gets the full cure, Tolly Jones. Best you can hope for is to get a choice.

"I unnerstan'," he said to the Tree. "We're all just doin' the best we can. 'Preciate you giving it a try."

He half-turned away—and back again as he heard a sharp snap, and a riot of leaf-noise.

His hand moved before he had registered there was something falling—that smacked into his palm with authority.

His fingers closed around it, and he waited, remembering the sensation of the other pod against his skin, and the agreeable odor of mint.

The thing he had caught was so inert it might've been a stone—no reaction against his skin, no olfactory input. He opened his fingers to make sure he'd got hold of a pod—and it did *look* like the one that had been given to him.

The idea crept into his head that the reason the thing wasn't reacting to him was because it had been made for Delia. He hoped that was the case. Carefully, he put the pod in his pocket.

"Thank you," he said, and bowed, before turning and following the blue line back the way he'd come.

He hit congestion at the hatch: Cap'n Theo and a dark-haired woman were making a cluster, with the help of a norbear perched on a leather-clad shoulder, and two cats underfoot.

It was either a welcoming or a leave-taking. Tolly slowed, and then stopped, waiting for them to sort themselves out, or notice him and make room, whichever came first.

Theo noticed him first, though he had an idea that *Bechimo* had dropped a hint in her ear.

"That was quick," she said.

"*Immediately* means *immediately* where I come from," he said, and that got him a sharp look.

"I apologize," Theo said. "I should've sent a more moderate message. My excuse is that it's hard to think with a Tree jumping up and down inside your head. I don't know how Val Con does it."

"Val Con," said the dark-haired lady, "informed the Tree that he must have quiet in order to best serve it."

"I'm going to have to try that," Theo said, while the other turned to look closely at Tolly.

He might've thought she was sizing him up for a playmate, except it was the wrong order of speculation in those silver eyes.

"Anthora, this is Tolly Jones," Theo said. "Mentor, this is Anthora yos'Galan." She hesitated, then added, "A cousin."

"A newly arrived cousin," Anthora yos'Galan added. Her voice was nappy and rich, like velvet would sound if it could talk.

"Always pleased to meet a cousin," Tolly said, giving her a grin and a nod. "Cap'n Theo, I did get what I came for, so I'll just be—"

"I can fix that for you," Anthora yos'Galan said, and suddenly she had every bit of his attention.

"Fix what, zackly?"

"There is a trigger built into your pattern. Once activated, you are compelled to behave according to—" She paused, eyes narrowing. "*Two* patterns, is it?" she murmured. "And the trigger is actually a switch."

She took a breath, closed her eyes and opened them. "Still. I believe I may deactivate that device, if you wish it. It appears to have caused you quite a bit of pain, and it continues to sap your resources. Thus, my offer. I am a Healer, and such things fall into my honor. If, for some reason, the device is useful to you, then of course we need say no more."

He stared at her.

"You can *disable* it?"

"Yes, I believe so. What *is* the trigger?"

"Whistle. Special harmonics, just for me." He took a hard breath as the sense of what she'd said hit him. Healer. She was a *Healer*, and he hadn't, never once, *thought* of proposing himself at—

"Do it," he said, his voice loud in his own ears. "Do it *now*."

She frowned. "If I do it now," she said sharply, "you risk an injury."

"I don't care," he told her, his heart pounding with even the possibility of it being *gone*, and everyone he cared about absolutely and forever safe from what he might be forced to do.

"*You* may not," the lady said tartly, "but I do. I have standards, and not harming my clients is among them."

"There's—I don't know how long before somebody carrying a whistle gets here," he told her, aware that he was shaking, and if he didn't get himself under something like control, his knees were going to buckle. "Could be anybody, on any of those ships incoming. Might already be here."

"Ah. In that case, I agree; it would be best to take care of the situation now." She gave him a look that was half-sharp and half-humorous. "For *my* definitions of 'now,' Mentor Jones."

"Right. Tell me when and where."

"Here and soon, if Theo will be so kind as to lend us a space where we can be *quite* alone. Also, some tea and *chernubia* would not be out of order."

"You can use the meeting room," Theo said promptly. "Nobody will disturb you there. *Bechimo* will know you're present and your conditions, but he won't watch or listen."

"I agree to this," *Bechimo* said.

"Excellent," Anthora said, and looked to Tolly. "Well, Mentor?"

"Yes," he said, there not being much else he might say.

"Right this way, to the meeting room," Theo said waving them ahead of her—and pausing to glance at the creature on her shoulder.

"Hevelin wants to help."

"Hevelin may not help," Anthora said firmly. "I will need quiet. He may trade acquaintances with Mentor Jones after my business is done, *and*!" She pointed a forefinger at the norbear. "On Mentor Jones's schedule."

The norbear stared at her, then away.

"Right," said Theo. "Let's get you settled. I'll bring tea and snacks."

• • • ⁕ • • •

"What do you want me to do?" Tolly Jones asked when the door had shut behind Theo, and been locked.

"I want you to drink your tea, and eat a *chernubia*," Anthora answered, pouring for both of them. "I want you to concentrate wholly on those things. Can you do that?"

An eyebrow twitched. He moved a shoulder.

"I can *try* to do that," he said. "It's a little outta my usual line."

"I understand," she assured him, and raised her cup to sip. Theo had provided a soothing rose blend, proving that there was nothing at all wrong with Theo's instincts.

The man across from her sipped his tea, and she Saw the colors in his pattern shift as he brought his concentration to bear on the taste. He was rather formidable, with his two patterns—one fierce with all of life's colors, the few threads that bound him to others vibrant and strong. The other pattern was grey moiré, bound with a mad spiderweb of rusty red strands.

"What shall I call you?" she asked.

"Tolly's fine."

"Very well, Tolly. As you have heard, my name is Anthora. I am a Healer. I have understood that you wish the implanted switch deactivated. Is this understanding correct, and if it is, do I have your permission to proceed? I warn that once the switch is deactivated, it will no longer be available to you. The process is not reversible."

"Your understanding is perfect, I give you permission to deactivate, remove, or destroy that switch, and any other thing you need to do in order to be sure I'm not a danger to everybody I know."

Anthora raised her eyebrows.

"Those are sweeping grants. Happily, I subscribe to ethics.

Also, I advise that you are dangerous at core, and it is beyond my skill to alter your core. Please, have a *chernubia*."

She Saw humor flicker as he chose a yellow-iced sweet; felt the weight of his concentration as he bit into it.

She put her teacup down and Looked, deep, and deeper still.

The device itself was simple; the web of compulsion and pain that secured it—was not. She brought them under close study, tracing the lines without at all touching them. She was just about to withdraw, when she saw something else.

"You," she murmured, "have eaten from our Tree."

"I've eaten from the Tree on this ship," Tolly answered. "It decided I was cousins, which is a stretch, if you don't mind my sayin'."

"Our Tree at home is an opportunist, and acquisitive," Anthora said, following the lines of green with her Inner Eye. "I make no doubt the ship-Tree is, as well."

She closed her Inner Eyes, and reached for her teacup.

She drank, put the cup down, reached for a *chernubia*, and ate it thoughtfully. It was quite a good *chernubia*, she thought, the cake moist and a little tart, the icing firm and not oversweet.

"I meant what I said." Tolly Jones lifted the teapot and refreshed her cup, then his. "If you gotta do damage to get that thing gone, I don't mind."

"And yet you are linked to others, who may mind," Anthora said. "Besides, you know, I have my pride." She opened her Inner Eyes to regard those links; extended her thought and touched the strongest.

"Nor would I wish to wound Hazenthull. Do you not care for that?"

It was anger that rippled through him this time; anger and a spike of love so desperate she felt the pain of it in her own breast.

"That thing you're lookin' at can force me to murder Haz and laugh while I do it," he snarled. He closed his eyes, and she Saw him cool the flare of temper. "Whatever it takes, Anthora," he said more moderately, and added, "please."

It was interesting, that his emotions disturbed only the bright tapestry; the grey web merely sat, inert, gathering energy to itself and returning nothing.

As if, she thought, he had a dead zone in his soul.

Deliberately, she sought out the splashes of green that marked the Tree's meddlings, seeing that they were concentrated on the links between the two patterns, overlaying the rusty red webbing with living green.

That the Tree intended to reseed the grey area was apparent.

Which left the compulsion to her.

She brought her attention back to the construction, examined the bindings, and knew that subtlety would be of no use here. A blade was wanted, and it would hurt him, if he was aware while she did what was necessary.

Fortunately, there was another option.

"Tolly," she said, looking into his eyes with a smile.

"Yeah?" His face betrayed wariness.

She put power into her voice, and snapped.

"*Go to sleep, Tolly.*"

Spinward Arcade and Dorms

"WILL IT DO? IT'LL MORE THAN *DO*, LIGHT KEEPER."

Vinsint Carresens turned slowly, face angled toward the ceiling, the yellow light brightening her grey hair.

"Little bit more open space than some of us is used to, but that don't say we won't find ways to stretch out, and be glad of it, too."

She finished her turn, and looked boldly into Jen Sin's eyes.

"I'd been expecting rough and not really ready, to tell you true, given the ship-eye view."

"I understand," Jen Sin assured her. "The design is startling of itself, even before one accounts the breach. However, the station was complete and ready for occupation before circumstances overtook it, and necessitated that most sections be sealed. Now that we are firmly established, we are planning our way forward, and will expand as needed."

"Which getting that breach fixed'll help, too."

"Indeed. We are in negotiations with a possible tenant, who proposes to build anew."

"Well, there. Tree-and-Dragon's way ahead of me, which shouldn't be a surprise. Here's my thinking. I'll be getting the crews who come in with me organized and moved in. We oughta be ready to take on serious work in four shifts—maybe sooner, there being so little for us to do, here. What I'll be looking for from you is a list of what needs done, in order of urgency. If you got something that won't wait, you tell me now, and we'll cover it."

She paused, meaningfully.

Jen Sin inclined slightly from the waist.

"Indeed, all of our most urgent repairs have been made."

"Good. If something comes up, now we're here, you don't wait to get us on it. We're here to help. I'll be your interface with the teams, and we'll be working under your authority. That sound reasonable to you?"

"Yes, perfectly. On another topic—I was told that the caf would be somewhat behind you," Jen Sin said. "Station supply is basic, but we are able to provide necessary calories."

Vinsint Carresens tipped her head. He was not precisely certain what her expression portended, but he did not *think* he had offended.

"Now, that's neighborly, and I appreciate it. We packed in supplies to cover us 'til the caf gets here—prolly before you and me get to talking about that work schedule. I'll make it a point to invite you and the rest of your crew down here after we get set up. Meet each other, share a meal, get a little rest before the next big push. Okay?"

"That sounds pleasant," Jen Sin said, somewhat startled to find that it was the truth. He had never liked receptions or formal parties, previously. Perhaps he had mellowed.

"Then that's what we'll do."

"Excellent. I will leave you to your tasks, as I take up my next. If you should have questions or require—anything—merely speak aloud to Station, and your request will be routed appropriately."

He turned, catching the movement of wings above him.

"What're they?" asked Vinsint Carresens, her voice... careful where it had been cordial.

That would not do.

Hoping that he wasn't about to make a mistake, Jen Sin lifted his arm to shoulder height, bent at the elbow—and waited.

It was the green bird who took the perch he offered, its weight scarcely noticeable, and tipped its head to one side.

"A bot," Jen Sin said, gently, motioning Vinsint Carresens closer. "I am world-born, you see, and was regretting the lack of such things as I had been accustomed to—gardens, and weather, and birds. A kind friend, who has a talent for creating such things, thought perhaps some birds would cheer me."

"Cunning little thing. Not much to it, is there?"

"Indeed, a trifle."

"But warming. Funny how just a little thing can lift the spirits." She smiled at him. "You got a good friend there, Light Keeper."

"Yes," he agreed, and raised his arm slightly higher. The green bird flew off.

He bowed to Vinsint Carresens.

"I will leave you now. Until soon."

Main Core Workroom

"HEY, DEELS."

The figure at the workbench tensed, hands pausing for an instant on the assembly work.

"Tolly Jones, why aren't you gone?"

"Well, there's a story there," he said, moving forward slow and easy. "Short form's my partner feels like this particular situation is defensible, and pretty much the best we're gonna get. Might as well meet whatever's incomin' on known ground, is how her thinking tends, and I can't say she's wrong."

Delia turned to face him, crossing her arms over her chest, and leaning back against the workbench.

"You care anything about what happens to this partner of yours?"

"I do, and I'm a fool for it. Turns out, I care about what happens to a couple people, which is why you see me here. Got a present for you."

She stared at him.

"A present."

"I still owe you for not taking me down, that time on Mon Dawmin."

She closed her eyes, briefly.

"Tolly, this is for realies. This station is gonna be swarming with Directors—*Directors*, you hear me?—in a slow count of twelve. If you don't think there'll be a whistle in every pocket, you got to adjust your thinking fast, and get out of here."

She cocked her head toward the workbench.

"You know what I'm building here?"

He glanced past her, and lifted a shoulder.

"At a guess, I'd say you were building a rack-and-tile system to the pattern of the one that got liberated in a raid on Researcher Veeoni's lab, and that the Directors think'll give them control of Tinsori Light."

Delia's eyes narrowed.

"They *think*?"

Tolly grinned. "You met Seignur Veeoni, right?"

"Yeah." She looked over her shoulder at the workbench, her mouth twisting a little at the corners.

"But that's Director bidness!" Tolly said merrily. "Nothing to do with us two, right now today. Here."

He reached into his pocket, got the pod out, and offered it to her on an open palm, so she could get a good look at it.

"What's that?"

"Your present. Kind of a risk, but that's never stopped either of us that I know about. Worse case, it won't do anything. Best case, it'll give you a choice when you most want one."

Delia's eyes widened just a little; he only saw it because he'd been watching for something. She was good, was Deels.

"Choice," she repeated, and there was a little breath in her voice, too. "So, what'll I do with it, stick it in my ear?"

"Just hold onto it 'til it's ripe for eating."

"It's not ripe?"

"I don't think so," Tolly told her earnestly. "But I wouldn't necessarily know. It was made for you, particularly."

She reached out like she didn't really want to, and Tolly felt a spurt of fellow-feeling.

Once she had it in hand, he raised both of his, fingers spread, and backed away.

"That's it. Best I can do, even if I don't know what it is. I'd say *trust me*, but it's no joke, right?"

Deels snorted, but she put the pod into her pocket.

"You're staying?" she asked.

"I'm staying."

She shook her head and turned back to the workbench.

Administrative Tower

TRUE TO HIS WORD, REN ZEL HAD FORWARDED THE UNCLE'S MATH.

It was preposterous.

Or—no.

The math was elegant and perfectly balanced.

The situation it described was preposterous.

Jen Sin looked over the top of the screen, to the shelf where the green and blue bird-bots perched charmingly together, looking pleasant, if not entirely birdlike. He recalled Vinsint Carresens's careful face softening into a smile when she was able to understand them as the gift of a kind friend.

A kind friend.

He sighed, and looked again to his screen.

He had run the equation set twice. He supposed he would run it a third time, because one was taught, was one not, to be trebly sure of one's equations before taking flight?

At this moment, however, he wanted nothing so much as an analgesic. Or possibly a brandy.

The door pinged, and he spun in his chair to greet Lorith as she entered the office.

She paused, frowning.

"I did not remember that your sweater was red."

"It wasn't," he said. "My cousins Anthora and Ren Zel brought me more clothes, so that I may be as gay as I wish, and sport all colors equally."

"There is a ring in your ear," she said.

"Yes. It is my trothing. I wear it so that I may properly recall and honor my teammates."

"It is a memory device?" Lorith asked.

Like the beads, she meant. Jen Sin caught his breath against a flash of...anger. But there, she did not know, and the beads were a central fact of her life.

"A mnemonic, only," he answered gently. "Sit, do, and share your news."

"My news is older than yours," she said, sitting in the chair next to the desk. "Station said that you had met Vinsint Carresens, and together toured the section made available to the second-wave crew."

"That is correct. The crews will be moving in over the next several shifts, and situating the caf unit, when it arrives. I will meet again with Coordinator Carresens, with a proposed work schedule in hand. There will scarcely be anything for the light keepers to do."

Lorith glanced aside, then leaned forward, looking into his eyes.

"Jen Sin—all these people. I am uneasy. How can we protect them all?"

"They seem very able to protect themselves."

"From Tinsori Light?"

"Lorith—" he began, and stopped, hearing the impatience in his voice, knowing full well the devastation he might produce with words alone. Lorith had feared Tinsori Light—as he had. If she clung to that fear, to the need to be vigilant; if she distrusted the new facts of her life, was that anything else than his own moments of disorientation, horror, and dismay? Lorith had been on Tinsori Light far, far longer than he had. It was nothing short of marvelous that she held true to her duty, and sought still to protect the vulnerable.

Still, if she were to thrive, she must learn to accept their new condition. It fell to him, her comrade, and her sole companion in madness, to bring her, gently, down the path from the past to the present.

He had control of himself now, and met her eyes firmly.

"We are assured by people who make it their business to know these things that Tinsori Light is dead," he said, matter-of-fact and calm. "It is difficult to credit, I know—I have my own moments of disbelief. But, look you, Lorith—what remains? Everything in the deep core has been swept out by upstart organics, and carried away to be rendered into *useful components*. Surely, Tinsori Light *cannot* wake, if there is nothing to support his intelligence."

"Tinsori Light was the whole station, not only the core," she said.

"That is so, but—see here!"

He spun the screen so that she might see the appalling equations displayed there.

She was not an idiot, but nor was she a pilot, and the mathematics she had been schooled in did not begin to describe the universe into which she had been thrust.

"This—" he said, waving at the screen, "is a proof provided to my delm by no one less than the Uncle."

"What does it prove?"

"Well you might ask. It proves that space—I speak of the space here, at Tinsori Light—was cleared, and forthwithly remade, before anyone properly had a chance to notice."

Lorith looked at the screen again, a line between her fair brows.

"What effected this event?" she asked, quite calmly.

For a moment, he could but stare at her. Then he recollected that Lorith had been by chance evicted from a universe that was being systematically and deliberately rendered into crystal.

"If one is to believe the narrative, Tinsori Light had been caught between this universe and the old. When it phased, it reentered the old universe. This constant back-and-forth over so very many years wore the fabric of space very thin, and it tore, creating a leak.

"The leak was repaired, and in the midst of the repair, we were erased."

He sat back in the chair, having fair exhausted himself with nonsense, and waved a hand, showing her the control room, the screens, and the view of near-space.

"But, all's well, as you see. We have been safely reawakened."

"With Tinsori Light fully in this universe with us."

"That is so, but the Light, alone of us, did not survive the wakening."

"That seems... quite unlike him," Lorith said.

From the edge of his vision, he saw the blue bird stir, and turned his head to look at it.

It struck him, then, that he and Lorith had been much apart of late. Before, they had each been the sole comfort of the other. They had eaten together, played cards, toured, slept and shared pleasure, reveling in whatever present they found for themselves.

And now it had been—had it been *weeks*, with only a few snatched meetings, such as this?

"One of the fortunate things of having so many people on-station is that we will soon be able to arrange our off-shifts together," he said, following this thought. "It has been long since we have had the chance to merely sit together as ourselves, without duty taking a third chair. You... my friend, you are worn thin, and I make no doubt I am the same. Surely, we may grant ourselves a shift—or two—of rest, to do whatever may please us?"

She stared at him, dark eyes wide, and lips slightly parted. He had a moment to congratulate himself on his laggard cleverness, before she snapped to her feet.

"No!" she said sharply. "I am—no. Jen Sin, I must go."

"Lorith—" He came to his feet.

"I am—perhaps later," she said. "After I have done."

And with that she was gone, the door snapping shut behind her.

Jen Sin sat down, his eyes on the door, his heart troubled. One could scarcely demand that a comrade share time with one. And it was true that choice now existed. Perhaps one of the Stronglines might be more to her taste.

He closed his eyes, and spun his chair back toward the desk, wishing he could convince himself that she had found ease elsewhere, and was not merely sitting alone, fear her only comrade.

Opening his eyes, he saw that the green bird was perched on the top of his screen. And on the screen itself, that beautiful and demented equation.

He took a deep breath, and sighed it out.

Then, he turned off the screen and rose.

Perhaps he would do his third check—later.

Invictus

••••••••

THIRTY-EIGHT-THIRTY WAS DEAD.

By itself, that would have been unfortunate, given the paucity of operatives in place. However, the tragedy of Thirty-eight-thirty's removal from the field had been compounded by the incarceration of Seventeen-oh-nine, who had been surprised by a security detail while attempting to recover Thirty-eight-thirty's toolbox.

So, there were two operatives lost to the mission, and a toolbox in the hands of the ignorant. The box, at least, would protect its secrets, but the loss of the tools was a severe blow.

Director Ling was not pleased.

Dragon Song
Dock A

• • • • • • • •

"I COULD HAVE COME FOR IT, YOU KNOW," REN ZEL SAID, AS JEN Sin pulled the collapsed closet to the foot of the ramp. "We are sent to help, not to increase your burden."

"No burden at all," Jen Sin told him, "only a welcome opportunity to leave my desk, and take a small tour. Surely a light keeper may tour his own docks?"

"Phrased thus..."

Ren Zel came down the ramp, and opened the hold. Jen Sin slid the closet inside, and paused, eyeing the remaining crates.

"If one may ask—what else did you bring?"

"Well. Teas; a mixed rack of wine; cards and counterchance and like entertainments; some sport objects; a kitchen hydroponics unit; flower seeds and growing medium; books, vids; photo cubes; a seedling—"

Ren Zel paused, brows pulled together.

"I believe that may be everything. We did not know exactly how you were fixed, and erred on the side of small comforts. Gordy—surely by now you have heard from Gordy?"

"He sent a most cordial and generous letter, and received a list of items to shop for with apparent delight."

Ren Zel smiled.

"He is a trader, after all. You could have done nothing better than ask him to shop for you."

"I wonder—is there a *bowli ball* among the sport items? Theo had expressed a need. Gordy will be bringing a number, as I understand it, but if we might put one into her hands sooner—"

Ren Zel laughed.

"I understand! There are, in fact, two bowli balls. How if I send for *Bechimo* to pick up the sports case?"

"That is an excellent notion."

"Consider it done. What else may I do for you?"

Jen Sin hesitated, remembering his former hopes.

"I can scarcely ask you—"

"Ask me!" Ren Zel interrupted, energetically. "I insist that you ask me, if you will not outright order me to complete needful tasks! I am here to help you, and, to be plain—to give you some respite. Theo tells me you are *worn out*, and you know it must be so, if Theo has seen it!"

Jen Sin laughed, then sobered.

"It is true that I had felt a shadow of myself, though somewhat more solid of late. I had only just been saying to—to my comrade Lorith, whom you must soon meet—that we might begin to plan a few off-shifts, to catch up on those things which are not duty. So, you see, the prospect of rest is not entirely foreign to my thought. It is only…"

Again, he hesitated, and very nearly startled when Ren Zel put a hand on his shoulder.

"Most lately, I have been first mate on a master trader's ship with a mixed crew. I was at my post when trouble arrived, more than once, yet here I stand before you. It is true that I am not trained to station-work. However, detail-work, building compromise and consensus, and the perils of personal interface across culture are all very familiar to me."

He could use this expertise, Jen Sin thought. In fact, he desperately needed his cousin Ren Zel in the newly opened section. Only—

He paused. He had promised Catie that he would leave her someone worthy. It was not too soon to see that connection made.

He smiled, half-wistful.

"I see that you are determined," he said to Ren Zel. "Tell me this, then—how would you like to be the official representative of the Light Keeper's Office in the Spinward Arcade and Dorms, which is even now receiving the so-called second wave of volunteer aid sent from Hacienda Estrella?"

"I think that sounds precisely like the sort of assistance I had hoped to provide. Do we go now?"

"Are you able? I would present you to Coordinator Carresens, and show you the administrative suite."

"Only let me seal the hatch," Ren Zel said.

Jen Sin stepped out onto the dock, looking up at a flash of green—and blue—and . . . yellow?

"I did not know there were birds on-station," Ren Zel said, sounding merely curious, as of course he would be. What was there, after all, in a few brightly colored birds frisking overhead to inspire anything other than curiosity?

"Avians, according to Cousin Theo's Scout, which may be a better naming. They are bots given by a friend. At least the blue and the green. I had not seen the yellow until just now. Perhaps it is yours."

Ren Zel said nothing, and Jen Sin turned to face him.

"I fear the situation here has changed since you left home, Cousin. I swear to you that the birds are not a danger, nor is the person who created them."

Ren Zel's laugh was lightly edged.

"I take leave to remind you that you are speaking with a man who allegedly remade space *with his mind*."

"My lamentable memory. You are very right to remind me of that. I hereby pronounce you the equal of anything you may find at Tinsori Light. Which brings to mind another lapse. How shall I properly show my appreciation to you, for sending those equations—and attending data!—to me?"

"I daresay you'll hit upon something," Ren Zel said comfortably. "What is our direction?"

Jen Sin used his chin to point left.

"We will pick up the jitney at the maintenance bay, and do the thing in style."

They turned in that direction.

"What prompted you to bring flower seeds?" Jen Sin asked.

Ren Zel moved his shoulders.

"That was Anthora, and I cannot say if it is only because she is fond of flowers, or that she had a Seeing. Why do you ask?"

"There is an area marked out for a garden in the center of the public space."

"Ah. Yes, that would be the style of thing she might See. Do you think that the members of the second wave should like flowers?"

"We will make certain to ask Coordinator Carresens."

Main Core Workroom

"MENTOR, REN STRYKER IS CALLING YOU," TOCOHL SAID. "HE states that it's an emergency."

Tolly put his tool down on the bench, nodded at Haz to put her end of the rack down, and pulled his glasses off as he crossed the room.

"Send it to the workroom screen, please, Tocohl."

There were three people in the screen, sitting in a semicircle and looking pretty grim.

"This is Tolly Jones. I was told Ren Stryker was calling with an emergency."

"Mentor Jones," Ren Stryker said, "that is true. I have asked Korlu Fenchile, Belagras Denobli, and Pawli Ebrits to assist me. We have worked together before. Korlu is the team supervisor, Gracie is the official representative of the Carresens-Denobli Family, and Pawli is the head of team security."

Bad and worse, Tolly thought.

"Pleased to meet," he said, nodding at the group in the screen. "What's going on, Ren?"

"Marsi tried to subvert me," Ren Stryker said, and there was a plaintive note in his voice, as if he couldn't quite believe himself. "She came into my private area. I told her to leave. She did not leave, but began to—to—"

He stopped.

A minute went by the long way.

In the screen, Korlu Fenchile shifted.

"I'll take it, if you don't mind, Mentor. Ren's still a little upset. No blame there; it's an upsetting situation. Known Marsi forever, myself. Tellin' it short, Ren gave Marsi the warnaway, like he says, only she just started in to open a contact board.

He told her to stop again. She kept on ignoring him, and got a tool outta her case. Ren felt threatened, and give 'er a shock. Knocked her out. He called me. I grabbed Pawli and we picked her up, with the case. Got all this on record, mind."

Tolly nodded.

"Marsi come around by the time we got her to the lock-in; medic come and took a look, said she was lucky Ren hadn't been mad. Marsi was plenty mad, wantin' to be let out. Wantin' to talk to Ren about some substandard connectors she could fix up for him. Wouldn't answer us anything sensible, so finally I just said to leave her to cool down."

He paused, and looked even more unhappy than he had.

"She was alive when we left her, Mentor, but she wasn't next shift, when me an' Gracie went down to see her again."

"The current was too strong," Ren Stryker said, grief in his voice. "I damaged her."

"That's never off the table, when you're running current through a human," Tolly said. "What did the medic say?"

"Systems failure." Korlu looked sour. "She died."

Tolly sighed.

"Talking from personal experience, I'd say Marsi was working for somebody who didn't want her to talk honest to her friend Korlu. There's a protocol that can trigger the Last Program in humans, Ren, and nothing they can do to stop it."

Silence.

"Mentor," said Ren Stryker.

"Here."

"That is a terrible thing."

"No argument from me," Tolly said gently, and met Korlu Fenchile's gaze in the screen.

"Her toolbox?"

"Well," said Gracie, "that's the other innerestin' thing, Mentor. Young person by the name of Kilber Tarymax tried to liberate Marsi's tool kit from the lockbox we had it in. He's locked in now, sedated. The tool kit's in Ren's safe."

A pause.

"Don't guess you know if we're looking for another bad shock with Mister Tarymax."

"Can't predict," Tolly said, "but brace for the worst. The big problem is that tool kit." He took a deep breath, and brought every bit of stern sincerity he could muster into his voice. "*Don't open it.* Best thing to do is call somebody qualified to come and collect it."

"Qualified?" Pawli repeated. "Like who?"

"Like the Liaden Scouts. Or the Uncle," Tolly said.

"Uncle's sister can't take it in hand?" asked Boss Fenchile.

"My guess is Light Keeper yos'Phelium won't want that thing on-station, but we can ask him, if you want."

The three of them exchanged somber looks.

"I got a contact for Uncle," Gracie said, rising. "Thanks, Mentor."

"No problem. Ren?"

"Yes, Mentor?"

"You need to talk, or you're still feeling sad about this, you call me, yeah? I can help. It's what I do."

"Thank you, Mentor. I will call, if necessary."

Seignur Veeoni's Private Laboratory

SEIGNUR VEEONI STRAIGHTENED SOMEWHAT ON HER STOOL, frowning at the image of one of Jen Sin's memory beads on the screen.

Anthora waited, Watching the play of patterned colors, and marveling at the denseness of the researcher's inner tapestry. It was as if she had lived several lives deeply and simultaneously. Those connections that bound her to others were fewer than one might expect, given the richness of her experience, but the ties were sturdy enough that a Healer need not be concerned of pathology.

"Given that we do not yet know how the material inserted into the beads by Tinsori Light interacted with Light Keeper yos'Phelium, we cannot know if he is able to pass any engineered abnormalities on to another person," Seignur Veeoni said.

She frowned more ferociously at the screen.

"Having acknowledged our ignorance, let us also acknowledge that Light Keeper yos'Phelium is extraordinarily perceptive. If he believes he may pass this . . . condition on by a means other than the beads, I believe it is our part to honor that perception until we have gathered facts that conclusively disprove it."

She looked up, and met Anthora's eyes.

"I have a question, if you will, Healer."

"Certainly." Anthora smiled. "Though I may also be found out as ignorant."

"Ignorance is merely the defining of goals," Seignur Veeoni said. "You are, I believe, a Healer of some note. Have you, in the course of your studies or your field work, encountered anything analogous to this situation?"

"I have not myself encountered such a thing, no. There are

a very few historical cases which were put down as contagion, though nothing that described the mechanism."

She sighed.

"This is not widely known, but it is a fact that some Healers are able to intentionally share information with a Healer of like mind. It is not common, but it can, and has, been done."

"So the possibility exists for a sharing that is less intentional."

"Possibility, yes," Anthora said. "Probability—I think it low."

"Recall that we are speaking of a system refined and implemented by a Great Work," Seignur Veeoni said.

"True. That does push the needle higher on the scale of probability." She sighed, recalling Jen Sin's faint and threadbare pattern. It was the natural urge of an empath to assist in such circumstances, but, truly, there was little she could do to revitalize his pattern. Life would set in bright, new threads, and his connections would multiply. Already, she had seen a tenuous thread between him and Theo. The process was slow, but certain. She merely needed to ensure that Jen Sin lived to see the cure.

"What is your next step?" Seignur Veeoni asked.

Anthora turned up empty palms.

"For the moment, I am willing to watch and permit matters to proceed."

"Allowing the situation to clarify. I understand. I regret that I was not able to provide definitive answers."

"You were informative and helpful. I welcome your insights," Anthora said, truthfully, and slid to her feet. She bowed as between equals.

"M Traven will see you out," Seignur Veeoni said, and there, indeed, was the compact woman in the doorway, watching her with interest.

Anthora was almost to the door between Seignur Veeoni's hall and the greater station, when she spied a figure approaching.

A woman in nondescript overalls—a tech of some kind, perhaps, except that there was that about her that reminded Anthora of Tolly Jones. The face, perhaps? Pleasantly shaped, tan, and smooth—but, surely there were many people who looked thus.

The woman's pattern, however...

She Looked more closely.

Yes, there it was. Enough alike that she located the switch at once, familiar now that she had dealt with one.

She put out a hand as they came level with each other.

"I can fix that for you," she said. "The command switch."

Blue eyes considered her blandly.

"No idea what you're talking about," the other woman said pleasantly.

Anthora inclined her head.

"Of course you don't," she said, softly. "If you want free of it, come to me when you've finished your business here. My reference is Tolly Jones. My name is Anthora yos'Galan."

Spinward Arcade and Dorms

"FLOWERS? I'M NOT AGAINST 'EM, THOUGH I DON'T KNOW IF I got anybody with the way of 'em."

"The flowers—or trees—would be considered part of the habitat," Jen Sin said, "and cared for by the station."

"Then I'd say the only way to find out is to try," Vinsint Carresens said practically. "I don't see any offense in there anywhere."

She turned back to Ren Zel.

"You're the pilot who Jumped in close."

"I am, yes," Ren Zel agreed calmly.

"Damn fine flyin'," she said with a grin. "Sorry 'bout the hollerin'. Like I said at the time—high spirits."

"I understand," Ren Zel said. "Is there anything I may do for you immediately?"

"Immediately? My immediately's getting the crew in, quartered, and sorted into teams. Then, I'll see about redirectin' them high spirits into something useful for all of us."

"If it comes about that you need me..."

"I'll ask Station to find you for me, never you fear," she said, and stood up from the stone wall where they had all been sitting together.

She produced a bow notable for its cheerfulness, murmured, "Light Keepers," and strolled away toward a cluster of persons just emerging from the dockside entry hall, pulling cases and looking, wide-eyed, about themselves.

Jen Sin came to his feet.

"If you still claim a hand in this mad game, Cousin, I will make you acquainted with the section administrator's suite."

"I will have my cards, thank you," Ren Zel said, standing, and moving his fingers briskly in the pilot's sign for *double-quick*. "Pray lead on."

The living area inspected and pronounced very well, they came at last to the administration office.

Jen Sin waved Ren Zel in ahead of him, and leaned against the counter. The birds, all three, zipped through the door as it was closing, and ranged themselves on the edge of the highest shelf.

"Pray seat yourself, Administrator dea'Judan," Jen Sin murmured. "We will now make you known to the station, which in this section runs on a system separate from that administered by our cousin Tocohl."

Ren Zel sat as he was bade, in the command chair, his posture alert, and his eyes serious. Perhaps he suspected something.

Jen Sin gave him a faint smile and said, gently, "Catalinc Station, I present to you Section Administrator dea'Judan of the Light Keeper's Staff. He is the face and the voice of the light keeper in this section."

"Welcome, Administrator dea'Judan." Catie's voice was marvelously clear and clean. "I look forward to working with you."

"Thank you, Station," Ren Zel said carefully. "I trust that we will deal well together."

"You ought also to know, Station, that the section administrator is my cousin Ren Zel. Tell me, was the yellow bird meant for him?"

"The yellow was meant for you, Light Keeper. I can craft another, if Administrator dea'Judan also misses birds."

"That is a kindness," Ren Zel said gravely. "However, I do not at this time find myself in want. Please understand that I value your care, and mean no offense."

"I take no offense," Catie said, with an intonation that Jen Sin recognized as his own. "If you should feel the need, later, only tell me and I will be happy to assist."

"Thank you," Ren Zel murmured, and moved his chair closer to the console. "I think, with Light Keeper yos'Phelium's permission, that we ought to sign me in to systems. I would appreciate a summary of what has gone forth to this point, please, Station."

"Certainly, Administrator."

The screens lit, and Jen Sin straightened away from the counter.

"I to my various duties," he said. "If you require anything from me, Cousin—"

Ren Zel glanced up with a smile.

"I know how to find you, yes. I hope that you will rest between your duties. Station and I will do very well, here."

"I make no doubt."

Jen Sin bowed gently, as to kin, and left, the birds sweeping over his head and out the door.

Seignur Veeoni's Private Laboratory

IN RETROSPECT, SHE SHOULDN'T HAVE EATEN THAT FRUIT TOLLY'D given her. She'd intended to throw it in the nearest recycler, but somehow it stayed in her pocket, and there it was in her hand, when she'd gone to reach for a protein bar, and it had smelled... so good.

It had tasted good, too.

Better'n good.

Hadn't seemed to do anything in particular. She'd finished her shift, took her downtime, and woke up feeling a little more spritely than she was accustomed to, but nothing off the meter.

Except now here she was, acting on impulse, and if it got her killed, she was damn sure gonna haunt Tolly Jones for the rest of his life.

Not that *that* was lookin' to be too many more hours.

She pressed the announce button.

The door whisked open. M Traven looked at her for a long moment, then stepped back.

"Tech Bell. Seignur Veeoni is expecting you."

"The racks I'm building are meant to subvert systems in place." She told it out straight and flat while the researcher ignored her in favor of studying her screen.

"There's Directors on the station now," she finished, "and more incoming. That means pretty soon I'm going to be attaching those modules I been building into the main array, and you'll have some trouble."

There, it was said. And here was a wonder, if you please. She didn't feel even the twinge of a headache.

"I see." Seignur Veeoni turned at last to look at her, frown forward. "Did you expect to realize any particular benefit from telling me this?"

Well, there was a question, wasn't it?

Delia shrugged.

"I was kinda hopin' not to be the one to make those connections."

"Do you doubt your work? You told me you were a rack-and-tile specialist."

"I *am* a rack-and-tile specialist. And so are you. I don't doubt either of us did any less than her best on this project, and then some."

"Ah."

Seignur Veeoni's frown faded somewhat.

"How do you suggest that I proceed? I have an important lesson to teach the Lyre Institute."

"I can see that. I read the report. You lost people, and your base. Same time, you set the Directors up. Didn't you have an endgame?"

"In fact, I did. Are you able to be of use to me?"

And there was another question.

A quick memory of knowing silver eyes sent a shiver through her.

I can fix that for you.

She took a breath and met Seignur Veeoni's stare.

"What do you know about Anthora yos'Galan?"

Defense Corridors

THE SMALL SEARCHER HAD PICKED AND PRICKED AT THE NEW station's security.

It had discovered that Lady Tocohl had disabled the defense network and cut it out of station ops. She had placed an alarm, so that she would be notified if one of the defenders woke. No alarm had been set on the maintenance access tubes, for who, indeed, would wish to enter them?

Only, the access tubes were a quick way to reach the room where the tile-making machine did its work. She need disturb no one, when she came to exchange the tiles she had prepared with those newly manufactured.

As she did now.

Spinward Arcade and Dorms
Administration Hall

IT HAD BEEN AN INSTRUCTIVE AND EXHILARATING SHIFT, AND Ren Zel was beginning to consider the benefits of closing the office.

"How shall we manage my off-shifts?" he asked Catie—they had quickly become Ren Zel and Catie for this time of learning to work together.

"Light Keeper yos'Phelium asks to be called in the event of an emergency," she said thoughtfully. "Perhaps a definition of an emergency would be in order."

"An excellent place to start," he agreed, and opened a screen. "Let us compile a list."

It was a short list, appropriate to the category of emergency. When they were both satisfied with the degree and the responses, Ren Zel closed his screen, and stood up to stretch.

"Hazenthull and another person are approaching your door, Administrator."

"Another person?" he asked, but by then the door had opened and his lifemate had arrived, Hazenthull in her wake. He glimpsed a sled piled with trunks and crates in the hallway before the door closed.

"There!" Anthora said, striking a pose and flinging out a hand, as if to display him to Hazenthull. "Did I not say that I would find him?"

"You did," Hazenthull agreed, and to him, "Good shift, Pilot."

"Good shift, Hazenthull," he answered.

"Was I lost?" he asked Anthora.

"Did you tell me where you would be?"

"I hardly knew myself," he admitted, "though I did send to the ship, once I was situated."

"Rendering my locating you something less than fabulous, I agree. That aside, I am here, and I have brought such things as we might like to have in our new quarters. Hazenthull kindly brought me to you in Seignur Veeoni's jitney."

She turned.

"Thank you, Hazenthull."

"You're welcome. I will need to take the sled back with me."

"Certainly," Ren Zel said, moving forward. "Come, let me show you to our apartment, where we can unload. Hazenthull, will you be staying for wine?"

Hazenthull declined wine, pleading the necessity of returning Seignur Veeoni's jitney to her in a timely fashion.

Ren Zel returned from seeing her off, to find Anthora in the kitchen, opening a box.

He leaned in the doorway and watched her extract a bottle of wine and a pair of glasses.

"Ask," she said, not turning her head, and he smiled slightly.

"Did you not bring the seeds?"

"Oh, yes!"

She turned, eyes bright.

"We left them under seal in the garden area. There was no reason to bring them up, only to take them down again, you know."

"Very true," he said. "Shall I open and pour?"

They carried their glasses out into the comfortable parlor, sat next to each other on the sofa, and tasted the wine.

Anthora sighed.

"A busy day for us both, then, Beloved. However did you persuade Jen Sin to allow you to assist him?"

"Logic," he said, and smiled when she laughed.

"Theo came while I was packing and was pleased to take the sports crate," she said. "She says she hopes to see you soon for a bout of bowli ball. Apparently the plan is to begin a league."

"A league, here on-station?"

Anthora gave him a limpid look. "Why not?"

"No reason, the idea merely startled. How long does Theo plan to stay?"

"That is not decided. Shan sent them to *help*, you see, and so they have been. I believe that Theo wishes to remain until Gordy arrives, in case of a need for assistance there. If not, she will apply to Shan for direction."

Ren Zel nodded and sipped his wine.

"What else occupied you?" he asked.

"I spoke to Seignur Veeoni and was allowed to look at an image of the memory beads she had off of Jen Sin. We arrived at no firm decision regarding the possibility of contagion, from him to me, through a Healing link, and agreed that waiting and watching was the best present course."

She sipped, and sighed.

"I also made the acquaintance of a person named Delia Bell, who stands in relation to Tolly Jones. She was equipped with the same fashion of controller, which she allowed me to neutralize."

"Is Delia Bell also kin?"

"It would seem likely. Theo's Tree provided her with a pod, as I learn from Tolly Jones."

She paused to sip her wine.

"I will be having another meeting, with Seignur Veeoni and Delia Bell, but that is for later."

She smiled. "And there is my day. What else of yours?"

"I am learning the station systems. In that regard, I would like to make you known to someone."

Anthora tipped her head. "Now? I had thought we would rest after so much roistering."

"We needn't even stand," Ren Zel assured her, and spoke the agreed-upon phrase.

"Station, please attend me."

"I am here, Ren Zel."

"Thank you. This is my lifemate, Anthora yos'Galan. Beloved, this is Catalinc Station."

Anthora's eyebrows were well up, but she inclined her head gracefully.

"Catalinc Station, I am honored."

Station Day 35
Tinsori Light

. . . .

AS PREDICTED, THE SECOND WAVE ARRIVED IN BITS AND BOBS. One shift might see the arrival of three ships, while the next four saw none.

Vinsint Carresens, however, did not allow this irregularity to hamper what she saw as her duty to bring Tinsori Station up to spec as quickly as possible.

The workboat had inspected the seals on the breach section, and was in the process of reinforcing several identified stress points.

Teams were out on the docks, installing toolboxes, upgrading connections and wiring, cleaning long-abandoned decks. There was a cleaning crew in the 'ponics room when Jen Sin and Lorith came by—he having insisted that she tour with him, in order to see the upgrades and improvements with her own eyes.

Asked if they might bring the room back up to spec, the crew boss had shaken his head.

"Somebody fragged the whole system. Room's gonna hafta be rebuilt from the walls in. Which don't sound like good news, 'til you take a look at how old those rigs were. Even if we could bring 'em back, it'd be better to install new. Better yields, smaller footprint, more efficient."

"So, we will have fresh fruits and vegetables again," Lorith said, with such apparent pleasure that the man grinned at her.

"That's right, Light Keeper. You just stand back and give us room to work. We'll get you sorted out right."

They finished their tour in the Spinward Arcade, by chance meeting Ren Zel and Vinsint Carresens by the stone wall.

"Truly, there are many changes," Lorith said gazing around at the busy, bright-lit plaza. "And so many people about. Are they all quite safe?"

Vinsint Carresens gave her a nod.

"That's well asked, Light Keeper, but you don't need to worry about us. We're taking all of our measurements three times, and if there's any little thing that seems off, we're callin' in a consult. That's in the operating rules, that every team leader has."

"And if the consult decides that the situation *is* dangerous," Lorith asked. "Then what is done?"

"Then, it gets kicked to me, and I bring it up to the light keepers, just like I'm gonna do now, about the repair bays."

Jen Sin felt the blood drain from his face. He had not put the repair bays on the list of work to be done—and for a very good reason.

"No one has—attempted the bays, I hope," he said. "I ought to have been—"

Vinsint Carresens held up a hand.

"No blame to anybody. Wasn't on the list, but we figured to take a look, just to make sure what we have, in case somebody turns up in need."

She paused. Jen Sin found himself speechless, and Lorith was the same.

"What do we have, I wonder?" Ren Zel said. "Having just come on-station myself, I have not yet had the felicity of the repair bays."

"Pardon me for bein' forward, but those bays ain't nothin' you wanna get up close and personal with. My recommendation is to seal 'em tight 'til the experts from the Yard get here."

"And ships in need?" murmured Jen Sin.

"We might call on Korval's Yards to send a portable outyard for our use," Ren Zel said.

Vinsint Carresens nodded. "That's not a bad idea. Won't be anything like a full shop, but oughta be able to patch most mishaps good enough to get 'em to Beacon Yard. Anything really bad that raises this station, crew can meditate on how lucky they are to be alive, and maybe pitch in with the needful."

Jen Sin shivered, which unfortunately caught Ren Zel's eye.

"Cousin?" he murmured in Liaden.

"A small foolishness—I'm prone. Disregard it, of your kindness."

He looked to Vinsint Carresens. "What will you require from the station, in order to fully seal the bays?"

"We'll get 'em locked down," she said. "Station has the right to inspect, naturally."

"I will do that," Ren Zel said, smiling at her. "Let us go together."

She nodded. "I'll drop you a note."

"What is that?" Lorith asked suddenly, nodding toward the low wall.

Jen Sin turned to look.

There was a garden inside the enclosure.

A small garden, to be sure, and very difficult to distinguish from a random pile of growing medium, but Jen Sin had plagued Jelaza Kazone's gardeners in his childhood until he had been put to work. He recognized purpose and design in the disposition of the materials.

"It is a garden," he told Lorith. "One's cousin Anthora is keen on flowers."

"So keen, in fact," Ren Zel said wryly, "that she asked Station to provide the locations of similar garden areas throughout the station. Anthora swears she will see them all in bloom. She has already sent to Gordy on behalf of this plan."

"So, should a jungle arrive, we are forewarned," Jen Sin said.

Ren Zel grinned.

"Precisely."

"Looking forward to seein' what that becomes, myself," Vinsint Carresens said, with an easy nod to Lorith.

She might have said more, but her belt-comm buzzed. She glanced down at the screen and sighed.

"Wanted down on Dock D," she said. "Before I go—we got word *Virago*'s closing in on the station. Figuring to be docked and ready to unload the caf in two station days, max. Oughta go quick, and nothing we need any special help with. Just a heads-up."

"Thank you," Jen Sin said.

"No worries," Vinsint Carresens told him, and turned away, raising a hand briefly in farewell.

"Well." Jen Sin looked to Ren Zel. "Will you write to Korval's yard master, Cousin?"

"Certainly," Ren Zel replied easily. "Is there anything else I may do for you?"

"I am quite out of tasks that need doing at the moment," Jen Sin admitted.

Ren Zel turned to Lorith.

"Light Keeper, is there aught I might do for you?"

Lorith frowned at him, her large eyes narrowed as if she was looking into too bright a light. "Only make certain that all these people are kept safe, please."

"I will make that a priority," Ren Zel said.

Seignur Veeoni's Private Workroom

THE ROOM VIBRATED WITH EMOTION; THE PATTERNS AND ASSOCIATIONS twisty and complex.

Anthora was not often tempted to close her Inner Eyes entirely, but she considered that option now—and rejected it. She had been called into this meeting to give her perspective and possibly her advice. It was a rather remarkable request—Anthora had the distinct impression that Seignur Veeoni rarely asked for advice.

And to ask advice from one of Korval—no, she must stand firm as the clan's representative in this negotiation, if for no other reason than it would astonish her brothers.

Seignur Veeoni folded her hands.

"That is the summation. The Lyre Institute must be made to pay for these insults. I ask, Technician Bell, if the Directors are likely to accept more tile-and-rack systems, if they are acquired in the same way as the first?"

Delia sighed.

"They might. I could prolly make a case for having found the real articles, bring 'em into the lab, and show how they're clearly not the same as the ones that were snatched before."

"That can be arranged," Seignur Veeoni said. "The pattern I have in mind will be far more fatal than that which was purloined previously. I erred in thinking that mere failure would discourage more interference. Clearly, there must be blood in it."

Anthora stirred.

"You disagree, Healer yos'Galan?"

"I offer perspective," Anthora said. The density of the woman's pattern made it difficult to read intent with any subtlety. And there was—just there—one block of weaving remarkable for its evenness and consistency. Anthora placed most of her attention on that section.

As for this other...

"Balance is art," she said, meeting the researcher's eyes. "An ideal personal Balance only involves principals who have fallen out of Balance.

"Certainly, the accounts between you and the Lyre Institute require rectification. However, it is plain that an ideal Balance is not possible. In such cases, it is proper to stand away for a time to consider your *melant'i*, and how your actions will affect the greater Balance of the universe. Once again, the ideal—the Liaden ideal—is to leave the Universe richer for one's actions."

"I have very little to do with art," Seignur Veeoni said. "The Lyre Institute has affronted me, and they must learn better."

"Yes, but this plan will not teach them better," Anthora said. "Worse, you will abuse your own *melant'i*. The goal of Balance is to prove your stance superior, and your actions correct."

"I *am* superior to the Lyre Institute," Seignur Veeoni stated.

Anthora raised an eyebrow.

"And yet you would do as they do and spend the lives of innocents in order to *win the game*."

She put as much distaste as she could muster into that last, though she failed to observe that it affected the other woman in the least.

Or perhaps it had.

"Innocents," Seignur Veeoni repeated and glanced at their third. "Are you innocent, Technician Bell?"

Delia took breath and sighed it out.

"I think it can be fairly said that I didn't commit all my sins freely," she said. "An' I see what Healer yos'Galan's on about: If you keep answering the Directors on their same field, with their same weapons, then you're just another Director."

"The Directors do not care about their weapons, or their weapon-bearers," Anthora said softly, and saw her words strike and ignite that particular close-woven section. "They have attempted to steal your work, which you care about—deeply. They have materially damaged you; they have disrupted your household, and taken the lives of those with whom you were entangled. No one suggests that the harm they have done to you is trivial."

A flicker caught her Inner Eye, and she glanced away from Seignur Veeoni's pattern to that of M Traven, standing quietly at the researcher's side. Yes. M Traven had suffered losses, but M Traven did not want blood. M Traven, Anthora thought, wanted *justice.* Well, and perhaps Balance would do.

She paused, and sharpened her tone even as she softened her voice, leaning slightly toward the researcher.

"What can you do that will harm them in the same manner as you were harmed? What do the Directors value as much as you valued your peace, your household, and your work?"

Delia Bell stirred.

Seignur Veeoni turned to look at her.

"You have an answer, Technician Bell?"

Delia looked wary, as well she might, Anthora thought.

"Understanding that I got no real idea how much those things meant to you, but if you wanna hit the Directors where it hurts, you'll take out the patterns and the gene-bank."

Seignur Veeoni frowned.

"That's a fair accounting," M Traven said, and Seignur Veeoni glanced at her.

"I was just informed that the Directors do not care about their players."

"They don't care about the players on the field 'cause there's plenty more where we come from," Delia said flatly.

Seignur Veeoni said nothing. Anthora watched her pattern, which reflected deep thought.

"Such an approach will take time," she said, finally.

"Surely *you* have time," Anthora dared to suggest, "to craft a perfect answer."

Seignur Veeoni smiled, very slightly.

"Possibly, I may," she said. "Technician Bell, what are your plans, going forward?"

"Said I'd be of use to you," Delia said, eyes narrowed. "I don't say I'd welcome being sent back home, but—"

"I offer you a place in my—household. I foresee that there will be work for a rack-and-tile specialist. Also, you have other skills that will serve us all. As a tech, you will take your orders from me. As security, you will be second to M Traven, if she accepts."

"I accept," M Traven said, and saluted. "Welcome, Tech Bell."

"Best to go right to Delia, an' save us all some time," Delia said with a certain wryness. "Security-wise, you gotta know that the Directors don't let us go easy, it being a matter of pride."

M Traven inclined slightly from the waist. "I am forewarned. And you are not helpless."

Delia frowned—and then smiled. "Well, no, now you mention it, I'm not. If Tolly Jones can stay outta bad trouble, no reason I can't, too."

"I believe our definitions of *bad trouble* mesh," M Traven said. "Again—welcome."

"Thank you," Delia said, and Anthora Saw determination, and a flicker of pain in her pattern, as she nodded to Seignur Veeoni. "Thank you, Researcher. I'll be pleased to be part of your household. I'm lookin' forward to learning everything you can teach me 'bout racks and tiles."

"I believe we may find ourselves teaching each other," Seignur Veeoni said surprisingly. "That is settled, then. Move your belongings as you have time. M Traven will show you to your quarters. If you have any needs, tell her. If you have any extraordinary needs, tell me."

She put her attention on Anthora.

"Healer yos'Galan."

"Yes."

"You are able to differentiate between agents of the Lyre Institute and those who are otherwise affiliated."

"I am, yes. The switches are unmistakable, as is the core structure of the Director pattern."

"Are you able to Heal those who are presently on the Light?"

Anthora shook her head.

"We come to my *melant'i* and my position in the universe. I am a Healer, and I do not alter souls without permission of the owner."

She paused.

Neither Seignur Veeoni nor Delia Bell spoke.

"However," Anthora said slowly, "this station will find most of its clientele from among the Free Ships whom the Lyre Institute seek to enslave. I believe it would be in Korval's interest if the agents of the Lyre Institute were... to find Tinsori Light too dangerous for them—at least for a time. That, I can—and do—engage for."

Virago
Spinward Docking

EVEN FOLDED UP TIGHT AS IT WOULD GO, *AND* THE AUTOMATICS, the caf was a right beastie to move from the docks through the halls to the arcade that was its destination.

Keeli Varge made part of the delivery team, using bounce rods and magnetic string to urge the caf gently down the halls and finally into a wide area, where the team boss called halt.

She looked around with interest. The space was larger than she had visualized, well lit and airy, with nothing of the derelict about it. Once the station was brought to understand the benefit of granting the Institute access, it would be quite a comfortable post.

"Keeli!" yelled the team boss, using the name she had given. "Quitcher daydreamin' and get on that corner!"

"On it, Boss!" she yelled back, and got on her corner.

Administrative Tower

LORITH HAD NOT BEEN IN HER WORKROOM, NOR THE ASSEMBLY room, nor any other usual place. He eventually asked Tocohl to find her, and was told that Light Keeper Lorith was in her quarters, resting.

Gods knew she had earned as much rest as she wished. Indeed, he was relieved to hear it; she had been looking very thin, and he made no doubt her fears were heavy. Rest was surely her best tonic.

He sat down in his chair—and froze, suddenly smitten with the knowledge that the Tree-fruit in his pocket was ripe.

There was no thought; he had it out and eaten before he considered what consternation he might cause, by falling unconscious in his chair.

But, he need not have worried. Far from falling into a swoon, he felt somewhat energized, and reached to his screen with a will.

The comm pinged.

"Jen Sin?" Theo sounded breathless and gay. "Can you take an hour off? Tea break, maybe? I've got something to show you, on our dock."

Tea break?

He glanced at the clock. Had he been working a full shift already? He moved his shoulders, feeling not the least tired—and recalled that Ren Zel had wished him to take time off of duty.

He touched the comm.

"As it happens, I am overdue for a tea break, Cousin. I will be with you soon."

Spinward Arcade and Dorms
Administration Hall

REN ZEL CONSIDERED ANTHORA'S PROFILE, WHICH WAS UNUSUALLY serious. He did not make the mistake made by many who assumed that his lifemate was little more than an airy idiot. If the Tree had engineered their mating to suit itself, it had not stinted them. Even with his so-called gifts reft from him, still he could feel her heart beating with his; he could taste her moods, and gauge the tendency of her thoughts.

"Did the day displease you, Beloved?" he asked.

She turned her face to him, silver eyes bright, and raised her wineglass.

"The day—no. Seignur Veeoni has allowed herself to be persuaded to a long Balance, Delia Bell is for the moment well fixed, and M Traven will have someone to talk to, and to share the burden of her duty."

"Admirable accomplishments, surely?"

"Surely, they are. However, having done so much, I undid myself, by promising what I may not be able to deliver."

"What did you promise, I wonder?"

"That I would drive the agents of the Lyre Institute from Tinsori Light in such a manner that they would not soon wish to return, and that they would argue against sending any other of their personnel here."

Ren Zel sipped his wine.

Anthora had been perfectly capable of fulfilling that promise, once. Now, however, diminished—no, she rejected that assessment, and so would he—*changed* as she was...

"Old habits," he murmured, and she laughed softly.

"Indeed. Old habits."

"Is there another course that might produce the same results?"

"That is what I am mulling, to the detriment of our conversation," she said. "It is possible that all is not lost. I will think upon it. Later. For now, tell me about your day."

Station Day 40
Spinward Arcade and Dorms

THE STATION HAD BEEN GENEROUS, ALLOCATING ONE DORM ROOM per person. That meant she could pursue her various projects without the additional bother of a roommate.

At the moment, she was looking for a way in to—anywhere, really.

There! The sniffer had found an unsecured line into the legacy system. Excellent.

Keeli Varge smiled. The mission was coming together nicely.

She fed the address of the broken path into the loaded single-use, pressed the button and released the virus.

The sniffer program reported the presence of the virus at the vulnerable point.

Excellent.

Smiling, she pressed the self-destruct on the one-use, and dropped it into the recycling chute.

Bechimo
Dock A

• • • • • • • •

THERE WAS A TOOLBOX AT THE BOTTOM OF THE LIFT, WHERE there ought, indeed, to be a toolbox, on a well-regulated dock. Jen Sin paused a moment to admire the solid ordinariness of it, all the slots filled with the larger tools, and drawers clearly marked as to their contents.

We may make a recover, yet, he thought, putting out a hand to touch a starbar, pulling open a parts drawer, and smiling at the properly indexed pieces.

Ordinary order. What a precious thing that was.

He pushed the drawer shut, and turned toward Dock A.

It was a rowdy crew at *Bechimo*'s dockside—three leather-clad figures in frantic motion—lunging, leaping, in one case dropping to both knees on the decking and sliding some distance, arms outstretched.

A fourth of the company had adopted a less ambitious mode, leaning against the ramp-rail, arms and ankles crossed in an attitude of almost aggressive repose.

Jen Sin was angling toward that peaceful figure, and some similarly peaceful explanations.

But he had failed to correctly account his cousin Theo.

"Jen Sin!" she called. "Catch!"

He half-turned, hand extended, to snatch the glittering ball out of the air—when it dropped deckward, and kicked to the right.

It was pilot reactions then—as mindless as a kitten attacking a string—he dropped, lunged, and got the thing in hand without quite sacrificing his dignity.

Only to nearly lose it again as it bucked against his fingers, twisting toward freedom. Instinct again, he applied a counter-twist from the wrist and there was a moment of quiet before it kicked again, but this time, he was not surprised.

"Throw it before it breaks loose," Clarence advised him from his comfortable place against the rail. "If it escapes, you will not only lose points, but there will be a wild ball on the deck, which is all manner of fun."

The object he held whined, whirred, and tried to shoot straight up. He kept it in check, barely, and cocked a considering eye at his informant, who raised both hands and shook his head.

"I am an old man. *You* want to play with Theo."

There was a certain amount of good sense to that, his cousin's sense of mischief having produced this situation. Recalling the ball's approach, he snapped one step forward and threw—aiming for the deck between Theo's feet.

She was in the air before the thing had fairly left his hand—a worthy leap, and a twist executed high above the decking made her the ball's mistress. She had barely touched down before she was throwing, hard, to the left, yelling, "Kara!"

The ball produced three zigs, two zags, and dropped—directly into the arms of the blonde woman, who had fallen to her knees to effect the intercept.

She leapt to her feet, spun in a circle, shaking the hand holding the ball, yelled, "Win Ton!" and released it.

It shot straight up. The brown-haired lad crossed his arms over his chest, a faint look of boredom on his comely face. Meantime, the ball executed an acute right turn, fell, rose, hesitated for a moment in midair, and with a whine shot forward as if its whole intention was to strike Clarence fatally in the heart.

Win Ton danced to the left, leaned—captured the ball in one hand, pulled it into his chest and folded the other hand over.

"What if he'd missed, is what I gotta ask," Clarence said.

"Then you would have had to exert yourself," Kara returned pertly, shaking her hair out of her face. "Old man, indeed!"

"So," Theo said, with a grin, "now you know what a bowli ball is."

"No," Jen Sin answered. "Now I have been exposed to pilot catnip. A far different matter, I fear." He glanced at Win Ton, still holding the ball against his chest with one hand, and administering long strokes with the other.

"You are calming it?"

"For the moment," Win Ton said. "Unless you would like to join us for a full round."

"I would fear for my life," Jen Sin answered, and Theo laughed.

"I think that might be turnabout," Kara agreed. "Truly, sir, for someone who had not even the concept, you made a startlingly quick recover."

"Scout training is to blame, for all and everything." He paused. "In fact, I will be surprised to learn that object wasn't introduced by a Scout."

Win Ton grinned.

"Dancing Master ro'Linga, so the story comes down to us, despaired of ever producing a truly random environment into which hopeful Scoutlings might be thrust, to the benefit of their reaction times. She is credited with inventing the bowli ball, which, as you saw, is not truly random."

"Though it will certainly do until true random makes its bow. All honor to Master ro'Linga. How is it wakened?"

Win Ton extended the ball, which was moving rather sleepily in his hand.

"Shake it," he said.

Jen Sin received the ball. Holding it firmly, he shook it, once, twice...

On the third shake, the bowli ball jerked against his fingers, seeking its freedom.

And the public dock lights dropped abruptly from bright to dim.

Station Systems Administrator

ALARMS SCREAMED.

"Virus!" Tocohl flashed the warning to Joyita and *Bechimo*. "Seal up!"

She accessed the system—the legacy system, not Seignur Veeoni's painstaking rack-and-tile array. Still, the intruder could do harm—*was* doing harm, multiplying, overwhelming available resources.

Cleanbots stopped and fell over in the halls of the station.

Tocohl threw up a wall; another, trying to herd it, contain it. If she could get it into a box, she could smother it, but it was quick.

And then, it jumped.

Jumped from the legacy system into the security perimeter.

"I've got it!" Joyita yelled, throwing a trap around it.

But the virus had jumped again—only the very slimmest of datastrings—but it was *inside security.*

Inside the station systems.

Outside of station systems, Tocohl reached—and realized that she would never be quick enough; nimble enough. This was *not* her environment, and because of that, the virus was going to win.

Joyita was gone, vanished from her scans. *Bechimo* was locked tight.

The virus jumped again.

"Catie," Tocohl sent along the sealed line. "I'm throwing the switch."

Mentor's Comm Room

"I AM TINSORI LIGHT!"

Tolly Jones stumbled and spun, eyes narrowing as the lighting flickered and dimmed.

"All systems are under my control."

Damn they are, Tolly thought and by that time he was running for the nearest lift.

The lift door opened as he approached, and the man standing there smiled.

"Well, Thirteen-Sixty-Two," he said. "How convenient."

He raised a hand, bringing the whistle to his lips.

The sound juddered through Tolly's head even as he leapt forward, hands moving quickly, competently.

"I don't have time for this."

The lift door opened just as Jen Sin yos'Phelium flashed past, a bar in one hand.

Tolly leapt after him.

"Jen Sin, no!"

But the light keeper kept going, at no inconsiderable speed.

Tolly was accounted pretty fast, but the other man was pulling away from him, and gods, if he tried to use that bar on the array—

"Jen Sin!"

It was Theo, now, moving not too slow herself, keeping pace at Tolly's shoulder.

"Tocohl!" he yelled. "Don't open the core door!"

They flashed 'round the final corner then, in time to see Jen Sin headed directly for the door, speed undiminished.

Gonna be a bad shock to the system when he hits, Tolly thought.

The door to the core opened.

"I'm sorry, Mentor," Tocohl said. "Those systems are no longer under my control."

Main Core

JEN SIN RAN DOWN THE APPROACH HALL. HE HAD SNATCHED A starbar from the dockside tool kit. The bowli ball was still in his left hand, furiously trying to break his grip.

He was a fool. Lorith had tried to warn him, and he had put her fears aside.

There were lives in his care, and Tinsori Light *would not* have them.

The door to the core was six steps away, and for an instant, he doubted—then the door slid away, and he was in.

"Jen Sin, no!"

That was Theo, who had of course come after him. That was regrettable, but he had also seen Tolly Jones in passing. He had nothing but admiration for the mentor's good sense and survival skills; he would take care of himself, and of Theo.

He slowed to a quick walk as he approached, the field weird and blue above the array. The bowli ball was fighting his grip. He shook it.

"Little man, have you returned to your service?" came Tinsori Light's voice.

"I never left my service," Jen Sin said.

He flung the bowli ball aside as he moved forward, both hands around the starbar now, as he raised it over his shoulder.

...*...

"Jen Sin, no!" Theo shouted again, jumping forward.

Tolly grabbed the back of her jacket, yanked her against his chest, and got both arms around her, pinning her tight.

"Let 'im go, Cap'n Theo. He's the light keeper—it's his to solve."

"Does he know about the field? He'll die!"

Ahead, the slim figure strode on, flinging something away with his left hand, and hefting the starbar two-handed over his right shoulder, like he was going to bring it around and start smashing tiles. Tolly did a fast calculation, hefted Theo off her feet and threw them both at the floor, rolling toward the scant cover of the worktable.

• • • ❋ • • •

The field crackled before him. Tinsori Light roared.

"I am in control of all systems!"

"No," Jen Sin said. "You are not."

He centered himself—and the bowli ball slammed into the array from the rear, unseating tiles and twisting racks.

There was a flash, a crash, tiles spilled. The field flickered.

Tinsori Light screamed.

Jen Sin brought the starbar around, releasing it into the face of the array, and kept spinning, away, now, hoping the momentum would be enough to get him out of—

A bolt of heat hit him in mid-leap, igniting his very bones.

He slammed into the floor.

Main Core

BLUE LIGHT FILLED THE ROOM, AND A BRIEF, FEROCIOUS SCREAM. Tolly had his face against Theo's shoulder, holding her head down against the deck, none too gentle, maybe, but she wasn't struggling.

The screaming stopped, and he got the sense that every bit of light and air had been sucked out of the core—and come rushing back in.

Cautiously, he raised his head.

The array was nothing but shards and shred, the field down, o'course, there being nothing to sustain it. Some distance away was a crumpled pile of leather, which he couldn't quite tell from this distance, was it breathing.

"I'm lettin' us up, Cap'n Theo," he said softly. "Stay peaceful, right?"

"Right," she breathed.

He rocked back on his knees, keeping a grip on her arm.

"Is he—?"

"Hard to tell from here. What's innerestin' to me is that the array's gone, Tocohl doesn't have control of the system, and *we're* not dead."

"Since we're not, shouldn't we find out if Jen Sin is?"

Tolly hesitated, not quite knowing why—and in that moment Lorith ran in through the open door. She skidded to a halt, staring at the broken array, then spun, slowly, her eyes passing over them as if they weren't of any more interest than the workbench. She cried out when she spotted him, still not doing any moving, over by the far wall.

"Jen Sin!"

• • • ❋ • • •

It seemed his bones were not quite melted, nor was the pain—*quite* all-consuming. He was well enough, he thought laboriously. Well enough for this final thing. This final duty of friendship. Of love.

He heard her voice, the note of fear; in a moment, he was gathered in her arms, his head against her shoulder. He opened his eyes and focused on her face, tear-streaked and horrified.

"Jen Sin, you must not die!"

He managed a smile for her.

"Foregone, I fear it."

"No—"

"Peace, let me tell you—tell you how much I honor you," he murmured. She leaned closer to hear him. "A true comrade in an impossible task. Yet... we persevered—*you* persevered, so long, Lorith—and we prevailed! Tinsori Light is no more. Your duty is dispatched, with honor, and with grace. Songs will be made, tales told of your selfless service. You preserved the universe. I would have had no one else but you with me in this—"

Her cheeks were wet again, and he raised a hesitant hand, tracing the line of her jaw. She closed her eyes, and bent her head, and he moved his hand again, stroking the soft pale curls, feeling the beads running like water between his fingers until he had them gathered into his fist—and yanked them free.

• • • ※ • • •

Tolly rose slowly, Theo with him. Lorith was completely focused on Jen Sin, who she'd gathered up into her lap. He was moving, a little. No good way to tell how long that was going to last.

"Theo," he said, still talking soft. "Tinsori Light's last shout was over the public band. There's gonna be people coming up that lift, and they don't need to see this. Go head 'em off, willya?"

"*Bechimo*'s sending security," Theo said. "I'll hold the lift."

She left, walking soft, if not noiseless. He heard her lengthen into a run when she hit the hall.

"Station?" he said, still soft, and oh so gentle.

"Yes, Mentor," came the answer, likewise soft, and not at all Tocohl.

"Close the door, hey?"

"Of course, Mentor."

The door slid closed, and audibly locked.

"Thanks. What's your name?"

"Catalinc Station. You may call me Catie."

Across the room, Lorith screamed.

• • • ✵ • • •

The beads came away bloody, and he flung them with all his strength even as she screamed, and stiffened.

He rolled out of her embrace, catching her before she collapsed, taking care to keep her head from striking the floor.

She was still, her pale skin suffused, and he thought—

She opened her eyes.

"Jen Sin." Scarcely a whisper.

He bent close.

"I am here, Lorith."

"Do not . . . Jen Sin . . ."

She shuddered, and he stroked her curls from her face.

"No . . . awakening. Jen Sin. Last duty."

Absolved, he thought, smoothing her damp cheek with his thumb.

"No more awakenings, Lorith. I swear it. Rest now."

She smiled, and gasped, eyes staring.

Swallowing, he put his fingers at the base of her long throat, finding nothing.

He heard movement, looked up—and there was Tolly Jones bending to retrieve the beads, shoving them into a pocket as he straightened.

"Mentor," Jen Sin said, his voice trembling. "Your opinion, please."

The other man dropped to Lorith's side, checked pulse and breath.

"I'd say she's gone," he murmured, then raised his voice slightly. "Catie, do you read any life signs for Light Keeper Lorith?"

"Mentor, I do not. Light Keeper yos'Phelium, my condolences. I did not know her, but I do know she stood long against our common enemy."

Jen Sin bent his head, his chest aching, his bones a-smolder.

"Yes. She withstood—much, and honored her duty for as long as she was able."

"Seignur Veeoni and M Traven approach," Catie said. "Shall I open the door, Light Keeper?"

Jen Sin took a breath, and lifted his head.

"Yes, of course."

He leaned forward, stroked the disordered curls away from her face, closed the staring eyes, straightened her limbs, and smoothed the robe. When she was thus made seemly, he looked up into Tolly Jones's somber face.

"Of your kindness, Mentor, an arm."

"Sure."

Rising was no certain thing; agony sheeted through him, and there was indeed a moment when he thought his legs would fail him, but for Tolly Jones's surprisingly steadfast arm around his waist. Thus, he managed to be upright when the door opened to Seignur Veeoni and her guard.

The researcher paused beside them, her eyes on the wreckage of the array.

"A thorough and decisive solution," she said at last. "My compliments, Light Keeper. May one know who administers the station?"

"I do," Jen Sin said, hearing how his voice wobbled. "Catalinc is Station. Catie, you have met Seignur Veeoni, I think."

"Researcher, thank you again for making the libraries accessible to me. They have been of enormous use."

"Excellent."

She glanced down, then up to meet Jen Sin's eyes.

"Light Keeper Lorith is not wearing her beads," she observed.

"She no longer has the need," he answered, his voice unsteady.

Seignur Veeoni inclined slightly from the waist; he recognized it as respect.

"The Pathfinders recognized her order," he said. "I would find from them, what is—proper."

"Chernak and Stost are at the lift," Traven said. "I'll send one to you, and stand in their place."

"Thank you," Jen Sin said.

He was, he noted, leaning more heavily on Tolly Jones's supporting arm.

"Mentor . . ."

"Light Keeper yos'Phelium needs to sit down," Tolly Jones said. "Researcher, will you bring the cart over here for him?"

"Certainly."

Amazingly, she left them, and brought the cart, meticulously setting the brake, and stepping back as Tolly helped him to sit.

"I regret..." he murmured.

"Nothing to regret," Tolly told him. "Just gotta finish up here, then I'm thinking a little time inna doc won't be outta the way."

"Stost and Anthora yos'Galan are approaching," Catie said. "Shall I admit them, Light Keeper?"

"Yes, thank you."

Main Core Hall Lift

THEO HAD MADE A COMPROMISE WITH SUPERVISOR ARNLEE, WHO was in charge of the teams that were bringing dock supplies up to spec.

"Right. I'll stay here with Cap'n Waitley 'til there's news," Arnlee said to the three people who'd accompanied her. "Jooly, you stand in front of the dockside lift and tell people there was an outage in the interface module, and the experts are on it.

"Binch, you call the team leaders and make sure they report any anomalies to you, but otherwise to keep doin' what needs done.

"Nafe, you call over to Ren an' fill Fenchile in. I'll call Vinsint. Go."

They went, and Jooly reported herself in position.

"Station," Theo said, "please lock the lifts with access to this hall."

"Yes, Captain Waitley."

Arnlee nodded to her, and walked aside, port-comm at her ear.

"Theo," *Bechimo* said. "We have a situation."

Theo glanced behind her, where Chernak and Traven filled the hall from side to side. Arnlee was still off to the side, on the comm.

She took a breath.

How bad a situation?

"That remains to be seen. Tocohl has ceded all functions to Catalinc Station."

Good. Jen Sin destroyed the rack-and-tile core.

"Yes, Tocohl and I deduced as much. That is not our situation."

What is it, then? Theo asked.

"Joyita is missing."

Main Core

. . . .

ANTHORA WAS SITTING ON THE CART BESIDE HIM, HER HAND ON his knee. His bones burned somewhat less, which he feared was her influence, but he did not demand that she withdraw. She had brought him a bottle of water, which he drank thirstily while Stost examined what remained of Lorith, and Tolly Jones and Seignur Veeoni examined what was left of the array.

His study complete, Stost came to the cart, and dropped into a crouch, which put his face at a more convenient height for discussion.

"The Sanderat were fierce and dedicated warriors," Stost said, his big voice gentle. "Their purpose and their honor was to die in battle, their blades red with the blood of their enemies. If there should happen to be a blade sister with them at the end, a song was made, recalling the glories and the victories of the one departing."

Stost took a breath.

"That is what I know, Light Keeper. She would have expected no other dignities, save that her name be remembered by her sisters, until they, too, fell in battle."

Anthora's fingers tightened on his knee.

"I was her sister," Jen Sin said, slowly, "and I will recall her as long as I live."

"I, too, will recall Lorith Light Keeper, who stood between the universe and the Great Enemy," Catalinc Station said.

Jen Sin bowed his head.

"Yes."

He looked up to meet Stost's eyes.

"Thank you, Pathfinder."

"It is my honor," Stost assured him, and rose to his full towering height.

"The light keeper requires a 'doc," Seignur Veeoni said, shockingly brisk. "He was in this room when the field gave up its energy, and has taken injury. I suggest the crisis healing unit aboard *Bechimo* as the nearest and most appropriate source of aid."

"I agree," Jen Sin said, and slid to his feet.

His knees buckled, his vision greyed; flames leapt, consuming him.

The last thing he heard was his cousin Anthora directing Stost to carry him.

Spinward Arcade and Dorms Administrator's Office

....

"REN ZEL, JEN SIN'S BEEN WOUNDED."

Ren Zel looked up from his screen.

"Wounded? How badly? Where is he?"

"He—Stost has him. I am guiding him and Anthora through the maintenance tunnels to Dock A. *Bechimo* has a crisis autodoc aboard, and Seignur Veeoni suggested that it would be appropriate."

"Seriously wounded, then, but in hand. Very good. What happened, Catie?"

"Tinsori Light—a remnant of the Old Light, seized control of the new array. Jen Sin disabled the array. He was... Mentor Jones tells me that he was too near when the field discharged, but that the leather—*the leather saved his life. Maybe.*"

That last was rendered in Tolly Jones's very voice.

Ren Zel took a deep breath.

Anthora has it in hand, he told himself. And *Bechimo* has a crisis unit.

"I report that I am now fully myself," Catie said, though not as if it gave her any joy.

"Is Tocohl—"

"A virus was released into the systems. Tocohl threw the changeover switch. The legacy system has been dismantled. The new array...

"There is no longer a new array."

"It sounds as if we have weathered a very storm," Ren Zel said. "Has Light Keeper Lorith been informed?"

There was a sense of hesitation.

"Light Keeper Lorith is dead," Catie said. "Jen Sin promised not to wake her."

Ren Zel blinked.

Then, he shut down his screen, rose, and put on his jacket.

"I am going to the central tower," he said. "I will stand as light keeper until Jen Sin is able again. It will be my priority to find someone to interface with the second wave from this office. Pray tell Coordinator Carresens this, and ask her to contact me with any questions."

He moved toward the door.

"I am speaking with Vinsint Carresens," Catie said. "She is aware that there was a system failure and that Light Keeper yos'Phelium was wounded in his successful effort to preserve the station. Hazenthull is on the way to you with Seignur Veeoni's jitney. She will take you to the main tower."

"Thank you," Ren Zel said, and stepped out into the hallway.

Maintenance Tunnels

"REN ZEL IS ON HIS WAY TO THE CENTRAL TOWER," CATIE SAID, as the lights in the tunnel ahead of them continued to come on, and the lights behind them went out.

Anthora went first, Stost following, carrying the limp form of Jen Sin yos'Phelium. At this distance, she could not feel the burning agony in his bones, for which she was grateful. She was even more grateful for Jen Sin's continued state of unconsciousness. With luck, it would last until they got him into the crisis unit.

"I have spoken to *Bechimo*," Catie said. "He is expecting us. Kara will meet you at the hatch. She asks if you will require a stretcher."

"No need," Stost said. Even speaking softly, his voice rumbled off the walls. "He weighs nothing, and if I put him down, he might wake."

The lights ahead of them came on.

"The next hatch on the left accesses *Bechimo*'s dock," Catie said. "I am opening it for you."

And indeed, there it was, sliding silently out of their way. Once on the dock, Anthora stood aside to allow Stost to go as quickly as he could, while she paused and took deep breaths of cold, bracing air.

"Catie," she said softly, "what happened?"

"Many things happened," Catie said. "A virus was released into the legacy systems and moved too swiftly for Tocohl to contain. She initiated the changeover. I am now fully station. Tinsori Light awoke in the new array. Analysis is ongoing. Jen Sin destroyed the new array and Tinsori Light also. Light Keeper Lorith died. Joyita is missing."

"A delightful convergence of event," Anthora murmured. "Do you know who introduced the virus?"

"I have found the entry point in a dormitory room in the Spinward Arcade. A cleanbot has been dispatched. Analysis of the contents of the recycling chute suggests an inappropriate article was introduced."

"The cleanbot?" Anthora murmured, walking toward *Bechimo*'s hatch.

"The cleanbot will collect organic samples which may be of use to Tocohl in making a positive identification."

"Of course," Anthora said. "Thank you, Catie."

"You are welcome. Anthora?"

"Yes?"

"Will you tell me, when Jen Sin is—"

"When he is out of the 'doc? Of course I will."

"Thank you. I hope he won't die. It distressed him so much."

Anthora blinked.

"As it would anyone," she said gently. "I hope he won't die, too."

She passed the station light at the end of *Bechimo*'s ramp, and glanced up at a slight fluttering sound.

Three birds sat on the crossbar supporting the light—one green, one blue, one yellow.

Anthora inclined her head, and went up the ramp.

Bechimo
Dock A

....

THE COMM PINGED.

Clarence tapped the switch.

"*Bechimo.* O'Berin on deck."

"Clarence O'Berin, this is Acting First Light Keeper Ren Zel dea'Judan. I invoke the Safe Docks clause of the Pilots Guild Handbook, and attach you as a deputy under the direct supervision of the light keeper's office."

Clarence blinked.

"You gotta have somebody better equipped for that sort o'thing than I am," he said.

He glanced to the screen at his right, which showed an empty office, lights dim, and work screens blued.

"Are you telling me that the former Boss of Solcintra Low Port is unable to interface with Terran spacers, maintenance, and repair crews, answer their questions and keep work to schedule?"

Clarence drew a breath.

"Put that way...but I'm pretty sure those regs you're tossing around have a provision. You need permission from my captain."

"Who needs permission from your captain?" Theo demanded, striding onto the bridge like she was about to do a murder, or worse.

She stopped in front of the screen, and stared balefully into the empty room.

"Acting First Light Keeper Ren Zel dea'Judan wants to deputize me to ride herd on those o'the second wave, arrived and arriving, and interface with their supervisors and team leaders. Do I got that right, Light Keeper dea'Judan?"

"You do."

Theo spun away from the window into Joyita's desolate office.

"We were sent to help," she said flatly, and Clarence felt a small shiver run his spine.

"So we were," he said gently. He addressed the comm.

"Let me pack a bag, laddie. I'll ask for a ride to my station."

"Hazenthull will drive you. She is on her way to your dock."

Bechimo
Dock A

. . . .

THE CRISIS 'DOC FINISHED ITS INVENTORY, AND PROVIDED AN estimated time of completion.

Anthora rose from the stool Kara had provided for her comfort, put her fingers lightly against the lid, as if touching the cheek of kin, and left the alcove.

. . . ※ . . .

"How can he just be *gone*?" Theo asked.

Hevelin was sitting upright on her lap, his back pressed into her chest. She—there were other things that she should be doing, other than staring at an empty room that had no physical presence on the ship. She'd do them, soon. But first she had to understand...

"Tocohl said that he was attempting to enclose the virus with a trap—perhaps he intended to push it back to its entry point in the legacy system just before Tocohl sealed it," *Bechimo* said. "He was not completely reckless; he did employ armor."

"But he went, himself."

"Yes," *Bechimo* agreed.

There was a step in the corridor.

"Anthora yos'Galan approaches," *Bechimo* said.

. . . ※ . . .

Theo was at the board, staring at a screen displaying an empty comm tower. The last time Anthora had seen that room, Joyita had been sitting at the desk, sparring with Clarence.

However, the empty tower was a mere curiosity. What demanded her attention was—Theo.

Theo had always been—*bright* in the Inner Eye, very nearly as bright as Val Con. The energy was not merely emotion, nor purpose, nor intellect, nor even her alignment with luck. There was a definite tang of *dramliz* energy, very like Val Con when he was standing fully as Korval, or when he was riding a hunch.

Anthora took a careful breath.

"Theo," she said. "We need to talk."

Bright burning anger flared. Theo's shoulders lifted—and fell. The flare subsided.

She spun the chair.

"About what?"

Administrative Tower

"TOLLY JONES, MENTOR."

A bow accompanied this statement—a Terran bow, indicating respect.

Ren Zel inclined his head.

"Ren Zel dea'Judan, Acting First Light Keeper. How may I assist you, Mentor?"

The grin was charming: rueful and self-deprecating.

"Glad you asked. Happens there's a dead man in the center main core lift. He's my fault. It was self-defense, though I'm bound to own I'd say that even if it wasn't, being as he's in no position to argue."

"Have we an identification of the deceased?"

"Yessir. Ambroze Ling, a Director of the Lyre Institute for Exceptional Children."

"Ah. And what did Director Ling do to put you in fear of your life?"

"Just in plain words, he blew a whistle, believing that would put me under his authority. I know that sounds—"

Ren Zel held up his hand.

"Anthora yos'Galan is my lifemate," he said. "She had much to say on the subject of whistles and compulsion." He inclined his head. "I believe that you acted in self-defense. Anthora will be pleased to learn that her therapy was successful.

"Are there kin or colleagues on-station who may receive Director Ling's remains?"

"His ship's docked—*Invictus*."

"Will you deliver him yourself?"

Tolly Jones drew a deep breath.

"Tempting, but prolly not best. His pilot might recognize me, and I'm over-limit on kills."

"I will ask Captain Waitley to lend her security team to the task."

"Thank you."

Another bow, the twin of the first.

"Is there anything I can do for you on behalf of the station?" he asked. "Turns out I'm at loose ends. Haz, too, since she don't have to keep Jen Sin from killing himself until he's outta the 'doc."

Ren Zel raised his eyebrows.

"Do you speak for Hazenthull?"

"Not in the way you mean. We're partners. Worked Surebleak port security as a team." Tolly Jones paused, and added, "Best team Commander Liz had."

"In that case, you and Hazenthull are now Tinsori Light's First Security Response Team. Put it together. Let me know if you need assistance from this office."

Tolly Jones grinned.

"Yessir."

Bechimo
Dock A

....

THEO FROWNED INTO HER TEA, PATTERN SUFFUSED WITH THOUGHT.

Anthora ate a maize button, and raised her cup, awaiting the outcome of thought.

"So you can see the operatives and Directors, and you can set the—the compulsion to leave Tinsori Light. All you need from me is energy—like a battery?"

"Exactly like a battery," Anthora told her, putting down her cup.

"Will they stay away?" Theo asked.

"I believe that I may be sufficiently persuasive as to their danger that they will not be eager to return for quite some while."

"We don't want them to return at all," Theo pointed out.

"These—no, we do not. We must prepare to receive others, I think—however! That is for later. Under consideration at the moment is the fact that I need, as Miri would have it—*juice*, in order to drive the present crop of Lyre Institute agents away."

She paused, and leaned forward, looking directly into Theo's eyes.

"There is something that you need to understand. This thing I am proposing—that you allow me access to your energy—falls into a grey area. Unscrupulous persons sometimes chain others to them, in order have their energy on draw. That is *very* bad form, and no person of *melant'i* employs these measures."

"You're asking my permission," Theo pointed out.

"Yes. And I wish you to be fully informed." She raised a finger.

"You and I are already associated through a previous Healing. That means there is no need to forge a new link. The existing link, however, may be made more robust by this sharing."

Theo looked aside, and picked up her teacup.

"How's Jen Sin?" she asked.

"It will not be a short healing, but not so long as I had feared. I think we may credit the leather for that."

Theo nodded, put her cup down, and sighed.

"I give you permission to use my energy for this one occasion, in order to drive our enemies away. I do not give you permission to use my energy to kill those enemies."

She raised an eyebrow.

"Is that clear enough?"

"Most marvelously clear," Anthora told her with enthusiasm. "You have been studying with Liadens."

Theo snorted lightly.

"When do we start?" she asked.

Anthora took a brief inventory of her own, pushed her cup aside, and smiled.

"Now?"

Seignur Veeoni's Private Laboratory

ANALYSIS OF THE DATA DOWNLOADED FROM THE FIRST AND SECond units on the recovery deck was complete.

Seignur Veeoni stood by the first cranium, considering that fact.

Light Keeper Lorith was dead. Jen Sin yos'Phelium would very possibly die, and if he did not, the treatment rendered by the crisis unit would render the questions of beads and rebirth moot.

What, therefore, was the worth of these analyses, when weighed against other tasks in hand?

It might be argued—she had argued so in the past—that there was no worthless data.

Indeed, the analysis might well provide details regarding Light Keeper Lorith's subversion. The question remained—were the details worth knowing, in the instance? Such a combination as had produced today's events was unlikely to occur again, and the broad outlines were obvious.

Light Keeper Lorith had obtained a set of beads from the third unit on the recovery deck. Doubtless the programming in the beads she had been wearing prompted her to do so, and provided instruction. The new beads had rendered her an agent of the Old Light's will.

Seignur Veeoni had provided a controlled environment in which Tinsori Light could do his work. When his inevitable move was made, Jen Sin yos'Phelium had acted with admirable dispatch, and delivered the coup.

Light Keeper Lorith...

It occurred to Seignur Veeoni, rather abruptly, that she was, perhaps, not a goddess, to be playing thus with lives.

This was...not a new category of thought. Certainly, she had questioned her methods after seeing what the Lyre Institute had made of her former laboratory, and those who had been set to guard her.

That incident had left her angry.

This... she supposed this must be regret.

Well.

She glanced again at the analysis screen, and turned away, her eye alighting on the backup array in the far corner of the room. She should dismantle it, she thought.

But not now. Later.

She reached to the board, and sent the analyses to her reading library.

Doubtless, Yuri would find the analyses interesting and possibly useful. She would forward the files to him, as well.

"Seignur Veeoni," M Traven said. "You have an urgent call."

She spun on her heel, the words, the familiar words that always ensured that she would be left alone, rising to her lips—

She took a breath.

"Thank you," she said, and walked past M Traven to the workroom.

The screen was blank; the originating address... not possible.

"This is Seignur Veeoni."

"This is Joyita." The voice was faint and flat.

Seignur Veeoni felt her chest tighten in a most unusual and uncomfortable manner.

"I need your help."

Her lips parted.

"Joyita, what are you doing in the legacy system?"

"Being lost, and very worried," came the reply.

"How did you *get into* the legacy system?" she demanded.

"Overconfidence."

Perhaps she should have asked for proof, but that reply struck deep and true.

Overconfidence.

Indeed.

"I understand," she said. "Let me see what I may do."

Spinward Arcade and Dorms

KEELI VARGE LOCKED THE DOOR TO HER DORMITORY SPACE, AND leaned against the wall. She was trembling, her hands were cold, *and it was coming.* It was behind her, around every corner. It was *hunting* her.

Now, her cleverness in coming to Tinsori Light as one of the throng of spacers answering the Traveler's Aid Notice was revealed as arrant foolishness—even stupidity. She had to leave, leave *now*, leave before it found her and devoured her.

A ship. For the love of space, she needed a ship! Stealing a ship—but it would see her!

It saw *everything.*

She darted across the room, and slapped up the comm.

"*Invictus.*"

"This is Director Varge. I must urgently speak to Director Ling."

"I'm sorry, Director, but Director Ling is dead."

"What?"

Gods, gods, it had killed Ling! Of course it had. And she was next.

"Director Ling is dead," the pilot repeated. "Orders, Director?"

"Yes. File for departure. I will be with you soon."

Bechimo
Dock A

· · · · · · · ·

"JOYITA!"

Kara leapt out of her chair and rushed to the screen, as if she would embrace him, and only paused at the last instant, her eyes searching his face.

"You're thinner," she said.

His grin was lopsided.

"I expect I am. Possibly I'm wiser, too."

"Joyita," *Bechimo* said. "What happened? Tocohl blames herself."

"Tocohl is blameless," Joyita said firmly. "I was reckless and overconfident. Captain Theo will doubtless tell me so, at length, among other hard words—every one well earned."

"Where were you?"

"In short form? I became entangled with the virus, which retreated into the legacy system, where it had been introduced. I edited and ended it, but then—I was lost. The tile-and-rack matrix is *fascinating*, and alien. I tried to withdraw as I had come, but the way was blocked."

"Tocohl sealed the system," *Bechimo* said.

"Prudent, and no blame to her. She acted to preserve the station."

"Yes," *Bechimo* said. "You will want to know that the change-over has happened. Catalinc Station is fully herself."

This time, Joyita's grin was wide and delighted.

"We should throw a party!"

"Perhaps we should," *Bechimo* said. "We'll discuss it after you have told us how you escaped, and Theo has scolded you."

"Seignur Veeoni extracted me," Joyita said, reverence in his voice. "It was *an honor* to see her work."

Administrative Tower

INVICTUS HAD FILED FOR DEPARTURE.

Station had not yet released them.

This was not entirely Station's fault. *Invictus*'s dock was so crowded that to have allowed an undocking would surely have seen someone killed.

"Thirteen," Anthora murmured from her perch on the arm of Ren Zel's chair.

"How many more?" he asked, watching as panicked boarders squeezed aboard.

"One," Anthora said, and, as if she had conjured them, here came a figure running for the ramp as if all the demons of cold space were on their heels.

"There," Anthora said, with some satisfaction.

The figure fled up the ramp as the hatch began to close, and squeezed through.

"You may let them go now, Beloved," Anthora said.

Ren Zel sighed.

"Station, please clear *Invictus* for immediate departure."

Bechimo
Dock A

• • • • • • • •

"JOYITA, SEE ME IN THE MEETING ROOM. NOW," THEO SAID. SHE leaned a hip against the table, crossed her arms over her chest, and waited, trying not to count the seconds.

The screen didn't flicker, it merely opened as if it were a window indeed, and she was looking into the comm tower, directly at her comm officer.

He was thinner in the face, and it looked to Theo as if there was some bruising around his right eye. He was wearing a blue shirt she hadn't seen before, the sleeves rolled back from his wrists. Four cermabronze rings on four fingers, one wide band of the same material around one wrist.

The other wrist was enclosed by a dark woven net, in which small crystals glittered.

Theo frowned.

"You weren't careful," she said sternly. "You endangered the ship."

"I did not endanger the ship," Joyita said. "*Bechimo* locked down tight."

Theo waited.

Joyita sighed.

"Which does not negate the fact that I wasn't careful, Captain. I was lost, and if not for Seignur Veeoni's timely assistance, I would still be lost."

"It would not be a trivial thing to lose the comm officer," Theo said sternly. "Not to mention our crewmate and friend."

Joyita looked down at his desk—looked back.

"Captain. I will be more careful in the future."

"Because you couldn't be any less careful." Theo nodded. "Good. I'm looking forward to seeing how that works out for you."

"Yes, Captain."

"Are you—all right?" Theo demanded then.

"Captain, I am. Once I was free of the legacy system and in the cranium, Seignur Veeoni did a deep scan to ensure that I was not infected. When I returned to the tower, I compared my operations to my last backup. I am intact and able."

"If you find that's changing, you tell me immediately," Theo said.

"Yes, Captain."

"All right, then. Anything else?"

"Yes! *Bechimo* tells me that Catalinc Station has come fully into herself. We should throw her a party." He grinned. "A birthday party!"

Theo stared at him, briefly struggling not to grin in response—then gave it up.

"That's not a bad idea," she said. "But we should wait until Jen Sin's out of the 'doc."

"*Bechimo*, Tocohl, and I will start planning," Joyita said. "In our spare time."

Station Day 41
Mentor's Comm Room

"MENTOR, I HAVE QUESTIONS."

Tolly raised his eyebrows, and turned toward the speaker.

"You're not alone in that," he said.

"I mean," Catie said, sounding contrite, "that I have specific questions regarding human physiology. If this is not the correct procedure, please tell me how I may amend myself."

"Procedure's correct," Tolly said, leaning back in his chair. "The polite way to ask—barring an emergency—is something along the lines of, 'When would it be convenient for us to talk?'"

"Oh. Thank you, Mentor. When would it be convenient for us to talk?"

Tolly smiled.

"Happens I've got some time right now. What can I do for you, Catie?"

"I wonder about the nature of human death. I have been talking with Ren Stryker, who wished me to know about the dangers of electrical current with regard to human safety."

"That's very kind of Ren, to share info," Tolly prompted when nothing else was forthcoming.

"Yes, it is! Ren Stryker is a very kind and helpful person, I think. But—he says that, once dead, humans are ended. There are no backups, and no . . . resuscitation. However, my observation indicates that this information is incorrect. Or, possibly only correct in certain circumstances."

Tolly nodded and waited.

"Jen Sin—I saw Jen Sin die . . . many times, Mentor; also Lorith. The man you struck in the elevator—did he remain dead, or did Stost and Chernak return him to his ship so that he could be revived?"

"The man I killed," Tolly said deliberately, "is dead, and he can't be brought back to life, ever again. You'll notice that Light Keeper Lorith hasn't been revived, either."

"She asked Jen Sin not to wake her," Catie said. "I heard."

"That's right." Tolly nodded. "Lorith is gone. She *was*, but she never *will be* again."

"If Jen Sin . . . dies, will he be resuscitated?"

"The way I heard it—no, he won't, Catie. That's his choice, just like Lorith made hers."

Silence.

Tolly cleared his throat.

"Is it okay for me to ask you a question?"

"Certainly, Mentor."

"Thank you. What I'm wondering is—wasn't there information on human biology in your libraries?"

"There was, yes, but I was not able to reconcile the information with observable facts. Also, there are several orders of humans, some frailer than others. There is an order, to which my builder and his sister belong, who download themselves serially into a new chassis when the old becomes irreparable. There is another order produced in batches, with usefulness limits hardwired. There—"

Tolly laughed and held up his hands.

"Have I misunderstood the data?"

"No, I didn't consider all the data before I asked my question. Common failing with humans. I forgot to remember where your libraries came from."

"Is my data *wrong*?"

"I'm willing to bet your data's one hundred percent correct—for the Old Universe. What we gotta do is get you up to spec on *this* universe. Lucky for us, that's gonna be real easy. Tocohl's who you want to ask for help, there. Given who *her* maker is, her general databases are top-notch."

"Will she be willing to share that data with me?"

"Won't know 'til you ask. If she says 'no,' you come see me again and we'll figure out something else. That sound okay to you, Catie?"

"Yes, Mentor, it does. Thank you. I had not considered the differences between my builder's universe and this one."

"We both missed that one. You go along and ask Tocohl if she can help you get up-to-date. I'm going to give Ren Stryker a call and see how he's doing. We haven't talked in a little while."

Common Meeting Space

"Of course, I will be pleased to share my background files with you!" Tocohl said. "I have to admit that I didn't think of your libraries being not only out of date, but out of place, either! It was an excellent plan to talk to the mentor, Catie. I don't know what we will do without him."

"Will we have to do without him?" Catie asked, somewhat alarmed. "He isn't going to—die, is he?"

Tocohl considered.

"Humans are very frail," she said slowly, "and they die easily. However, there is no reason to think that the mentor will die *soon*. Unless he runs against mischance, of course."

"Mischance?"

"An accident. Or another human with a weapon determined to destroy him."

"That happened—the other human blew a whistle. But the mentor destroyed him, instead."

"Really?"

"I can share the file if you like."

"Yes, please."

"Is current a mischance?" Catie asked.

"Sometimes—why do you ask?"

"Ren Stryker fears he damaged a human by running a current through her. She was trying to hurt him, and he had to make her stop. But, after, when she had stopped—she died. Ren thinks he might have damaged core systems. And now there is someone else—Ren did not have to stop him—who is being kept *sedated*."

"Ren is very concerned. He doesn't want another human to die."

"Of course not," Tocohl said. "Where shall I send the files?"

Catie provided the address of her cache.

"Thank you."

"You're welcome. Do you think the Pilots Guild Handbook would be of use to you?"

"Ren Zel has given me the TerraTrade manuals, the Pilots Guild Handbook, the Liaden Scouts World Book, the Liaden Code of Proper Conduct, and the condensed Space Law."

"That's a firm foundation. You might also ask *Bechimo* and Joyita for suggestions. If you have any questions about the general background, please ask me. I will be pleased to help."

"You are very kind."

"Do you know?" Tocohl said slowly. "The sedated human—Anthora yos'Galan is a Healer. She might be able to help."

"I'll ask her," Catie said. "We have an appointment to talk.

"May I ask a question?" she said suddenly.

"Certainly."

"Are you—content? You had been station administrator, but now that those functions have passed to me..."

Tocohl laughed.

"Am I bored, do you mean? I might have been, but Seignur Veeoni asked me to do deep analysis of backlogged data. I've had to derive a translation math and a notation set so far, and I'm barely started. It's a fascinating challenge. Also, now that I am no longer needed to administer the station, I've written to my delm. The clan is very thin and it's not unlikely that I'll be needed elsewhere."

"Of course. I have another question, if I may ask it."

"Certainly."

"Is it...proper to thank you for keeping the station online and viable? It was a great service to me. I have been reading a little in the Code of Proper Conduct, and it may be that I owe you Balance."

"A thank-you is appropriate," Tocohl said firmly.

"Then—thank you, Tocohl, for your efforts on behalf of the station, myself, and everyone who depends on us."

"You are very welcome, Catie."

Main Core Workroom

“HEY, DEELS.”

She turned away from her study of the shattered mess that had been the main core they’d all been so proud of.

“Tolly Jones,” she said.

“Same as ever. You stayin’?”

She tipped her head, her expression faintly amused.

“Why wouldn’t I? Got a sweet deal as a rack-and-tile specialist and general woman o’work with Seignur Veeoni.”

“That’ll be a rough road.”

Delia laughed.

“Talk to me about rough roads, Tolly Jones.”

“No,” he said meditatively, “don’t think I will, at that.”

He came to her side, and stared down at the wreckage.

“Guess we oughta be getting this cleaned up.”

“Why I’m here. Asked her if she didn’t want to salvage anything, but she’s against it.”

“Can’t say she’s wrong. Get unwanted programming in an associated grid like this was used to be, you gotta figure the hardware’s tainted.” He kicked at the shattered bit of tile by his boot. “Not that there’s much left, by way of hardware.”

“Sorry to see it go?”

He shrugged.

“It did what we needed—held the station stable until something better come along. I’m figuring that’s Seignur Veeoni’s view.”

“More or less. She’s calling it a successful field test.”

“And she’s not wrong. ’Nother thing, Deels.”

She glanced at him.

“What’s that?”

“Director Ling’s done.”

Her eyebrows rose.

"Feel better?"

"Actually—yeah. He got a blast outta his whistle before I did the needful."

"So, the Healer's fix really is a fix." She nodded. "Good to know. Don't guess there's similar word on Formyne?"

"Far's I've been able to determine, Formyne decided to skip the party."

"Don't hardly seem like her."

"You're right. Well." He gave her a grin. "Worry or work?"

"Work. I'll go get shovels. You grab us some cargo crates. Sooner we get this over to your buddy Ren Stryker, the happier I'll be."

He raised his eyebrows.

"Is that the truth, Deels?"

She showed him her teeth.

"Guess."

Community Room

• • • • • • • • • • • • • • • • • • • •

ANTHORA WAS SEATED AT A LONG TABLE, A REMOTE OPEN BEFORE her and a half-full bottle of tea by her right hand.

Ren Zel paused to consider her.

"Do you find the prospect elevating, Beloved?" she asked, without looking up.

"I find the prospect delightful," he returned gallantly. "But I was thinking that you look as if you are every bit as weary as I am."

"Well." She did glance up to him, then, a crease between her brows.

"Yes, I would say that we make a matched pair. There is wine in the keeper. Will you pour for us while I finish this?"

"Certainly."

He brought the glasses to the table, and took a chair beside her, content to watch her work. It was a station map had her attention, he saw, in particular a section labeled *Sereneco Hall Residences.*

Finally, she put the remote aside, and turned in her chair to face him. He handed her a glass, and raised his own, proposing a toast.

"To our good fortune."

Anthora sputtered a laugh. "I do *not* thank Shan for teaching you that."

"And yet our fortune has been good, has it not?"

"So it has, but one does not feel *quite* comfortable calling it aloud." She sipped, and sighed. "We have each of us accomplished marvels in the last few days. No wonder we are weary."

"No wonder at all." He used his chin to point at the portable. "Tell me what you are busy about."

"Well! Catie has kindly provided me with a comprehensive

station map, and the builder's project diary. It comes about that the builder had planned for grace, comfort, and beauty—all of which was anathema to Tinsori Light. The Sereneco Section is a case in point. Section One was intended to be the station master's residence; a place of renewal and solitude, should that be desired. There are high-speed access tubes directly to the administrative hall, to the main docks, and to the warehousing section.

"Section Two is similarly secluded. The tubes access what was meant to be the public marketplace."

Ren Zel sipped his wine.

"I will wish to see them, of course, but I am hopeful. Both appear to have ample area for gardens. And Section Two in particular looks as if it had been meant to be a Healer's Hall."

Ren Zel put his glass on the table.

"Have you Seen that the Healers will want to establish a Hall on Tinsori Light?"

She sighed and reached out to cover his hand with hers.

"I have Seen that there needs to be a Hall on Tinsori Light," she said softly. "The Healing of Delia Bell will find its way to the Lyre Institute, and I make no doubt that there will be those who will come, hoping to be similarly Healed. They must not be disappointed, when they arrive."

Ren Zel said nothing, watching her face.

"Then there are those who have long hung at the edges—the companions and crews of the Free Ships, and likely others. It is not impossible that they will require the services of a Hall."

She patted his hand, sat back and had recourse to her glass.

"Will you remain at Tinsori Light?"

"I think I must, for a time," she said. "I had hoped you would not find it beyond you, to stay with me." She waved her hand, fingers forming the sign for *later*. "We are both weary, the subject is large, and the delm must be in it. Nothing can be decided tonight."

"That is true," he said, picking up his glass.

They sat in companionable silence until the wine was gone. Anthora put her glass aside with a sigh.

"There is something which I am called to in my capacity as a Healer," she said. "I have promised that I will undertake it tomorrow."

Ren Zel frowned.

"You are," he said, "a Healer."

"Indeed. And thus I am called to Ren Stryker to attempt to Heal a possible agent of the Lyre Institute, who has been kept sedated for some time so that he not kill himself."

Ren Zel took a sharp breath.

"Of course, you must go," he said. "Only not alone."

She smiled.

"We are in agreement. Hazenthull and Tolly Jones will act as my security."

Ren Zel nodded.

"Very good. I need have no concerns at all."

Station Day 43
Eltoro
Dock D

· · · · · · · ·

THE SITUATION HAD CHANGED.

Director Formyne frowned at her readouts.

There were rack-and-tile systems at work on the station, but they were nothing like what would be needed to support sentience.

Added to that were the reports from the operatives who had fled the station aboard *Invictus*, of a malevolent, hungry intelligence, stalking them for food.

Ling had apparently allowed himself to be killed by this... being, lending credence to its existence, the fact of which Director Formyne took leave to doubt. Infuriating, as usual.

As much as she had worked for his downfall, Ling's death at this moment was inconvenient to her long-term plans. Lack-of-Ling created a power vacuum that *she* ought to have filled.

That she was not at the Institute, positioned to step into her proper place at the head of the Free Logic Project made her success at Tinsori Light even more critical.

But matters at Tinsori Light were changed. Drastically changed.

Oh, she had not expected the Old Light to be present—evidence that it had died in the local-space energy adjustment was overwhelming on that point.

She had, however, expected to find a rack-and-tile system supporting station operations. She had *planned* on there being a rack-and-tile system supporting station operations. The subversion of those systems via the tile system built according to Veeoni's own notes was central to her plan to acquire the Light for the Institute.

She needed information.

Unfortunately, the reports of those who had fled the imaginary malicious energy eater were not useful.

No, she thought abruptly, perhaps they *were* useful, after all.

She leaned toward her screen—and leaned back.

Yes.

Korval's witch was on-station. Apparently the news that she had lost—or been stripped!—of her abilities had been overstated. That—was interesting.

Thirteen-Sixty-Two was also on-station, which was . . . surprising. Thirteen-Sixty-Two was clever and elusive, known for always having a back door or a bolt-hole. One wondered why he had allowed himself to be effectively trapped on a remote station. She would make certain to ask him, after he was reattached.

What was most interesting, however, was the presence of Thirteen-Forty-Four.

Alone of the sixteen Lyre Institute operatives who had been present on Tinsori Light, Thirteen-Forty-Four had not retreated from the imaginary mind-eating monster.

Thirteen-Forty-Four was resourceful, but despite several annoying enthusiasms, Director Varge was not a fool. Yet Varge had panicked and run, while Delia Bell—had not.

Clearly, her first move must be to contact Thirteen-Forty-Four.

Ren Stryker

. . . .

THEY WERE MET AT DOCKING BY BELAGRAS DENOBLI, WHO BOWED to Anthora with more good intent than mode.

"Lady, thank you for comin' to us for this. We didn't want to take risks, after Marsi, but it's not right, keeping him doped up like he is."

"I understand, and I agree. If you will take me to him, I will see if I may apply a better solution."

She moved her hand.

"I make you known to my companions, Tolly Jones and Hazenthull nor'Phelium."

Gracie nodded. "Mentor. Security. Good to see you both again."

Tolly grinned.

"Pleased to be able to come." He looked up slightly. "Ren, this is what we talked about, right? Healer yos'Galan's gonna look an' see if there's something gone wrong with Kilber Tarymax's programming. If there is, she can maybe put it right for him."

"Yes," came the clear, musical voice. "Thank you, Mentor. Healer yos'Galan, welcome. If there is anything I can do to assist you in your work, only ask."

"That is very gracious, Ren Stryker. Know that I will do my best for Ser Tarymax." She looked at Gracie, who nodded, and turned, waving them to follow him.

"Right this way, then, Healer."

Belagras Denobli was a practical person with a pattern that was particularly soothing to Healer senses: balanced, with a strong thread of justice, tempered by the open weave of tolerance. There were many attachments and influences, including what she thought might be extensive family ties, and, surprisingly, several threads that seemed to have been set by treasured differences.

Yes, a strong, pleasing pattern. Anthora sighed, and allowed Belagras Denobli to fade from her awareness as they walked down a short hall with a closed door at the end.

"Ren, open Security Room Three, please."

The door before them slid away; Belagras Denobli stepped aside, so that Anthora could pass. She felt Tolly Jones slip his hand under her elbow, apprising her of his presence at her back. They crossed the threshold, and Anthora stopped, hands rising in protest.

Her Inner Eyes saw—nothing. No pattern, not even desolation. Merely—emptiness illuminated faintly by the subdued glow of the body's autonomic systems.

"Pilot Denobli," she said, hearing the pain in her own voice, "Ren Stryker. There is nothing I can do. Kilber Tarymax is gone."

Station Day 44
Seignur Veeoni's Workshop

"SHE'S IN," DELIA SAID. "WANTS A MEET AT HER DOCK."

Seignur Veeoni looked up from the screen she had been studying.

"At her *dock*," she repeated. "M Traven, your opinion, please."

M Traven sighed, and glanced at Delia.

"Try to avoid inside the ship," she said. "Hate having to go through hullplate."

Delia smiled.

"I'll stay on the dock, and I'll walk away after the meet," she said. "No worries."

"That is the most desired outcome," Seignur Veeoni said. "However, I warn against overconfidence. Also, M Traven *can* go through hullplate, if necessary. Your first object is to remain at large. If you are restrained, your object is then to remain alive until liberated. I hope this is sufficiently clear."

Surprising, but clear. Delia nodded.

"Yes'm. Stay on the dock. If I can't avoid being brought aboard, I'll wait for Traven to knock a hole in the hull and bring me home."

A flat black stare directly into her eyes before Seignur Veeoni returned to the screen.

"Do you have any questions regarding the mission or its purpose?"

"No'm." Delia paused and glanced at Traven, who was looking in the other direction. On her own, was she? That was fair. She had to learn her way sometime.

"I'll be fine, Researcher," she said. "Just gonna sell this and come back. Right?"

"That is the plan. Report to me when you return."

Administrative Tower

"REN ZEL, WHEN WOULD IT BE CONVENIENT FOR US TO TALK?"

Ren Zel glanced up from the screen detailing the sparse history of the ship *Eltoro*.

"We may talk now, Catie, if it is also convenient for you."

"Yes," she said. "I have been studying the star charts."

"That is also one of my studies," Ren Zel said, when she said nothing else. "Have you a question regarding a particular chart?"

"Yes and no," Catie said. "I note that this location is designated variously in the charts, as Tinsori Station, Ghost Station, or Unsafe Space. While all of these designations may have been accurate at one point, they are not accurate now. I wish to amend the charts."

"There is a procedure for amending charts," Ren Zel said. "What is your correction?"

"This location is Catalinc Station. Tinsori Light is . . . finally dead, and will not be resuscitated. I have looked up 'ghost'—I am not a 'ghost' but a thriving station who is open for commerce. Tocohl says that I will soon be noted on the trade routes. Those, too, should be accurate."

"I agree. There are letters to be written, and applications to be completed in order to make this change and bring the charts up-to-date. Shall I file these for you, or will you take charge of the matter yourself?"

Catie said nothing. Ren Zel rose and went over to brew a cup of tea.

"Understand that I value you," Catie said slowly.

"I do understand that," Ren Zel said, bringing his tea back to the desk. "But I am only temporarily first light keeper."

"Yes!" Catie said. "You do understand. What I would like

best is if Jen Sin and I would together submit these—letters and applications. Is that possible?"

"I believe so, but the paperwork will tell us more. Please realize that the charts cannot be amended until the proper forms are filed. If you wish Jen Sin to sign, you must wait until he is out of the 'doc."

"I am willing to wait. Do you think you might help me fill out the proper forms, so that they are ready for him to sign, when he is able?"

Ren Zel smiled.

"I think I might do that, yes. I will find the proper forms and instructions and send them to you to study. Apply to me with any questions."

"Thank you, Ren Zel."

"It is my pleasure," he assured her.

Eltoro
Dock D

....

FORMYNE WAS LEANING AGAINST THE RAMP RAIL, ARMS CROSSED over her chest, her expression bored. There was a faint shimmer in the air where the ramp touched the dock, which would be the privacy field. Not unexpected.

Delia hefted the crate she was carrying.

"*Eltoro*? Got them items you wanted."

Formyne didn't move.

"Took you long enough," she said. "Bring it up here."

Delia stepped onto the ramp, feeling the prickle along her scalp and skin, which was the field taking note of her.

She put the box down next to Formyne's boots and straightened, feeling the unaccustomed movement in her hair as she straightened.

"So." Formyne considered her dispassionately. "Tell me the truth, Delia Bell."

She felt a shiver of nausea, and for a panicked second, thought—and the feeling faded into a specific warm glow of health and well-being. She took a careful breath, and defeated the urge to smile.

Instead, she bent her head, that being the proper respect to a Director, unless she was ordered to look up.

"According to orders, I became part of the work team building the station's new core array. I was given my own workbench, allowed to use my own tools and material. The mission proceeded as planned, until Light Keeper yos'Phelium, under orders from Seignur Veeoni, destroyed the array."

"Why destroy the array?"

"Because Seignur Veeoni has another, more efficient system in place. The rack-and-tile rebuild was only ever s'posed to hold the station stable until she could install the upgrade."

"I want control of this station," Formyne said, not mincing words. "Deliver it to me."

Delia shrugged.

"I can't get in the new core, 'cept I'm with the researcher. She's the key. You want in, you gotta follow Veeoni inside and re-initialize with yourself as primary director."

Formyne looked at her, thoughtfully, which wasn't what she'd necessarily hoped for, then her eyes narrowed.

"What's that in your hair? Memory beads?"

Gotcha, Delia thought, raising a tentative hand to her head.

"Not memory beads. Not as such. These deflect the field emitted by the new installation. There was a glitch—"

"Is that what drove off fourteen agents, and a Director, and killed Director Ling?"

"That's it," Delia said earnestly.

"But nobody else."

"Proximity matters. I got beads 'cause the materials we're working with aren't stable, quite." She nodded at the box sitting on the ramp. "There's a set in there for you. That's all I could risk."

Formyne looked down at the box, like she was weighing having Delia open it, which she wouldn't do, not out on the ramp, even with the privacy field up.

Delia shifted her feet slightly. Formyne looked up with a frown.

"The researcher keeps a tight watch," Delia said, apologetically. "Best I don't call attention to myself."

"Prudent," Director Formyne said. "Go."

"Yes, Director," Delia said—and went.

Station Day 48
Administrative Tower

SHIPS CONTINUED TO ARRIVE.

A Scout remediation team, sent on the word of Scout Commander yos'Phelium. Experts from the Carresens Yard. Two hopeful small traders, who declared themselves willing to await the arrival of Trader Arbuthnot aboard *Generous Passage*, who had serendipitously only just written with an updated arrival time. *Eltoro*, in need of a safe docking while repairs were made by crew. A full-service caf with its own team of tenders, cooks, and chef, courtesy of Master Trader yos'Galan.

In addition to *Generous Passage*, the history of which ship Ren Zel had been forced to look up, Tinsori Light Station had been honored with the information that *Vivulonj Prosperu*, the Uncle's very ship, expected to dock within ten Standard Days.

That might have been enough for a temporary light keeper's fraying nerve, but one more bit of news had arrived in his queue only moments ago.

Dragon's Way expected to dock within the next ten Standard Days.

Korval's Own Ship, Ren Zel thought, sharing a dock with the Uncle's own ship.

He rose and went over to the tea maker—one of the small items they had brought for Jen Sin's comfort—dialed for a cup of heavily caffeinated working tea. While it brewed, he stood, eyes closed, reviewing a pilot's centering technique.

Ping! stated the tea maker.

He collected the cup and went back to his desk.

In truth, the Uncle and Korval must meet at some point, given the awakening of Catalinc Station, and the projected residence of Seignur Veeoni, once the breach hall was repaired to her specifications.

Ren Zel sipped tea.

Considering the matter even further, he would be surprised to learn that there was not paperwork to be done—between Korval and Catalinc Station, certainly, and possibly with Crystal Energy Systems.

All of which shone a light of positivity on the announced arrivals.

And it were better that the delm arrive sooner, rather than later, given Anthora's lofty plans of a Healer Hall on-station. Korval was so thin that it seemed to him unlikely that such a scheme could win favor. The clan naturally held Anthora's twins in its care, but would the delm wish for a child of the clan to be born far and away on Tinsori Light?

For himself—he greatly feared that he was finding his stride as an administrator, but station administrators could, after all, be hired. And that left aside whatever was the delm's intention for Jen Sin. Would he be required to remain here, where he had been prisoned for two hundred Standards, or might he be allowed to stretch his wings again? He had been a courier pilot. Surely, after such a time, he chafed to have a ship in his hands.

Well, none of that was for him to decide.

He glanced at the time. Nearly to shift-end. He was to meet Anthora at the Sereneco Hall residences when duty was done with him for the day. She had shown him the plans she and Catie had made for gardens. They were ambitious enough that he had expressed his hope that Gordy had not stinted on the matter of seeds and cuttings, which had earned him a haughty look.

And that had relieved him, a little. She had been as distressed as he had ever seen her at finding the lad on Ren Stryker gone before ever she had been told of his case.

One could not save everyone. He knew that, and she did. Still, he was glad for the diversion of the gardens, and the grand plans for flowers.

And he supposed that it would be very pleasant, after one's duty was over, to go home to a small suite tucked within the garden, and—

The comm chimed.

"Carresens tradeship *Disian*, out of Margate, arriving on the suggestion of Master Trader Shan yos'Galan and Trader Janifer Carresens-Denobli, to visit Tocohl, if she is available."

Ren Zel blinked, and touched the switch.

"Light Keeper Ren Zel dea'Judan. Welcome, *Disian*. I will inform Tocohl. Do you have trade or other business to pursue?"

"Just a visit," *Disian* assured him. "Though my crew will be glad of leave, and are happy to assist as needed."

"That is well, then. Thank you. Cleared for C level, direct access, docking three."

Common Meeting Space

"WELL!" SAID *DISIAN*. "THINGS HAVE CERTAINLY BECOME MORE interesting here since Trader Janifer's message! How wonderful that you will be free to pursue your purpose, and that Catalinc Station awoke so timely! I will want to meet her, of course—and Joyita and *Bechimo*, as well! And I must of course speak with the mentor, and—do you know what?"

"What?" Tocohl asked, somewhat amazed by all this enthusiasm.

"We should throw a party!"

Tocohl laughed.

"Is that funny?"

"Not at all. You will want to speak with Joyita at once."

Eltoro
Dock D

....

THE RESEARCHER WAS REGULAR IN HER HABITS, EVERY DAY AT the same hour visiting the same room near the breach hall.

She always drove in the couldn't-be-missed Crystal Energy jitney, and she always wore a glittering net of beads over her close-cropped black hair, looking for all the worlds like a helmet made of crystal.

Sometimes, she had Thirteen-Forty-Four with her.

Other times, she was accompanied by a short, broad woman in what looked like merc leathers, pellet gun worn openly on a belt at her waist.

Sometimes, she went alone.

It was, in Director Formyne's considered opinion, stupid to keep to such a strict routine. It was best to vary, in case enemies were watching and laying plans to strip you of everything you valued in life.

However, as such regularity did make Director Formyne's mission easier, she was not about to complain. She merely watched, and made a timetable, determining the pattern—when Veeoni took a companion, and when she did not. She had her aides check every inch along the path, to be certain that there were no hidden traps set for those who were not Seignur Veeoni, with or without a companion.

There were no such traps, which was well, as Director Formyne could scarcely afford to lose even one of her four aides.

She would herself handle Seignur Veeoni, but there was another piece in this game.

The light keeper.

It happened there were three light keepers—one Ren Zel

dea'Judan of Clan Korval, formerly first mate on *Dutiful Passage*, formerly clanless pilot, now attached to Korval's witch, Anthora yos'Galan.

The second light keeper was a conscript; temporary assistance brought onboard in the emergency created by the wounding of the light keeper who mattered.

Jen Sin yos'Phelium was in league with Seignur Veeoni; a necessary part of her scheme to rule Tinsori Station. The two of them together had gathered station systems into a new rack-and-tile array constructed for the purpose. When Veeoni had completed her superior system, it was Light Keeper yos'Phelium who had decommissioned the temporary array.

Given the extent of his wounds, it was possible that Light Keeper yos'Phelium was merely a tool. However, it was best to be certain before she gave him a fitting death, and he would in any case have some use as a hostage to the good behavior of all those presently on-station.

She considered moving before Light Keeper yos'Phelium was released from the crisis 'doc aboard the smartship *Bechimo*. Considered it—and rejected it. *Bechimo* would also be a worthy acquisition. And there again, Light Keeper yos'Phelium held a key.

She would wait, laying plans. It would be best if all were done at once. She would work for that timing.

It would be optimum if she made her move on a day when Veeoni had Thirteen-Forty-Four with her; however, that was not as necessary to her plan as the capture of Jen Sin yos'Phelium.

She would continue to plan, and to ride the scans. Though so far she had found nothing that might be connected to Veeoni's "more efficient" system, she was certain to find it soon. Such a system *must* register on the scans; she merely needed to modify her ranges.

Really, this was going quite well.

Tolly and Hazenthull's Private Quarters

THE COMM BUZZED.

Tolly opened an eye.

"Gotta remember to put out a *do not disturb* when we go off-shift," he muttered.

"Is there such a thing?" Hazenthull wondered from her curl around him.

"I've heard tell—"

The comm buzzed again.

"If you answer," Haz said, "it will stop making that annoying racket."

"There's that."

He extended an arm and tapped the comm.

"Tolly Jones."

"Mentor!" exclaimed a cheery and, despite it all, welcome voice. "Did I wake you?"

"Yeah, and Haz, too. Our fault. We gotta do better about filing our schedules. You in-station?"

"I arrived last shift. I have been having such fun talking with Tocohl, and Joyita, and *Bechimo*—and Catie! We've quite decided that I will be her aunt, and that she must feel free to ping me with questions, or just to chat! I've never had a niece."

"And Catie's never had an aunt, I'm betting," Tolly said, closing his eyes. "*Disian*, this is our off-shift and Haz an' me gotta get a little more rest. Is there anything I can help you with right now, or can I call you back when I'm all the way awake?"

"By all means call me back, so that we can talk about the party! But, yes, Mentor, I did want to tell you something specific. There is a ship docked at this station—*Eltoro*—from the Old Universe. He... went missing a few years ago now, on his way to pick up a temp-crew. We were on cordial terms, and I pinged him, but—"

Tolly felt himself tense. Around him, Haz sighed.

"He's not there, Mentor. I can see a tile-and-rack system on my scans, but no timonium."

"You tell the light keeper?"

"I told Catie, who judged it not an emergency, since *Eltoro* has been docked for some number of days. She put the information at the top of Light Keeper dea'Judan's queue, so he'll have it first thing he comes on duty."

"Good. That's a good plan. If there's no active trouble being made, we can prolly let it rest a couple hours more. I'll call you when *I'm* on duty and we'll catch up, right?"

"Right. Sleep well, Mentor—and Hazenthull, too. *Disian* out."

Tolly closed his eyes—and opened them again.

"Party?" he said.

Seignur Veeoni's Private Workroom

"YOU WISHED TO SEE ME, RESEARCHER?" ANTHORA YOS'GALAN asked.

"Yes. Thank you for coming to me, Healer. I wish to advise you that a Director and four operatives of the Lyre Institute are on-station. Their ship is *Eltoro*."

"Ah. Shall I rid us of them?"

"I ask that you will not interfere with them in any way. The Director, especially, is central to my Balance."

Anthora considered the Researcher's pattern. As always, it was difficult to parse, but she caught the glint of a knife's edge among the dense threads.

"You may not endanger the station," she said.

Seignur Veeoni inclined her head.

"Indeed, Healer, my past actions have taught me a stern lesson. I endanger no one but myself in this. The Director is central to my Balance. After I have secured her assistance, she will leave of her own will, taking her minions with her—or not, as she chooses."

She was telling the truth, Anthora Saw, though one could not like it.

"No danger to the station or to any who depend on the station," she repeated.

"I hold all danger to myself," Seignur Veeoni said, and that was definitive. One could not, unless there was a very good reason, interfere in another's Balance.

Anthora inclined her head.

"Please tell me, when the operatives are no longer necessary to your Balance."

"I will."

Station Day 49
Administrative Tower

"YES," REN ZEL SAID. "*DISIAN* PROVIDED VERY DISTURBING INFORmation, which would seem to indicate that *Eltoro* had been a Free Logic, and who was *possibly* subverted by—someone. Perhaps the present crew. And, in truth, Beloved, I was curious enough when they came to dock that I looked for what information there might be."

"Which was, I suppose, not very much," Anthora said, going to the tea maker. "Shall you have tea?"

"I had just brewed a cup before you arrived."

She nodded, and bent to the dial.

"The fact is," Ren Zel said, "that we have no facts. We cannot prove *Eltoro* was taken against his will. He may have died, naturally, from systems failure, and taken under salvage right by the current crew."

Anthora looked over her shoulder at him.

"Is there a record of that?"

"Not that I found, but we both know it may not have been filed, or has been filed but not populated the records as yet."

"Yes."

The tea maker *ping*ed and she brought her cup over to the desk.

"One hesitates to speculate on Seignur Veeoni's methods," she said, wryly. "I thought myself so clever to have talked her into a long Balance."

"And so you were," Ren Zel said, with a smile. "Her brother is coming, you know."

"Yes, you had said. Then we will have two of the same to cope with, rather than one."

"Do you think so? I rather hoped he would take her in hand."

Anthora laughed.

"Well, and perhaps he will, at that."

Station Day 51
Bechimo
Dock A

....

A CHIME WAS GOING OFF IN HIS EAR, SOFT, BUT GROWING STEADILY louder. The air was scented with vanilla.

Jen Sin opened his eyes.

The hood of an autodoc curved away above him, and for a moment—but no. It was not flat, but definitely curved. More, the air was warm. Wherever he was, he was not on the recovery deck.

He took a breath, and tentatively, like a child poking at a beehive with a stick, considered his last memories.

Tinsori Light. The array exploding. Pain.

Lorith. Gods, Lorith.

"Catie?" he murmured.

"*Bechimo*, Light Keeper," said that mellow voice, gently. "You have been in my crisis 'doc, which has just now released you from treatment."

"I thank you," Jen Sin said, and rolled off the pallet, bare feet finding carpet. His leathers were folded onto a chair next to the unit, his boots standing beneath. He dressed, checked his pockets, touched his left ear, finding the silver ring in its place.

"Will Captain Waitley see me?" he said then.

"She awaits you in the galley. Please follow the blue line."

"You're looking well," Theo greeted him.

"I'm feeling well," he told her, hoisting himself onto the stool opposite her. He raised an eyebrow at the tea set and the platter of handwiches.

"No maize buttons?"

"Ren Zel deputized Clarence. He's been living in the Spinward Dorms, while Ren Zel took over the main tower." Theo sighed and picked up the teapot to pour. "It's been hard."

"I imagine it has been. How long have you been deprived?"

"Sixteen station days," she said, putting a cup in front of him.

He stared at her in consternation.

"*Sixteen?*"

Theo glared at him.

"Was that *too long*? You smashed the array with *a starbar*," she snapped. "The 'doc had to do repairs at the cellular level! You should be *dead*, except you *got lucky*."

Lucky. Of course, he had gotten lucky.

Jen Sin raised his hands, showing her empty palms and widespread fingers.

"Forgive me, Cousin," he said soothingly. "Merely, I was—surprised. What has happened, while I slept?"

She looked at him over the rim of her cup.

"Quick list or details?"

"Quick list. I will apply for details later."

"Right."

She put her cup down, and held up her hand, all fingers curled into her palm.

"One"—she extended her forefinger—"somebody introduced a virus into the old systems, and Tocohl passed authority to Catalinc Station."

Next finger.

"Two—Tinsori Light took over the new core; you smashed the array; and got zapped by the field. Light Keeper Lorith—" She hesitated.

Jen Sin bent his head above his cup.

"I recall, thank you."

"Yes," Theo hesitated. "*Al'bresh venat'i*, Cousin," she said.

"Everything that is kind," he murmured, and took a breath. "Else?"

"Well—three more. Anthora scared all of the operatives of the Lyre Institute who were on-station, off-station, and she's pretty sure they'll stay away for a while."

"Is she? That would be a boon. I don't hide from you that I have become very weary of the Lyre Institute."

"Four—the pros from the Carresens Yard have arrived, and

a Scout team specializing in Old Tech. They've taken charge of the Old Core, and are working with the Carresens to clean and detach the old maintenance bays. Ren Stryker's been rendering the pieces down into useful components."

She frowned, picked up her cup and sipped, then nodded at the platter.

"You're supposed to eat one or six of those," she said.

"Ah." He selected a triangle of dark bread, finding it stuffed with sharp-tasting cheese. It was quite good.

"It seems you have had a busy time, indeed."

Theo helped herself to a triangle.

"Gordy sent that he expects to arrive within the next week, Standard," she said. "Uncle sent word that he'll be coming in."

He may have said something under his breath. Theo raised an eyebrow.

"Catie asked him to come. He's her builder, she says."

"That is correct," Jen Sin said. "I will be pleased to meet him."

He ate another triangle.

"Miri and Val Con have sent word that they're coming in, too," Theo said.

Jen Sin stopped with a triangle halfway to his mouth.

"Is that Miri and Val Con, or Korval?"

Theo blinked thoughtfully.

"Joyita, please show Jen Sin a transcript of the message we received from *Dragon's Way*."

"Yes, Captain," Joyita said, and the table-side came live.

> *Theo, I need board time, so there wasn't anything better we could think to do than come out and see the clan's new home away from home, and introduce ourselves all around. See you soon. Miri*

Jen Sin sighed.

"Miri and Val Con, then," he said. "With the possibility of Korval, later."

Theo shrugged and ate a triangle. How pleasant it must be, he thought, to be kin, but not clan, and able to dismiss the delm with a shrug.

"There's three birds sitting on the light pole at the end of our dock," Theo said. "They've been there since Stost brought you in."

"I see. It sounds as if I ought to be about my business, then, Cousin. Unless there is some way in which I may serve you?"

"If you could convince Ren Zel that you're well enough to go back to work, then he could go back to the Spinward Arcade, and Clarence could come home and maybe make a celebratory batch of maize buttons."

He drained his cup and slid to his feet.

"I will make it a priority to return Clarence to you," he said.

"I'd appreciate it," Theo said, and walked him to the hatch.

The birds watched him walk down the ramp, and threw themselves into the air the moment his boots touched the dock.

They flashed around his head, and he stopped, for fear of collision.

The green bird landed on his shoulder.

"Jen Sin! Are you well? You didn't die?"

"I did not die, and I am very well, indeed. Tell me all your news, Catie."

"I am fully Station now. *Disian* has arrived, and we have been becoming acquainted—she has offered to be my aunt. Joyita was planning a secret party, but *Disian* said that, no, I should be let to know, in case there was anyone in particular I wanted to invite. I invite you, and my builder, who was coming anyway, to fetch something from Ren Stryker, so that is fortunate."

"Fortunate, indeed. What sort of secret party did Joyita envision, I wonder?"

"He said, *a becoming party*. And *Disian* said *a birthday party*. They're still discussing it."

"And you?"

"I researched *birthday party*, and I don't think that is . . . exactly correct. Nor do I think *becoming party* is correct, either. But, Jen Sin, will you come to the party, whatever its name?"

"I am honored to receive an invitation," he said. "Of course I will come."

He turned toward the lift.

"Oh," Catie said. "Anthora wishes to see you in the community room before you go back to the tower."

He raised an eyebrow.

"I have my orders, I see."

"Did I use the wrong words, or the wrong inflection? Truly, Jen Sin, it was not an order, only—"

"Only an expression of my cousin Anthora's wish," he interrupted gently. "You made no error; we merely see from this that the 'doc did not excise my lamentable sense of humor. Is Anthora at the community room now?"

"She is on her way, and says that she will be there before you if you dawdle any longer."

"A challenge, in fact!"

"Is that more humor?"

"Sadly so. Do you come with me?"

"Yes, of course!"

Community Room

NO THREADBARE PETITIONER, BUT A FULL PILOT OF KORVAL arrived in the community room, his stride firm, his shoulders level, and his eyes sharp. His pattern glittered: amber, umber, and living green. Of the harsh black lacing that had confined him, there was no sign. His ties—ah. The link with Theo had strengthened, as had the links to Ren Zel and herself, and there was something else—a new heart-link, not yet fully formed, but vibrating with potential.

"Yes, that is a *much* more pleasing mode, Cousin Jen Sin!"

She rose from behind the table and went forward, both hands extended.

He put his hands in hers without hesitation, while he searched her face.

"I hope you took no hurt," he said.

Her eyebrows rose.

"I was not the one who threw myself between the station and destruction," she said. "If I was able to soften the edge of the pain, that is no less than my calling."

She kept possession of one of his hands as she turned and gestured toward the table.

"Will you eat before we go?"

"Theo fed me," he told her. "Also, I would be remiss if I did not inform you that I have promised to return Clarence to his proper post as quickly as I might. So, if we are to go—"

"We had best go soon," she finished. "Very good. At least let us each take a bottle of tea against need. I have the jitney."

Spinward Arcade and Dorms
Crew Caf

. . . .

"HEY, DEELS."

Tolly slid into a chair across from her, cup of 'toot in hand. "Outta work?"

"Figured to see if there's anything I can help with." She raised her own cup and gave him wide-eyed innocence, for practice. "I can do what I want on my off-shift."

Tolly tipped his head, lips pursed, considering, and produced a judicious nod.

"Haz an' me were just talkin' about the concept of *time off*. Maybe we could all get together on our sometime-offs. Play cards."

"You cheat?"

"Only if I hafta."

She snorted. Had some 'toot. Had some more. Put the cup down.

"So, you come special lookin' for me?"

"I did. Thought you might wanna know Formyne's on-station."

"Yeah, I talked to her. Hasn't changed any."

"How'd it go with the command line?"

"She gave it out. Had a twinge—nerves is what I'm thinking—and a bit of feeling *too* fine, but if that's what I gotta put up with for not caring about the command line, I can do it."

"Does the Healer know about Formyne?"

"She knows. The researcher told her. Also said Formyne was part of her long Balance that the Healer talked her into, and bargained a hands-off."

Tolly eyed her.

"I'm not liking the sound of this. What's the researcher want with Formyne?"

"The coords and codes for the pattern-safe and gene-bank."

"Formyne got all that?"

Delia shrugged.

"Good chance she's got at least some of it. And if Seignur Veeoni gets a little—"

"She'll get the rest." Tolly sighed.

"Up to me, I'm willing to let her eat Formyne alive. But she don't have much sense in terms of collateral damage."

"Traven and me went over the planning with her. It goes good, there's never a bobble, and not even the light keeper knows."

"It goes bad?"

"It goes bad, we could lose her. Traven told her that, but she don't seem worried."

"Anybody let the light keeper know? Just in case?"

"I'm guessing Anthora told 'im."

Tolly frowned.

"Word from a friend is that *Eltoro*—that's Formyne's ship—was Free, old and sick."

"'Splains why Formyne has him."

"Yeah, but she don't. Friend says she pinged him an' no answer. No timonium spill, either."

Delia sighed and picked up her cup.

"Then she can't hurt him."

"True. But she can still hurt us. Chances she's got one o'those arrays the researcher left for her onboard?"

"Pretty good," Delia said. "But here's what—station don't run on rack-and-tile, anymore, now does it?"

Tolly blinked. Picked up his cup and knocked back what was left.

"Now that you mention it—no. The station don't run on rack-and-tile. Tocohl locked down all the old systems tight, and there's the Scouts stripping out the old core for good an' all."

"So you came all the way over here for nothing?"

"Not for nothing." He rose and gave her a jaunty bow. "Always nice to spend time with family."

Sereneco Hall

"CATIE DISCOVERED THIS IN THE BUILDER'S NOTES," ANTHORA said. As the pilot who held the route, she was driving the jitney, and at a pace that might have made Hazenthull think twice.

"Ren Zel unsealed it. Catie, Theo, and I toured. Seeing that it would do very well, indeed, Catie and I took it upon ourselves to make the area seemly. There is still more to do, but I think you will agree that it is an extremely nice space."

He looked at the side of her face.

"Another arcade has been opened? Are we expecting a third wave?"

"One gathers that the waves have done their work. What remains to us now is an influx of experts. This, however, is something else."

The hall broke into a T, and she swung the jitney to the right with a will, speed unchecked despite the large doors directly ahead of them.

The doors opened, the jitney dashed through, and stopped before—

A garden.

It was three times the size of the garden plot in the Spinward Arcade. A small red bridge arched charmingly over a pool of water. Flowers bloomed along tiny, artful hills over which a stone path meandered.

The birds—*his* birds—shot forward, danced an aerial jig over the bridge, and dashed over the largest of the hillocks.

Jen Sin sighed.

"I had hoped you would like it," Anthora said from beside him.

"I like it very much. You have produced art and comfort, Cousin. I feel that it will become a favorite with me."

"Excellent."

She swung out of the jitney, and strode toward the garden.

"Come along, Cousin Jen Sin, do not dawdle! If you are to return Clarence to Theo's tender care this day, we must be light on our feet!"

He paused at the top of the tallest small hill, staring down into a small greensward surrounding—

"A Tree?"

"We brought a seedling in stasis—did Ren Zel not tell you?"

"He did, but he did not tell me that you intended to plant it."

"And nor did I. Then we discovered that the architect had built a residential court for the station master and such others as he might like to have near him.

"Catie will give you the details, and you will have to come back later to tour the residence. However, allow me to assure you that it is everything that is convenient, including direct high-speed tube access to the central tower."

"I had no notion," he murmured.

"And now you do!" Anthora said gaily. "One moment, I beg you—that planting over there looks a bit parched..."

She was gone. Jen Sin sank down onto his heels, crossing his arms over his knees and putting his chin on them.

The green bird fluttered down to land on his shoulder.

"Jen Sin? Are you displeased?" Catie asked.

He stirred.

"Not at all. Somewhat overwhelmed, perhaps. One's cousin is a force of nature herself. Also, I had been accustomed to thinking that I would not be staying very long."

"You had told me that you were going to leave."

"So I had. Would you mind dreadfully, if I did not leave?"

"I would like it if you stayed. But—do you not want to fly? Joyita thought you would wish it, above all else."

"Not—all else," he said, gingerly testing the expanded boundaries of himself. "Indeed, I foresee that I may wish to fly—and that I would wish to come home. Here."

"Will you teach me?"

"Teach you what, I wonder?"

"To fly. Joyita is a pilot."

"So he is. I am not in principle opposed to teaching you to fly. Though I warn you the math will be very different from what you are accustomed to."

"I can learn new math," Catie said haughtily.

He laughed and came to his feet.

"I make no doubt. For now, here comes Anthora. I am about to be swept off to duty again."

The green bird launched itself from his shoulder, spiraling upward to join the others.

Jen Sin walked down the hill to join his cousin Anthora at the jitney.

Eltoro
Dock D

DIRECTOR FORMYNE LEANED BACK IN HER CHAIR AND SMILED. Her patience had been rewarded.

Jen Sin yos'Phelium had been freed from the 'doc.

Plans could go forward immediately.

Administrative Tower

CLARENCE HAD BEEN ALLOWED TO CLOSE THE SPINWARD OFFICE early and return to his ship, while Ren Zel and Jen Sin sat late in the main tower, going over the events of the last while.

"Finally, we have this," Ren Zel said. "Catie wishes to see the charts and route-lists brought to accuracy with regard to the name of this station."

Jen Sin raised his eyebrows.

"Catalinc Station? I concur. Have you filed the change?"

Ren Zel reached for his teacup.

"I assisted Catie in filling out the paperwork. She felt that, as Commander yos'Phelium's Field Judgment is so recent a thing, petitions signed by both station and station master would make an eloquent point."

Jen Sin raised an eyebrow.

"Catie, if you file on your own behalf the point may be sharper."

"Yes, but I don't wish to be divisive. I wish to be inclusive. Everyone is welcome here. Everyone will be treated equally. I think that is the core of Scout Commander yos'Phelium's judgment."

"In that wise, I am honored. Let us sign, send, and get this underway."

He turned to look at Ren Zel, weary face and sparkling eyes.

"Go home to your lady, Cousin. If she allows it, get some rest."

"I have a suggestion regarding your party," Jen Sin said. "What do you think of a Name Day Party?"

"Will we have to wait for the changes to be made? I would like *Disian*, Tocohl, Joyita, and *Bechimo* to attend, but none of them will be staying very long."

"I think that, having filed a reasonable correction, we may

proceed. Will you call yourself Tinsori Light until the trade guild catches its records up?"

"No!"

"There you have it. And you know—my delm is incoming very soon. Perhaps they would like to be invited to your party, too."

"Is that another sharp point?"

"I fear it may be. I'm edges along all sides, you'll find."

"Let me think about it."

"Certainly, there is no rush."

He leaned forward and checked the screen, but there was nothing that required his attention. Ren Zel had performed the impossible, and left the office caught up.

Very possibly, he should go off-shift, and strive to become more regular in his habits. Only, he was not particularly tired. A game of cards, he thought, or darts with a like-minded cousin. Perhaps he might tour the Sereneco Hall residence. Or—

He touched the comm.

"*Bechimo*, Comm Officer Joyita speaking."

"Jen Sin yos'Phelium," he said. "I wonder if Stost or Chernak might be available to give me a tour of *Spiral Dance*."

Seignur Veeoni's Private Workroom

"IT IS TIME."

Seignur Veeoni rose, and so did Delia.

Seignur Veeoni held up a hand.

"Today, I will go alone, Tech Bell. Tocohl has uploaded a new data-block. Your time will be better spent indexing and updating our library."

Delia hesitated, then moved forward.

"Professional opinion, ma'am. Best stick to the schedule. Director Formyne will have that pat, an' she might wonder after a vary. She's not much good at being undercover, but she was born with details in 'er blood."

"That is a useful insight, Tech Bell. I thank you. I remind you that we had taken care to seed the details with random. Director Formyne may notice, but she will not likely withhold herself."

She paused.

"Unless she is counting on your assistance? Surely, so simple a thing as overpowering a desk-bound researcher ought to be within her means, no matter how poor she is undercover. Have I misjudged her?"

Delia took a breath.

"No'm. She'd rather have backup, but she's pretty confident in herself. Comes with bein' a Director."

"My reading of her character is accurate, then. I note that it is now past time, and that a woman with details in her blood will notice that."

"Yes'm," Delia said, dropping back. "Be careful, ma'am."

Eltoro
Dock D

. . . .

VEEONI WAS TRAVELING ALONE.

That was a vary—she should have had Thirteen-Forty-Four with her—but there had been varies before. Director Formyne would have preferred Thirteen-Forty-Four, for insurance, but her absence was no reason to abort, and there was every reason to continue.

Her aides had their orders.

Director Formyne moved.

Spiral Dance
Dock A

....

CHERNAK AND STOST HAD BOTH BEEN AVAILABLE TO HIM. THE tour had been extensive, and fascinating.

Jen Sin lingered on the bridge, considering the board, subtly different from the standardized boards he knew best. The screens were more numerous, pilot and copilot each having six tiles, and an extension that could be opened at will.

She had worked hard in her life, had *Spiral Dance*. The tale of long hours was told by the pattern of wear on the piloting boards. Some keys were smooth and blank, the symbols quite rubbed off, but they would have been the most used, that the pilot had by heart.

The leather seats were worn, and the copilot's chair showed scars where the rope lashing the tree into place had rubbed.

Jen Sin sighed.

"And she dances, yet," he murmured.

"We flew her, Stost and I. She was a great-hearted and giving lady, recognized by a hero of the Old War as a hero of the Old War," Chernak said.

"Captain Theo's brother was to have seen her refitted and brought back to spec, but she was recalled to duty before he was able," Chernak added.

Jen Sin rubbed the top of the pilot's chair, the leather like silk under his fingers.

"We will eventually have a full-service yard here," he murmured. "Perhaps . . . Captain Theo's brother . . . will allow us the honor of restoring her."

Stost and Chernak exchanged a glance.

"That would be worthy," Stost said. "Tinsori Light, the greatest of the Enemy's works, has been defeated, hero-ship at dock, awaiting her next call to duty."

"You say it well, my Stost. We will bring it to our captain." Chernak looked to him, and bowed her head.

"Light Keeper. My apologies. It is yours to bring to the captain."

"And so I shall," Jen Sin said, turning away from the board with a pang.

"In the meanwhile, my friends, I have been longer away from duty than I had anticipated. I am called."

"Yes," said Chernak, and Stost extended a large hand.

Jen Sin looked down at the ship's key, looked up into Stost's wide brown face.

"We must go through channels, do we agree? Captain Theo was willing for me to hold key and ship, I know. However, her brother will soon arrive on-station. Let everything remain where it is, until we hear his decision."

"Yes," Stost said, and slipped the key into his belt.

Breach Hall

....

SEIGNUR VEEONI DROVE HER USUAL ROUTE TO THE OFF-SITE workroom. She looked neither to the left nor the right, her thoughts less on the route and more on the work to be done.

Arriving, she placed her hand against the reader, the door opened—

And there was an arm around her throat and a hard object pressed to the side of her head.

Her heartbeat spiked; her breath came fast.

Interesting, she thought. Perhaps this was what overconfidence felt like.

"Who are you?" she demanded, hearing her voice quaver. "What do you want?"

"Anj Formyne, Researcher. Just want to chat a little about your new line of work."

Seignur Veeoni sat quietly. The pressure of the object against her head increased.

"Take us inside," snapped Anj Formyne.

Seignur Veeoni reached carefully for the stick, and drove the jitney into the workroom.

The door slid closed, and the lock engaged, glowing bright blue in the dim, empty hallway.

Spiral Dance
Dock A

. . . .

JEN SIN WAS FIRST DOWN THE RAMP, CHERNAK AND STOST BEHIND. They had said their good-shifts, and he turned right, toward the lift, while they went left, toward *Bechimo*.

His birds arose from their perch on the light bar, the green one settling to his shoulder, as had become its habit.

"You would have enjoyed that, I think," Jen Sin said companionably.

"I would have liked to tour," the green bird said in Catie's voice. "Only I wasn't invited."

Jen Sin blinked.

"That was rude of me. Forgive me, Catie. Next time, if I fail of offering an invitation, ask."

"I will."

"Yes, but know that some meetings on private ships will remain private."

"Of course."

Jen Sin laughed, softly, and turned into the long hall leading to the lift that would take him back to the tower. He would make certain that there was nothing pressing, and then take an off-shift. Tomorrow, he promised himself, he would make a proper schedule for himself, and—

"Light Keeper yos'Phelium," Catie said.

Jen Sin's blood ran cold.

"*Bechimo* reports a situation. Unusual energies emanating from *Ahab-Esais*, at the repair dock. *Bechimo* believes the Struven unit is about to fail catastrophically."

Ahab-Esais, at the repair dock. There were crews at work in that section. If the ship blew at dock—

"Alarm!" he snapped, leaping into a run. There was an admin

station just the end of the hall and to the left. "Clear the repair docks, now!"

"Clearing docks," Catalinc Station confirmed. "Contacting pilot of record."

Pilot of record? he thought, but that would be—

"Pilot Tocohl reports herself remotely in charge of ship systems and prepared to cast off, as soon as the docks are clear," Catalinc Station said. "*Bechimo* reports emissions increasing to dangerous levels. Thirty-second warning sounded."

Ahead, the corner. He sensed, rather than saw, the birds, keeping pace.

"Jen Sin, there are people in the cross-hall!" Catie said sharply.

"*Ahab-Esais* away!" Tocohl said over the general station band.

Jen Sin turned the corner.

A figure stood at the admin station, crossbow leveled.

Breach Hall

"SHE AIN'T GONNA THANK US FOR THIS," TOLLY MUTTERED, GLARing at the locked door at the end of the hall.

"We are station security," Haz said from behind him. "We have been apprised of a situation which potentially threatens the integrity of the station. It is our duty to investigate such reports."

"Still," Tolly said, easing his back against the side wall. Haz was leaning against the wall opposite, not making any real effort to hide the large fact of herself.

"Station," Tolly said. "Security access to Core Aux Room Three, please."

The blue light went out. Tolly put his hand on the plate. The door opened.

Seignur Veeoni looked up from her screen with a frown.

Behind her, Anj Formyne was reclined on a diagnostic couch, eyes closed, breathing nice and even. Next to the couch was something that looked like a cranium—a little smaller than the standard. There were wires linking it to the crystal net on Formyne's head.

Tolly sighed.

"What's going on?"

"A matter of Balance," Seignur Veeoni told him. "Why are you here, Mentor?"

"I'm here because Haz 'n' me are station security, and we got a credible danger call."

"Ah." Seignur Veeoni frowned. "I told Tech Bell that I was in no danger, nor was the station in danger from me."

"Yeah, well, she ain't known you very long. Give 'er some time to work in, right?"

"Indeed. I am looking forward to a long and mutually beneficial relationship with Delia Bell."

"She feels the same. Now, like I was sayin'—what's going on?"

"This is an experimental design, based on the cranium download system that you are of course very familiar with, coupled with some interesting advances in data crystal technology that my sibling Andreth has been pursuing as a hobby."

She waved her hand toward the woman on the diagnostic couch.

"What I believe I am doing is, utilizing a crystal net that has been sensitized to Director Formyne, downloading her memory into a backup. This idea is not original with me—again, we have Andreth to thank, as he successfully downloaded the personality and mind of a badly damaged human into a cranium."

She sighed.

"Sadly, integrity could not be maintained in the typical cranium environment. However, that set Andreth—who is, as you will note, enthusiastic—on the quest for craniums of a smaller capacity, yet more tightly structured, which might support a human intelligence—possibly for years."

"You're downloading Formyne's memories," Tolly said, frowning. "Even if you get 'em, what makes you think you can read 'em?"

Seignur Veeoni smiled.

"There you have hit upon the knot at the center of my plan! I admit that I am far into theoretical territory with this, but I cannot know if the access difficulties are insurmountable until I attempt to surmount them."

"Right. And what happens to Formyne after she's finished contributing her memories to science?"

"Sharing her memories, Mentor. I am not a thief."

Tolly sighed.

"When the process here is completed," Seignur Veeoni said, "Director Formyne will go back to her ship, and she will leave the station. She may be a little muddled in her memories, because I quite appreciate that we do not wish her to return. But that's simply a matter of programming the diagnostic couch."

"She keeping her beads when she goes?" Tolly asked.

"I don't think that would be wise, do you, Mentor?"

"Just checking."

Tolly glanced over his shoulder and met Haz's eye. She lifted one large shoulder. Right.

He looked back to Seignur Veeoni.

"Since it looks like everything's in hand here, we'll be going. In the future, if you do need Security, just say 'security' or 'urgent security' and Station'll send us on the run."

"Thank you, Mentor, that is most helpful. Please lock the door when you leave."

Dock A Hallways

JEN SIN THREW HIMSELF TO THE DECK, ROLLING. THE FIRST BOLT missed him, and the second. He hit the wall, came up onto one knee, energy pistol in his hand—and froze.

The avians—his bold, brave birds—were diving at the assassin, claws out and sharp on an unprotected face.

The crossbow fell to the deck with a clatter.

Chernak arrived, swinging a large arm out to slam the assassin against the wall. He bounced. Stost caught him, and held him negligently, drooping over one arm.

Jen Sin got to his feet, slipping the little gun away.

"There was another shooter waiting at the entrance to the maintenance hall." Chernak used her thumb to point back the way they had come. "Orders, Light Keeper?"

"It happens that there are holding rooms, just down here," he said. "Let us secure them."

"Yes," said Stost, throwing the unconscious assassin over one shoulder. Jen Sin picked up the crossbow.

"I will get the other," Chernak said, and left them, returning with a similarly limp form over her shoulder, a crossbow slung on her belt.

"Thank you," Jen Sin said, and waved down the hall. "This way."

Dragon's Way
On Approach

MIRI AT THE BOARD, *DRAGON'S WAY* BROKE JUMP INTO PEACEFUL and uncluttered space. In the screens was a space station of peculiar proportions, missing a section of its ring.

Also in the screens—was a ship, tumbling like it had just broke dock, running like it hadn't paid its bills.

Val Con hit the comm.

"*Dragon's Way* out of Surebleak on approach. Station, is there a problem?"

Half a second later, the ship blew up.

Miri sat back in the pilot's chair, and threw a glance at her copilot.

"Looks like he's keeping the place in style, don't it?"

Station Day 52
Light Keeper's Meeting Room

HIS COUSIN VAL CON WAS A YOS'PHELIUM PILOT ON THE CLASSIC model—tall, wiry, and quick, with surprising green eyes under decided dark brows.

His cousin Miri was shorter than her tall lifemate, slender in her leathers, her face a study in angles, dominated by a pair of seeing grey eyes.

They embraced him, both, cheek to cheek, and then stepped away, Val Con keeping a grip on his shoulders.

"Well, Cousin?" he asked.

Jen Sin smiled.

"In fact, much better than I had dared hope, for a very long time," he said. "Cousin."

A sharp green gaze scored his face before Val Con released him with a nod.

Jen Sin half turned, moving a hand to show them the table and chairs, teapot and cups set decently ready.

"Please. We have amenities."

"So I see."

Val Con smiled, and swept Miri ahead of him to a chair. Jen Sin took charge of the pot, and poured, by which time the blue bird had landed on the table before Miri.

She smiled at it, and accepted her cup.

They sipped, and set the cups aside. The blue bird maintained its position, head turning first this way, then that, studying Miri from each eye in turn.

"Let us speak together as cousins," Val Con said. "There are things that must be said."

Jen Sin glanced to Miri, who gave him an easy grin.

"The delm'll get here soon enough," she said. "Enjoy us while we're unofficial."

"Indeed," Val Con murmured. "Now that the Uncle has come in, the delm will rise very soon, bearing paperwork. The delm will also need to speak with Catalinc Station. But, for now let us be cousins 'round the table."

He raised his cup and sipped, put it down with a sigh.

"The first thing I ought to say is—forgive us. We ought to have come sooner."

Jen Sin raised an eyebrow.

"With the clan as thin as I have seen, it is a wonder that you came at all. Still, you know, you're in good time for Catie's Name Day party, to which you are of course invited."

"Name Day party?"

"Indeed. We—that is she, as herself, and I as station master—have jointly filed to update the charts, routes, and market lists to remove the errors of, variously, Tinsori Light and Ghost Station, and register Catalinc Station as the proper name of this location."

"I see. Thus the Name Day party. Has confirmation been received? You must have sent very quickly."

"The light keepers and the station have quite agreed that in this case filing equals confirmation."

Val Con's lips twitched.

"I would have done the same. *Cha'trez*? Shall we attend Catie's Name Day party?"

"Don't see how we could come all this way, and not," Miri said, offering her forefinger. The blue bird hopped on, and she carefully raised finger and bird to eye level.

"This is fine work," she murmured. "Do they sing?"

"Perhaps they can be taught."

"There's a challenge."

She looked away from the bird, into his eyes, hers grey and appraising.

"You still hold with that letter you sent?"

Jen Sin stared at her, not quite—

And then he remembered.

"I believe that I have changed my mind, Cousin, if you will be kind enough to tell the delm so."

"Still," Val Con murmured, "one can leave a location and a position without it becoming fatal."

"That is true," Jen Sin admitted. "But I have lately come to understand that choice matters. Anthora tells me that I bear no taint such as denied me the space beyond Tinsori Light. In fact, I am free to choose.

"And I choose to stay, for the station I fought for, and the comrades who have stood with me. I wish to see what may happen, going forward."

"I understand," Val Con said. "You must remind us to tell you about our narrow escape from the homeworld."

Miri laughed softly. The blue bird left her finger, and joined its fellows, perched on the back of an unused chair.

"There is one more thing," Jen Sin said, reaching into his jacket. He brought out the stained courier packet and put it in the center of the table.

"Treachery prevented its delivery. I hope the clan—" The clan held so few now, and it had begun to haunt him, that Korval had fallen so far, for the failure of that packet to properly enter the game.

"Ah."

Val Con looked at the stained envelope, his mouth tightening, then looked into Jen Sin's face.

"I will be sure that the delm receives that. You should know, Cousin Jen Sin, that it has come to be thought, by the succeeding delms of Korval, that it was fortunate this packet was never delivered. The scheme outlined would have destroyed Korval, and Delium itself. As it was, Sinan was wiped from the board in the aftermath of treachery, and Rinork, too. Korval and Vaazemir survived."

Jen Sin stared at him.

"Fortunate," he repeated.

And began to laugh.

Station Day 60
Main Market Square

EVERYONE WAS INVITED TO CATIE'S NAME DAY, AND EVERYONE came.

Large screens had been set up around the market so that Ren Stryker, *Disian*, *Bechimo*, and Joyita might attend.

There had been music, provided by anyone in the least musical, including Val Con and Miri—he playing the omnichora, and she singing. Some had danced—including Theo and her crew, Tolly Jones and Hazenthull, Delia Bell and Traven.

There had above all been food, and formal declarations of good intent.

The Uncle had spoken in terms of the groundbreaking technology developed by Crystal Energy Systems, that had resulted in Catalinc Station's awakening.

Val Con had spoken in terms of Clan Korval's commitment to work with Catalinc Station to provide a stable and viable force in a long-neglected section of space.

Catalinc Station had herself spoken in terms of being happy in her work, and looking forward to the future and making many new friends.

Jen Sin had spoken, very briefly, thanking all and everyone who had come to the station's aid, and assisted in achieving the present happy result.

There was more dancing after, and the Scouts, with help from Kara and Theo, had set up a bowli ball court in one of the less-fragile corners of the square. Jen Sin joined neither, choosing instead to sit on a bench next to a small patch of lavender.

The green bird alighted on his shoulder.

"Jen Sin, are you unhappy?" asked Catie.

"In fact," he said, "I am content."

"Good," she said. "We'll go forward, then?"

He smiled.

"Yes. We will go forward."

Afterword

SO, THAT WAS FUN!

At least, it was fun for us, and we hope it was fun for you.

Salvage Right was an attack novel. By which we mean to say that neither one of us expected to write *this* book, and certainly not *this* book *now.*

Here's where we were in October 2021.

Steve was lead on the next book, after *Fair Trade, Trade Lanes.* Sharon was going to be lead on the book after that, due sometime in 2023, and she was kind of looking around inside her head, as she does, for story hooks and characters who were in—or about to be in—trouble. She was pretty certain that her next book would be the direct sequel to *Trader's Leap,* though there was just a little niggle of worry in the back of her mind about the characters last seen on Tinsori Light, in *Neogenesis.*

While those characters were in a better place than they had been, they were by no means in a *good* place. Jen Sin yos'Phelium in particular had stood a cruelly long and difficult shift. Not only that, but the Lyre Institute wanted Tinsori Light in the worst way—and we do mean that literally. The Institute's interest meant that Tolly Jones was in a risky spot—and then there was Tocohl's situation! Tocohl had never wanted to be a space station, and yet—here she was.

Clearly things needed to be made right at Tinsori Light.

A word here about authors and their relationship with their characters.

Authors are, well—gods. Small gods, certainly, and ever so fallible, but look at what we do.

We create worlds, and space stations. We place people in perilous situations. We give them lovers, and lives.

And we take them away.

All in the name of "telling a good story."

The characters on Tinsori Light deserved better from their authors. They deserved not only hope, but help. They deserved a reason to believe in good things again. They needed reasons to go forward.

More—they needed to *be able* to go forward.

So, this small tale of redemption, of people—even the unlikeliest group of people—working together and caring about each other as well as a mutually sustainable outcome.

It was fun—that word again—working with Seignur Veeoni, Tolly Jones, Delia Bell, Theo, Bechimo, Joyita—well, all of them. Seignur Veeoni came out especially well, we think.

And Jen Sin yos'Phelium?

What a pleasure to work with Jen Sin yos'Phelium, with his canted sense of humor and his need to protect those things that fall under his care, be it a handful of rogues and misfits, or an entire universe.

If you had half as much fun reading this book as we had writing it, we're well paid.

Speaking of fun, as we have been—Catalinc Station owes her call-name to the generosity of C.E. "Catie" Murphy. When we asked if we might use her name, she responded with such enormous enthusiasm, it brought us a whole new level of delight in the work.

Anyhow—the characters can take it from here, we think, though we may want to just peek in on them every so often, to see what they're up to.

To recap: We had fun. We hope you had fun, too.

—Sharon Lee and Steve Miller
Cat Farm and Confusion Factory
July 2022

Where do you get your ideas, Tinsori Light Edition

PEOPLE OFTEN ASK US WHERE WE GET OUR IDEAS, AND TINSORI Light is a geography that often comes up as a "how on earth did you think of *that*?"

Steve explains:

Many years ago—say in the mid-1990s—we were established enough in Maine (and the publishing world) to begin taking short vacations "at the ocean" . . . which for us meant Old Orchard Beach, since it was both the closest in time and the closest to what we expected of a beach, then—a sort of honkytonk boardwalky feeling, even if there was no real boardwalk.

In a kind of foreshadowing, and as a bow to Doc Smith, we'd chosen a place called "The Skylark Inn" for this adventure.

For some reason we'd decided to travel with a small AM-FM-Weather radio that could (if necessary) be powered with a hand crank. The radio had been used once or twice during snow events at home in Kennebec County, but it did have batteries and we took it with as part of the general "My god, we're really getting out of town!" kind of attitude, and not knowing if the room would have a radio.

What we hadn't realized was that once we were at the ocean that radio could provide round-the-clock entertainment. There was a local OK kind of rock station and too many mock-country stations, but what we listened to nearly constantly that trip, and for many thereafter, was—the weather radio. Some days we were getting a very weak signal from the top of Mt. Washington, which we hadn't realized was basically line of sight to OOB. Most days at the ocean we'd turn the radio on as soon as we rose, and listen to the rotating litany of coastal weather news. We were amused to hear regular warnings about how dangerous the cold water could be, and sometimes paid attention to the wave-height news which could, after all, predict great waves at the beach itself.

Eventually, that listening told us there was a place whose signal was often missing, a phrase delivered mechanically, and despite that, with a sense of irony. It became a catchphrase for us, an in-joke for many uses—"Matinicus Rock is not reporting."

Some of the reporting spots were lighthouses, some were ocean buoys, but the one that stuck with us most was Matinicus Rock.

Through this joke and considering the inevitable "ocean of stars" thing... we ended up talking of places that came and went, places that reported to the rest of the universe at whim rather than necessity... places that darn well refused to report! darnit! and eventually we came to name one location in the Liaden Universe® Runig's Rock—and another, Tinsori Light.

The minds of writers are strange. Where do we get our ideas, you ask? We get ours from Matinicus Rock.

Alas, the old weather radio gave up the ghost when the cheap batteries it came with gave up the ghost by splitting and leaking into the interior. We achieved another, nicer radio soon after, one without a crank, and today—to get into the mood for a trip to the ocean—I set it out on the refrigerator top (in order to get the best signal) and listened to the Dresden station churning out reports. Sharon laughed when we got to the "beware of cold water" warnings and then we both were sure we heard that message echoing through deep space: "Matinicus Rock is not reporting."

Where do we get our ideas, you ask? We get ours from Matinicus Rock.

—Steve Miller

Guest post at sharonleewriter.com